The Devil's Eye

H. L. Richardson

WORD PUBLISHING
Dallas • London • Vancouver • Melbourne

All Scripture references are from The King James Version of the Bible.

Published in association with the literary agency of Alive Communications, P.O. Box 49068, Colorado Springs, Colorado, 80949.

Richardson, H. L., 1927–
The devil's eye / by H.L. Richardson.
p. cm.
ISBN 0-8499-3855-4
I. Title.
PS3568.I3175D48 1995 95-1550
813'.54—dc20 CIP

5 6 7 8 9 RRD 9 8 7 6 5 4 3 2 1

Printed in the United States of America

For Barbara . . . truly my "better half."

Chapter 1

MIKE MURPHY HATED HOT DAYS, particularly Kansas' muggy spring heat. His ruddy, plump face was covered with beads of perspiration. The dirty shirt stuck to his portly frame with the tenacity of glue made of dust and sweat.

Mike wiped the dampness from face and neck with the bar apron hanging from his massive waist. Randomly looking about the bar he bellowed, "Any of you gentlemen want anything to drink?"

No one answered, although Murphy's voice could rouse the dead. The few customers of The Royal Kansas Bar and Game Emporium in Brookville were either deeply engrossed in the card game at the back of the room or were too drunk to pay attention.

Hearing no reply, Mike leaned over and extracted a beer mug from the galvanized tub underneath the bar and began to wipe the grease-filled water from the glass with his apron.

"One of these days, I'm goin' to move to northern Canada," grumbled Mike to himself, "gonna sit on a snow bank in the dead of summer and cuss the spit outa Kansas just fer the fun of it."

Thinking how that cool snow bank would feel brought pleasure to the bulky Irishman, but his daydreaming was sharply interrupted by the ominous rumbles coming from the direction of the card game.

"Young man, if you can't hold your liquor, I suggest you retire from this game of chance until you can," stated the dealer. "You've been having a run of bad luck which can be more properly attributed to your combining whiskey with poor judgment than to any devious action on the part of anyone in this game."

"What the heck did he say? Did you insult me?" slobbered the young cowboy. "Did he insult me?" He staggered to his feet and gazed at the other players. "Did that tinhorn insult me?"

"Aw, sit down and play your cards . . . cash in or shut up," said Don Biron. "You're not sober enough to know anything!"

The young cowboy sat down. "Nobody insults Clete Lamson," he mumbled. "Nobody cheats him either!"

Murphy was taking it all in, much as the desert absorbs water. He prided himself on running a reputable establishment. No messing around was his motto . . . come on in, drink, play some poker, but no rough stuff. Most of Mike's customers were farmers and ranchers who lived in or about Brookville, Kansas. His place of business wasn't on Main Street . . . which was just the way he wanted it. Mike left all of the wild doings to the other saloons, not that there were many raucous Saturday nights left in Brookville. Things had quieted down since the farmers and ranchers moved in and the trail-herding cowboys from Texas moved out. The affable Celt preferred it that way; his customers were usually all repeat business.

The men at the poker table were locals with the exception of the young cowboy. House dealer, Dandy Matson, had worked for Mike since the first Texas cattle drive crossed the Kansas border and made its way to Brookville. Dandy was perfectly capable of taking care of himself. Being an educated man, he was not only good with words, but with a deck of cards and a gun, as well. Three men had found out the hard way. Under his vest, tucked snugly in his belt, was a Colt Patent House pistol with four, .41-caliber chambered shells. It was a small gun but packed quite a wallop for its size, propelling a 185-grain bullet from its short muzzle. Nowadays, there was little cause to carry the firearm but old customs were hard to shake. Dandy felt undressed without it.

Wade Johnson, sitting beside Dandy, was a quiet, hardworking farmer. Saturday was his once-a-month sojourn into Brookville for supplies . . . and a friendly game at Mike's.

Next to Johnson was C. T. Meyerhoff, the town's barber. Don Biron, who worked night shift at the Union Pacific railroad yards, sat beside C. T. The inebriated cowboy was seated directly across from Dandy. He was a stranger to everyone, but drifting cowpokes were nothing new.

For years, Brookville was the end of the line for Texas cattle drives. It wasn't as well known as Abilene and Salina, but plenty of cowboy blood and bad liquor had mixed with the dust of Main Street.

Kansas was a free state prior to and during the Civil War. It became known as "bleeding Kansas" and the citizens were proud of the fact that proportionately, they had sent more men to the Union army than any other northern state. Living proof of the bloody nature of the war was evident in even a rowdy frontier town like Brookville; amputees were not an uncommon sight, nor were disfigured faces. A .58-caliber slug made a nasty wound, often complicated by lead poisoning or gangrene. Amputation was the quickest and usual solution for a bad leg or arm wound, especially if bones were broken. For every visible scar, many more were hidden, especially the bitter memories of lost sons and fathers, friends never to return.

There were more than 600,000 casualties in the gory Civil War conflict. Kansas contributed more than its fair share. All the ingredients for violence were present when the Confederate Texans rode into town, bringing with them suppressed anger, sour hate, undiminished pride, and humiliation. They were confronted by cocky Kansas cowboys, smug with victory and still mindful of their fallen comrades. Texas was proud of the men who wore the Confederate gray. They had scars as well, more painful because of defeat suffered in a losing cause.

Texans had no choice but to drive their cattle north. There was no market for beef at home and the closest railhead, the Union Pacific, was in Kansas. Salina, Abilene, and Brookville were the end of the trail. Southern cowboys, after torturous and deadly cattle drives up the Chisholm Trail, had plenty of pent-up emotion to release . . . and release it they did. Fistfights were commonplace and gunfights too. Confrontations erupted, ignited by unbridled hatreds, hard liquor, and foul words. Texans plainly didn't like bluebelly Kansans and the Jayhawkers remembered the carnage from the Quantrill raid on Lawrence to the bloody Civil War battles.

Conflict was inevitable, but so was trade. Texans had beef which the north needed and Kansas had the nearest railroad. It was the southern cattleman's only option if he wanted to sell his meat at a decent price.

The violent days of the cattle drives were past and by the year of our Lord 1879, things had quieted down substantially. Kansas was now cattle country, filled with men accustomed to hard times . . . but this, too, was changing. Recent years had witnessed a steady influx of farm families as more discovered that the fertile land of Kansas produced abundant red wheat. The troublemakers had moved on as the railroads pushed farther south and west. The Santa Fe cut into southwest Kansas, while the Union Pacific stretched to the western extremes. Dodge City became the hub of the cattle drives as the Texans used the Western Trail.

Eastern Kansas was becoming one of the more stable areas of the frontier, and Mike Murphy didn't mind the newfound tranquillity one bit. In the old days when the shooting started, Mike would dive head-first behind the bar and remain crouched down until the violence subsided. Heroism was not a part of his ancestral history. Mike often boasted about the enlightened pragmatism of his forefathers and how they, as he, had escaped any mayhem, military service, and controversy. "Yep, we Murphys have a sixth sense when violence approaches and through our innate dexterity, ingenuity, and controlled cowardice, we have all emerged in one piece."

Mike's sixth sense was telling him trouble was brewing at the poker table. The cowboy was getting louder and more belligerent. Joe Coombs, sitting beside the angry young man, tried to reason with him. "Come on, pard, no need to get riled. You're havin' a run of bad luck, and I'm pickin' up the good cards for a change."

The biggest stack of chips was in front of Joe. A born loser, he was normally the first to drop out. Everything he touched seemed to turn bad. His hay crop was lost to fire while everyone else had a banner year. His oldest boy was the sole casualty in the only Indian raid in the town's history. His wife ran off with a drummer from Wichita. Bad luck was Joe's constant companion . . . until tonight. The cards were falling in his favor and the coins were stacking up before him. Joe wasn't about to see the game spoiled by a drunken cowhand, and he continued trying to cheer him up . . . to no avail.

Sitting quietly at Joe's left was Zack Budrow, feed and hardware store proprietor. Most of the players were regulars—all friends, all honest men.

"Darn you, tinhorn, I caught you this time." The soused cowboy staggered to his feet again, bumping the table, knocking over his chair, sending coins and drinks spilling to the floor.

"Caught me doing what?" Dandy replied angrily. "Are you accusing me of cheating?"

"Danged right I am," he slobbered. Leaning back in his chair, Wade Johnson calmly said, "Come on now, let's quiet down. This ain't a big-stakes game. A man would be a fool to cheat for nickels and dimes. Dandy, don't let this young bellyacher spoil my once-a-month outing . . . let's finish the game. I'm out four dollars and fifty cents and I want to win it back." Wade reached out to grab the cowboy's arm to seat him back down while Dandy bent over to retrieve some of the coins on the floor. He reached for a bright silver dollar that had rolled behind his chair . . . the last thing he ever did. The liquored-up cowboy drew his gun and fired wildly at the bent figure of Dandy Matson.

Wade Johnson lunged at the cowboy and caught a stray bullet in the neck, shattering his spine. Joe Coombs instinctively grabbed for the smoking pistol, only to have the barrel catch him flush on the temple as the gunman tried to escape the grasps of the remaining players.

"Did you see it, did you see it? The tinhorn went for his gun," screamed the frantic cowboy. "Tried to cheat me! I fixed him, darn him, I fixed him!"

The alcohol-crazed cowboy stumbled backwards toward the saloon door, waving his gun side to side.

"Keep back, all of you! I know you're his friends . . . know you're in with him. Keep back!"

The young killer, wild-eyed, stopped at the doorway and blurted at the dumbstruck patrons, "Didn't mean to shoot, but he made me." With saliva foaming at the corners of his mouth and panic written all over his sweat-streaked face, he shouted, "Don't try to stop me!" He turned and ran through the door into the fading afternoon light.

Mike Murphy was stunned. At the first shot he had collapsed to his knees, seeking cover behind the bar. He rose at the sound of the departing cowboy and peeked over the top of the bar. Carnage was everywhere. Three men were grotesquely sprawled on the floor—two motionless, one convulsively twisting in agony. Blood mixed with cards and coin littered the floor; smoke and the smell of black powder hung in the air, combining vomitously with the odor of whiskey and sweat.

Mike rushed to the side of his friend Dandy, who lay face down with one arm awkwardly draped over a fallen chair, two crimson rings forming where the bullets had entered his back. Mike rolled him over and recoiled from the ugliness of the wounds. The .44–.40-caliber slugs left gaping holes in his chest. Dandy had dealt his last hand of cards.

Wade Johnson was lying on his side in a pool of red, the last drops of life oozing from the vicious wound on the side of his neck. The remaining card players had dropped to their knees to aid their fallen comrades. Don Biron turned to C. T. Meyerhoff and said with quiet urgency, "C. T., you're the youngest and fastest—go get Doc Jones!" C. T. immediately got to his feet and rushed out the door. Zack Budrow was ministering to Joe Coombs, the ugly gash on the side of his forehead still bleeding. The barrel of the Colt single-action .44 had cut clean to the bone. Joe stopped his painful thrashing about and was softly groaning.

"Somebody better get Sheriff Tate," yelled Zack.

"I'll do it," said the one remaining patron. The others had quietly slipped out the back and only this frightened bystander was still there. He quickly shuffled through the swinging front doors.

"How's Joe?" Mike asked, "Will he live?"

Zack lifted the soiled bandanna from the wound and gazed at the ugly cut. "He'll make it. Looks like his good luck held . . . he's still alive."

The distraught Irishman looked out into the approaching darkness. Shock was rapidly turning to anger. "Stupid young fool! He won't get far in his condition. He'll run that poor animal into the ground and the sheriff will catch up to him before noon tomorrow. We'll have him hanging from a tree before the month is out." Mike was contemplating the pleasant thought of the young cowboy dangling and kicking from the end of a rope when the sheriff rushed in. Zack, sitting on the floor holding Joe's bleeding head in his lap, looked up at the sweating, out-of-breath lawman. "Sheriff, there's been a terrible killin'!"

The lawman looked from one twisted body to the next, flinching. "Good God, Wade Johnson!"

"Yeah, and Dandy Matson's dead too," angrily blurted the bartender. "Don'tcha think you better form a posse an' git after that crazy cowboy?"

"Mike, you can bet we will, but first tell me what happened."

Mike stuttered, "I didn't get a good look at the shootin'; ask Zack."

Zack Budrow filled the sheriff in best he could, including the cowboy's panicked dash from the bar.

The sheriff was silent for a moment, then said, "If he's headin' west, there's not too many places to go with the rivers overflowing from spring rain. I'll telegraph the towns within a two days' ride to be on the lookout for him. We'll go after him at first light."

Sheriff Tate looked at the bloody, crumpled body of Wade Johnson and swore under his breath, "Darn!" Lying dead on the floor, without question, was the most respected man in the county. Tough as the job required him to be, Sheriff Tate couldn't keep the tears from welling up in his eyes. Taking a bandanna from his back pocket, he turned away from those present and quickly blew his nose and wiped his eyes. With a choked voice he quietly said, "Before anything else, someone will have to ride out to the Johnson ranch and tell Agatha."

Nobody said a word in response.

"Well," shrugged the sheriff, "I guess that *someone* is me."

Brookville was quickly disappearing behind the young killer as he unmercifully spurred his horse onward. Passing the last little house on the outskirts of town, he spotted an elderly couple sitting on the porch enjoying the evening sunset, their reverie disturbed by the frantic pace of the rider and horse.

He kept his eye on the couple as long as he could . . . noticing how intently they watched him . . . until finally too much distance made the old folks disappear like dots on the far horizon. Horse and rider disappeared over the distant western hills, a brief frantic black silhouette against the red-orange sunset. He could envision the old folks rocking back and forth in their rocking chairs, nothing better to do than watch the emerging fireflies and anticipate the cool of evening. That sort of life was not for him!

The cowboy continued his frantic pace until he was well out of earshot and sight of town, then he reined the exhausted horse to a stop. His manner changed entirely as he calmly looked back toward Brookville and smiled. He reached into his shirt pocket for the makings of a cigarette and with steady hands, rolled a perfect smoke and lit it with one quick stroke of a match.

He drew his pistol from the holster, removed the empty shells, and reloaded. Reaching into the saddlebag, he removed a slightly oiled cloth and carefully wiped clean the Colt .44. Satisfied the gun was in perfect working order, he deftly holstered the firearm and simultaneously spurred his panting mount into a trot, leisurely heading the mare in a new direction . . . south, toward the Smokey Hill River. It didn't take long to reach the swollen waterway, which was dangerously high. Spring rains and melting snows had converted the peaceful river into an ugly brown, silt-filled torrent. The banks were overflowing, the muddy water was invading the nearby fields and rushing loudly amid the partially submerged cottonwoods. The cowboy let the horse pick its way down to a knoll at the water's edge.

"This will do," he muttered to himself. He carefully viewed the river in the remaining light. "Yes, this will do nicely."

Although the animal was overheated and exhausted, he allowed the horse to drink freely and gorge itself with water.

"If you were a mule, you wouldn't be so stupid," muttered the cowboy. While the horse drank, he removed his bedroll and saddlebags, then looked around and spotted a large rock outcropping. "I should be able to find that in the dark."

The killer carefully picked his way up the side of the slope and deposited his gear at the base of the rocks. Sitting on one of the smaller boulders, he began to remove his clothes. In a matter of moments, stark naked except for socks and hat, he placed his boots and gun beside the bedroll, neatly folded his pants and shirt, and placed them protectively over his gun. He looked toward the river and stretched his lean, well-proportioned, muscled body.

"Good night for a swim," he murmured wryly.

Gingerly stepping over the rocks and around shrubbery, he worked his way back to the mare. She was startled by the appearance of the white flesh looming out of the darkness.

"Whoa girl, whoa there, calm down! It's just me."

The horse quieted at the sound of the familiar voice. The cowboy untied the reins, mounted, and nudged the animal into the cold waters of the Smokey River. Although spring had brought sunshine and rain, melting the snow pack, a chill was still in the raging water, and sent a shock through both man and beast. It wasn't long before the muddy ground fell away beneath the mare's feet and she was afloat. The horse was tired and bloated by the excess of water . . . but she struggled to swim. He forced her head to the middle, upriver, not letting her cross to the other side. The horse fought the strong current, and soon began to labor, head bobbing up and down. Each time her nostrils hit the water, the terrified mare surged with new strength. Fear was evident as the whites of her eyes shown in the darkness. In panic, she struggled toward shore, but the naked cowboy ruthlessly dug the bit deep into the corners of her mouth, again forcing her head upriver. Finally, no longer able to compete against the raging torrent, the last of her strength spent desperately trying to keep her head above the tumultuous black water, she sank beneath the surface. As the young killer slipped from the horse's back, he felt the huge body shudder for the last time.

The cowboy struck out downriver toward the rocks where he had stacked his gear. A powerful swimmer, he soon reached the embankment. With no moon to light his way, he cautiously picked a path through the darkened night to the outcropping, a pale silhouette against the dark sky. Unseen branches and berry vines cut across his naked flesh; the wet socks on his feet offered little protection from the rocks and debris. The river's fast flow had carried him farther downstream than he had planned. The night air still held the heat of the day and warmth still radiated from the soil. By the time he reached the outcropping, he was sweating slightly. Steady fingers swiftly untied the bedroll and removed a dry shirt, black coat and pants, and a crumpled black hat.

He dressed quickly, then spread out the bedroll on a shelf of flat granite. After a slow but prolonged stretch, the young killer climbed beneath the blanket and was asleep within minutes. Several hours later, he folded the cowboy gear into his bedding and carefully placed his revolver in the saddlebag. He pulled the black hat down on his head, then set out, back toward Brookville.

Walking as swiftly as the night would allow, he approached town, stopping at the sight of the first group of dwellings. The wind was in his face, improving his chances of not being discovered by waking dogs. He moved slowly, taking his time, circling the sleeping community. The eastern horizon displayed the first dim red of the coming sun as he reached the far edge of town. The train station's outline was in the distance. A locomotive had already arrived and several cars were being unloaded in the early light. Smoke and steam from the engine drifted lazily skyward as it temporarily rested on the tracks.

He reached into his coat pocket for his watch as he strolled onto the railroad platform. "Six-fifteen—departure time 6:30." He smiled and said to himself, "Perfect timing."

He stopped at the ticket window; the clerk's back was turned, oblivious to his presence. As he knocked gently on the window, the startled clerk whipped around.

"Oh, I didn't know anyone was there." His face quickly broke into a broad smile, "Oh, Reverend, you gave me a start! What can I do for you?"

"That's perfectly all right. I'm sorry I startled you. Would you be so kind as to tell me if the train to Denver will be leaving on time?"

"Departs 6:30, right on the button. All we have to do is load the baggage car," volunteered the young clerk. He gazed into the downcast face of the minister. Anyone could see how gentle was his demeanor—so serene and peaceful, so free of wrinkles. Gold-rimmed spectacles were perched upon his nose and a battered black hat sat squarely on his head, covering the full head of flaxen hair.

The Union Pacific clerk could see as easily as anyone could that this face staring down at him was the face of a man of God; he had the look of a holy man. The clerk passed the ticket through the window opening. More than one circuit rider, whose flocks reached over great territories, had passed through Brookville. With Bible in hand, they would circulate from one small community to the next, preaching the gospel. Circuit riding was a tough life, hard on man, family, and horse. The circuit riders were respected men of God who would marry, bury, or tarry with whoever would listen. Their earnings were meager at best and more often than not, they visibly showed the wear and tear of their lifestyle. This minister was no exception; his clothes were soiled and badly in need of pressing.

"Reverend, been preachin' here abouts?"

The young minister smiled warmly, displaying a perfect set of teeth. "Yes, I gave quite a lesson to a group of sinners yesterday. Several of them came to know their Maker."

"Why, praise the Lord," smiled the clerk.

"Yes . . . praise the Lord," beamed the circuit rider. The minister looked up and for the first time, the railroad clerk saw his eyes . . . pale . . . cold blue . . . empty. Only once before had he ever seen similar eyes . . . on a cadaver.

Suddenly, the clerk shivered, as if chilled to the bone by a blast of cold.

CHAPTER 2

WELL, I'LL BE DARN! Kenneth Seymour was shocked to see Sam Dodd walking toward him down the crowded boardwalk. *Never thought I would ever see him again.* But here he was, accompanied by two young boys, obviously his sons. Dodd was hard to miss—broad-shouldered, taller than most, a strong handsome face with chiseled features weathered by time and experience.

These were prosperous times. The streets of Denver were busy, teeming with people rushing in and out of shops with packages, riders dismounting at hitch rails, wagons being loaded. Everyone was moving vigorously, spurred by the sharp sting of autumn wind. Flecks of snow swirled about, disappearing soon after touching the ground. The slate gray sky and the cutting, crisp breeze proclaimed Dame Winter's imminent arrival.

Seymour felt the cold wind bite through his suit coat; he was ill-prepared to dally around the street reflecting on bygone days. He hoped to escape Dodd's notice, but it was impossible; he was dead ahead, coming down Sixteenth Street . . . there was no avoiding him.

Taking the initiative, he called out, "Sam, Sam Dodd, what brings you to Denver?"

Sam flashed a friendly smile and warmly shook Kenneth's hand. "I'm here to sell some horses, pick up a few supplies, and show my boys the big city. Matthew, Daniel—I'd like you to meet Mr. Seymour. He's legal counsel for the Sassy Mae Mining Company, the outfit I used to work for. We were also in the same regiment during the war."

Sam turned to his sons who were beside him on the crowded boardwalk and motioned them forward. "Kenneth, these are my two middle sons, Dan and Matt."

They extended their hands and said almost in unison, "Pleased to meet you, Sir." Both boys were almost as tall as Seymour and were taken aback by the lawyer's fancy attire—an impeccably tailored gray suit, brocade silver vest with woven gold threads, and the maroon cravat with a small diamond stickpin tastefully displayed. All of this splendor was crowned off with a gray silk top hat, jauntily perched on his head. Impressive . . . but nothing awed the boys more than the bright yellow kid gloves. Neither could keep from staring at the leathered hand offered them. They instinctively wiped their right hands on their trousers before offering their own. In turn, each gripped Seymour's gloved hand firmly, as their father had taught them to do. Daniel was surprised by the limp, cold fingers within his grasp . . . and let go quickly, embarrassed by the contact.

"Your middle two? Good Lord, Sam, how many kids do you and Bertha have?"

"It's Mary, Kenneth, my wife's name is Mary. We have six, four boys and two girls." Sam smiled, "You remember Mary, don't you?"

"Oh yes, Mary . . . fine Christian lady."

Seymour remembered Mary Dodd all too well. On several occasions in Silverville, they had crossed verbal swords, and each time he had come out on the short end of the exchange. Counselor Seymour was not accustomed to losing political or verbal debates, especially to women; his recollection of Mary was clear, and he hadn't forgotten her name.

"How come you're not in Silverville tending to Charlie's legal affairs?" inquired Sam.

"That's exactly why I'm here in the capital city, trying to convince a few politicians we need to change some of the state's mining laws."

Sam jovially chided, "Buying politicians is more like it. Remember me, Kenneth? We used to work together."

Noting Sam's sly grin, Seymour also smiled, "Well, whatever works."

Sam was right; the lawyer would much rather compromise a politician than reason with one.

"Bought politicians are much more reliable," Seymour had sarcastically remarked in the past. "Show me a politician who votes on principle and I'll show you a man you can't trust to do the right thing!"

The "right thing" was always what he wanted, and the right thing was whatever worked . . . for Seymour. He prided himself on his pragmatic approach to life, never comprehending what benefit could accrue by dogmatically insisting on honesty, integrity, and fidelity. Those who possessed such attributes were too difficult to deal with. Sam and Mary Dodd epitomized the moral certainty that Seymour abhorred.

"Consistency is the hobgoblin of small minds," the lawyer often quoted.

When Sam left Charlie's employment and bought a ranch near the Wyoming border, Seymour thought he had seen the last of him. *Good riddance*, Seymour thought to himself. *No longer will that family be a burr under my saddle.* Things were much better since the Dodds left. Although Charlie Meyers usually followed Seymour's counsel, he trusted Dodd's judgment implicitly. On several occasions Charlie had listened to Dodd's advice while rejecting Seymour's, costing him healthy legal fees. He wasn't soon to forget. Now, years later, here he was amicably chatting with Sam on a windy street in Denver, discussing bygone days just like long lost friends, while two wide-eyed boys stood obediently alongside their father, taking in every word.

Children made Seymour uncomfortable; in fact, to him, they were a cumbersome, unwanted by-product of lust. It was difficult for him to see how anyone could enjoy them, much less express happiness being saddled by one of the little snot-nosed brats. Children were an impediment to pleasure. Pregnancies kept women out of action and positively ruined their shapes. He had been personally involved in several such circumstances . . . messy affairs! Seymour shifted from foot to foot, pretending to be far colder than he was. He reached into his vest and extracted an ornate gold watch.

"Time to go . . . late for an appointment . . . been good seeing you, Sam—give my regards to the missus."

Seymour offered a limp hand to Sam for a parting handshake, patted both boys' shoulders, and without waiting for a reply, quickly turned and scurried off.

The boys curiously watched him disappear down the crowded street.

"Pa, is he always like that?" asked Matthew.

"Yep, he's a strange one." Sam looked up to the sky and frowned as more small flakes of snow circled around in the wind. "Boys, I reckon we'd better get the rest of our supplies, pack up the mules, and head back to the ranch before it starts snowing in earnest. We have some high passes to cross; they're tough enough in good weather."

"Yes, Pa," the boys replied in unison.

By nightfall, Denver was far behind them.

★ ★ ★

Lawyer Seymour sat at his favorite table in the Gold Strike Saloon, reflecting on his long association with Sam Dodd. He didn't dislike the cow man, but then again, neither was he fond of him; they were breeds apart with little in common. During the war it was a different story. Sam was vital to his survival, so maintaining a close relationship was healthy business. Now that the war was over he saw no need to sustain the acquaintance, especially if it included Sam's wife. He didn't like being around Mary Dodd. She was too religious, too pretty, and too bright for her own good. She made him very uneasy.

Seymour and Dodd served together for more than three years in the Union Army of the West under General Ulysses S. Grant and then later, under the command of William Tecumseh Sherman. Together, they burned and pillaged Georgia on their way to the sea.

After the war, some of the company survivors received offers to work for Charlie Meyers, one of their army buddies who had struck it rich in Colorado. Sam was hired as the head of security, guarding the bullion while Seymour took care of legal chores. Both prospered working for Charlie; Sam saved his earnings and bought land while Seymour invested in speculative mining ventures which, to date, had failed. Seymour was a gambler and loved the excitement, the visceral thrill of taking chances whether investing in speculative mining claims, betting on horse races, or wagering at the gaming tables. His legal skills earned him substantial fees and losses were of little consequence. Kenneth Carrington Seymour could usually be found most evenings seated at the poker tables in select Silverville saloons . . . by and large, losing.

Notwithstanding his questionable personal ethics and bent for compulsive gambling, Kenneth Seymour excelled in court. His expert handling of Charlie's legal affairs placed his services in demand. He had the tenacity, the intelligence, and knowledge of mining laws that his employer needed. He was smart enough not to play games with Charlie since he was the one man, if crossed, who could be ruthless and vindictive. Besides, Charlie was his golden goose—and no bright lawyer cheats his principle client.

Charlie Meyers was also as close a friend as anyone could be to Seymour. They were much alike in many ways. Both were small in stature, physically unattractive, distrustful of women, and thoroughly jaded. They became close companions during the war, sharing a few soiled doves and many of the same hatreds and prejudices. For both of them, the war held little political or philosophical significance. It was an escape from the past, a temporal way out of difficult circumstances—Seymour from criminal prosecution and Meyers from an ugly and scandalous marriage. Neither thought the freeing of slaves or preserving the Union worthwhile reasons for shooting anyone. Meyers was the most vocal.

"Bein' caught by a jealous husband or welshin' on a gamblin' debt—now, that's cause for bein' shot at, but fightin' for niggers' rights ain't reason enough to spit, much less kill 'nother white man!"

Charlie wasn't known for his compassion, affection, or good humor outside of his war companions. He was a bitter, sarcastic shrimp of a man with a pasty complexion covered by a full black beard.

Before the war, he grubbed out a living for wife and child in the coal mines of southern Illinois. His mood often matched his black countenance after a hard day extracting bituminous coal from the bowels of the earth. The work was dirty and foul. His nasty temperament grew uglier when his wife, Sassy Mae, took their only child and ran off with another man. To make matters worse, she left him encumbered with debt and mortified beyond description. Sassy Mae's new lover was an assistant undertaker. Charlie had been cuckolded by a second-rate mortician from Kentucky!

"Serves him right," Meyers would quip. "He'll find her colder than his clients and not quite as affectionate!"

Beneath the facade, it really wasn't a joking matter; Charlie was extremely bitter over the loss of his wife. It was a pain he could not forget, so he carried the ache inside like a malignant tumor. Sassy Mae was his prize possession, a small but buxomy brunette with deep dimples and rows of big white teeth. Charlie often boasted, "When my little gal smiles she lights up the room!" He had little else to be proud of, so he incessantly bragged about his good fortune having such an attractive wife. His fellow miners resented his braggadocios attitude and when she ran away they found it very amusing, particularly when it became known that her new lover was an immigrant Italian undertaker. Although they ribbed him unmercifully, Charlie smiled and joked about it as well. He was thin and physically unimpressive, unlike most of the miners who were rugged, tough laborers; he was certainly no match for any of them.

Gettin' mad could be dangerous, he thought. *My time will come.*

Meyers didn't think the jokes about his errant wife were funny at all. Like a bad dream, the memory loomed around his mind like a rum hangover. The War Between the States gave Charlie an excuse to leave the coal mining area of southern Illinois. He heard talk that most Kentuckians favored the South and were joining the Confederate army, giving him added reason to join the North.

Maybe I'll get a chance to shoot the kin of that wife-stealin' gravedigger. If he's joined up too, maybe I can get lucky an' put a bayonet through his stinkin' gizzard!

The idea pleased Charlie—so much, in fact, that he actually smiled. It had been far too long since the corners of his mouth curved upward. Contemplating violence toward his enemies sustained him during the entire war. The loss of Sassy Mae had been a cruel blow to his ego; he planned on getting even . . . and did. After striking it rich, Charlie bought the Illinois coal mine and fired each and every man who had teased him.

He had other plans for Sassy Mae.

Sam Dodd was special to both Charlie Meyers and Kenneth Seymour, having been their squad sergeant and the reason both of them were still alive. Seymour remembered one chilly winter evening when members of several squads were huddled around a fire, shifting from one foot to the other, trying to keep warm. Although it was years ago, he still remembered the conversation vividly. The soldiers were discussing the capabilities of their officers, from Grant down to the lesser grades. On the proficiencies of their leaders, opinions were mixed. In only two cases were the men in total agreement: General Grant and their own sergeant, Sam Dodd.

They admired but feared Grant and had contempt for all lieutenants, but Sam was different; he was, to a man, liked and respected. All agreed there were few men like him in the Union Army of the West.

As his contribution to the fireside recollections, Kenneth Seymour brought up the battle at Stones River, where Confederate General Bragg had launched a fierce attack, driving the Union forces back better than three miles. "A blasted Rebel artillery shell blew over a supply wagon I was hiding behind, pinning me underneath. I was hollering my darn fool head off for help while soldiers were passing me by, retreating on all sides, most of them running for their lives. The Rebs had us temporarily moving back; shells were exploding all around while enemy troops were advancing through the nearby peach orchard. Yankee soldiers were falling everywhere and the screams of the wounded were drowning out my feeble attempts to attract attention." Seymour visibly shuddered at the thought.

"What happened then?" asked another soldier.

"Well," Seymour continued, "The wagon was on fire, loaded with powder and ready to blow me into a bloody piece of gore. Next thing I knew, Sam was beside the wagon directing our squad's fire on the advancing Rebs. We were under withering attack, but as if it didn't weigh a thing, he braced his back against the smoldering rig and lifted it just enough so I could crawl out from underneath. Then he tossed me over his shoulder as if I were a bag of grain and directed us to a stone wall where we continued to return fire. The Rebs swept around us for just a few moments before finally retreating. We would have been dead, or worse. We could have spent the rest of the war in Andersonville if Sam Dodd hadn't been there."

"Our captured boys were packed off to this Confederate stink hole to rot out the war. Good fellers died in droves 'cause of no food and the fever," added Private Clarence Devlin.

"Better to die in battle than starve to death in Andersonville," piped in Corporal Andy Quade.

Seymour's story was interrupted by the chatter of Charlie Meyers, reflecting on the siege at Vicksburg. "Remember when sniper fire almost picked me off, when I was tryin' to take a leak? Sam saved my life for sure!"

"How'd he do that, Charlie?" inquired one of the newer recruits.

"Sam don't miss much. He's thinkin' all the time. While the rest of us is dreamin' about ladies and liquor, Sam studies this durn war; no small detail escapes his attention . . . lucky for me!" swore Charlie.

"What do you mean by *small detail,*" asked one of the men from another squad.

"A puff of smoke, just a small insignificant puff of smoke," inserted Corporal Wade Johnson.

"Yeah," answered Charlie, "at the siege of Vicksburg, Sergeant Sam noticed occasional puffs of white smoke from the Rebel fortifications. An' ya'll know, black powder causes a heap of smoke outa the muzzle of a rifle; from afar, looks like a ball of cotton. None of us paid any mind to the tiny white cotton puffs comin' from the Rebel fortifications."

"Why not?" asked another.

"Too danged far. We thought we was well out of range of rifle fire an' unless the cannons roared, none of us paid no mind," added Private Briggs.

"We should have," chimed in Seymour. "Every so often, one of our Union boys would crumble in his tracks or we could hear the dull thud of a bullet striking our fortifications nearby. These fatalities were attributed to lucky shots for the Rebs and just bad luck for the Union soldier that wandered in front of a stray Minie ball."

"How far away was the Rebs?" asked another.

"They were over a half-mile from where we was," responded Corporal Johnson. "Those Johnny Rebs can shoot and their rifles are good, but not at distances over five hundred yards! We were camped at better than triple that distance. Wouldn't you say so, Charlie?"

Charlie spat out a stream of tobacco juice, aiming for a horsefly on the side of a nearby tent, before replying.

"Yep! Usta-mosey in full view of them Rebel lines, feelin' safe from all but artillery fire. The siege lasted a long time an' we all got a bit relaxed, everyone but Sam."

By this time, members of the other squad were listening intently and waiting. . . .

"Well, what happened?" one soldier inquired impatiently.

Ignoring the request for more information, Charlie let fire another saliva salvo before he answered.

"We thought Sam was actin' kinda funny, hunched down behind the ramparts while gazin' real intent at the Reb's fortifications, scribblin' on a small paper tablet. Every so often he'd look at his pocket watch, then stand up and look around. He was jest like a ground hog on watch. He did that for days. Finally, he called us all together to explain what he was up to. He told us we'd been under some kind of fancy sniper fire. First off, we thought he was jokin' but after he explained the timin', from sight of the smoke 'til the thud of a bullet or the collapsin' of a soldier along the line, it started to make some sense. Lots of times he said there would be smoke and nothin' would happen. It was real difficult to figure where the bullets was hittin' cause of our size, the huge number of our Union forces." Corporal Johnson continued, "But, after a while, Sam figured the relationship was too coincidental to ignore. Puff of smoke, three-and-a-half seconds and . . . thud! Twelve hundred feet per second. He said they were shooting at us at distances close to three-quarters of a mile—and we had the dead to prove it!"

"Yeah!" interrupted Private Devlin, "Sam figgered out some Reb sharpshooter up there had a telescope attached to a rifle an' could shoot more 'an a thousand yards! Some were laughin' at this thinkin', includin' the officers, but not us guys who knew Sam . . . we listened real good when Sam spoke. He warned us that the Rebs needed a still target and a movin' man would be jest about as hard to hit as a spooked coon 'cause of the time lapse, so when in sight of them Rebs, we was to keep movin'."

"We sure all obeyed," Charlie smiled, "but over the long siege I forgot . . . darn near got my butt shot off an' near cost me my life. Ya see, it wuz this way. I gotta hold of some Mississippi moonshine and after a spell, I was feelin' purty good. After killin' off half the jug I had to water the roses, so to speak. Me, Charlie Meyers, bein' the shy gent I am, sashayed around in front of our barricades, aimed at the enemy, and let fire. I was standin' there piddlin' away when Sam shouted at me. *Charlie! Duck!* The sound of Sam's voice scared the heck outa me! Man, I jumped aside like I was goosed by a red-hot poker . . . that shout made me to wet my trousers, but it saved my life."

"Yep," joined in Sean Sullivan, "The .577-caliber slug tore a huge hole in the fortification exactly where Charlie's head had been. Later, after we captured Vicksburg, we found one of them sniper rifles. They were heavy-barreled muzzle-loaders made by the bloody English; stamped on the barrel was *Made by Kern of London.*"

"That's right," said Clarence Devlin. "It was a clumsy looking weapon with a long thin periscope attached to a long rifle barrel; it had a killing range of over two thousand yards."

Seymour remembered clearly the ugly foreign rifle. In the latter days of the war, a Union general was killed by Rebel sniper fire. The .577-caliber bullet traveled 2,200 yards—6,600 feet—better than a mile.

Charlie Meyers and Seymour weren't stupid and from that day forward, along with many others, they kept well out of sight of Rebel lines and as close to Sam as possible. All the veteran squad members made jokes about it.

"Heck, dot feller can schmell dem Rebs five miles avay!" added Otto Schmitz. "Maybe more like six."

When on patrol, everyone became alert when Sam stuck his nose in the air and started looking around.

"Like a dog on scent!" one of the men cannily observed.

When asked about his propensity to sense trouble, Sam Dodd always made light of it.

"Ain't you guys ever took a good whiff of each other? It's no wonder we've been losin' to the Rebs—they don't smell as bad as we do. Those fellows know where we are at all times, they just get downwind and fire into the stench."

"That why you're bathin' all the time?" inquired one of the soldiers.

"You bet! No smell . . . nothing to hit." Sam grinned widely.

"Aw, Sarge . . . you're just joshin' us."

Sam smiled again. He really could smell the enemy. The Reb army had a certain unmistakable aroma of sour sweat and gunpowder. Bathing was not a common occurrence for fighting men. When on patrol Sam always worked the wind to his advantage. "The Lord gave man the five senses, why not use them all?"

But Seymour and the older squad members knew Sergeant Dodd had more than the usual five; he possessed a sixth sense, an uncanny ability to *just know* when the Grim Reaper was close by. Sam once told Seymour he could feel the chill of death like a frigid, wet hand on the back of the neck . . . the knell that summons to heaven or fire and brimstone. The others knew it was smart to shadow Sam Dodd, to stick to him like a cocklebur on a long-haired dog. The officers were also aware of the sergeant's innate talents and whenever circumstances called for a special patrol, Sergeant Dodd was called.

Charlie summed up for all of them when he said, "If Sam Dodd dove head first through a crap hole in an outhouse, I'd follow him, so help me God, I would!"

"You'd never make it," guffawed Wade Johnson. "All the rest of us would be stuck in the hole tryin' to be second!"

Seymour was envious of Sam's popularity and the casual way he accepted leadership. The sergeant didn't talk much, but what he said was regarded highly. He was obviously a religious man, for he carried a small Bible with him in his backpack; whenever there was a lull in the fighting or one of those long monotonous periods between battles, Sam was usually engrossed in reading Scripture. Often, Seymour noticed some of the troops discussing the Bible with Dodd. In fact, it was a regular occurrence for many of them. Seymour believed there could be a God or gods but he never saw any relevance of "invisible spiritual things" or how they could impact his own life. The Bible, to him, was just a book of impractical restrictions—a bunch of *shall nots* and antiquated morals.

"What anybody sees in a book that's thousands of years old is beyond me," he'd grumble to himself. "If everybody believed in that narrow mythology, there'd be no joy in life. The Greeks had the right idea; if you have to have a god, have a separate one for each and every thing."

Seymour's reflections on his Civil War experiences were interrupted by one of the scarlet ladies who slowly made her way down the staircase from the row of rooms above the saloon. She had obviously just awakened from her morning's rest, for she was unconsciously scratching the tiny bites acquired while asleep. These were mementos of the little pests known as bed crumbs, often found in beds that have known many occupants. He waved and motioned for her to sit beside him.

"Sit down, Molly—I'll buy you breakfast."

She dropped into the chair like a sack of grain, stretched both arms above her head, and yawned loudly.

"I'll have bourbon, Counselor . . . beautiful, amber bourbon!"

Seymour ordered another bottle from the bar, a stock they kept especially on hand for him. Bourbon was yet another taste acquired while accompanying General Sherman through Georgia. He momentarily forgot Molly while his thoughts once again returned to Sam Dodd. He suspected that Sam wasn't very fond of him, *but so what*! The war was long past and Sam's sixth sense was no longer needed. He also suspected he wasn't very well-liked by anyone other than Charlie Meyers. *A pox on 'em! Who cares!*

Kenneth Carrington "Slick" Seymour may have been short in size but not in legal ability. One cowboy said he was "slickern' a fresh cow pie on a wet rock." When fighting a legal battle or electing one of his allies to office, he could be formidable and unscrupulous. "It's all a game," he'd say, "and those who make the rules, win the game!"

The cowboy's comment struck a chord; Slick became his nickname. Seymour welcomed the monicker, took all of the acrimonious criticism as a compliment, and even welcomed the slurs about his professional ethics. He became accustomed to the many descriptive, uncomplimentary adjectives that preceded his name. "Proper tools of the trade," he bragged when inebriated. "Show me a so-called moral, upright lawyer and I'll show you a man I can beat in court. Legal battles are won before twelve men, not twelve apostles." Although a non-believer, Slick Seymour delighted in using biblical quotations in or out of context. He discovered the advantage of quoting from Scripture as an asset in court. Juries were often swayed by biblical references punctuating key points, and this was especially true in the West. Many pioneers held a special reverence for Holy Writ, and he used every opportunity to exploit it.

Seymour was extremely successful in court and his large clientele reflected it. Not many were upstanding citizens; most of his cases involved criminal defendants or mining claims. His number one client was Charlie Meyers, who demanded results—just the kind of results produced by Slick Seymour.

Molly left with a customer for the bedrooms upstairs, leaving Seymour alone with his thoughts. He ordered another bottle of bourbon, and again, the faces of the two tall Dodd boys came to mind. *They're the kind of "handsome" boys my father would have been proud of, instead of a pox-marked shrimp like me*, he said to himself. Then, as an afterthought, *No, they're Sam's sons; they have the look of their father.* He recalled again that his former sergeant had saved his life. Feelings of remorse were new to Slick Seymour, and he didn't like them at all. Sarcastically he quoted the oft heard passage, "and this too shall pass." He was hoping the bourbon would wash away his uneasiness, salve his conscience, blot out the faces of the two boys . . . but it didn't.

How could he forget his recent acquiescence to the imminent murder of their father?

CHAPTER 3

"SHADUP!" pleaded a gravel-voiced woman. "Dontcha' know we're tryin' to sleep? It's close to midnight!"

The two inebriated miners stopped singing and looked around for the source of the voice. "Whatsa' matter sweetie, don't ya like our harmony?" slurred the taller of the two as he staggered full-circle, peering into the dark. Hearing no answer, "Awright, I'll sing the second verse by meself." Turning to his less than sober partner, he put a finger to his lips and loudly whispered, "Shush, Rufus. Keep quiet." Softly, in a clear, beautiful Irish tenor, Andrew Quade sang as he and his buddy Rufus staggered down the street:

"Oh fer the life of a miner,
diggin' hole after hole after hole.
Could anythin' be any finer
then high-gradin' a big stash o' goooold!"

"You shore do sing pretty, Andrew, but ain't it findin' a big stash o' gold, not high-gradin'?"

"Maybe thas so, Rufus, but high-gradin' a few nuggets in the ol' lunch box is much more fun to sing about."

Rufus was Andrew Quade's pard, the man he worked with in the mines. Today they discovered several nuggets and had successfully secreted them past security in Andrew's false-bottomed lunchpail. Because of his close association with Charlie Meyers, the mine owner, he wasn't inspected as carefully as the others. More than once he had taken advantage of his friendship with the boss and gruffly reprimanded the guards if they appeared too curious about his heavy pail.

Rufus knew how light-fingered his pard could be because they worked side by side deep in the bowels of the earth, blasting for ore.

"Yep . . . yer as good at singin' as ya are at stealin'!" commented Rufus.

"No, no, Rufus, it ain't stealin'. It's extra pay fer the dangerous work we do."

Andrew Quade smiled the smile of an accomplished high-grader. Pocketing nuggets was an accepted practice by numerous employees. Ingenious smuggling methods were devised, hiding the metal in lunchpails, pant cuffs, shoes, false pockets, even inserting them into body cavities. Many a miner supplemented his income by high-grading the boss's gold.

Andy Quade was an expert and the extra money allowed him to bring his brothers from Ireland to America. It also made it possible to support his mother and relatives on the Emerald Isle. To Andy, high-grading was a moral responsibility, a patriotic Irish duty. It never dawned on him that he was actually stealing from his benefactor and former military colleague, Charlie Meyers. It was nothing more than special compensation for perilous underground work.

Quite a few miners bragged about their thievery, knowing full well they would not be punished by the law. Some had been arrested but a jury packed with their peers had yet to convict one single culprit.

In general, Andy kept his mouth shut about how good he was at pilfering. The braggarts, if discovered, were beaten to a pulp by Jethro Briggs . . . or worse! Jethro was in charge of Sassy Mae Mines security, and his meanness was legendary.

"Besides, it's only fair to Jethro and Charlie that I keep me high-gradin' talent hushed up. It's not nice ta create trouble between me war buddies."

Tonight, Rufus and Andy were celebrating their good fortune with wine, women and—now that they were homeward bound—song. Arm in arm, they swayed drunkenly down the street, warbling ribald ballads.

The road cut through a series of small, slant-roof shacks built close together. Deep snowdrifts surrounded each little house and at midnight, with no lighted windows, they looked much alike. Rufus had to stop and squint, trying to pick his home out from the rest. Then it was his turn to whisper. "Better hush up, pard—I don' wanna wake up me missus."

"Aw right, me bucko, see ya in the mornin'." With a wave of the hand and a pat on the back, the two men parted. Andrew hummed another Irish tune as he tottered away.

Quade was a bachelor and bunked at the Hoskin Boarding House, sharing a room with six other men. Two of them worked on the night shift at the Lucky Boy Mine, so contending with only three other snorers wasn't all that bad. On Sundays when all six were present, the din became unbearable. This night, nothing would keep him from a sound sleep and sweet dreams; the two large nuggets in his pocket were worth several months' wages.

Andrew steadied himself before attempting to mount the icy boarding house steps, but just as one boot touched the stair, a voice called out, "Excuse me, Sir, could you help me?"

Andrew was momentarily startled by the unexpected greeting emanating from the darkness. Muggings of lone miners were not uncommon on the streets of Silverville at night.

"Who's there? Show yerself!" Andrew demanded.

Out of the inky shadows of the boarding house porch appeared a face, caught in the dim light coming through the window of the front door. Dressed in dark clothing, the body seemed to blend into the night. This sudden appearance of only a face frightened Quade. "Merciful God!"

"Yes indeed, He most certainly is merciful," came a cheerful reply.

Quade let out a sigh of relief, as he saw the white collar and ministerial attire. "Aye Father, you surprised me. What's a priest doin' out so late this night?"

The man of God smiled, "Don't you know the devil works at all hours?"

"He most certainly does, Father," laughed the miner, "he most certainly does." Andrew extended his hand in friendship, which the minister warmly received. "Father, how can I help?"

"I'm not Catholic, my son, just an Episcopal pastor trying to locate a friend. I seem to be lost."

"What and who are ye lookin' for?" inquired Andrew.

"I'm to meet my friend at the Sassy Mae Mines at the end of the swing shift."

"Oh, Father, er . . . Reverend, the mine's on the other side of town, a good ten-minute walk in the dark an' I suspect the swing shift let off about a half-hour ago. They shut down the night shift last month. I'd bet the mine is deserted by now. Are you sure yer friend will be there?"

"Oh, I'm confident he'll be there. I better hurry; my friend will freeze, waiting for me on a night like this. Could you tell me which way to go?"

"Pastor, ye'll never find it in the dark," answered Quade. "Tell you what . . . I'll show ye the way. I work at the Sassy Mae an' I could walk there wit me eyes closed."

"How kind of you!" joyfully answered the reverend.

The Irish miner felt a warm glow well inside his chest. The Saints had led him to the gold nuggets, and now he was returning the favor by helping one of their own. Andrew kept up a continual chatter all the way to the mine, leaving little room for response.

When they reached the entrance, everything was totally dark and no one was in sight.

"Looks to be yer friend has gone," Quade remarked.

"No, he wouldn't do that. Maybe he's still in the mine."

The pastor strode quickly towards the mine shaft, Andrew following on his heels.

"Slow down, Pastor—mines are dangerous if ye don't know yer way around."

Oblivious to Quade's warnings, the pastor lifted the single rail guarding the mine shaft and peered down into the black hole. "I see a light down there. Someone's still working below . . . I would guess it's my friend." Quade looked cautiously over the edge and said, "I can't see any light."

"Yes, there is," said the pastor. "Here, hold onto my hand . . . lean over a bit farther and take another look!"

Chapter 4

THE SUN HAD YET TO RISE when Mary Dodd crawled from beneath the warm quilt and moved quietly into the kitchen. The fire had been banked in the stove, a few coals still glowing among the ashes. She tossed in some kindling and blew gently, the glow softly reflected on her face. She moved quickly about in the semi-dark, lighting lanterns, then feeding more kindling on the hungry fire. The welcome aroma of brewing coffee soon filled the room, cutting through the chill in the air.

This was Mary's favorite time of day . . . the peaceful moments when the ranch was all hers. She poured herself a cup of steaming coffee, opened the kitchen door, and walked along the porch to the steps facing the eastern sky. A thin golden strip of light rimmed the horizon, melting into the cerulean skyline. Gradations of colors with stars poking shining holes into their deep blue canopy were in stark contrast to the black pines, silhouetted against the rising light. What a dramatic panorama was the iridescent skyline! White frost covered the low meadows between ranch and creek, sparkling like diamond-littered fields when touched by the first rays of sun.

Mary deeply inhaled at the sight, sensing the cold dry air enter her lungs; it was heady, chilling . . . wonderful. She pulled the woolen robe tighter about her. The morning's majesty more than compensated for the bite of the frosty mountain air.

The last few years had been the happiest of her life. The years of sacrifice were all worth it. She shuddered, recalling the desperate war years, wondering if Sam would ever return, and the long winter nights, fighting off the horrible thoughts of death and pain. She remembered all too vividly the separation . . . she hated the very thought and tried to force it from her mind. The end of the Civil War brought untold joy to Mary, only 'til she discovered that another prolonged separation would be thrust upon her by the necessities of life.

Happily, the worry over just surviving was all past. The hard years were behind them, and the ranch was successful beyond their wildest hopes. They now owned the necessary farm equipment to run a large horse and cattle operation. The popular Morgan horses they were breeding brought high dollars, the cattle operation prospered, and they had accumulated enough capital to purchase lumber for a house with a real floor. No more sod huts. Even their small mining investments had paid handsomely . . . enabling them to purchase more bottom land for hay production, and in the mountains close at hand, unlimited grazing was available. The Dodd ranch now covered five thousand acres under title, much of it capable of producing quality hay. And blessings of all blessings, a real home. The newly constructed rambling log house had wood floors, a large kitchen, and a screened-in porch . . . the future looked bright.

Dear Lord, my cup runneth over, Mary thought to herself, *we've come such a long way*. She remembered clearly the cold Sunday afternoon in 1861 when Sam came to visit her family's Illinois farm. She saw him far off in the distance, walking down the icy-rutted road, shoulders hunched, with his coat snugly wrapped around his tall frame, gloved hands shoved deep into his pockets and hat pulled down tightly, so as not to be dislodged by the biting wind.

The Arbuckle farm was about two miles away from the Dodds, a good walk in the summer but a miserable stretch during a winter storm. The snowdrifts were piled high against the fences and the wind whipped small particles of sleet through the air, stinging on contact. The only barriers to the winter gales were the low fences and farm dwellings. Most of the trees were long gone, cut for firewood by the early settlers.

"Mama, Papa, Sam's coming down the road."

Late in the afternoon, the Arbuckles were enjoying the warmth of the pot-bellied stove.

Mary's father said, "Wonder what brings that Dodd boy over on a miserable day like this?" He winked at his wife. "Martha, think he's coming to borrow a cup of sugar? He couldn't be coming just to see Mary!"

"Stop teasing, John! We know he's not here to see us!"

Mary waited while Sam stomped the mud and snow from his boots; then she opened the kitchen door to a gust of white and penetrating cold. With a shiver, she said, "Hurry in, Sam—it's freezing out there."

Sam quickly stepped into the kitchen and took off his hat, releasing a heavy shock of light brown hair. He took a blue bandanna from his pocket and wiped the moisture from his clean-shaven face, then deferentially greeted Mary's parents.

"Howdy, Mrs. Arbuckle, Mr. Arbuckle. How are you, Sir?" Sam walked over to where Mary's father was seated and extended his hand. The senior Arbuckle rose and offered his in return. Sam's grip was firm but restrained, hiding the power in his lithe body. Young Dodd's gaze was direct, his gray eyes unwavering.

"We're all just fine, Sam. Say, what brings you out on a day like this? Any problems at home?"

"No Sir, everything's just fine. I have to talk to Mary.

"Want to take a walk, Mary?"

She looked outside at the swirling snow and was about to say "No," opting for the creature comforts of the front room, then realizing Sam wanted to talk out of earshot of her family, she answered, "Surely . . . it should be invigorating. I'll get my coat." Noticing the curious look on her father's face, Mary smiled. "Don't worry, Papa, we won't go far."

Mary had second thoughts as the freezing wind sought out every seam in her clothing, but moments later she felt a hot rush of fear as Sam abruptly announced, "Mary, I've enlisted in the Union army and I have to report for duty soon."

Mary felt faint, hardly able to stand. Her body was numb from the shock of his announcement. She had been fearful of such a day. She realized that the early hopes that the war would be of short duration dissolved at the Battle of Bull Run. The North had taken terrible losses and Illinois was raising an army to join in the fight; many local men were enlisting. President Lincoln called upon his home state to help preserve the Union. The men of Illinois were ready to answer the call of their favorite son . . . and Sam was one of them.

Mary took Sam's hand in hers and led him toward the barn. "Sweetheart, we have to talk," she said. The barn was filled with alfalfa hay and provided a shelter against the elements. The cows were in the stalls and restlessly ready for milking.

Mary climbed the ladder to the hayloft with Sam following. It was full of sweet-smelling alfalfa, harvested a few short months ago. She nestled down into the loose hay, seeking warmth. "Please Sam, come here."

Reluctantly, Sam complied, allowing ample room between them. Though he loved Mary with all his heart, he had never done more than hold her hand and steal a few boyish kisses. He didn't feel it was honorable to do otherwise. Although they had not yet spoken about it, Sam's intention was to wed his young sweetheart. They both assumed it as inevitable, ordained, written in stone. Mary's love was far more passionate, being less inclined to contain her more primeval impulses, but her respect for Sam—and her Christian upbringing—kept her emotions under control. She had been his girl since primary school and never had anyone else attracted her attention. Now she was about to lose him to this frightful war . . . maybe forever.

The mere thought of the ugly consequences of war made her move closer to his side, snuggling against him . . . burying deeper into the soft hay.

Mary looked at his strong handsome face and into his gray eyes. She reached up, kissed his cheek, and passionately whispered, "Darling, I have such a hunger for you that I can't explain in mere words. I can't bear the thought of not seeing you, knowing we may never be together. Did you know I've already named our first three children?" Tears were streaming down her face. "Oh, Lord, Sam, I love you so much!"

Sam reached over and gently brushed the auburn curls away from her tear-stained face. He looked at the sixteen-year-old beside him and was fully aware of what she had just offered—absolute, complete, uninhibited love. Never had she looked so desirable, so beautiful. Sam reached for her and kissed her, first softly, then with such ferocity it surprised them both. Sam drew back quickly, confused by the overpowering intensity of the sudden burst of desire.

"Mary, this isn't right. We'll marry when the war's over . . . we must wait. I'll be back . . . but in case . . . in case something happens . . . it's better . . . if we don't." Using more will power than he realized he possessed, Sam stood up and extended his hand to Mary. She just looked at him for a minute or two, then pulled herself up on her elbows and in a most matter-of-fact manner asked, "Samuel David Dodd, when do you have to leave?"

"In six days. Next Saturday."

Mary rejected Sam's outstretched hand and helped herself to her feet. Without a word to her bewildered companion, she scrambled for the ladder and scurried down. Sam followed as she ran towards the house. By the time she reached the kitchen door he had caught up with her.

Mary burst in and without taking off her muddy boots or coat, abruptly startled her parents. In a voice trucking no dissent, she stated emphatically, "Mama, Papa, Sam's joined the army and we're going to be married . . . tomorrow!"

And they were.

★★★

Mary sipped her coffee and watched the tip of the sun rise above the eastern horizon. She vividly remembered their wedding day, only a few friends and family in attendance. They were wed by their Baptist minister and had a few days alone before Sam left for the war. David Samuel Dodd, Jr. was born nine months and four days later.

The following years had been difficult but were a small price to pay for the life they now had. Mary opened her Bible to Psalm 92. "It is good to give thanks unto the Lord, and to sing praises unto thy name, O Most High: To show forth thy loving-kindness in the morning, and thy faithfulness every night . . . O Lord, how great are thy works!" Looking up and gazing at the landscape before her, Mary quietly bowed her head and gave thanks for their land, the children, and her husband. "And thank You, O Lord, for our Savior, Christ Jesus."

Mary could hear Sam and the older children stirring in the kitchen. The long work day was about to begin; her meditation time was just about over. With a cup of coffee in hand, Sam opened the door and sat down beside her. "Good morning, Sweetheart."

"Sam, remember the cold day in Papa's loft when we were snuggled down in the hay?"

"Nope."

"Fibber!"

"Oh, 'course I do." Sam blushed, "Some things are hard to forget." Sam placed his arm around her and, hugging her tightly, tried to change the subject. "Goin' to be a pretty day."

"You were a real gentleman." She leaned her head on his shoulder and hugged his arm, impishly enjoying Sam's uneasiness.

"Wasn't hard; you're a real lady."

She looked up and smiled, "Not as much as you thought I was."

Sam felt there were certain subjects men shouldn't talk about. Whenever one of these occasions arose, he would combat it with silence or with a quiet grunt. Some things were just too personal to verbalize.

"Umph."

Mary smiled coyly, changing the subject—much to Sam's delight. "You're right. It's goin' to be a nice day."

"Yep, an' I better get at it . . . there are chores to do." He leaned over and kissed her on the top of the head and strolled down the hill.

Mary watched him walk down to the shed where the cows were stalled. *There*, she thought, *goes a danged good man—not much of a talker, but a danged good man.*

Life had not been gentle for her husband. Since the close of the war there had been few easy times in the task of supporting the family, while trying to save enough capital to buy their own land. There had been plenty of sacrifice on both their parts. Mary and the children had to live with her family in Illinois while Sam headed the security force at the Sassy Mae Mine properties in Colorado and to make extra wages, he accepted the Silverville sheriff's offer of a part-time job as deputy. Considering the ramshackle roughness and the boisterous nature of a preponderantly male mining town, the people were remarkably honest. For a place that boasted nineteen hotels, forty-one boarding houses, eighty-two saloons, thirty-eight restaurants, twenty-one gambling houses, and thirty-five houses of prostitution . . . there were just three undertakers.

"Lots of fighting but not much killin'," Sam commented.

Although the job of deputy called for handling the mining camp rowdies, the additional pay was too good to turn down in exchange for a few black eyes and banged up knuckles. The ruffians of Silverville soon learned to walk a wide circle around Deputy Dodd, already known as no one to fool with. He soon became a recognizable threat to the rowdy element. His trademark was the weapon he carried—a sawed-off shotgun gripped firmly in his right hand which he used more as a club than a firearm. A few cracked skulls with the barrel or sharp pokes by the muzzle resolved many a barroom brawl. Sam did not like being a deputy, but the job hastened the day when the family could finally be together.

Mary and the children moved to Silverville, into the small house Sam built, but his two jobs left him with little time for the family. Mary hated his work as a Silverville lawman, and threats to kill him didn't help. Sam had arrested Orville and Joe Billy, two members of the Craven clan. Sam had bodily and unceremoniously thrown both of them in jail for drunk and disorderly conduct. They were a sullen bunch of troublesome miners who owned a small claim in Stray Horse Gulch. The Craven family threatened to even the score; Orville openly bragged that "the family was going to kill that psalm-singin' waddie!"

Threats were nothing new to Sam . . . they came with the job. The Craven boast was not one to be taken lightly. During one summer, in the late hours of a Saturday night, the Dodds were abruptly awakened by a series of pistol shots, followed by an explosion of glass and the wails of the children. Two men on horseback rode boisterously around their house, discharging shots through the windows and all along the walls of the wooden structure. Amid raucous laughter and cussing, they galloped off toward the center of town. Mary and Sam burst from bed, unmindful of the glass-strewn floor, and rushed to the children's rooms.

"Is everybody all right . . . answer me! Is anyone hurt? David, Sarah, answer me!"

The response was immediate, "We're fine Pa . . . what happened?"

In the dark, Mary could hear Matthew and Daniel groggily asking the same question. Baby Betsy was screaming. Mary moved to the crib and felt her body . . . her face was wet . . . and sticky.

"Sam, something's wrong with the baby!" Panic was in her voice as Betsy's screams grew louder. "Quick . . . someone get the lamp!"

"No . . . no light yet," Sam commanded as he quickly grabbed the shotgun from the mantle, slipped through the back door, and disappeared into the darkness. Moments later he returned, "It's all right. . . they're gone." Sam put the gun down on the kitchen table and lit the lamp.

The baby was still crying as the family gathered around the crib. A small piece of glass had lodged in Betsy's cheek, bloodying her tear-streaked face. Carefully, Mary removed the splinter and pressed a clean diaper to the wound to stem the trickle of blood. As Mary lifted her into her arms, Betsy stopped sobbing and rubbed her sleepy eyes. The other children appeared to be unhurt but Mary, when rushing across the darkened room, lacerated the soles of her feet on the shattered glass. Handing the baby to Sarah, she sat in the kitchen chair to inspect the damage.

As Sam looked at his wife's bleeding feet and then at the blood in the crib, rage welled up in his chest, up to his neck and jaw. Never had he witnessed such a dastardly act. He immediately dressed, snatched the shotgun from the table, jammed extra shells in his coat pocket, and lurched for the door. Through clenched teeth he muttered, "I'll be back." Once more he disappeared into the night. The moon was almost full, oblong, hanging like an illuminated balloon in the star-studded sky, casting deep shadows. The air was cool at ten thousand feet.

As he approached town, the din of the player pianos and the high-pitched fiddles and banjoes mingled with raucous voices. It became irritatingly louder and louder as he neared Walnut Avenue. Harlot-filled cribs dotted the street and patrons staggered in and out of the saloons. Saturday night was "fun time" for the miners to "get drunk and bunk up with the scarlet maidens of Silverville." Walnut Avenue was the place to be. Rotgut and ladies of the night were for the asking . . . at a price.

Sam was sure the Cravens would be a part of the carousing mob. Three men were warming themselves before an open fire as Sam approached. One called out a friendly greeting.

Recognizing them from the Sassy Mae Mine, Sam quickly inquired without slowing his pace, "See any riders come this way?"

"Sure did, Mr. Dodd . . . Orville and Joe Billy Craven just rode by a laughin' and a cussin' . . . seemed like they was drunker'n skunks!" The others nodded in agreement.

"See where they headed?"

"Yep. Watched them go into Maddy's down the end of the street."

Without a word Sam continued on, quickening his pace to a shuffling dog trot. He knew the Cravens would probably be bragging to their friends at Maddy's Irish Bar. He was wrong. Sam instinctively ducked into the shadows as a shot whistled by his head. Leaning against the hitching rail in front of Maddy's was Orville Craven, aiming a smoking pistol in Sam's direction. At the sight of Craven, he halted and moved deeper into the shadows. Something was amiss; Orville Craven wasn't brave enough to take him on alone. Could it be he was walking into an ambush? Where was Joe Billy?

"Wha's the matter, Dodd . . . scared? Come on, I'm gonna shoot holes through that badge ya got on yer chest!"

Orville Craven leveled the gun and fired once more into the shadows, splintering wood near Sam's head. "Come on, ya coward, come out in the open! Shoot it out in the street like a man!" Orville swaggered into the middle of the street, aimed and shot again.

At that distance, Sam's sawed-off shotgun was useless.

Orville knew it . . . Sam knew it too! Where was the other Craven? At the alleyway, down and across the street, Sam saw the brim of a hat appear, then move out of sight. Sure he had located Joe Billy, Sam exploded into the street at a dead run, zigzagging toward the alley, darting in and out of the shadows. He had to get close. He knew both Cravens had been drinking, so their reflexes couldn't be razor sharp; hitting a weaving target was tough enough sober, doubly difficult at night. Orville fired again, kicking up dust, then again, a bullet humming by Sam's ear. By the time Sam approached the alleyway, Orville had expended all six loads. Sam swerved to the boardwalk and hugged the walls as he ran, forcing the man in the alley to step out for a clear shot. Sam fired both barrels. At least half of the double-0 buckshot tore off the side of the building; the other half smashed the ambusher into eternity, slamming Joe Billy into the ground. One down.

A terror-stricken Orville Craven frantically tried to shove new rounds into the chamber of his gun . . . fumbling . . . dropping shells on the ground. He succeeded in loading only two rounds as Sam hurried relentlessly toward him, reloading the shotgun as he ran. Craven wildly fired both shots, then continued to thumb back the hammer on his single-action Colt. The staccato of the pin falling on empty rounds allowed Sam to slow down. He walked the remaining short distance and faced the weeping, slobbering coward.

"My God, I'm out'a shells." He dropped the gun as if it were on fire.

"I'm unarmed!" Orville whined, "Ya wouldn't shoot an unarmed man, would ya?"

* * *

At the inquest, Sam was absolved of the double killing; no one doubted they deserved to die. Although Sam was somewhat remorseful over the elimination of Orville, he knew his family could never be bothered by either of the two troublemakers again.

Mary felt it was time to leave Silverville while Sam was still alive. They'd move to their land in northern Colorado, into a quickly constructed sod house if need be. Better a cold earthen floor than a cold, dead husband.

* * *

"Yes, life has been good . . . recently! Praise the Lord." Mary rose from the porch and stretched with her arms crossed above her head, moving side to side, trying to remove the stiffness from sitting on the cold stoop. "Don't loosen up as quick as I used to. Oh well . . . age!"

The sun had cleared the eastern horizon and warm pastels now replaced the vibrant tones of early morn. The children were noisily bustling about the kitchen. David, the eldest, burst out the door and bounded past his mother, giving her a moist, exuberant kiss on his way to the barn. "Gotta help Pa with the chores."

Mary smiled tenderly as she brushed her damp cheek with the back of her hand. "Breakfast will be ready soon," she called to the running boy. "Clean up before you come back into the house." David waved without looking back, having so often heard those words before.

Mary set about preparing their main meal. She sliced the ham and potatoes while Sarah broke the eggs and readied the batter for griddle cakes. They made sure there was plenty of beans, bread, and pan gravy.

Sam and the boys loved beans. More than once he said, "It's a man's food. Nothin' better for a hungry hand than a pot of navies simmerin' on the cook stove." Slathered on a slice of buttered bread, the dish was a favorite.

After the dishes were cleared away, the education of the younger children began. There was no schoolhouse within a two-day ride and like many frontier families, learnin' came from mother and the Good Book.

School texts were difficult to obtain and anyone who had a full set of *McGuffy's Readers* was fortunate. Mary had acquired a few books, but the major text was still Holy Writ.

The Bible was an indispensable tool, as essential to Mary as her kitchen stove. A day rarely passed when she did not read from it, to teach or preach. Scripture was used to emphasize a point or correct a child. Proverbs was her favorite book to quote and she inevitably found a verse to fit any occasion. The Scriptures were not a once-a-week experience for the Dodds nor for many others . . . it was the core of their existence, the

Rock upon which families were built. The Dodds observed the Sabbath by holding most work to a minimum. Only rudimentary tasks were performed . . . feeding stock, milking the cows.

The Lord commanded the seventh day as a day of rest and worship . . . and so it was for the Dodds to faithfully obey. Mary looked upon God as their special Friend. *Hadn't He protected Sam through the terrible war, looked over us through years of separation, given us healthy children, provided for our every need, and led us to our present surroundings? Of course He had.* There was no question in her mind that from Him all of their blessings flowed. She doubted that anything could alter the present happiness; the troubled times were past. *No question about it—the hardest years are behind us.*

CHAPTER 5

"INDIANS! . . . MOTHER! . . . INDIANS!" Sarah's voice was half-scream and half-shout, high-pitched, desperate, coming from the direction of the barn. Mary automatically reached for the Springfield rifle leaning against the wall, then slammed through the screened door onto the porch. Her heart was pounding as she saw her oldest daughter racing toward the house with baby John in tow. Rapidly gaining on them was a painted Ute savage, war club poised above his head, ready to strike. Mary jerked the gun to her shoulder and fired . . . *missed!* The bullet kicked dust in front of the warrior, bringing him to a stop, buying precious seconds for Sarah. Seeing the terrified woman clumsily trying to reload a rifle, he let out a bloodcurdling yell and resumed his chase.

KAPOW! The Ute was halted once more by another bullet, this one screaming by his ear. It whistled past Mary's head as well, coming from the doorway behind her. Five-year-old Betsy stood there, feet apart, holding a .44 Colt single-action in both hands, squinting down the barrel, smoke rising from the muzzle. She was in the process of thumbing back the hammer for the second shot when both Sarah and Mary exploded by her into the house. Mary grabbed Betsy by the back of her dress dragging her through the doorway, but not before she got off another round in the general direction of the astonished Ute. Mary slammed and bolted the door, quickly placing another shell in the breach-loading Springfield, poked it through the gun slot, and fired at the retreating savage.

"Did I hit 'em, Ma, did I hit 'em?" Betsy's face was bright with excitement as her mother grabbed the smoking gun from her hands.

"You did just fine, Betsy; now . . . you girls go check the back of the house! Sarah, look out the north side, both of you . . . do it quick!" Mary's urgent command was immediately obeyed.

Oh Lord, please let Sam and the boys be close enough to hear the shots!

Sam heard. Faint, far away, the sound of gunshots stiffened all three; heads up, alert, each reached for his rifle. Sam and the two younger boys were cutting lodge pole timber for a new horse corral when they heard the sounds reverberate off the mountainside. But in the high country, noises could be hard to define, bouncing off steep terrain, ricocheting up canyons, disguising direction.

"Pa, was that a shot? Did that come from the ranch?" asked Matt.

"Boys, follow me close, you hear?" Sam set off at a dogtrot with the boys fast on his heels, his mind racing over the possibilities. *Can't be David; he's helping round up cattle over at the Wilson place.* All thoughts were quickly synthesized with the pistol shots: There was bad trouble at the house. Sam's insides tightened each time the revolver fired, filling him with fear. The boys surged ahead at the sound of the rifle shot. Once more their father commanded them to trail behind. His pace quickened somewhat, but not enough for the boys.

"Pa, can't we go faster?"

"Stay behind me . . . do as I say!" Sam wanted desperately to dash down the mountainside but experience and reason prevailed; an exhausted, winded, middle-aged rancher with two young boys was no competition for hostiles. He had seen men rush pall-mall into battle but when called upon to shoot, they were too breathless to effectively aim and fire their rifles. Although there had been Indian raids on isolated ranches, so far the Dodd spread had been left alone. Sam had trained the family well; with almost military precision, they were instructed in the use of firearms, and just what each member should do in case of an attack. Some settlers who hadn't taken precaution had been brutally massacred. Sam had planned for every conceivable contingency. "If Mary and the youngsters follow instructions, they should be pretty safe, at least 'til we get there."

The Dodds were well-armed. Sam bought two .44-caliber Winchester Henry repeating rifles, each firing sixteen rounds. One, he kept with him at all times; the other he gave to David. Few Indians had anything comparable. Inside the house, by both front and back doors, were loaded Springfield breechloaders, with ammunition within easy reach. A loaded Remington army .44-caliber revolver or Springfield rifle was in every room. A loaded double-barreled shotgun hung over the fireplace. All the children except baby John had been given strict orders in their use. Daniel and Matthew carried converted Springfield breechloaders, firing a .577- caliber bullet that could knock a man clean to kingdom come. They were clumsy for teenage boys to carry, but strapped over shoulders, the boys didn't seem to mind. No one went anywhere unarmed, not even behind the house to chop wood.

Sam knew the importance of being properly equipped, having lived through three years of Civil War combat from Vicksburg to Atlanta; he had no intention of being killed by some savage after surviving Johnny Reb. No member of his family was going to lose a scalp to any Ute, Kiowa, or Comanche warrior.

Once more the boys forged even with their father, who was still jogging at a frustrating pace. Infuriated by the slow descent, Daniel blurted, "Pa . . . shouldn't we hurry?" Desperate looks were on their youthful faces, panic in their eyes. Both wanted to rush ahead of their dogtrotting father.

"Pa, let's run!"

"Boys, do exactly as I say!" His voice had a quality of command that called for immediate obedience, so dutifully, they fell behind once more. For what seemed an eternity they picked their way down the mountainside and through the timber. While still in the shadows of the pines, Sam stopped, looked in all directions, then cut to the right keeping a small grove of aspens between themselves and the ranch.

"Do as I do and no noise!" Sam hissed to the boys. Bent over, making low silhouettes, they ran toward the barn, keeping the slope of the hill to their advantage. When in sight of the buildings, Sam dropped to one knee and motioned the boys to kneel behind him while he quickly scanned the movement ahead. Four armed, war-painted Ute braves were yanking out the corral posts while another, mounted, was leading the horses away. One of the renegades, spotting Sam and the boys, let out a war cry and pointed in their direction. Sam raised his rifle, braced his elbow on his knee, and coolly shot the horse from under the rider, scattering the animals. The wounded horse collapsed, tumbling the Ute to the ground. As he scrambled to his feet, Sam's 200-gram, .44-caliber shell slammed into his chest, knocking him backward onto the downed kicking horse. Both Indian brave and horse lay there in a tangled heap, convulsing in the dirt. The other warriors started firing, filling the air with the gruesome hum of bullets passing overhead. All the gunfire kicked up dust, forcing the boys to hug tightly to the ground. The Indians darted among the milling, frightened horses, attempting to hide themselves from Sam's deadly fire. Three carried short-barreled, smooth-bore muskets, neither effective nor accurate at more than a hundred yards. One shouldered a Winchester repeating rifle and rapidly began to shoot, jacking round after round into the chamber. Sam fired, spinning the Ute brave groundward with a bullet in the lower abdomen. The next shot completed the job. "Boys, hunker down right here 'til I call for you, understand?"

"Yeh, Pa." Both boys, wide-eyed, had just seen their father cold-bloodedly kill one of their prized mares, then drop two men just like prairie chickens. Now he was calmly ordering them to sit still as if they were at the supper table.

Sam rose and took off, weaving down the hill toward the remaining Indians who were desperately trying to reload their muskets. At about a hundred and fifty yards he stopped, brought the rifle crisply to his shoulder, and off-hand, shot a third Ute, knocking him over backward. Another fired at Sam, kicking dust over his right boot. With a shout of defiance, the Indian tossed away his empty musket, pulled a knife from his belt, and rushed toward Sam, bending low to the ground . . . zigzagging closer. Matthew and Dan watched in horror as the wild, screaming Indian charged their father. Making sure the horses were out of the line of fire, Sam slowly moved to the left, raised the Henry rifle, and shot the savage in the forehead. He dropped as if he had run into a barricade, shuddered once, then lay still, no more than twenty feet away. The last of the attackers stepped from behind the corral fence and threw his weapon to the ground. He stood rock still, arms folded across his chest, staring impassively at Sam, resigned to death. Sam held the stoic Indian in his sights, the oldest of the lot, gray streaks in his raven-black hair, deep wrinkles etched in his weathered face, battle scars on his body. He held his chin high, defiantly, indifferently . . . a Ute warrior to the end.

"Shoot 'em, Pa!" screamed an excited Matthew from the distance.

After several deathly quiet moments had passed, Sam dropped his gun to his side and stood equally still. No one spoke. Finally, the Indian turned and trotted away, down the slope and through the aspens.

Sam watched him disappear from sight, then quickly spun on his heels and ran towards the house, relieved to see Mary and the children emerge from within.

"We're all right, Sam. What about you and the boys?"

"Don't worry about us," he answered. "Go back in the house. I don't want the girls to see what's happened."

"All right, Sam." Mary turned and herded the children inside.

Sam turned his attention to the bodies at the corral, watching to see if there was any movement. Several minutes passed before each one lay motionless, the convulsions of death finally spent. The boys watched their father circle carefully around the downed Utes, then from behind, approach and poke each one sharply with his rifle barrel. He stepped back and shot one of them again. Convinced they were all dead, he called to the boys. "Matthew! Dan! Round up the horses before they wander too far off—and keep your eyes open!"

"Yes, Pa," came an awed response. The boys had just witnessed a side of their father they hadn't seen nor even vaguely suspected. They had always thought of their mother as the iron-willed one of the two. Both were strong, but Mama seemed to have the edge. Now they knew different; they had a glimpse of how their father survived three years of one of the blackest wars in human memory. The boys had always been aware of their Pa's physical strength and his seemingly tireless energy. Now they saw the depth of his courage and control under conditions that would panic most men. After dragging the four bodies into the shed and covering them temporarily with straw to keep the flies away, he hadn't even broken a sweat. He seemed calm and collected. Not so the boys: Dan felt a bit nauseous; Matt was nervously jabbering asking his father one question after another. Finally, with the horses corralled and the dead mare dragged away, Sam turned to the boys.

"Come with me—we need to talk." They entered the dark, cool shed where rays of light fell through the cracks in the sod walls. Their father motioned for them to sit on the bench against the damp wall. Both sat silently while their father threw more hay on the corpses. Inside, their hearts were racing, their senses at razor's edge. They had seen death firsthand, the blood and screams of the dying, twisted forms on gore-soaked ground. They didn't like it . . . they didn't like it at all. Now, the smell of sweet hay and decaying manure, combined with the awareness of four dead Indians just a few feet away, mixed a nauseous brew for Matthew. He desperately wanted to vomit, but the mortification of throwing up in front of his Pa and brother kept his stomach under control. Dan started to squirm when at last their father spoke.

"Boys, under that pile of hay are four men who, but for an act of thievery, would still be alive. I took no pleasure in shooting them, nor have I ever felt glory over the killing of any human being. The Lord says it is wrong to take human life and I believe that is true." Sam slammed his fist down hard into the palm of his hand to make the point. "'Thou shalt not kill,' saith the Lord!"

Sam was quiet for a moment, contemplating what he had just said. "Boys, sorrow is the lot of killing, sometimes to the one who kills and always for the ones who lose a loved one." And as a quiet afterthought, "Someone always mourns. Some Indian Mama will cry tonight . . . some child has lost a Pa . . . some Pa, a son. It will be a bitter, sorrowful, night in more than one lodge. Not one of those Indian boys was over thirty, 'cept the one I let go."

The sadness in their father's voice shrouded the darkened interior of the shed; for once little Dan remained quiet as Sam collected his thoughts.

"Unfortunately, some folks pay no attention to right and wrong; those poor savages were out to steal our horses and only God knows what else they had in their thievin' minds. No doubt they would have murdered us if they had the chance. It's a fact, they certainly didn't come here to bargain or trade." Sam took a deep breath and looked toward the pile of straw, "I had to kill them—they gave me no other choice . . . that's for sure, no other choice."

Sam paced slowly back and forth before his sons.

"Pa, why didn't you shoot that last one?" asked Matthew.

"Yeah, why not, Pa? Why'd you let him get away?" piped in an animated Daniel.

Sam looked at his wide-eyed sons. "He surrendered when he threw down his gun. That one was the smartest of the lot; he knew I could kill him with ease and I guess he was resigned to die like a brave. He put his life in my hands. It was the only chance he had to stay alive. Besides, he'll tell others it's dangerous to steal from this ranch."

Sam continued to pace in front of his sons, reaching for the words to explain, to justify what had just happened. He remembered killing Orville Craven—without hesitation he blew him in half and yet he'd let the Indian go free. "Boys, it's proper and just for a man to defend his honor, country, and home. Pray to God you always do the right thing, 'cause sometimes you won't have time to think about it. Violence can come on you sudden-like."

"Like today, Paw?" asked Matthew.

"Yes, Son, like today." Sam solemnly nodded his head.

"Sometimes deadly force is the only answer ya got. I've watched good men die 'cause in a moment of indecision, they didn't act and for their hesitation, they got a bayonet through the gut. If yer called upon to kill . . . kill. Shootin' another is no game nor is it wise just to wound an enemy. Men die hard and angry . . . swearin' and cussin'. I've seen fellows reach deep down inside and find the energy to fire one more shot. I've seen dead men rise up and fatally wound the very one who shot 'em."

"Pa, is that the reason you shot that one Indian on the ground?"

"That's right, son. I wasn't convinced he was dead. I just made sure. Boys, we live in a rugged land an' if we're to survive, if you're to live a full life, you may be called on to use a gun. I pray that time will never come. But if it does, you must think only of the task at hand and never about the well-being of those you face. Some of the men who joined the Union army couldn't effectively fire a rifle and a sergeant said,'It's just like shootin' squirrels, only them squirrels got guns.' Cold-hearted as it sounds, that's how you have to think of it . . . shooting squirrels. Any remorseful thoughts must come later . . . and come they will." The last sentence spoken was so low the boys had to strain to hear. Their father slowly leaned forward and whispered with an intensity that burned the words into their minds.

"Never point a gun at anything you're not willin' to kill nor be undecided about shootin' anyone who points a weapon at you. Be calm. Never show fear, even though it's eating you alive, and never, never show your back to an enemy . . . the sight of it gives em' courage, the front of you makes them weak. If it's smart to retreat, back down and live to fight another day like that Indian. Always keep your guns clean, loaded, an' handy. Make sure your knife is always sharp."

The boys waited silently while their father pitched more hay over the dead Indians.

"Your mama and me pray that none of you'll ever have to kill, or hurt anyone. We're all God's creatures and it'd be wonderful if we could let each other be, but since Adam hankered to chew on that apple, men have been killin' and robbin' each other. Like it or not, you'll have to fight. You better be good at it or your Ma and me will have to bury you." Sam shook at the thought. "God forbid that day ever happens."

Sam knew he had to teach them more about the discipline needed in confronting an enemy, but now was not the time. He wanted his boys to benefit from the knowledge he had gained, but in many ways he wished he would never have to discuss it again. Talk about it he would, for the sake of his sons. Preparing the children to cope with the ugly side of life was his responsibility, and he was certain the subject of death would have to be broached again.

He had trained his eldest, David, on the use of firearms and the training had come in handy when they had to run off some prospectors intent on trespassing. Now, Matt and Dan had just been given their first lesson in dealing with death. Hopefully, by the time baby John reached the age where he had to learn such things, Colorado would be civilized enough that he wouldn't have to train him, too, in the use of deadly force.

"Sons . . . 'til Christ comes again, man'll continue to sin, and sin again. Stealin' and murder will be with us 'til the Resurrection . . . you can count on it!"

The immediate problem was four dead men who had to be buried before rigor mortis set in.

"Dan, hitch up the wagon an' Matt, go get a pick and a couple of shovels. I'll check with your mother on where she wants 'em buried." Don't mention to your mother about that last shot."

Without a word they went about their chores.

★★★

"We have to give the four of them a Christian burial," Mary insisted firmly.

"But Mary," Sam protested, "they're war-painted, almost-nude heathens!"

"They may have been heathens, but then . . . maybe not. What matters is that *we* aren't."

No sense arguing with Mary about any subject she believed fell within the perimeters of Holy Writ.

The chosen family resting place bordered a small, lazy stream that meandered down from the mountains. A grove of aspen formed a semicircle around the grassy knoll. To the north, the land sloped away, giving a pastoral view of the valley below. The persistent wind sashaying here and yon caused the native grass to sway gently, giving the appearance of vibrant life to the land. At sun up, the first morning light hit the top of the aspens, slowly working down the foliage, spilling across the leaves to make them shimmer with iridescent vitality. It was the most beautiful place on the entire ranch, a fitting place to return to dust. Nearby, against Sam's mild objections, they dug the graves for the four Ute renegades.

Mary spoke to the Lord on behalf of the departed and read words from the Good Book. Sam wasn't too pleased to have Indians buried within sight of the proposed family graveyard, but Mary reminded him that the Utes had been there long before any Dodd had set foot in Colorado.

The family wore their best to the funeral. After the service Mary and the children retired to the ranch house, leaving the job of burying the four braves to Sam and the older boys. The bodies were wrapped in dilapidated, dusty canvas tied with rope—lumber being too dear to fashion the coffins. Sam bent over each cadaver and opened the canvas, exposing their heads. On every face he painted a red stripe before closing them up again.

"Pa, why you doing that?" asked Dan.

"Ute custom, Son. It's a greeting to their great spirits. A warrior must be properly painted when he meets his ancestors."

"It ain't Christian, is it?" asked Dan.

"Well, Son—guess not—but I don't think the Lord will mind."

★ ★ ★

Concealed in the timber, watching the ceremony through a powerful telescope, was a lone spectator. Attached to the telescope was a rifle.

"Stupid Indians," he muttered to himself. "Five of them couldn't steal one horse or kill one man! This won't be easy."

He removed his hat and scratched his head. "Aussie Walker was right; this Sam Dodd may be the toughest." He pondered the task before him. *He hardly leaves the ranch alone and rarely without the dogs. Can't approach the ranch without being seen. Too tough to shoot from a distance 'cause he rarely sits still long enough to get a good bead on him.*

He smiled, smoothed his flaxen hair, and replaced his wide-rimmed hat. "Dodd, you're a real challenge, not like the others."

He moved quietly through the woods to his horse and carefully placed the rifle in a specially constructed scabbard, designed to carry the long-barreled rifle and telescope. Reaching behind the saddle, he removed the bedroll. "Well, looks like we may be here awhile."

Chapter 6

The cool touch of late fall was in the air, that special brittle crispness proclaiming the close of the third act of God's seasonal play. The announcement of impending snow filled the evening breeze, bidding farewell to fall. Dawn may have been Mary's special time, but for Sam, dusk suited him best. It was the time to reflect upon the day's labor, smoke his pipe, and enjoy the aroma of supper cooking on the stove . . . besides, sunsets in the Colorado mountains were spectacles that should not be missed.

Thin strips of gray clouds crossed the sky and the sun, just before ducking behind the Medicine Bow Mountains, seemed to emit more intensive rays, painting the gray clouds and rock faces iridescent crimson and gold. Everything seemed more alive, more vibrant.

A fitting time for a man, Sam thought as he watched cool shadows creep up the mountainside. High on the eastern slopes, white-trunked aspens offered a stark contrast to the green pine and yellow leaves shimmering in the evening sun.

High on the western slopes, a cow-elk casually moved into the open, leaving the security of the black pine to satisfy her hunger . . . then another . . . then another. Before long, the entire slope was covered by grazing Wapiti.

The old bulls wait 'til the last few minutes of light before they come out to feed, Sam mused. *Let the ladies discover if any danger lurks in the open.* Sam puffed deeply on his pipe, reflecting on the symmetry of it all—the seasons, the living, the dying, and how it all fit together in perfect harmony . . . dust to dust.

The four Utes buried just over the hill came to mind . . . a deep melancholy welled up within him. Although two weeks had gone by, the bitter memory hadn't diminished.

At forty, he had his fill of dying, enough to last a hundred lifetimes. Now was the time to enjoy life . . . the time to watch his children grow, marry, and share the joy and tribulations of raising their families. The mental image of grandchildren made him smile, as did the thought of growing old with Mary.

One of the family's dogs silently approached and tried to place its head in Sam's lap. "Whatcha doin', Rusty? Want some petting?" Reaching down, he scratched him behind the ear as the dog's tail beat a tune of appreciation on the porch floor.

Sam opened his Bible and turned to the Book of Ecclesiastes where Solomon, the wisest of the wise, spoke poetically of life, death, and the difficulty of seeking wisdom. "One generation passeth away, and another generation cometh; but the earth abideth for ever."

Sam grinned. *If Solomon had trouble seeking wisdom and found it a grievous task, it's sure more than a simple rancher like me can resolve. At least Solomon was wise enough to find out, "Fear God, and keep his commandments: for this is the whole duty of man."* Sam reached over and patted his dog again. "Rusty, smart words sure cut through a lot of sagebrush and thistle. If obeying the Lord was good enough for that smart old bird, it's good enough for me."

The evening wind had died down to a whisper, then imperceptibly shifted, the warmer air rising up the hill. Rusty's tail stopped wagging and a low growl vibrated in his throat. Sam leaned forward in his chair, took the pipe from his mouth, and scanned the grove of pines at the foot of the hill. He had built the new ranch house on a bare knoll, a solid log exterior with lumbered pine floors and porch. It was large, rambling, and rugged—a mini-fortress in the wilderness. Sam and the boys had cleared away all remaining trees and shrubbery within a thousand yards, with nothing to mar the immediate view. Whoever approached could be seen at a safe distance . . . before getting within normal rifle range. Suddenly, a cotton ball—a puff of white smoke—appeared against the dark green of the pine. . . .

Chapter 7

FOR SEVEN DAYS the snow had swirled downward, dancing round and round with the whistling wind, obscuring the landscape, blanketing everything it touched. Shadows disappeared and sky, earth, and smoke merged into a dull white oneness. Winter had arrived in Silverville with a vengeance. Occasionally, dark figures could be seen darting from building to woodpile to privy and back; even traffic to the saloons and cribs had slowed somewhat.

Intermittent bursts of wind built deep drifts against Charlie's palatial home, covering the north-side windows with a curtain of white. It was teeth-chattering cold . . . vicious, mean, life-robbing weather.

At last the snowing had stopped and the early morning sun blindingly cream-tipped the snow-blanketed mountains, crowfooting the eyes, wrinkling the nose.

Charlie Meyers squinted as he looked out the bay windows then quickly returned to the comfort of the divan, not far from the roaring fire.

"Lordy, it's cold!" Charlie pulled the blanket tightly about his frail frame and moved his feet closer to the hearth. His bluish lower lip quivered as the coughing—deep-seated, ugly, bending him over in pain—began anew. He took the handkerchief from his mouth; telltale blood speckled the cloth.

"Blast it!" Racked with pain and frustration, Charlie threw the handkerchief into the fire. "Jest when you git to the top of the heap, you git sick an' die!"

He looked around the spacious and beautiful living room, filled with the finest furniture, draperies, and paintings money could buy. Building his mansion had taken better than a year to complete. Charlie brought Chicago's finest architects and decorators to Silverville and commissioned them to build a mansion better than that of Clarence Tabor, Leadville's most noteworthy mine owner and leading citizen. They had succeeded at great expense, but to Charlie Meyers, money was no concern; he had plenty of it. His mining investments had mushroomed beyond his wildest dreams. Every claim Charlie owned was producing valuable minerals. The Sassy Mae Mine held a body of silver that was the envy of every prospector in Colorado.

"Sassy Mae, you cheatin' wench, you brought all this to me. If you hadn't left me for that rotten gravedigger, I'd still be grubbin' around in that Illinois coal mine, tryin' to make ends meet."

Thinking about Sassy Mae still hurt, but not as badly as before. His financial success had somewhat moderated the burning hatred he had borne for her. His revenge was satiated in her lover's plight; Charlie's wealth had seen to that.

Sassy Mae's paramour was a weak man who, at the first sign of intimidation, had left her for safer environs. "The cowardly gigolo ain't got no backbone," Charlie muttered. "All I gotta do is send Jethro after him to scare him into the next state."

Which is exactly what Charlie had done. It wasn't too difficult tracking down an Italian mortician. Each time his prey found new employment and was somewhat settled, Jethro Briggs would appear, asking around. As soon as Sassy Mae's one-time beau got word of it, he'd flee, leaving whatever he had accumulated behind. Charlie had originally sent Jethro to kill the bugger, but chasing him from state to state was much more fun. Charlie loved asking Jethro about all the details of each flight. Jethro gladly obliged, discovering that any ribald embellishment sent Charlie into howls of delight.

"Ya mean you caught him in the arms of a harlot?"

"Shore did," Jethro smirked. "I waited until he was all excited, then I shouted out, loud as I could, Adolpho Garabaldi, this here's Jethro Briggs. I'm here to shoot you dead . . . come out and fight like a man!"

"Good for you, Jethro. What did that wife-stealin' Latin do?"

"What'd he do? Why, Charlie, he didn't even wait to open the danged window. I heared the breakin' of glass as that durn fool jumped clean through into the snow."

"Must'a hurt him a bit to do that." Charlie beamed with joy. "Then what?"

"Well, I went into the room and this here naked dove was settin' in bed with the covers up about her neck, shakin' with fright. I told 'er I didn't mean her no harm, I was jest after Mr. Garabaldi. After she calmed down, she asked me if she could get paid for a job half done."

"You mean she wanted you to pay the bill for half-services rendered?" Charlie incredulously asked.

"Yep, her price was fifty cents and she demanded two bits. She claimed I was at fault for her loss of employment."

Charlie was laughing so hard tears were rolling down his whiskered cheeks. He could hardly speak. "Wha . . . what happened then?"

"I went over ta the window ta see if there was any blood on the broke glass. Lookin' at the soiled lass, I said, bet he ripped the seat outa his pants on the way out . . . and Charlie, you jest can't guess what she said next!"

"Wha? Out with it. . . . What'd she say?"

"Charlie, you won't believe this—I *swear* you won't!"

"Darn it, Jethro, what did she say?"

She said, "What clothes? . . . Haw! . . . He was naked as a peeled potater!"

"You mean ol' Adolpho warn't wearin' nothin'?"

"Nuder than the day he was born! Poked my head outa the window and saw barefoot prints an' blood spots in the snow. All he was wearin' was scratches."

"Well, I'll be darned." Charlie was grinning from ear to ear in sheer delight. "Did you pay the girl?"

"Didn't have to. Adolpho Garabaldi's pants were hangin' over a chair in the corner an' he had a small poke in his pocket—two silver dollars and some change. I barely beat the wench to the clothes. Once she remembered where they was, she exploded outa bed, nuder than a cue ball. We both made a beeline for his drawers . . . she was tuggin' on one leg of his pants and me on the other. Had to kick her on the shins so she'd let go. She shore did know how to cuss! . . . hoppin' 'round on one leg givin' me what for."

Charlie was limp from laughing and Jethro was real pleased with his storytelling; making the boss laugh was smart business.

"Whatcha do, give her a quarter?"

"Yep, I felt sorry for the poor dear, hoppin' 'round, freezin' wind blowin' on her bare bones an all. Bein' gentle-hearted, I gave her one of the silvers."

"That was durn nice of you, Briggs."

"Yep, thought so m'self."

Briggs lied . . . he gave her two bits and struck a deal for two bits more.

Chasing mortician Garabaldi came to an end when he left for Italy, but the tormenting of Sassy Mae continued. Without means of support she and her son, Charlie Jr., were forced to return to her parents' farm. Sassy, being their only child, was warmly welcomed home. Charlie's harassment was somewhat contained as long as she remained with her folks, but he continued to send her any and all newspaper clippings referring to his success. He wanted to make sure she knew of his wealth, his prestigious position in the community, and the fact that senators, congressmen, and governors were his personal friends. Charlie lost no opportunity to flaunt his prosperity before her eyes. *Revenge is sweet,* Charlie thought. *It's been sustaining me for a long, long time.*

He coughed again as he continued to look about the parlor. Charlie admired the oak-paneled walls, the heavy brocade drapes bordering the spacious windows, the Persian carpets covering polished hardwood floors, the romantic eighteenth-century French paintings that adorned the walls and, in particular, the painting of a reclining nude on a stallion above the hearth. He had given a tintype of his former wife to an accomplished English portrait artist and commissioned him to render a voluptuous lady with Sassy Mae's head—a difficult task.

Although Charlie thought Sassy Mae beautiful, others found her quite plain. He was more than satisfied with the final results, but the painting was glaringly out of place with the other furnishings. At the party Charlie had thrown to show off his new residence, the oil painting evoked a great deal of subtle mirth. The state dignitaries in attendance were discreet; however, the social editor from the Denver *Rocky Mountain News* boldly wrote, "Charlie Meyers' mansion is a thing of opulent beauty, marred only by the painting of a bare lady upon a horse's back. The nubile body is of a goddess, but differentiating between the head of the horse and the face of the nude is difficult at best."

Charlie was not amused. Neither was the social editor when her employment was terminated without notice. It didn't pay to anger Charlie Meyers.

Charlie "Goldie" Meyers was filthy rich, successful beyond his wildest dreams. After the war, he migrated to the Colorado gold fields with but a few dimes in his pocket. Several of his claims bore workable gold deposits—nothing immediately spectacular, but productive enough to employ a number of his old war associates. Charlie believed that some of the worked-out gold claims in the headwaters of the Arkansas River still had possibilities and whenever the opportunity arose, he bought the rights to the mines. Later, in 1874, local miners Al Stevens and Bill Woods assayed some black rocks and discovered they contained sixteen ounces of silver to the ton. It wasn't long before every miner knew that part of Colorado was a mountain of precious metal. Silverville sprang into existence. Charlie's gold claims were rich in ore-filled black rocks. Charlie, however, discovered that finding a bonanza was one thing; keeping it was another.

Charlie trusted few men before and none after his newly acquired wealth. Gold shipments were robbed, miners helped themselves to nuggets, and muggings and killings were common occurrences. Law enforcement was practically nonexistent; counting on it was a joke. The riffraff of the world saw new mining towns as their own personal bonanza and were attracted to them as flies to a dung heap.

Charlie had no real friends in the mining community. He was smart enough to acknowledge that friends were a dime a dozen when you have some gold in the pocket. He was justifiably suspicious of everyone he met after discovering his first rich claim. He wanted people around him he could trust, men who could help him keep his claims intact, people he knew intimately.

Those who came to mind were the men he'd fought with in the war—comrades from the Illinois Thirty-first Infantry. He wired twelve of them and offered employment. Several of the old acquaintances accepted immediately. Work was hard to come by after the war—especially good paying jobs—so Sam Dodd, Jethro Briggs, Otto Schmitz, Kenneth Seymour, and Andy Quade headed for Silverville.

All who went to work for Charlie prospered. They helped him consolidate his claims, protected his property, and gave him trustworthy, loyal companionship. He reciprocated by paying them well. Now, he was one of the richest men in the West—associate of governors and senators, politically powerful, member of the finest clubs in Colorado . . . and destined to die of consumption.

The years of inhaling the powdered black coal of Illinois and the hard-rock mine dust of Colorado had ruined his lungs. The gallons of rotgut liquor and too many cigars hadn't helped.

The violent coughing spells became frequent and the blood-specked handkerchiefs had finally forced him to see a doctor. He remembered the conversation vividly.

"Mr. Meyers, you are a very sick man."

"I know it!" Charlie snapped. "Any idiot can see that. Tell me what I kin do about it."

The doctor flushed, unaccustomed to being addressed in such a harsh manner.

"A . . . all right," he blustered, "there's little we can do at this advanced stage."

"I've got plenty of money; I can afford the best doctors."

"You can't buy new lungs, Mr. Meyers."

"How much time do I have?"

"Not very much, I'm afraid . . . you're going to die, all too soon."

"What's soon?"

"A year at the most. If you take care of yourself, give up smoking and drinking, you might stretch it out a bit. There's a new sanitarium in Colorado Springs where doctors are making it easier for folks with consumption."

"You mean makin' dying easier?" Charlie asked sarcastically.

"Suit yourself," the doctor replied. "You can stay in Silverville and cough your lungs out or make your last days more comfortable . . . it's your choice."

"You're right, Doc . . . it's up to me."

Charlie ignored the doctor's warnings, even when he saw it in writing. Charlie stuffed the diagnosis in his pocket and stormed from the office. "Quack!" he muttered to himself. "I've struck it rich and I'm goin' to enjoy it! Nobody . . . nobody, not even God Almighty . . . is gonna deny me my due!"

That was better than a year and a half ago, yet only his closest associates knew of the medical prognosis. He disclosed the report to just two people—Jethro Briggs and Kenneth Seymour.

"He's loco, ain't he?" Charlie said about the doctor who had prepared the report. He needed to hear the two men tell him what he needed to hear—that he was still strong as an ox.

Of course, they both agreed.

"Heck, Charlie, you'll git kilt by a jealous husband before any ol' cold will do ya in," joked Jethro.

"That doctor doesn't know how much good liquor you consume, Charlie," grinned Seymour. "Everyone knows good bourbon is a preservative."

"Yer right! I've drunk enough to pickle me fer a good ten years."

Charlie was out to prove the doctor wrong, but with the advent of winter, the ugly reality of his impending death was unmistakable. The cough became his constant companion, tearing, rasping what little remained of his lungs. Bloody phlegm and uncontrollable seizures were denying him the pleasure of smoke and drink; even a good whore brought no pleasure.

He begrudgingly gave up the imported Cuban cigars.

"The ultimate symbol of a successful man." He held the expensive cigar by the tip of his fingers, twisting, rolling it around, observing the Havana masterpiece as one might examine a precious stone. He put it to his lips and tasted the tobacco; the saliva flowed in delightful anticipation . . . but so did his lungs. The coughing began anew. When the painful hacking stopped, Charlie crumbled the corona in his hands, grinding it into fine particles. He had inhaled his last smoke. Resigned to the inevitable, he angrily threw the box of costly cigars into the fire, pulled the blanket tightly about his shivering shoulders, and contemplated Colorado Springs.

Chapter 8

Jethro Briggs sat tilted back, right boot on the porch post of the Lucky Buck Diner, enjoying the aftertaste of breakfast. Belching frequently, he picked his stained teeth with a silver toothpick, then wiped it on his trousers with a flourish and returned it to his vest pocket. Briggs belched again, this time loud enough to be heard across Walnut Street. Taking out a pouch of chewing tobacco, he stuffed a large wad into his mouth and began to chew and spit, and spit some more. Leaning back, he balanced the wooden chair on its hind legs while changing from one boot to the other on the corner post, effectively blocking the foot traffic down the wooden walkway. Male pedestrians were forced to step into the muddy street or ask Briggs to lower his leg. Knowing better, most just quietly detoured into the quagmire, without even glancing sideways.

Occasionally there was a, "Howdy, Mr. Briggs," which received only a grunt in reply. Jethro "Dynamite" Briggs was not lacking in social graces; he just enjoyed being mean and ornery. He was paid quite handsomely to be the certified bully—the enforcer for the Sassy Mae Mines.

All residents of Silverville knew Jethro Briggs' reputation with both fists and guns . . . confrontation with him could be physically unrewarding and often deadly. All passersby weren't rudely treated; he ceremoniously stood, smiled kindly, and doffed his derby hat to any woman pedestrian. There were few ladies in Silverville, Colorado, so his meditation was rarely disturbed.

Jethro was an effective thug for the mining empire of Charlie Meyers. He had succeeded Sam Dodd as the muscle Charlie needed, should lawyer Seymour be unsuccessful in court or some employee become too rowdy. J. B. was inordinately strong . . . and it showed. A derby-capped head protruded above powerful shoulders, like a small bucket on a large barrel. Store-bought clothes designed for ordinary men were uncomfortably draped on his powerful frame. He took to buying the largest size available, giving him a perpetual sloppy appearance. Coal-colored eyes peered out from under frowning bushy black brows. The tips of his drooping handlebar mustache were adorned with tobacco particles from errant expectorations. A chaw of tobacco perpetually bulged from his cheek, removed only to eat or sleep. J. B. wasn't too careful where or when he spat, much to the chagrin of the local saloon and restaurant owners. Spittoons were missed by him with irritating regularity.

J. B. took great pride in his reputation as a brawler. Many people knew that he had once beaten a miner unmercifully, pounding him into a helpless, bloody pulp. The reason for the fight was never known, but the knowledge of it was sufficient to intimidate most.

Jethro knew but one man who gave him cause to doubt his invincibility with guns and fisticuffs . . . and it all had to do with errant tobacco juice. Several years back, he was second-in-command of the Sassy Mae Mines' security patrol, under the direction of Sam Dodd . . . a fact he deeply resented. Briggs believed he was far more qualified than his immediate superior. "Dodd's just too soft to enforce discipline among miners or to scare off anybody. He was good at soldiering' durin' the war . . . but so was I. Charlie hadn't no reason pickin' Dodd over me."

In Silverville's early days, law enforcement was practically nonexistent, so wise mine owners hired their own protection. Lawless elements were drawn to these open, high-rolling rich strikes as hogs to slop. Robberies of ore shipments were frequent, as was thievery. A town teeming with men, few decent women, liquor, and wealth was an explosive combination. Local governments were makeshift at best, and sufficient funds to hire competent officers were in short supply. Goldie Meyers hired his own security.

Charlie was delighted when Sam accepted his offer of employment and immediately put him in charge of security enforcement. Jethro temporarily held the job, but on Sam's arrival, he was shifted to the second spot. The demotion was a brand that never healed; he could still feel the burn whenever he had to secure Sam's advice and permission about certain personnel problems. One night at the Silver Spoon, an ore-wagon driver was roaring drunk and threatening mayhem. The mines' security was contacted to "come git him or we'll have to shoot the bugger." J. B. would have gone down to the saloon, rapped him on the head with his six-shooter, and dragged him out into the snow to sober up. This had happened once before but the employee never fully recovered from the head wound. Good drivers were hard to come by so Jethro had to get permission before he could manhandle a Sassy Mae employee. Anyone else, he had free reign to do as he darned well pleased.

Briggs resented having to go out into the freezing night and walk halfway across town to get Dodd's instructions on what to do. By the time he had arrived at the Dodds' threshold, he was bitterly cold. Briggs knocked loudly, swearing profusely, demanding to be let in, shouting, "It's colder 'n icicles out here."

Sam let him in. Without stomping the snow from his feet, Jethro tracked ice and mud inside. Hearing the commotion, Mary came out of the bedroom, lantern in hand, wearing her bathrobe.

"Care for a cup of coffee, Mr. Briggs? I have some left on the stove."

Briggs ignored Mary and curtly detailed the problem.

Sam knew the driver and believed him to be harmless. He also was aware of Briggs' propensity for violence and was concerned over how he would handle the situation.

"Wait just a minute, J. B., I'll get dressed and go with you."

J. B. just looked at him for a moment, then spat a stream of tobacco into the corner of the room while looking contemptuously at both of them. Sam dressed and left with Jethro. By the time they arrived at the Silver Spoon, the driver had passed out, slumped over a table in the back of the tavern, snoring obnoxiously.

"J. B., I know where he bunks—grab his other arm."

Ignoring Sam, Jethro picked up the drunk like a bag of grain and threw him over his shoulder. "Lead on . . . *Boss*!"

Sam turned and walked from the bar, not once looking back until they approached the boarding house where many of the single employees resided. J. B. opened the door, dumped him on the floor inside, and slammed the door shut, unmindful of any harm occurring to the man. "Is that all . . . *Boss?*" he sarcastically intoned.

"No, that's not all!" Sam swung mightily, hitting Jethro squarely in the mouth, sending him sprawling backward over the porch rail into the street. Sam walked down the steps as Briggs staggered to his feet. Before Jethro could shake the cobwebs from his mind, Sam hit him on the side of the head with all the strength he could muster. Again Briggs dropped to the ground with such force that his head flopped back, striking the frozen earth, knocking him unconscious.

He groggily awoke minutes later, feeling the snow on his face and the freezing ground underneath. Rolling over on his side, he spat out the chaw of tobacco that was still in his mouth; it didn't taste so good mixed with blood and loose teeth. He wasn't alone. Dodd was kneeling beside him.

"Jethro," Sam said, "Do you hear me?"

Briggs said nothing. Sam grabbed him by the hair and twisted his face upwards. "Jethro . . . listen real good."

In a matter-of-fact tone, Sam firmly said, "Jethro, you can be curt or sullen with me all you like; in fact, you can even curse me in public if it makes you feel any better . . . there's no reason we have to like each other to work for Charlie. But Jethro, don't ever spit on Mary's floor again . . . you understand?" Once more Sam spoke, this time a little louder. "Do . . . you . . . understand?"

Jethro understood. He had never been hit that hard before nor felt such pain from so few blows. The inside of his mouth was pulp and his cranium felt crushed. It was several days before he stopped hearing those little bells.

Jethro "Dynamite" Briggs remembered Sam Dodd painfully well. When Sam and his family left Silverville, Jethro happily inherited his job. After a while the memory of the beating faded and Jethro's ego was far more comfortable believing he was the victim of a lucky punch.

"If it hadda been light, I'd a kilt 'em, so hep me!"

J. B. was kept busy since Sam's departure and his ugly reputation as a killer became all the more legendary.

Once two brothers from Georgia had claimed part ownership to one of Charlie's silver discoveries and had taken their claim to court. They lost . . . lawyer Seymour had tied their attorney in knots. Not only had the brothers come up empty-handed, they were obliged to pay all legal fees. Embittered, they made dire threats on Charlie's life, thus it became J. B.'s job to resolve the matter.

"Run 'em out of town, Jethro," Charlie directed. "Do whatever you need to do."

Briggs found them drinking in one of the makeshift tent bars along Silverville's Main Street . . . he told them to leave town.

"Briggs, y'all ain't the law. Y'all got no right to tell us nuthin'. We got as much right to stay in Silverville as y'all do. In fact, I'm goin' to have another beer. Barkeep, two more for me and my brother!" Both contemptuously turned their backs on Jethro and bellied up to the bar. J. B. stared at them for the longest time. They did have as much right to the Colorado

Territory as anyone else, and if Jethro drew down on them without provocation, he could well be hung for his efforts.

J. B. drawled. "Y'all? My, my. You two must be from the Deep South, couple of Johnny Rebs?" Northen folks say 'you all,' not 'y'all' like a nigger."

No response . . . the brothers were aware of J. B.'s murderous reputation and didn't want to instigate a fight.

Jethro moved closer until no more than two yards separated them along the bar. Still with their backs to him, hoping he would go away, the brothers continued to drink their beer. In a low voice that only they could hear clearly, J. B. resumed the taunting.

"I hear yer from Georgia . . . beautiful place . . . been there m'self. Red clay dirt, beautiful ladies, purty mansions, an' peach orchards all around." Then, after a pause . . . "too bad I had to torch so much of it . . . some of them farms made such a purty fire! I remember one in particular, just outside Atlanta. . . ."

The younger of the two turned slowly to face J. B., his face flushed with anger and shame. "What did you say, bluebelly?"

"I said, General Sherman and me made one sweet blaze through Georgia . . . everything burned real good!" Jethro had a smile on his face. He knew he'd touched a sensitive chord that would force these brothers to react. Armed with holstered pistols strapped to their sides, both were flushed with liquor and seething with hate. Although neither had been old enough to fight for the South, both had witnessed the wanton destruction of their beloved Georgia by General Sherman's infamous march to the sea. They had watched their family farm set afire and burned to the ground, all of their possessions up in smoke, their food carried away in Union army wagons. They had lost their father at Chancellorsville and oldest brother at Gettysburg; their mother died of a broken heart.

Countless friends and relatives had been slain or severely wounded in the War Between the States. Post-war Georgia wasn't a pleasant place. The brothers tried to run the farm but soon gave up and left it to their sister and her husband. They headed west, cowboyed in Texas and Oklahoma territory, but found the work hard and unprofitable. It was more to their liking to rustle cows than punch them. The discovery of silver in Colorado drew them northward. Hard times and the will to survive led them to both sides of the law, and neither was a stranger to thieving. Both had become hard-case to the core. They had jumped one of Charlie's lesser claims and justified their act as merely revenge against another accursed Yank. Here they were, being insulted by another representative of the despised forces of Abraham Lincoln. Worse still, he had been a soldier in Sherman's Army, one of those despicable bluebellies who ravaged their beloved Georgia. And to make matters worse, he was bragging about it! They were sure two southern boys were more than enough to handle one stinking Yankee. They were wrong . . . dead wrong.

The Reb nearest J. B. edged away from the bar, giving both of them an unobstructed view of the taunting Yankee. He drew first as he stepped from behind his brother. This was all Jethro needed. The Georgian was quick . . . but not quick enough. Briggs had blazing speed gained by plenty of practice and years of practical experience. The younger of the two had barely cleared leather before the .45 slug from J. B.'s Colt army single-action pistol tore into his chest, blowing him over backward and sending his riddled body crashing into table and chairs. The older was more successful. The bullet bored a hole in the floor, inches from the toe of J. B.'s boot, as the second shot from Jethro's Colt tore into his chest, staggering him back, spinning him down the bar by the brute force of lead hitting bone. As the southerner tried valiantly to lift his gun, another slug caught him above the eye, blowing his hat and part of his skull across the room. White gunsmoke and shocked customers filled the room.

"Did you all see it? They drew first!" Jethro shouted. "I said . . . they . . . drew . . . first!" His voice was a command.

The barkeep and several other customers quickly nodded affirmation and nervously moved towards the fallen southerners to see if any life was left. Briggs holstered his Colt and sauntered outside into the dust-filled street. Killing was not new to him, especially killing Johnny Rebs. If there was ever a doubt in Silverville about his prowess with a gun, it was dispelled that late afternoon. His mark as a gunfighter was firmly established, as well as his reputation for protecting the interests of the Sassy Mae Mines.

Chapter 9

JETHRO STARED AT THE ENVELOPE the hotel clerk handed him and asked, "Where did that come from?"

"Don't know, Mr. Briggs—it was just here in your key slot."

Jethro opened the letter. He rarely received communications, especially here at his hotel. He read,

Dere Mr. Brigs.
You rotten pole cat, you kilt my Paw. I, Claude Dillon, Jr. intend to shoot you dead in a fair fite. Be noticed that this here ain't no joke. If you will meat me alone at the old Kasser Mine tomorow at noon so we can fite fair and square. Only a coward wood fail to showe up.
Signed, Claude Dillon, Jr.

"I'll be danged! Ol' Claude had a son," Jethro grinned. "Meat him, haw! Darn right I'll 'meat' him. The kid's as stupid as his old man."

Claude Dillon was a meek, mild-mannered accountant with the Sassy Mae Mining Company who, when inebriated, became morose, belligerent, and sullen. Six months ago he went on a tear, boarded himself up in a mining shack with a supply of whiskey, and refused to come out. When they tried to enter the shack to get necessary tools, Claude opened fire. Fortunately, no one was hurt, but Claude became Jethro's problem.

"Get that darn fool outa there, Briggs, that's what you're paid for!" shouted Charlie Meyers.

"You care how I do it?"

"That's *your* problem. Just get it done!"

Jethro tried diplomacy at first, but Claude responded by firing a shot in his direction, so he waited until dark, then threw a stick of dynamite under the shack. Claude Dillon, Sr. came out in pieces.

Jethro remembered the bawling out he received from Charlie.

"Dang it, Jethro, you blew my tools all the way to China. Another accountant I can get, but good drill equipment is hard to come by."

Charlie paced angrily about the office, turned, and shook his finger under Jethro's nose, "Sam Dodd would'na done a stupid thing like that!" He could not have said anything more painful to Briggs.

"So, Claude has a son and he wants to shoot it out with me. If he's anything like his Pa, he won't be much to bother with." The letter amused J. B. He looked forward to tomorrow. Lately, it had been pretty dull around Silverville. The town was becoming too civilized.

Jethro scribbled a note to Sheriff Poole and attached it to the letter received from Claude, Jr. He handed it to the desk clerk. "If I don't show up for a day or two, give this to the Sheriff, understand?" The clerk nodded in assent.

"That letter gives me a reason to shoot 'em. Stupid fool signed his own death warrant."

★ ★ ★

No one was at the abandoned Kasser Mine when Jethro rode up. The Sassy Mae Mine enforcer was visibly disappointed.

"When ol' Claude's boy really thought about facing me, he weaseled out," Jethro grumbled to himself. "I'da done the same thing if I was in his boots. Shouldn't expect much from Claude's kin." Jethro dismounted and tied his horse to a post at the entrance to the mine. He waited awhile, spitting brown holes in the snow bank, then—thoroughly disgusted—he meandered over to his mount. "Not much reason to stand around an' freeze up here." Just as he put one foot in the stirrup, he saw a rider working his way up the trail.

"Hey, maybe it's Claude's boy. Maybe he's got some guts after all." Jethro watched the horse and rider approach, choosing their way slowly up the snow-covered road. As horse and rider drew near, Jethro's disappointment returned.

"A preacher—a doggone circuit rider!" Jethro guffawed. "Probably that Dillon boy sent him up here to pray for me."

When the circuit rider was within twenty yards, he dismounted and tied his horse to a post beside where Jethro had tied his, at the mouth of the mine. He then removed his overcoat and, much to Jethro's surprise, he was packing an ivory-handled Colt .44 with the holster snugly strapped to his leg.

"Good afternoon, Mr. Briggs—glad to see that you could make it." Casually he reached into his vest pocket, extracted tobacco makings, and deftly rolled himself a cigarette. "Smoke, Mr. Briggs?"

"Naw. . . . I chew. Are you Dillon's boy?"

"No, Mr. Briggs, that I am not, but I did send you that letter."

The preacher took a deep drag on the cigarette, letting the message sink in. Jethro's brow furrowed; he was becoming confused . . . he didn't appreciate games.

"What tha heck are you sayin', Preacher? If you ain't Claude's boy, what are you doing up here?"

"Why, Mr. Briggs, I'm here to kill you."

"You're *what?* What . . . you're gonna do *what?*"

"Kill you, exterminate you, mortify your bones, send you to your Maker."

"Preacher, you tetched or somethin'?"

"No, Mr. Briggs, nothing of the sort. I have been paid a sizable sum to kill you. I have been instructed to make it, if at all possible, look like a natural set of circumstances and not like murder."

Jethro smiled, "So, you think you're gonna murder me? Ha! How the heck you goin' to do that?"

"Well, I intend to shoot you dead when you go for your gun!"

"You will?" Jethro laughed loudly. "Now . . . if that ain't the funniest thing I've heard in ages . . . J. B. Briggs, outdrawed by a preacher." Tears of mirth glistened in his eyes. "Oh Lordy, this is funny! Preacher, you sure do have a sense of humor." J. B. wiped his eyes. "Now, come on, tell me why you're here. You really a preacher?"

"Sort of. I attended seminary but found it dull. However, I find it most convenient to wear this attire. It serves my purpose of bringing souls like *you* to the Lord . . . quickly. Yes, very quickly . . . *prematurely*, you might say."

The preacher smiled, took another deep drag from his smoke, and flicked the ashes in the snow.

"You see, Mr. Briggs," he continued, "I kill people professionally. I'm very good at what I do; in fact, I'm convinced I'm the very best . . . even better than you with a gun."

"No one's better than me, much less a phoney pretendin' ta be a man of God."

"You may be right," admitted the circuit rider, "but I doubt it. Every so often one's skills should be tested against other competent professionals, so I'm giving you a chance to prove yours and to sharpen mine. Who knows? You may get lucky."

The gunman took one last drag on his cigarette and tossed away the butt. He moved to his left, taking the horses out of the line of fire.

Jethro couldn't make head or tail of the man before him. *He must be nuts to think he could make me believe such a crazy story*. It occurred to Jethro that he may well be slightly demented, thus potentially dangerous.

"All right, Preacher, or whoever ya are, you've had your say; now get on your horse an' leave afore I get mad."

The circuit rider laughed, "You really *are* as ignorant and uncouth as everyone says you are. You're too dumb to even know when you're mortally threatened. You may draw first, you cocky braggart." The last sentence he spat out contemptuously, viciously.

The minister stood, feet apart, arms folded across his chest, spewing out more foul derogatory comments regarding J. B.'s character and questionable ancestry.

Jethro had enough. He drew, his hand a blur as he pulled the gun from leather. The muzzle of his weapon was just coming up as the .44–.40 slug entered his head, right between his bushy eyebrows. The impact knocked him backwards, feet flying in the air. Jethro "Dynamite" Briggs crashed to the ground, flat on his back in the snow, a pool of red outlining his lifeless head, with eyes and mouth wide open, as if in shock . . . grim testimony to the futility of second best.

The circuit rider looked down to where Jethro's bullet had hit between his boots. "Good . . . surprisingly good. You're the best I've come across."

He removed the empty shell from the chamber, then wiped the gun with the oiled rag secured from the saddle bag. After reloading the Colt with a theatrical twirl, he slipped it deftly into its holster.

Chapter 10

Sherry Arbuckle leaned back against the side of Rowe's Hardware, shifting the weight from his bad leg to relieve the pressure on his stiff knee. He was happily but uncomfortably engaged in listening to local and world events being discussed and cussed by old friends and neighbors. Just about everybody in the vicinity was in town. People for miles around Paris, Illinois, had wagonned to the county seat to celebrate the Fourth of July, the great celebration of the nation's 103rd birthday. Buggies and horseback riders circled the town square, while youngsters frolicked on the courthouse lawn.

"Hardly a place to spit! Folks everywhere . . . gol durn, the country sure has growed," commented Slim Macy. He looked left, then right, before shooting a brown tobacco stream in the general direction of the gutter, just missing the group of fellow farmers gathered in front of the store.

"Did ja hear about New York City?" Asa Grubbs asked. "Did ja' hear?"

"No, hear what?" asked Sherry.

"One million folks—that's what they got in New York City, one million pop-u-lay-shun. Know it for a fact!"

"How's that?" inquired Slim Macy.

"Read it in the *Chicago Tribune*, was on the third page, big as life!" emphatically stated Grubbs.

"Warn't in the Paris paper, not a word of it," chimed in Josh Felese. "Besides, if it war true, ya cain't count 'em as real folks; most of them foreigners crowded in the land cain't speak a word of American."

"Josh, we don't recall you winnin' any English awards in school," joked Arbuckle.

"Yeah, Josh," piped up Don Doolittle. "We don't remember you winning any spelling bee either!"

They all laughed. Most of them had gone to the same schoolhouse, eight grades packed into one room. They had known each other most of their lives. Asa smiled at the ribbing. "Laugh all you want, but jest watch whut happens when all them makes it here to the West . . . you jest watch!"

"Watch what?"

"You heard me the first time. You jest watch."

Macy took out his bandanna, removed the new straw hat that covered a wealth of red hair, and wiped his sweaty, freckled brow. "Sure is a hot Fourth o' July."

"That's a fact . . . but if the rain holds up, it sure could be a good year," commented Doolittle.

All nodded in agreement. The year of our Lord 1878 had been just fair, but this year—1879—had been good . . . so far. Spring rains had been moderate—no late frosts, the weather had been practically perfect. The soil around Paris was deep, rich loam, ideal for growing corn. Heavy rains could turn Edgar County into a mud bog, inhibiting planting and destroying crops.

Sherry Arbuckle had barely scratched by . . . he needed a good year. Farming eighty acres and providing for an elderly mother and invalid sister took both a healthy body and mind. Sherry had one but not the other; the war had left him crippled. Just two weeks before the war's end, he was crushed under an overturned cannon, smashing his right knee. The army doctors wanted to amputate but Sherry fought them off. He had witnessed too many deaths from the aftereffects of this radical surgery.

"I'll kill the first one of you that puts a saw to that leg!" he screamed, wildly waving his 1851 Colt at any orderly who tried to move him to the operating tent. "See this revolver? Doesn't that muzzle look big enough to crawl into?" Looking down the dark hole of a .44-caliber barrel made a very convincing argument. They left Sherry alone. His cousin, Sergeant Dodd, and members of his squad kept guard over him while he recuperated. The leg healed, but not without leaving a pronounced limp, a locked and unbendable knee. Sherry did not complain; he felt fortunate to be alive. Farming was difficult work for a cripple, but not impossible. He took over the Arbuckle farm, caring for his mother and sister after his father passed away. He never married.

"Do you think 'Ol' Rud' will only serve one term as president?" asked Doolittle. "Being a lifelong Democrat, I don't care much for Republican politics, but this here Republican ain't been too bad. I wouldn't mind seeing him run again."

"Won't happen," volunteered Macy. "Hayes is a Christian man of his word . . . he said one term, one term it will be. Heck fire, I cain't see how he could get reelected with that woman of his. Won't let a drop o' liquer in the White House. Bet nary a congressman comes to visit, much less no French diplomats . . . hear them Frenchies cain't eat without havin' their wine. What's that they call her?"

"Call who?" asked Doolittle.

"The president's wife."

"Lemonade Lucy," chuckled Josh Felese.

"Yeah, I heard that too . . . read it in the *Chicago Tribune*," added Grubbs, "was on page four."

"Well, give 'em credit. President Hayes ended Reconstruction, just as he promised," offered Doolittle.

"Yep . . . he sure did that!" grumbled Macy.

The humor had gone out of the conversation. The Civil War divided Southern Illinois right down the middle. Southern sympathies were strong, as well as pro-abolitionist ideals. Abe Lincoln was a native son, but many a Southern Illinoian drifted south and fought for the Confederacy.

Asa Grubbs had lost a brother fighting for the Rebel cause. Josh Felese's brother died battling for the Republic. The Reconstruction Period had been viciously and bureaucratically administered. A decade had gone by and the South was still under northern domination and scars of the war were still boldly evident. Congress fought President Hayes on civil reform. His right to the presidency was still under heated debate. Rutherford Hayes won the election with the help of the Electoral College. His opponent, Samuel Tilden, won the popular vote, receiving more than a quarter-million vote plurality, but the electoral vote in four states was under question. Congress stepped in and formed a commission to settle the question; during the debate both sides threatened to seize the government—by force, if necessary. The Hayes' forces received the nod and "Ol' Rud" was installed as the nation's nineteenth president. His administration was rocked by controversy. Hayes refused to create cheap money and insisted the government return to gold-backed currency. The nation was still recovering from the debt-ridden, war-torn government of Lincoln. Hayes' conservative policy won and prosperity soon followed.

Politics was an acceptable subject, but rehashing the Civil War was not. Too many deep feelings were involved. Reconstruction opened old wounds, stretching unstretchable scar tissue, resurrecting bitter memories.

Sherry Arbuckle's leg ached and conversation about the war didn't help. He changed the subject, to everyone's relief.

"I think I'll wander down to the Twin Lakes for the fireworks."

"Good idee . . . it's gettin' close to dark," said Macy. "See y'all down at the lakes."

They were lifelong friends and wanted to remain that way. Many a Sunday sermon had been preached about forgiveness and brotherly love. 'Binding up wounds' was heard from many a pulpit . . . North and South alike.

Sherry walked stiff-legged to his buggy, untied his horse, and headed toward the park next to the Twin Lakes. He wasn't alone. The grand procession had begun, buggies and riders passing, cheerfully waving, calling out friendly greetings. Sherry was popular, an eligible, handsome bachelor with his own farm . . . a 'propertied man.' The Arbuckles were founding members of the First Christian Church; Sherry often soloed with the choir and ushered the second service.

A solid citizen, "real catch when his ailing mother passes away" . . . many a Paris damsel entertained that thought and more than one conspired to win his favor. Sherry enjoyed the attention but marriage was out of the question; two women around the house was enough.

The park was a beehive of activity, many families using the occasion for reunions. Every table was laden with food in abundance; the smell of fried chicken and freshly baked goods filled the air. Each table was decorated in the national colors. Small flags were pinned to dresses and coats . . . red ties, white shirts, and blue denims abounded. The band blared from the grandstand as youngsters danced on the lawn.

Sherry couldn't pass a family table without being asked to join them for supper. Some old rascals offered him beer or a sip of hard liquor. Occasionally he obliged, but more often he would turn it down. "Can't get too snockered, want to hear what Superintendent Rice has to say."

Elmer Rice was the County Superintendent of Schools and a renowned local orator. Uncle Rice, as everyone called him, was to give the major Fourth of July address.

The superintendent, who had held the office as long as anyone could remember, gave a fireburner of a talk. His voice trembled and eyes watered as he detailed the suffering, the hunger, the frozen feet, the dead and dying of the brave heroes at Valley Forge. His massive snow-white eyebrows knit together in righteous anger as he eloquently cursed the foul Tories, the

Benedict Arnolds, and English vermin who "befouled our fair land." He spoke of Christ Jesus as the Guiding Light of Washington; of Madison and Adams, and how the Lord laid the foundation of this Christian land. Many eyes were moist as fresh waves of patriotism filled their hearts.

With plenty of old friends around, Sherry was soon full of fried chicken, mashed potatoes and gravy, topped off with apple, berry, and cherry pie.

"Good heavens, I won't have to eat for a week!" Sherry wished his mother and sister were well enough to be with him. Although cousins and uncles abounded, he felt envious of those who had immediate family around.

"Maybe someday I'll have my own . . . maybe someday." As Sherry limped towards the lake to see the fireworks, he noticed a strikingly attractive lady headed in the same direction. He was sure she didn't live around Paris; he would have known about it. He thought, *If I ever marry, I hope she's as pretty as this gal.*

She turned her head and smiled. "Is there a good place to watch the fireworks?" Her smile was radiant. Sherry felt slightly embarrassed but quickly seized upon the opportunity to respond.

"Just follow me; I know the best spot and you won't have to worry about getting mud on your shoes."

"Why, thank you, Sir. I'm new to these parts and I appreciate your kindness."

Sherry, trying to keep up with the crowd surging to the water's edge, stumbled and fell. The lady reached to help him, but he gently pushed her away. "It's all right, I'm used to falling." The sarcastic embarrassment in his voice was evident.

"Nonsense! My oldest brother had his leg shot off at Kennesaw Mountain and it took him years to get used to a wooden leg. I'd have to lend him a hand at least twice a day." She put a strong arm under his and with surprising strength, helped him to his feet.

"Why . . . I was at Kennesaw Mountain too. Who was your brother with?"

"Wisconsin Fourth Artillery . . . were you really there too?" Her face lit up like a thousand lanterns, adding to her beauty.

"Sure was! Illinois Thirty-first. I didn't get this bum leg until later."

The conversation flowed. Sherry was entranced by her company; they had so much in common. Her youngest brother was a farm equipment salesman from Madison, Wisconsin. He was in Paris on business and asked her to come along.

"Our sister lives in Terre Haute, Indiana, right across the state border from Paris. After my brother's business is completed, we intend to visit to see her new baby. I'm just dying to see her new child . . . it's a little girl, the first one in our family . . . she's named after me . . . Lorelei."

The young lady happily prattled on as Sherry became more smitten by the minute. As soon as the sun slipped behind the western horizon, the fireworks began. The rockets burst into vibrantly beautiful colors, painting the sky with iridescence. The sudden flashes of light accompanied by the deafening explosions soon made conversation impossible. Lorelei had placed her hand on his arm and kept it there throughout the entire event. Sherry didn't know which was pounding more, the exploding rockets or his awakening heart. Suddenly it was over and people began to leave. Sherry didn't want it to end; he was enchanted by this charming young lady, complemented by her attention.

"Would you like a lemonade? We still have time to get something to drink."

"That sounds wonderful. It's been a very hot day. Besides, I don't see my brother anywhere. I'm supposed to meet him at the boat landing after the fireworks show." They sipped their lemonade, neither one in a hurry to part company. Sherry couldn't remember a more delightful celebration of the nation's birthday. Only a few stragglers remained in the park as he walked her to the boat dock. Sherry thought, *If only this evening could last forever!*

July Fifth. Headline in the *Paris Daily Press:*

FOURTH MARRED BY BRUTAL MURDER!

The unidentified body of a young woman was found floating underneath the Twin Lakes' boat dock. She appears to have died from a cruel blow to the back of the head. Her clothing was badly torn, possibly in a struggle attempting to fend off her dastardly assailant. She was last seen with Sherry Arbuckle at the fireworks event. Police are looking for Arbuckle in connection with this foul murder. He is nowhere to be found.

Chapter 11

"Aussie wants to see you, Slick."

Kenneth Seymour barely opened one bloodshot eye, smacked his lips distastefully, and limply waved his hand. "Go away, Mindy Lou—can't you see we're trying to sleep?"

A tousled blonde head appeared from beneath the covers next to Seymour. His partner for the night groaned, blinked her reddened eyes, and pulled the blankets over her face, disappearing into the warm comfort of the feather bed.

Mindy Lou leaned over and pulled the covers back, exposing Seymour's nude torso.

"Wake up, Counselor! Aussie doesn't like to be kept waiting. He wants to see you . . . *now*!" With that, she jerked at the covers once more to make her point.

"All right! All right, tell him I'll be there as soon as I'm dressed." He pulled the quilt up around his neck. The room was cold, freezing cold. The wench snuggled beside him, snoring softly.

Seymour was now wide awake. Being summoned by Aussie Walker early in the morning was sobering . . . and frightening. Walker was one of the many "down under" convicts deported from Australia during the 1850s who, along with a boatload of other gangsters, docked in San Francisco shortly after the California gold rush. Before long, he'd made a sizable poke cheating at cards, jumping claims, robbing drunk miners, and pimping.

By 1855, the good citizens of San Francisco had their fill of hoodlums; they formed a vigilance committee and in 1856, hung some of the worst. Aussie Walker got the message, as did hundreds of other less desirable citizens. He made his way to the gold fields of Montana, then gravitated to the rich silver strikes of Colorado.

Aussie was a huge bull of a man, towering above most men, broad shouldered and ruggedly handsome. Abundant coal-black hair laced with gray framed his chiseled face. He was a ladies' man, dapperly dressed, favoring subtle gray and rich maroon clothing. He was often mistaken for a successful businessman . . . that is, until he opened his mouth. His heavy accent grated like fingernails on slate. His words were course, vulgar, and abusive . . . but commanded attention. He had moved up in life from rolling drunks and busting heads to running saloons, bordellos, and loan-sharking. He owned five of Silverville's saloons, plus better than 50 percent of the cribs along Walnut Avenue.

Over the past twenty years, Aussie had expanded somewhat. Layers of fat now covered his bulging muscles, making him all the more intimidating. Seymour shuddered as he rose from bed, partially from the cold but more from having to face Aussie. Rumors were rampant about Aussie's reputation for vengeance upon those who welshed on debts. Kenneth knew it for a fact. He had witnessed Aussie dispense punishment to one of his wayward dealers.

"That Australian ape put the little crook's head between his massive hands and crushed his face like a ripe melon!" Kenneth shuddered at the memory . . . he could still hear the shrieks of the bug-eyed dealer.

Leaving the hotel, Kenneth stepped from the boardwalk into the frozen, mud-rutted street. He hadn't completely slept off the night before and keeping his balance took his entire attention.

"Blast this eternally frigid ruthole!" Kenneth slipped to his knees before reaching the other side, soiling his trousers, skinning his shins on the frozen mud. "Aghhhh! I hate this primeval existence, this refuge from civilization." He bent over to wipe off the particles of ice adhering to his wool trousers. "They're all wrong—hell's not hot, it's cold! What can be worse than this?" Even in the spring Silverville's temperature consistently dipped below zero. Lawyer Seymour hated the cold but he loved money . . . and Silverville had plenty of both.

Seymour limped into the Lucky Dog Saloon and went straight for the bar, where the barkeep spotted him and had a shot of bourbon poured by the time he bellied up.

"Good morning, Counselor, what brings you out in the morning?" Seymour didn't respond, lifting his eyes upward toward the second-floor balcony office of Aussie Walker. "Oh," mumbled the bartender. "Put the drink on your tab?"

"Yes . . . put it . . . on my account. What's one, no, what's two drinks more? Pour me another, please."

Kenneth let the warmth of the second bourbon work for a moment, then looked up to the darkened balcony window. Slowly, wandering around the gaming tables, he headed for the staircase, then—one hesitant step at a time—he approached the doorway at the head of the stairs.

Although Seymour was moving at a snail's pace, his thoughts were racing ahead. . . . *What does he want? Does he want me for legal advice or is he going to pressure me for the $57,000 I owe? The debt is close to two years old, long overdue. Whatever, it must be important to rouse me this early.*

Seymour had successfully defended some of Aussie's acquaintances in court—a scurvy, vermin-infested lot! Through his contact with these "clients," he had become uncomfortably aware of how well-connected Aussie was with the criminal element in the West's major mining communities. Gambling, prostitution, robbery, murder for hire—Aussie had his finger in it all.

Aussie's office overlooked the gambling tables. The large curtained window gave him a complete view of the action below. He watched as Seymour gulped down the second whiskey and meandered to the stairway.

"Insolent bloke! Owes me a bloody fortune and 'e takes 'is bloody time aboot comin' ta see me." The knock on the door was barely audible. "Come on in, Slick."

"Good morning, Mr. Walker. What conjured, specious reasoning invoked this morning summons?"

Aussie's brows furrowed. He didn't like Seymour; in fact, he hated his pretentious guts. "Ya owe me a lot of bloody money! Yer loan grates in me bloody craw. I wants ta know when I'm goin' ta get paid."

Seymour continued his nervous pacing. "Got anything to drink up here?"

Aussie frowned. "I've a bit o' bourbon in me desk." He reached into the lower drawer and brought out a bottle, placing it within easy reach of the lawyer.

Seymour nervously poured himself a drink, splashing some on the polished mahogany. Oblivious to the spill he created, he turned to his host and held up the bottle.

"Want some?"

"No." Aussie took his handkerchief from his pocket and very deliberately wiped up the spilled whiskey while Seymour chattered on. "I gave you half of the three mining claims I own; what more do you want?"

Walker looked at him for a moment before replying.

"Yeah, 50 percent of nuthin' is nuthin'. So far, not one has paid off. I've sunk a bloody fortune on 'em an not one cent of profit."

"They're good claims . . . Charlie told me they were. Keep up the digging an you'll hit pay dirt." Seymour poured himself another drink, this time without spilling a drop. He held the glass aloft, admired the amber liquid, looked at Aussie, and toasted his irate partner.

"To you, my dear Australian pessimist—remember, the mines aren't the only deal we have going."

"Yeah, an every one of 'em has cost me dear. Slick, ya gotta come up with some hard cash . . . and soon. Yer not the only one with debts." Aussie had extended himself financially and borrowed heavily. He was unmercifully calling in old loans—none of which grated on his nerves like the huge sum owed by Seymour. He wanted to kill the mouthy lawyer, squeeze his head 'til his brains ran out his ears, but the sum owed was too great to indulge such pleasure.

"At the moment, I'm a bit short, old pal," Kenneth glibly remarked. "In fact, I was contemplating asking you for a small loan."

"Get out!" Walker angrily hissed. Menacingly, he raised his bulk from behind his desk. "Get outta my office!"

"My pleasure, but first a question: What do you know about the death of Andy Quade?" The surprise inquiry stopped Aussie in his tracks.

"Nothin', I know no more than you do."

"Are you telling me the truth?"

"Why should I lie? Everybody knew that Irishman couldn't hold his liquer." Aussie quickly changed the subject and in a more conciliatory tone asked, "Kenneth, can ya pay somethin' on yer tab? I'm gettin' squeezed by some blokes I owe. Ya make good money lawyerin', ya gotta pay something inta the bloody pot."

Seymour thought for a moment before answering. "Things are tight right now, but I'll see if I can borrow something from my boss, Charlie Meyers." As he opened the door to leave, he added, "Be patient. As to our other plans, it could be any time now."

"Fer yer sake, ya better hope so."

Seymour walked down the stairs briskly, glad to be out of Aussie's sight. *So,* he thought, *he wants money! What money! I've never been in such a hole before. Everything I've touched has turned to stinking dung. Borrowing from Charlie has reached a point of irritation; I dare not ask for more.*

Aussie wasn't the only one he was into for gambling debts; his credit in Denver was at an all-time low. *That overgrown thug will have to wait his turn.* Kenneth then remembered how quickly he changed the subject when Andrew Quade's name was mentioned. *He knows more than he's willing to talk about. That muscle-brained, fat slug is lying to me.*

★ ★ ★

From the shadows of his office, Aussie muttered as he watched Seymour return to the bar, "Stupid bourbon-soaked idiot! A useful fool, I must admit . . . that bloke is goin' to make me filthy rich. His gambling is money in me pocket."

Last year, when he first pressured Seymour to pay, he was given the mining claims as collateral. Aussie seized the opportunity and in the following months, the Australian poured money into the development of the mines. So far, all three proved to be worthless. With every deeper thrust of unproductive digging, Aussie's dislike for the slick barrister grew. Six months ago, when he called Seymour to his office and demanded payment, he got the same bag of glib excuses.

"I can't give you a dime right now, but next week I'm expecting payment of several legal fees. You'll have to wait."

"That won't do, mate. I'm sick of you and yer tall stories." Aussie's anger was clearly visible, face flushed dark with blood, jaw muscles bulging, and an evil smirk cut across his face. He had moved between Seymour and the door . . . there was no escape, nor mistaking his intent to do violence.

"All right, Aussie . . . cool down." Backed into the corner, Seymour begrudgingly reached into his inner pocket and produced a sheaf of papers. "Look at this."

"You got nothin' I want to see." With that he lunged at the small counselor. Agilely ducking under the outstretched arms, Seymour then stood his ground in the center of the room.

"Look at this, you Aussie ignoramus!" Once more, he waved the documents in the giant's face.

Anyone else would have dashed for the door, but Seymour's insistence caused Walker to pause and glance at the written material waved under his nose. "Well, what is it?"

"Go ahead, read it—it's self explanatory. You *can* read, can't you?" Seymour sarcastically asked.

Aussie snatched the papers from the counselor's outstretched hand and scanned the material. Then, as its substance penetrated his thick head, he moved behind his desk, turned up the gaslight, sank heavily into his chair and read every word.

"Well, Aussie—how's *that* for collateral?"

Aussie smiled, neatly folded the papers, rose from behind the desk, and handed them back to Seymour.

"Fifty percent!"

"Fifty percent! You must be mad!" Seymour incredulously blurted, "You should be euphoric to get ten!"

Aussie faced the diminutive Seymour. Suddenly, but without anger, he cupped the lawyer's head in both hands and effortlessly lifted him off the floor. He shook him like a rag doll, then kissed him on the forehead.

"Fifty percent, mate . . . in writing," he purred.

CHAPTER 12

OFF IN THE DISTANCE, he heard the barking of dogs as his shadowy figure melted deeper into the timber. "Blasted hounds!" Jacob "Deacon" Quinn swore softly under his breath. "Staying downwind around here isn't easy."

For more than two weeks he had been observing the Dodd ranch, circling as a wolf stalking its unsuspecting prey, struggling to stay undetected. Finally, he located a grassy knoll more than a half-mile away where he could observe the family. Squinting through a telescope was irritating, but it was important to know the daily habits of Sam Dodd. "The opportunity will come—it always does—and killing that wise old buck will be a real feat."

"Deacon" Quinn lay comfortably on his stomach at the edge of the hill, watching every movement, missing nothing.

By far, Dodd was his toughest assignment. The attempt to kill him had been bungled by the renegade Utes. Quinn wasn't used to failure, nor was he tolerant of incompetents. "Five Indians couldn't kill a middle-aged rancher, shoot a child, or even steal one horse!"

Quinn was told of Dodd's fighting prowess, but he had underestimated him. He observed the attack from the knoll and with professional fascination, watched Sam's cautious, deliberate stalking of the Indians, using the landscape to hide his approach. Then, when the shooting began, his selection of targets and accuracy with the rifle were also impressive.

"This man is most proficient." His frustration over the Indians' incompetence was moderated somewhat by his appreciation of the fighting spirit of the Dodd family. He was particularly impressed by the cautious approach to the downed Utes, but completely puzzled when Sam let one Indian go. *Had the bungler in his sights . . . strange . . . no, maybe not . . . the whole family's religious . . . that could count for it. Who but Christians would bury and pray over their enemies! Jacob boy, best you remember that little cultural weakness.*

Quinn's thoughts centered on the surviving Ute, wishing Dodd had killed him, saving Quinn some time and effort. He watched the Indian run away, then trailed him for miles. Well out of sight and sound of the ranch, he shot the only one who could tie him to the attack. He took the old Ute's leather pouch of pemmican and deer jerky.

The break he was waiting for came sooner than expected. The small grove of pines at the edge of the clearing was approximately a thousand yards from the ranch house. He planned to work his way along the stream bed to the trees and if enough light remained, pick off Dodd cleanly. The distance was long but with a good rest, proper equipment, and a stationary target, he was sure his marksmanship would pay off.

Quinn knew he was the best and his equipment was first-rate. From a soft leather scabbard, he carefully removed an 1874 .50–.110-caliber Sharps rifle, a gun designed specifically for the killing of grazing buffalo at great distances. A good hide-hunter could drop scores of bison undetected. Buffalo hunter O. A. Bond killed tens of thousands of buffalo with such a firearm. With the disappearance of the plains animal, the Sharps rifle became a favorite of target shooters . . . and Jacob Quinn. It fired a 500-grain bullet, traveling 1,300 feet per second. It would take less than three seconds for the heavy missile to reach the Dodd porch.

The "Deacon" knew exactly what the rifle would do, especially mounted with a quality telescope. Under a no-wind condition, a good rest and sufficient light, he could count on the 500-grain bullet doing massive damage to any living creature at three thousand feet. Men had been killed at much greater distances. During the battle of Adobe Walls, buffalo hide-hunters fought off seven hundred Comanches with Sharps rifles. Billy Dixon, one of the skinners, killed an Indian at 1,538 yards with a .50–.110-caliber Sharps.

Jacob Quinn reviewed the situation. Time was running out. This kill had to be made soon. Practically two months had been wasted on this one man—hardly a profitable venture. *Three days I've waited in that grove for a good shot. Yesterday, too much wind, the day before too dark, the day before that Dodd moved around too much . . . maybe tonight.*

Once more he crept along the creek bed, out of sight of the ranch house, every so often pausing, scuffing dust to test the wind. He slipped into the grove of pines, crawled behind deadfall, and waited. Bracing the rifle over a large log, he carefully removed any bramble that might deflect the shot and placed three extra shells within easy reach. After Dodd was down, he'd hit him again. One shot should do, but with a man like Dodd, it paid to be thorough.

He reached into his pocket and removed the leather pouch he'd taken from the old Ute, containing deer jerky and pemmican. Quinn placed it where it could be easily found.

Quinn rolled a cigarette, lighting it so the flame was shielded. He blew the smoke downward as an added precaution. When finished, he broke the butt apart and scattered the tobacco on the ground. Then, rolling the paper between his fingers, he tossed the small ball into the thick brush.

Halfway through the fourth smoke Jacob stiffened. Sam was on the porch, leaning against the rail, lighting his pipe.

"Not good enough; that's what you did the first time. Sit down, Mr. Dodd . . . please sit down!"

Sam moved about for awhile before he finally stretched and sat on the step and opened a book. "That's much better,

Mr. Dodd—it's an appropriate time to do some reading," whispered Quinn as he lined the cross hairs on his victim's chest. Just as he was about to squeeze the trigger, Sam moved to pet the dog sitting beside him.

"Blasted mutt!" Jacob waited once more. He began to sweat slightly. The wind died down; it was deathly still, the light fading fast. Sam was now sitting perfectly still, and so was the dog; both seemed to be intently looking in Quinn's direction, staring as if they could see him. *It was now or never!*

KAPOW! The butt of the Deacon's rifle bucked against his shoulder, knocking the sight off target. Within three seconds, he relocated the target through the scope and watched as Sam was knocked backwards by the awesome force of the bullet.

"Got him . . . got him good!"

He placed another round in the chamber; however, he couldn't see the body, the angle up the hill and the slope of the porch prevented a clear view. Quinn could see silhouettes were moving hurriedly out the open door, rushing about. A woman screamed, shouts of panic. A figure disappeared into the house and the lights were extinguished. He heard the rapid fire of a repeating rifle as bullets whizzed overhead. . . .

It was time to leave.

Barely audible over the chatter of the children was the muffled sound of a heavy object falling on the porch. Almost simultaneously came the distant sound of a large-bore rifle.

"What was that?" Mary's head turned sharply towards the front door.

"I'll go look!" David bolted from his chair, hearing the shot as well. Mary was close on his heels.

"Pa!"

Mary screamed. By the light of the doorway, a trail of glistening blood stretched from the porch steps to Sam's body which lay slammed against the wall.

"Git back inside . . . NOW!" Sam's voice cut through the din. "David, douse the lights and pour some rounds into those pines . . . do it quick!"

David immediately obeyed, but not Mary; she rushed to her husband's side, placing her body between his and the unknown. "Mary . . . go inside, I'll be all right."

She could still see in the dim light; Sam's right side was bathed in blood and gore. His right arm hung twisted, brutally mangled and bleeding profusely.

KAPOW . . . KAPOW . . . KAPOW! In rapid fire, David emptied fourteen rounds from the Winchester rifle into the hiding place of the assassin.

"Matthew, David," Mary shouted, "come help me get your Pa into the house before he bleeds to death."

Sam feebly protested, once more commanding them to stay inside, but shock was setting in. He tried to raise himself but collapsed. The violence done to his flesh by the .50-caliber slug was already taking its gruesome toll. All three of the boys lifted his limp body and carried him into the darkened house.

"Sarah, shut the doors and light the lamps! Boys, put your father on the kitchen table." Sarah and the boys quickly complied.

David angrily reloaded the Winchester, "I'm gonna look around outside."

"You'll do no such thing!" Mary snapped. "Let the dogs tell us if anyone's around. I need you right here!"

Mary knew the immediate job was to stop the bleeding. She quickly cut the blood-soaked shirt and Sam's underwear away from the wound. The bullet had grazed the chest, cutting a red swath before smashing through the upper right arm, tearing a gaping hole below the shoulder; there was barely enough room above the wound, but Mary applied a tourniquet and was able to stop the flow of blood.

Betsy stared wide-eyed as her Mother worked. Sarah held her hand to her mouth to hold back the nausea. Sam was unconscious and shivering from shock.

"Sarah, get some blankets . . . quick!"

Both girls dashed to the bedrooms and returned with an armload. They quickly covered their father's quivering body.

"David, stoke the fire; we need heat and hot water."

The warmth of the blankets and the cleansing of the wound caused Sam to stir . . . slowly regaining consciousness.

"Mary . . . is everybody all right?"

"Oh, Sam! . . . We're . . ." Mary turned away and grabbed her apron, bringing it tightly to her face to choke off the sobs.

"We're fine, Pa—how do ya feel?" David quietly responded.

"Felt better . . . where am I hit? My whole right side feels numb."

"You were shot in the upper arm; the bullet grazed your chest . . . your arm's all banged up."

"Break the bone?" Sam gritted his teeth from the pain of trying to get a look at his wound. Sweat beads covered his forehead.

"I don't know, Pa—it's all swollen and looks real bad."

Sam tried to lift the arm and almost fainted from the pain. "Don't look good." He was now sweating profusely. "Better take some of these blankets off."

Mary, regaining her composure, wiped his brow with a damp cloth. "Sam, what do we do now?"

David said, "Best we get Pa to a doctor."

"But that's impossible," exclaimed Mary. "It's better than a hard two-days' ride. It would kill him."

"David's right, Mary. If I don't try, I'll die right here—especially if the bone's broken." The thought of gangrene and lead poisoning brought bitter memories to mind. Sam had seen thousands die, many victims of unattended or poorly treated wounds. He had visited the makeshift hospitals and read the gospel to the dying. He had witnessed wholesale amputations, the flesh turning black, blisters, and the smell—that unmistakable odor of putrid flesh. A horrible way to go!

"Mary, bind my arm tight to my body. Wrap it up real good."

"David, git out the wagon and hitch up a good team of mules. Better fill the bed with hay. Someone's got to take me to a doctor."

"Can I help too, Pa?" asked Matthew.

"Yeah, me too," piped in Daniel.

"Let me think about it, boys. Some of us men have to stay here and protect your Ma and the little ones."

Sam struggled to sit, trying to help Mary bind him up. He swayed dangerously forward; only Matthew's quick intervention kept his father from plunging headlong onto the floor.

"Oh, Sam, you're not fit to travel anywhere!" Tears filled Mary's eyes. She felt every pain that flowed throughout her husband's agony-racked body and winced at the frightening thought of him being bounced around in a wagon over mountainous terrain.

"Sam . . . don't you think you better rest a few days first?"

There was nothing Sam would have liked better. He could hardly stay seated in an upright position and desperately wanted to lie down. He took a deep breath.

"We can't afford to wait, Mary—we have to get going soon."

"Pa, do we leave at first light?" asked his eldest.

"No David, we have to leave as soon as you hitch the mules to the wagon. Don't forget to put two saddles in as well—we may have to ride."

"Oh, Lord no!" cried Mary. "You're delirious!"

Sam didn't respond . . . there was no use arguing. He knew that if he didn't receive medical attention as soon as possible, he would be dead within a week.

"Mary, you and Sarah put together some food, blankets, and extra bandages. It could take us a few days. Daniel, tomorrow early, take the dogs and be real careful goin' down to the pine grove and see what signs you can find. And see if you can locate the slug that hit me."

"Pa, do ya think them Indians came back fer revenge?" asked Matt.

"Yeah," echoed Daniel.

"Maybe . . . but not likely; there are few hostiles who can make a thousand-yard shot. Whoever it was knew what they were up to." Sam had instinctively jerked aside when he saw the white puff of smoke, the cotton ball that suddenly appeared against the dark pines.

"Saved by a vivid memory," he said.

"What did you say, Sam?"

"Nothing, nothing important."

David appeared at the door. "The rig's ready, Pa."

His hat and shoulders were covered with white specks of snow and behind him, the flakes were gently, silently falling.

"Snowing very hard?"

"Not yet—this is the first real snow. Shouldn't be too bad."

David was worried, though he tried not to show it. There'd be two mountain passes and rivers to cross, dangerous enough being mounted and healthy, but real fearsome if the snow worsened.

"Well, we better git goin'." Sam paused and looked to his eldest son. "David, I want you to stay here with your Ma. She'll need a man around." Sam then looked at twelve-year-old Matthew, "Matt, you're next to the oldest; think you could give yer Pa a hand?"

"Sure could, Pa."

"Oh, no you don't," Mary cried in horror. "Sam, he's just a boy!"

"Darlin', leave well enough be. Matthew will do just fine . . . won't you, Son?"

"Yes, Pa . . . we'll . . . we'll do just fine." Matthew straightened up. Shocked and scared by the responsibility asked of him, but willing nonetheless. "Don't worry, Ma, we'll be back b'fore you know it."

Mary wanted to grab her boy and hug him tightly but . . . not now. She desperately had to let her young son know she had confidence in him. It was no time for a weak heart or tears . . . they would come later.

They all watched the wagon disappear into the night . . . the faint creaking of the wagon wheels, the snorting of the horses could still be heard long after they faded from sight.

Mary stood with one arm tight around Sarah's waist, her other arm resting on Betsy's shoulder, staring into the darkness. The snow swirled around their feet as the wind picked up its intensity. When the last faint sound had long passed, they still stood there . . . silently . . . until the cold forced them inside.

"Come on in, children—it's time we pray."

Chapter 13

IN THE PITCH BLACK, Matthew could barely see the flanks of the mules. He felt the wagon lurching beneath him and the biting snow pecking at his exposed face . . . but now the snow had turned to sleet . . . it hurt. The wind had become severe, moaning as it howled through the creaking fir trees. Matthew was afraid, but reassured by the steady plodding of the mules and the presence of his injured father in the back of the wagon. Fortunately, the mules knew the trail that wound through the valley; Molly and Polly had traveled it many times before, hauling hay from one end to the other. The road twisted up through a small pass to the Herbertson spread, the Dodds' closest neighbors. Matthew didn't remember what lay beyond that point. When they reached the far end of the valley, the mules hesitated, also unsure of what was ahead. Matthew used the whip, forcing them to climb the grade. Visibility was practically non-existent; the swirling snow and cloud cover obliterated any signs of the trail.

Suddenly the team stopped, refusing to go any farther.

"Giddap! . . . Molly! . . . Polly! . . . move! . . . dang your orn'ry hides!" Matthew applied the whip once more, beating angrily on their backs . . . but both mules refused to budge.

Frustrated, Matt turned and called, "Pa! . . . you awake? These danged mules don't want to go on and I can't get 'em to move . . . besides, I can't see nothing!" He felt a twinge of panic when there was no response.

"Pa . . . Pa!"

Matthew pulled on the hand brake, tied the reins about the handle as he swung around in the seat, and dropped into the bed of the wagon. He frantically groped for his father under the tarpaulin and blankets. There! A leg, a warm body. He was relieved to discover that his father, in spite of the pain, had fallen asleep. He was snoring softly. Matthew hated to disturb him, but wake him he must.

"Pa, the team quit moving. I can't see a thing."

"It's all right, Matthew," Sam replied groggily. "Come hunker down next to me and rest yer head on one of the saddles. It'll be light before long."

Matthew, happy to hear his father's voice, gratefully complied. It was warm under the tarp and blankets; fear evaporated as he snuggled next to his father and fell fast asleep.

★★★

The snow had settled on the wagon, layering the tarp with a thick coat of white. Matthew stuck his head out from under the covering and viewed the surroundings. The snow had stopped but the wind was blowing harder, drifting the swirling flakes around the wagon. Everything was blue-gray cold in the dim light of early dawn. Matthew slipped over the side of the wagon and worked his way to the heads of the mules, patting them, adjusting the harnesses. Suddenly the ground slipped from beneath his feet; only his grip on the harnesses prevented his fall.

He was horror-stricken! His feet were dangling precipitously over the edge of a cliff. In desperation, he clawed his way to safety.

"Pa! . . . Pa! Look!" Sam poked his head from beneath the tarp.

"Merciful Lord!" he exclaimed.

The team had wandered off the trail and was standing on the edge of a steep precipice, perched precariously near the edge; one step more would have plunged them all into the canyon below.

"Just be calm, boy. Molly an' Polly ain't goin' nowhere. Back 'em off the ledge slow and easy."

Matthew gingerly climbed onto the driver's seat, his heart pounding wildly as he slowly backed the mules away from the edge.

"Come back, girls . . . easy-like."

"Matt, if we would'a had horses, we'd be at the bottom of that gorge. Thank the Lord, mules are smarter."

"Where to now, Pa?"

Sam achingly crawled up beside his son. "That way," indicating up the mountain toward the draw. "We have to get over that saddle before I can tell if it's better to cut over the high country pass to Rustic or keep travelin' downriver toward Laramie."

Sam wanted to reach Rustic; it was closer and he knew there was a doctor in the vicinity. Medical facilities were available in Laramie, but it was another day's ride. The trouble was the weather; could he and the boy make it through Dead Man's Pass over Rustic way or should they follow the much longer but safer river route to Laramie?

The first snows of fall were usually of short duration and much of it would melt. The odds of safely making it through the passes were good. Sam's optimism grew as the day progressed. The clouds dissipated somewhat, allowing the sun to shine through.

"Matthew, if it weren't for these poor circumstances, we sure could enjoy all this beauty."

"Yeah Pa, it shore is pretty."

Ignoring the pain in his side, Sam drank in the spectacular scenery unfolding before them.

"Son, what could be more beautiful than this?"

The new snow had fallen heavily, covering the peaks and valleys with a clean blanket of sparkling white. Huge stands of dark green fir hugged the mountainsides, their limbs weighted down. An orange and cream carpet lay under every aspen, the pristine serenity disturbed only by browsing mule deer and an occasional string of elk.

Sam took an agonized deep breath, intentionally inhaling as much of the fresh air as he could cram into his lungs. "Intoxicatin' is what it is, absolutely intoxicatin'. What's more beautiful than Colorado? Nothing. . . . Well, nothing except Mary."

He felt substantially better than last night. Sleep had helped. The pain in his arm had subsided somewhat . . . he continued to feel hopeful. By noon, they reached the trail where they had to descend into the valley or turn eastward taking the high road over the pass to Rustic. Sam's mind was made up as the wagon dropped violently in a rut, jarring his arm, almost throwing him from the wagon.

"Turn the wagon to the right fork, Son; we'll try the pass. It'll save us a day's ride and me a lot of misery."

Sam looked toward the northern sky; the slate-gray clouds spoke of a new storm in the offing but with luck, they could be through the pass and on the eastern downslope before it hit. Sam knew of a deserted miner's cabin close to the summit where they could spend the night in some comfort and press on in the early light with time to spare. Driving a team of mules in the valley at night was one thing, but trusting mountainous driving to a boy after the sun had gone down was another. He remembered seeing a shed near the cabin where they could rest and feed the mules.

They reached the shack as dark closed around them. Just moments before, the storm struck with awesome force. The white gale that whipped the landscape surged through the narrow pass with enough ferocity to unsteady man and beast. Matthew clumsily helped his father to the door; both stumbling, fighting the wind, falling into the cabin exhausted. It was stripped bare—no chairs, bed, or table. Some prior inhabitant had used the furniture for firewood, charred bits of a table leg gave ample evidence.

"I've got to make a fire, Pa."

"You can do that soon enough, Son; first tend to the stock."

"Yes, Pa." Without complaint, Matthew returned to the bitter cold . . . and dark. He unhitched the team and led them toward the dim outline of a shed. Snow was drifting heavily against it. Matt staggered back to the wagon for feed, then back to the stock. He didn't even try to take off the harnesses, a job too big for him under the circumstances. In the corner of the shed he made out a small pile of kindling, enough for a fire. Matthew gathered the wood and headed back to the gray shape of the cabin, repeating the trip until the last bit of wood was gathered. Fortunately the cabin was relatively tight, with only a few crevices letting in the howling wind. The little cabin groaned under the force of the storm.

Sam moved over close to the fire and began to unwind his bandage, needing to have a look at the wound.

"Oh, Pa, that shore is ugly looking." Matt wrinkled his nose and turned away.

"Son, there's no such thing as a pretty gunshot wound. All are sickly to the eye. Actually, this looks better than I expected. Now, help me bind the arm to my body again."

Sam was pleased that the smell of rotting flesh wasn't present and the color of his skin seemed normal. The area around the wound was puffed and red but that wasn't unusual.

"So far, so good." Sam turned his attention to his son, watching the young boy's head drop repeatedly to his chest, then snap upward, fighting to stay awake.

"Lie down by the hearth, Son, and git some sleep. I'll tend the fire for awhile. You've done the work of two men today . . . I'm proud of you."

Matthew smiled the faintest smile imaginable. "Weren't nothin'." Curling alongside next to his father, the small lad immediately fell asleep.

★ ★ ★

The blizzard lasted three days, making travel impossible. Sam was sure he and his son would perish if they dared attempt to travel under such perilous circumstances, but knew that they could not afford to be snowed in much longer. Sam's condition was worsening; no longer did his wound seem to be healing, and the tell-tale darkening of flesh and putrid odor of dying tissue were evident.

They had to go back—retrace their steps down the mountain to the river. If he was incapable of going on, at least Matthew might make it to the Herbertson ranch.

"Matthew."

"Yes, Pa."

"Think you can help me saddle the mules?"

"Pa, are we gettin' outa here?"

"We're gonna try, Son . . . we're gonna try. Looks like the snow has let up a little and the wind is dyin' down."

Sam was sure their only chance was to mount up and ride out. Pulling the wagon through the drifts would be next to impossible, wearing the animals to exhaustion. It would also be his son's best chance for survival. The seriousness of Sam's condition became increasingly apparent. His chances were doubtful at best, but back-tracking could save his boy.

The first task was to get out of the cabin. It was difficult clearing the entrance; the drifting snow had piled against the door, sealing it shut. Sam placed his good shoulder against the door.

"Give me a hand, Son."

Matthew eagerly jumped to his father's side and pushed with all his might. The door refused to budge, and Sam was too weak to apply the necessary weight. He sank to the floor in pain.

"Well, we better figure on somethin' else." Sam looked about the room; his gaze fell on the boarded-up window.

"Matthew, take your rifle and see if you can pry off those wooden slats. If we can get you outside, there's a shovel in the wagon. Maybe you could dig the snow away from the door."

Matthew attacked the window, smashing through one board with the butt of his Springfield, then, with the barrel, leveraged the slats to the side. The freezing air rushed in, blotting out what warmth remained. He scrambled outside and in a matter of minutes, Sam heard the shovel cutting into the snow.

"Pa . . . try it now."

Sam struggled to his feet and pressed against the door once more. He moved it ajar, just enough to allow him to squeeze through into the sub-zero dawn. A strip of yellow rimmed the eastern horizon, though a continuous gray blanket of clouds stretched overhead. A light snow was falling. Looking back down the trail in the light of the blue-gray morning, Sam saw that most of the trail was obliterated. Only faint indentations in the canyon side gave evidence of a mountain path. They would have to carefully pick their way back down the steep slopes.

"Thank God we brought the mules; there's no more sure-footed animals."

"Matt, how's Molly and Polly?"

"They're fine, Pa, but this here frozen harness is tough to get off."

Matt wrestled removing the wagon rigging from the backs of the mules. They were tall animals, better than sixteen hands high . . . and Matthew was only four-foot-ten.

Sam watched helplessly while his son struggled to remove the frozen rigging.

"Be glad they're big animals, Son—we'll need those long legs to break through snow banks."

Sam shuffled back into the cabin to gather what food they could comfortably carry and stuffed the vittles into the saddle-bags. He lifted one of the saddles from the floor and staggered under its weight. Giving up, he dragged it through the snow to the shed. By the time he reached the mules, he could feel the trickles of perspiration running down his backbone.

"That's bad . . . gotta keep my flannels dry . . . that damp could cause trouble when ridin'." Sam worked his way to the side of one mule. "Son, put the blanket on Molly and help me with this saddle. There's little chance I can heft this rig by myself."

Matthew carefully placed the saddle blanket over the withers, then circled the mule to his father's side. Together, clumsily, they lifted the saddle to Molly's back, tightened the cinch, and repeated the effort with the other mule.

"Now, Son, the trick is to get me mounted."

Matthew led Molly to where the mountain sloped away. She stood stock-still while he helped his father mount from the uphill side.

Surprisingly, sitting in the saddle felt good; Molly's gait was bearable; in fact, more comfortable than the wagon. The mules sensed they were heading home so little effort was needed to guide them back down the path, even though the snow made travel difficult. The first major obstacle was an enormous snowdrift blocking the trail. The mules, belly deep, lunged forward and over, bucking Sam from Molly's back. He made every effort to get up in the deep snow, but his thrashing attempts just buried him deeper.

Polly had cleared the drift and when Matthew looked back, all he could see was Molly trotting toward him with an empty saddle.

"Pa!" he screamed, "You all right?"

"I think so. Son, throw me a rope and let Polly pull me out."

Matthew rode close and tossed the lariat toward his father's outstretched glove.

"Wait a minute, I gotta tie it around my leg. My arm can't take any more punishment . . . all right . . . pull!"

Matthew looped the rope over the saddle horn and gently dug his heels into Polly's side, "Come on, girl, pull easy-like."

Sam popped from the drift like a white cork from a bottle . . . snow crammed under coat and trousers, his hat missing. He lay still for a moment before struggling to sit up, then brushed the snow from his head and shoulders.

"Matt, see if you can find my hat." Laboring desperately and sweating profusely, he remounted, expending energy he could ill afford to lose.

It was slow-going to the juncture of the river, but at least uneventful. They rode around a few rock slides and busted through lesser snowdrifts. What had taken them five hours to ascend took a full day to retrace.

At the bottom of the trail, Sam called to his son in a faltering voice, "Matthew, it's best I rest awhile."

He was totally exhausted, with no strength left to stay in the saddle. The pitching ride downward and the jarring motion of crashing through the drifts had drained him of his last vestige of energy. Matt helped him from Molly's back, holding up most of his father's weight, and led him under the protective branches of a great blue spruce. Matthew hurriedly started a fire, using the dry underhanging branches. Erecting a makeshift lean-to with the tarp, he covered his shivering father with the heavy wool blankets, including his own. Sam fell into an exhausted slumber.

The snow stopped, replaced by a harsh, cold, and starry night. The sub-zero high country temperature was accompanied by its deadly companion . . . the bitter, cutting wind. Matthew couldn't afford to sleep. The fire needed to be constantly fed, but the activity kept his teeth from chattering out of his head. Every part of his body ached from the cold. He knew he had to keep moving about; their lives depended upon it. Off in the distance he heard the cries of a pack of wolves, bringing a rush of heat to flush his face and momentarily warm his body. He made his way to the mules and slid his father's Winchester from the scabbard, making sure there was a round in the chamber. Matthew retired to the fire and began to pray, for the first time neither by rote or duty.

"Dear Jesus, me and Pa are in deep trouble. We shore need your help. Lord, I just don't know what to do. Will you please help me take care of my Pa? Please?"

Matthew was scared . . . he'd never before had a real need to talk to God.

"Trust in the Lord, pray to Him, and He will give bountifully," his mother always said.

Through chattering teeth he prayed the Lord's prayer, over and over 'til dawn.

First light was welcome; it was time to be moving down river. "Pa . . . wake up, best we be movin' along." His father said it was still a two-days' ride to Laramie. It'd be a miracle if they made it, but having prayed about it had helped. The Lord Jesus would see them through.

★ ★ ★

On the high plains, a cowboy from the Stanley Brothers Rock Creek Ranch watched two slumped-over riders aimlessly make their way down the flats above the Laramie River. The mules stopped to graze. Neither rider answered when he called out to them, nor did they stir in their saddles.

"That's trouble," the hand said, putting the spurs to his horse and covering four hundred yards at a mad pace.

"Good Lord, what have we here?" he questioned as he reined in beside the pair. Both were unconscious, their clothing frozen to their saddles. The man's stubbled beard was covered with ice, his blue lips locked together. Blankets were tied with a lariat around the man's shoulders; nothing but a wool coat covered the boy. The rope from the man's mule was looped around the boy's gloved hand. The cowboy could barely pry it loose from the clenched fist. Fearful of dislodging the riders, he led the mules slowly toward Laramie.

Chapter 14

THE DISTANT WHINNY OF A HORSE, the creak of wagons, voices . . . all filtered through a haze of hurt, a cloud of pain. Sam tried to focus his eyes; squinting hard, he saw the white bed frame at his feet, a table, a coal oil lamp. He tried to speak . . . impossible. His throat seemed swollen shut . . . so dry, bone-dry. He worked his tongue around inside his mouth seeking moisture; finally he managed to swallow. He licked his puffy, chapped lips and called out, "Anyone here?" Once more, this time louder. "Is there anyone . . .?"

An elderly woman poked her head through the door. "Oh my! I see our patient is awake."

Disjointed pieces of information tumbled through Sam's mind, slowly fitting together—the gunshot wound, the mules, the freezing cold . . . *Matthew*!

"Matthew! Where are you?" Sam jerked his head from side to side in desperation. He attempted to sit up but somehow his arms wouldn't function. Panic filled his chest as he again tried to rise up in bed. "Where's my boy? Where's Matthew?"

Sam had known fear before, but nothing had prepared him for this. His last conscious thought was feeling feverishly sick and finding it almost impossible to stay erect in the saddle.

The swirling snow along with the bitter wind made it difficult to see his son riding up ahead. Matthew seemed to fade into the cloudy white. Sam could remember no more.

"Matthew! Son! Where are you?"

The woman rushed to the bedside, placed both hands on his shoulders, and gently pushed him back down on the pillow.

"There, there . . . calm down . . . everything's going to be fine; your boy's in another room down the hall. Rest quiet now—the doctor will be here soon."

"He's all right?" Sam sank back, relieved that his son was nearby. "He's all right, isn't he?"

"You're the one we've been frettin' over. Everyone thought you were a gone goose. Rest easy—the doctor's out on a call, but we expect him back any time." Sam's eyes focused on the woman for the first time: She was a nun!

"Where am I?"

"This is St. Joseph's; I'm Sister Bruner. We are members of the Sisters of Charity. We have only a few rooms in our small hospital, but we give good Christian care and we have a fine doctor. Rest easy now." With that she adjusted the bedding and speedily headed for the door. "Get some more sleep . . . there'll be soup for you when you feel like eating." She closed the door behind her.

Sam was now wide-awake. With his good arm, he scratched the stubble on his face . . . a good week's growth. The wounded right arm felt surprisingly painless; however, his shoulder ached horribly. Sam made an effort to lift the wounded limb. Nothing . . . only a short protrusion moved under the sheet. With his left hand, he ripped off the covers: "My God, they took it off!"

Sam twisted in the bed and stared down where his limb used to be . . . amputated! . . . only a bandaged stub remained. He flashed back to the war: A montage of crippled bodies, ugly images of broken, helpless men wove their way through his mind; fumbling half-men with empty pantlegs and pinned-up sleeves.

Sam was right-handed; his good arm was gone. *How can I write . . . carry a heavy load, handle a team of horses, cut into a piece of meat, raise a rifle?* He was flooded with fear of the unknown, a cornucopia of bitter fruit spilling forth.

How will I take care of Mary and the kids? Ain't never heard of many one-armed cowboys. Somehow the idea struck him funny. Out loud, he said, "Yeah, a one-armed waddy with six kids."

The opening door interrupted his thoughts and a large man filled the door frame. Sam had seen few men crowd space as this one.

"Howdy—I'm Doctor Hiram Latham . . . pleased to meet you, Mister . . .? Say, what *is* your name?"

"Dodd. Sam Dodd." His brow furrowed. "Didn't my son tell you?"

"No, Mr. Dodd, he did not. Your son has been a very sick boy. The exposure to the cold didn't treat him kindly. He's alive and hanging on, but it will be a few days before we can tell what damage he suffered. He's a strong young lad. He should make it."

Sam struggled unsuccessfully to get up. "I want to see my boy."

"Not today. He's asleep right now and you're in no condition to see anybody. Tomorrow—you can see him tomorrow." The doctor placed the stethoscope in his ears and leaned over the bed. "Let's see how you're doing. Frankly, it's a miracle you're still alive." He efficiently and quickly poked, probed, and listened.

"You're a lucky man," he said. "Gangrene set in and the flesh around the wound was blackened. I had no other choice but to amputate." He carefully inspected the bandage. "I'm very sorry I had to cut off your arm."

"No sorrier than I am," Sam responded.

"I told the sheriff I was caring for a gunshot wound. He'll want to talk to you."

Sam nodded. "I need to talk to him too."

"Where and when did it happen?"

"I have a spread near the headwaters of the Laramie River, on the east slopes of the Medicine Bow Mountains. That's where I got shot. I think it was about nine days ago."

"Good Lord, man, how did you get out? We've had practically two weeks of heavy blizzard."

"Warn't easy . . . fact is, I don't clearly remember the last few days. Better ask Matthew about that. I reckon he'd know that best." Sam smiled, "Brave little guy, ain't he?"

Doc Latham turned away, not allowing Sam to see his worried expression. "Yes, Mr. Dodd, you certainly could say that."

"Doc, he's going to be all right, ain't he?"

"He should be, barring complications. In fact, I'm sure of it. He has a lot of grit."

Sam smiled. "Yes, he does—takes after his mother."

"Mr. Dodd, I'm going to have one of the sisters bring you some food. I'd advise you to eat every bit of it, then get some rest. You've been through a great ordeal; it will take weeks before you'll be fit enough to leave here, let alone travel. Besides, the passes are snowbound. It would take a robust mountain man to make it back to your spread."

"If there's one around, I'd like to hire 'em. I have to get word to my family. They'll be worried to death."

"I'll see what I can do."

The doctor left the room as the sister entered with a tray. "Eat up, Mr. Dodd—you need all the strength you can muster."

Sam willingly complied.

★ ★ ★

Two doors down the hallway, Dr. Latham entered Matthew's hospital room where a young, dark-haired nurse sat attentively beside the bed, watching the pale, small boy under the white sheets.

"How's he doing?" the doctor whispered.

"He's holding his own," Sister Keppel quietly responded. "His cough is much better . . . so is his color. He was awake a short while ago and I fed him a little soup."

"Did he say much?"

"He asked about his father. I told him he was doing fine, just as you told me to."

"Good, that's good. No need to worry either one of them. Nurse, pull back the sheet. Let's take a look at that hand. Bring the lamp closer, please." He carefully lifted Matthew's right hand, inspecting every finger. As the boy groaned drowsily, the doctor gently placed the hand back at his side.

"Now, let's see about those feet." With the same meticulous care, he examined each foot and toe, then covered Matthew and sat back quietly in the chair, shoulders slumped.

"Well, Doctor?" inquired the nurse.

Without comment, he stood and motioned for her to follow him into the hall.

"Sister, let's get a cup of coffee," he whispered.

Silently, they walked down the hall to the kitchen where a large pot simmered on the wood stove. The young nurse poured the steaming black liquid into two cups and handed one to the doctor.

"What's the prognosis?" she asked. The doctor walked to the window and peered into the dusk; once more the snow was falling, this time slowly, gently meandering to the ground. He said nothing, ignoring her question. He didn't want to talk about it. Finally, he mumbled, still facing the window.

"I'm sorry, Doctor, what did you say?"

Doc Latham turned from the window to face her. "I'm not happy with what I will have to do, nor confident in the outcome."

Tears were in his eyes.

"Are you Sam Dodd?"

Half-asleep, Sam rolled over in bed. A tall, gangly man ducked through the doorway, brushing snow onto the floor from his bulky leather coat.

The first early rays of morning light cut through the window. With difficulty, Sam sat up. "I'm Dodd—who might you be?"

"Sheriff N. K. Boswell of Albany County. Hear you got a gunshot wound."

"Come on in, Sheriff—I'll tell what little I know."

Sam had heard about the famous "Boz" Boswell, the Indian fighter, trail blazer, and gunman who had cleaned the desperadoes out of Laramie—single-handed. The lawman took off his jacket and laid it on the floor, pulled up a chair, and sat down beside the bed. He took out a red handkerchief and wiped his beard and face, then gustily blew his nose.

"Darn winter colds—older ya get, the more ya get 'em."

He stuffed the handkerchief into his vest pocket and looked intently at Sam, "Now . . . what happened?"

"As I said, not much to tell. I got bushwhacked while sittin' on my own porch."

"Any idea who done it?"

"Nary a one. I suppose there's some folks who don't like me, but none I can think of who'd ride that far to drive a hole through my hide." Sam thought awhile. "There were some Utes who tried to steal my horses. I shot a couple of 'em and I let one go."

"Maybe it was him or some buck's family gettin' revenge," offered the sheriff.

"Could be. They were a sorry lot; all but one was carryin' poor firearms. Whoever hit me knew what he was doing. It was a long shot."

"How long?"

"Had to been better'n three thousand feet."

"Over half a mile?" incredulously asked the lawman.

"Yep, least that. He had to be usin' a telescope on a real quality rifle. I never heard of a Injun with a sniper's gun."

"Nor have I," muttered the sheriff. "Mr. Dodd, why would someone want to kill you?"

"Don't rightly know. I was a deputy sheriff once; had to kill a few men. Revenge maybe." Sam stared at the lawman. "Sheriff, I need your help. I have family that needs to know Matthew and me are alive and well. They've gotta be worried sick. Do you know anyone I can hire to go tell them?"

"Let me think on it. Maybe I could send one of my deputies—Joe Lefever or Buck Upholt. In any case, I promise to get back to ya real soon."

The sheriff asked a few more questions before leaving. Sam was glad the interview was over; he was anxious about Matthew. "The doctor said I could see my boy today!"

Sam swung his feet over the edge of the bed and carefully braced himself with one arm, grabbing the sheets to keep his balance. Small beads of sweat dampened his forehead.

"Better do this a step at a time."

Finally, he placed his bare feet firmly on the floor, steadied himself, and shuffled to the door, then down the hallway. Sam looked through the first door . . . nothing. The next one was closed, which he opened very quietly. Asleep in a chair was a nurse, and beside her in the bed was his slumbering boy. Sam stood still, watching his son, afraid of waking him but desperately wanting to hear his voice. Matthew seemed unusually pallid, but he couldn't really tell his condition in the early morning light.

Sam backed from the room, quietly closed the door, and returned to his room. *Best leave him sleep. Might scare the lad, seeing his Pa with just one arm.* Sam felt immeasurably better having seen his son alive and under good care. He thought of the rest of his family, fearful of what might have happened in his absence. Questions crammed his mind: *Was there more than one bushwhacker? Who were they after, just me or all of us? Is David capable of managing the ranch without me?* The queries came one after another. The lack of answers was a cruel companion. Sam's melancholy was distracted by the chattering of female voices and the clatter of dishes, announcing breakfast. Sam was hungry.

"Oatmeal and toast, hardly the fare for a starvin' man!" he muttered while inspecting the small, soupy bowl of cereal and dry unbuttered toast placed on the table next to his bed.

"Thank you, Nurse, but . . . may I have some eggs tomorrow?"

"Doctor's orders," grinned the nurse.

"Give him anything he wants," boomed the doctor's voice from the doorway. "We feed oatmeal to the dying." Doc Latham sat on the edge of the bed, checked Sam's pulse and felt his forehead. "Fever's gone, heartbeat good . . . let's see the wound . . . see how it's healing." He carefully removed the bandages. "Good, looks good—the week's rest has done wonders for you."

"How soon can me and my boy get outa here?"

"Not as soon as you would like, Mr. Dodd—your boy may be here awhile." The doctor's attitude had quickly changed from jocular to professional, from a grin to grim.

"Why do ya say that? What's happened to Matthew?" A hard knot suddenly gripped Sam's gut. "Doc, what's wrong with my son!"

"Mr. Dodd, we had hoped for the better but the news is not good. Your boy led your mule for quite a ways with the reins wrapped around his right wrist . . . too tightly, I'm afraid. The circulation must have been impaired, causing the fingers to suffer from frostbite."

"Will he lose some fingers?" Sam shuddered at the thought.

The doctor was silent, hating to tell the boy's father what he had to know.

"No, Mr. Dodd, I'll have to remove the entire hand and then hope we'll have to take no more. He's a sick boy; the cold was hard on him. I've been waiting to see his condition improve before operating. I can't put it off much longer."

Sam pressed his lips together, teeth clenched, trying to keep back the tears.

"Will he make it?"

"He should. It's tough enough amputating an adult, much less a sick lad. One never really knows."

"The Lord knows," Sam solemnly replied. "He brought us out of the mountains and He'll see us home . . . both of us."

★ ★ ★

The following month was the most burdensome time in Sam Dodd's life. It was hard enough adjusting to the loss of an arm but watching the agonizing, slow recovery of Matthew was worse. Matt was skin and bones, the amputation plus the hacking, deep cough that refused to go away sapped the boy's strength. Sam's presence helped, but he could tell the amputation of his arm troubled Matthew as much as the loss of his own hand. A marked improvement came with the arrival of news from home. The sheriff had sent one of his deputies, Buck Upholt, to the Dodd ranch. Traveling by horse, then by snowshoe over the passes, Upholt backpacked the rest of the way. His news of Sam's and Matt's survival brought tears of joy followed by sorrow over the news of the surgeries.

"Thank the Lord they're alive," sobbed Mary. "What a terrible price to pay . . . but, better than an icy grave. Better by far."

The deputy spent two days scouting the area, circling the ranch. Satisfied no one was lurking about, he headed back to Laramie with letters and a gift from the family. The letters, detailing that everything was fine with Mary and the children, lifted an enormous weight from Sam's shoulders. The package was a special early Christmas surprise in brown paper tied with a red ribbon. Matthew clumsily opened the gift from his mother and siblings—oatmeal cookies—dozens of crumbled oatmeal cookies. Matthew brightened, the first real heartwarming smile in weeks.

"Pa, do ya think I could have some milk with these?"

"Right away, young man, right away," promised Sister Keppel cheerfully as she bolted from the room.

★ ★ ★

"Your boy, David, wanted me to give you this," Deputy Upholt handed Sam an oilskin wrapped parcel containing a leather pemmican pouch, deer jerky, a lead slug, small bits of balled-up paper, and a note from his oldest son.

Dear Pa,

This is all Daniel and me could find but there was lots of sign. Whoever it was wore moccasins, probably a lone Indian. He must of forgot his food when I shot at him. He was riding a shod horse 'cause I found tracks in the timber north of the ranch. He must have been watching us for a few days. We think he was bedded down on that knoll you can see from the front porch. Even in the snow we could see all the grass pushed flat. We found the place in the pine grove where he hid waiting to shoot you. Daniel found the scraps of paper all balled up under a bush nearby and we found the pemmican bag and bits of jerky. Miracle we found anything. It was the dog's smelling around that caught our notice. The pine trees and the brush were topped with snow but the ground underneath was still dry; good thing we looked first light 'cause the snow came down heavy all that day. We dug the lead ball out of the cabin. It sure is big. He must of lit out right after the shot. We could find no tracks in the snow leading away. The snowing covered everything. That is all I can tell you except we miss you and hope you are home soon.

Your obedient son,
David Dodd

Sam examined the smashed lead slug and the small particles of paper.

"Deputy, what do you guess . . . .50-caliber?"

"I'd say so, prob'ly fired from a Sharps, tellin' from the distance. Buffalo gun, I expect."

"I agree."

"Moccasin tracks, pemmican pouch, an' jerky scraps—looks like an Injun."

"Could be, but it don't figure right. Deputy, would you try to unroll those wads of paper? I'd be a mite slow."

"You bet." Upholt carefully pulled one of the wads apart, trying not to tear the paper, and handed it to Sam. "That there paper is shore thin. Looks like makin's . . . cigarette paper."

"I think you're right." Sam held the paper to the light, "Somethin's stuck to it—looks like it could be a snip of tobacco. Deputy, see if the sisters has one o' those glasses that makes things bigger."

The deputy hurried off and returned quickly with a small magnifying glass.

"Let's see what we got here." Sam studied the thin piece of paper, a tiny bit of tobacco still clinging to it.

"Deputy, ya ever hear of a Ute smoking rolled cigarettes?"

"No, Mr. Dodd, I know they smoke, but ain't it usually a pipe? Can't remember ever seeing an Injun roll one. Seen 'em take a chaw o' tobacco, but that's about all."

"Ever know a Ute that'll wait days to bushwhack someone?"

"That's possible but then agin, it ain't regular," responded Upholt.

Sam paced about the room, deep in thought, fitting the pieces together. "Not many Injuns shoe horses."

"That's a fact, but some do," added the deputy.

"Mr. Upholt, do you know many Injuns who're sharpshooters making thousand-yard shots?"

"Mr. Dodd, I seen the spot where the bushwhacker set down an' looked up that hill to your place. Nobody shoots good at that distance with a peep-sight."

"I agree. He musta used a telescope sight."

The deputy scratched his head. "Yer right. That feller had to been using one of them new scopes. When you think of it, I know of no Injun rich enough to buy one, much less know how to use it."

"Uh-huh," answered Sam, "Powder and shot is dear to Injuns, so few practice target shooting. But what about the pemmican and jerky . . . and the moccasins? That says it was a vengeful Injun."

"Could be you were shot by someone tryin' to make it *look* like a Injun did it. Someone who'd intentionally leave that Injun food behind. If that's a fact, he shore went to a mess of trouble."

"Clouds the picture, doesn't it?" said Sam.

"Shore does. If you would have been killed, who'd have thought different? Your family would've buried you, an Injun blamed, an' that would have been the end to it."

"You're probably right. In fact, if there's an assassin he probably thinks I'm dead—he'd have every reason to think so."

"He'll likely figure you died from the wound or lead poison. Anyhow, he won't find out any different until spring, especially if we don't talk much about our suspicions. There ain't much talk about town. Unless the villain comes to Laramie, he'll have hardly no cause to know. Why'd anyone want ta kill you, Mr. Dodd? That feller went to a heap o' trouble to git you in his sights."

"You're right, Deputy—he went to a whole lot of trouble and likely, if he knows I'm alive, he'll try again."

The deputy thought for awhile, then said, "That's not very comfortin'."

"No, it ain't, but there's one thing in my favor."

"What's that?"

"He thinks I'm dead, so I guess I better find him afore he discovers I'm alive—and tries again."

"Do you know where to begin?" inquired the deputy.

"Yep, I know where to begin."

"That's good . . . real good. Well, guess I better git goin'." Buck Upholt walked to the door, turned, and looked at the empty sleeve hanging from Sam's right side. "Mr. Dodd, the sheriff an' I'd like to help . . . ya'll call on us . . . ya hear?"

"Thank you, Deputy—I appreciate your kind offer."

The deputy closed the door. Sam moved from the bed to the chair beside the table, lit the lamp, and reached for the Bible. He pondered God's Word as darkness crept in. December days were short on the high plains of Wyoming . . . making for very long nights.

Do I know where to start? Yes, I do, Sam dropped to his knees.

"Heavenly Father, help this poor sinner. . . ."

CHAPTER 15

"OTTO, ESPEREME UN RATO, por favor."

"Sveethurt, ven acá! Git yer self a goin'—we gut to get to Santa Fe before der auction starts. Hustle it up, me liebchen. Pronto!"

It would be a long ride to Santa Fe. Days. Otto Schmitz wasn't too eager to take his pregnant wife, Manuela, but she was intent on seeing the capital city and doing some long-awaited shopping for their ranch. Manuela was looking forward to attending the Three Kings' Day ceremonies at the San Miguel Mission on January 6. The festival of Epiphany was the revealing of Christ to the gentiles and a Holy Day for the residents of New Mexico. Santa Fe would be the largest town Mrs. Schmitz had ever seen—a hub of sophistication and culture, not to mention plentiful shopping opportunities.

Four heavily-armed riders would accompany them . . . Apache raids were common and Geronimo was still at large. The trip to Santa Fe meant traveling along the Rio Chamas to the Rio Grande, over miles of wild terrain.

The Santa Fe of 1880 was a hustling, bustling frontier town populated by thousands. Having been in existence for over 200 years, it served as last stop on the old 780-mile trail from Independence, Missouri. Founded by the Spaniards in 1610, the settlement had survived Indian raids, sweltering heat, and drought.

Otto held the team in check while a smiling Manuela climbed aboard. Her flashing brown eyes sparkled in anticipation. As soon as she was seated, Otto gently snapped the reins on the mules' flanks, and the buckboard jumped to a quick start, pushing them back up against the seat.

"Ve are off," Otto joyfully shouted.

"Sí, sí, que Dios nos vendiga," Manuela happily exclaimed.

"Sveethurt, in Santa Fe ve haf to sprecken American. Mexican is verboten . . . comprende? Aye haf learned American goot, now . . . it is your turn, ya vold?"

"Sí, er . . . ya my husban', yo comprendo."

"Is goot." Otto smiled the smile of a satisfied man.

Business was good; his Mexican wife was pretty and obedient.

Two sons had been born to their union and another child was on the way. "Life is goot." Otto reached over and patted the belly of his young wife. "Maybe dis von vill be blue-eyed." So far, both boys favored their mother, a subject of some concern to Otto Schmitz.

"Qué quieres decir?" his wife asked, then corrected herself, "Oh . . . what do you say, me marido, my husban?"

"Azul! . . . blue! I vant yust von uf our niños to haf blue ojos unt blond hair like der Poppa. How can un Schmitz haf brown eyes? Mine Poppa's eyes ver like der sky, like der sea . . . blue! Mine Momma's like der lake . . . blue! Schmitz hair ist like der fall leafs of der aspen tree, yaller und flaxen."

"Si . . . mine husban'."

Otto had spoken!

Indeed, life had been good since Herr Schmitz followed his brother from Germany to America. The first years were difficult, learning the language and serving in the Union forces. Like many immigrants, he joined the army in order to earn a living. Otto and his brother were two barrel-chested Germans who were thrust into war shortly after their arrival in the United States.

He lived with his brother in Chicago for awhile, but the temptation to get into the fight, the recruitment money, reports that the war would be of short duration and the slyly, amorous looks from his brother's buxom wife convinced him to enlist so as to keep peace in the family and money in the pocket.

Otto was a big, good-looking muscular blond who attracted every living thing—especially females. If there was one bitch in the vicinity, she would find Otto. He loved animals and they loved him. The army soon discovered this rare gift and assigned him to the stables, caring for the cavalry mules and horses. After the war ended, he worked as a veterinarian's assistant until Charlie Meyers called. Charlie needed a trusted hand to manage the stock for the Sassy Mae mines. Otto was the obvious choice. Mules were used to pull the heavy ore wagons and to dump the tailings. Otto readily accepted the job because it fit in perfectly with his post-war plans; his greatest desire was to move south to New Mexico, marry a señorita, become a hacendo, build a hacienda, and raise horses, mules, cows, chickens—and niños.

"I vill breed me up a whole passel of niños to do all der chores vile I set on der veranda givink orders und drinkink cervesa! Those Mexicans are a tough lot . . . I hear dey got schnapps called tequila—der stuff's made outa cactus juice und dey gotta suck on a lime to cut der taste. That sure vould cause a man to pucker up . . . should do vonders for a voman. Dah? Mit my gud strong German blood mixed mit der Mexican, ve can raise dark-skinned, blue-eyed, blond *Mexikrauts!* Dah! . . . it's New Mexico fer Otto!"

Schmitz got his wish. The pay working for Charlie was very good and with the money he had already saved, he homesteaded land at the base of the San Juan Mountains just south of the central Colorado border. It was fine cattle country; the mountains were filled with elk, deer, and Apache Indians. He married Manuela Becerra, a black-eyed beauty with a heavy dose of Apache blood. Manuela was the youngest of four sisters and seven brothers, all alive and healthy. Otto took that as a sign of good breeding, good stock. Her teeth were white and straight, and her sturdy frame would allow her to foal well. She would likely keep her good looks, since her mother had retained some of her attractiveness despite the eleven little ones. The Becerra home was orderly and neat. The family seemed industrious and relatives were everywhere.

That too was good, especially their ties to the Apaches. "If some uf der stock is stolen, I vill know who to ask."

At the first opportunity Otto asked Señor Becerra for permission to court his daughter, with the honorable intention of matrimony. Since Otto was a man of wealth, owning a sizable ranch, permission was quickly granted. Manuela was captivated by the good-natured blond and soon informed her parents that she loved the big German. Otto was discreetly asked if he were Catholic and if not, would he convert. Otto readily agreed . . . he was smart enough not to mention his Lutheran upbringing.

"Got is Got—who cares vot church door ve go through?"

Before the engagement was announced, however, Otto journeyed to San Miguel Mission in Santa Fe to receive instructions in Catholicism. After dutifully complying, he and Manuela were married. The population of the Schmitzes began in earnest. The jovial, good-natured immigrant was well on his way to becoming the Don of Chama Springs.

Otto's renown as a successful breeder and trainer spread throughout New Mexico and though a large man, his reputation for gentleness was legend. His effervescent good nature made him well-liked by man and beast. Working with mules was his special love. "Who but a kraut could vork mit des stubborn, hart-headed buggers. Ha . . . it takes von to know von! . . . Ha!"

Neighbors were fascinated as they watched Otto enter a corral, where mules gathered around him like loving dogs, nuzzling, gently brushing against his side. He talked to them, calling each by name. It was always tough for Otto to sell them . . . more than once, he said, "I hate to part mit der darlinks, but ve hav to put frijoles on the table."

The ride from the ranch to Chama Springs, the nearest outpost of civilization, took several hours. Chama Springs was little more than a gathering place for local ranchers, Mexican farmers, and a few Apaches. It was a spot in the road where trails met, some holding corrals and a general store. Santa Fe was still several days' ride to the southeast.

Although the January auction wasn't as well attended as the one in summer, the dollar amount per head was always higher, making the long drive into Santa Fe worthwhile.

Otto had three muleros. Manuela's younger brothers, Roberto and Jose, and their cousin, Angel Paredes, were entrusted with the prized animals, along with several other well-armed hands. They had already begun to drive the herd the day before. Otto wanted to start early the following morning, but Manuela's extensive preparations took longer than expected.

The first day of 1880 was typical for January—cold and dry, sucking the very moisture from the skin, setting nerves on edge. The auction would bring out ranchers and farmers from all over the state to sell and swap horses, cows, machinery, even land. Otto's animals always received special attention; his mules were bigger, stronger, and better trained than any others and received top dollar. Schmitz mules were used as "wheelers," the span hitched directly to the wagon. Santa Fe Trail wagoners knew the value of Otto's animals. When asked about the secret of his success, he joked about it. "I not so goot; fer years ben tryin' to breed me a Appaloosa mare mit der yakass stud und get a mule mit der white speckled butt, der blanket on der fanny."

Otto loved waiting for the inevitable question. "Did you ever get one?"

"No," he'd chuckle, "All I ever got vas a happy yakass stud."

They arrived in Santa Fe dusty, tired, and badly in need of sleep. All the hotels were filled to capacity but fortunately, room was available at the home of Manuela's second cousin, Miguel Becerra. Though crowded, no one seemed to mind. When relatives arrived, the custom was that the children slept on blankets on the floor while the guests got the beds. "Mi casa es su casa—my home is your home."

The days at the auction went well; Otto had a pocketful of money, a contented Manuela . . . and they were loaded with merchandise to take back to the ranch.

The morning they were preparing to leave, a young boy with a beat-up sombrero in hand came to their door. "Señor Schmitz?"

"I be Schmitz—vot can I do for ye, niño?" Otto reached over and playfully ruffled the wealth of black hair on the child's head.

"Señor, a man wants to see you at the stable 'bout a mule he bought."

"Tell 'em I vill be right dere pronto, niñito."

The boy scampered away.

"Manuela, I be right back, yah?"

The stockyards were close by; it was only a few minutes' walk. A Mexican vaquero was pacing back and forth by the corral, swearing under his breath, obviously agitated. He glanced up as Otto approached, then lowered his head in a docile manner, eyes on the ground. "Señor Schmitz, buenos días."

"Goot day ta you, Señor. Whut kin I do fer ye?" Otto recognized him; he'd purchased one of his mules at the auction. Having bid an exorbitant amount for the animal, he was hard to forget. He recalled his subservient demeanor, the lowered head, the abundance of black hair beneath the large sombrero, and the timid way he raised his hand during the bidding. He bought a good animal, one of Otto's pets.

"Señor, I tink you sole me a lame animal. I am not a rich man and I wanta get me dinero back, por favor. I heard you to be an honest gringo, but maybe no." There was malice and bitterness in his voice, the word *gringo* was spat out like an epithet.

"Now, hold on, Señor, if der ist somethink wrong mit der mule, you vill git yer money back. Ver ist der mule?"

"I will git him, Señor; will you git me money?"

"Ya, you bet I vill—but I vant to see dot mule first."

"Son las diez y media. Señor?"

"Ten thirty's fine wit me, dot's about twenty minutes from now. See you then . . . bring der mule!"

Otto was angry. He'd never sold a lame mule in his life and no one had ever questioned his integrity before. "Now, dere's a Mex mit a chip on his shoulder." He knew hatred for gringos existed among many Mexicans but it had never been directed at him.

New Mexico had been a part of Mexico proper until the Norte Americanos stole it away. The United States and Mexico warred on several occasions, with Mexico each time coming out on the short end. Bitterness remained long after the conflicts had ended, often surfacing at times such as this.

Otto huffed and puffed his way back to the house, cursing in German.

"What is the trouble, me husban'?" Manuela had never seen her mate this upset, neither had her brothers.

Otto pulled himself together, "Oh, it is nothink important. Some vaquero vants his dinero back fer der mule. It's a goot animal so I don' mind taken 'em back."

"Need any help, Patrón?" asked the brothers.

"Naw . . . ain't the furst time I buy back animal."

Otto returned to the corral thinking about how angry he'd become. It wasn't like him. "It mus' be this darn New Mexico air!" Since arriving in New Mexico, Otto had noticed the change in his normally sanguine nature and in others, as well. The high arid deserts of the southwest, with rainfall less than twenty inches a year, seemed to create an atmospheric sponge which drew moisture from man and beast alike. Skin wrinkled early, aging came quicker. The dryness angered the soul, bringing out the meanness in a man.

Otto was first to arrive . . . no one else was about except a few ranchers by the barn. Within moments, from around the corner of the corral, appeared the vaquero, limping mule in tow. Otto was surprised at the sight of the crippled animal. "Vot do ve haf here!"

"Do you see, Señor, she limps!" the Mexican shouted. "I want the money . . . now!"

Heads turned at the sound of the angry voice.

The mule, spotting Otto, limped over to his side and he reached up and scratched her ear. "Let's see 'bout der front leg." He deftly lifted the foreleg to examine the hoof, expecting to see some object lodged between the sole and the shoe . . . nothing. "Oh, oh, vot do ve haf here!" Twisted tightly around the pastern was a thin piece of rusted wire hidden within the hair. It caused obvious discomfort to the mule, pressuring the flexor tendon, restricting circulation. He felt the blood rush to his face. The vaquero had undoubtedly paid more than he could afford for the mule and had used this old trick to get his money back. Otto was furious; he would have gladly taken back the animal and returned the cash, but to cripple one of his darlings was more than he could stand! He untwisted the wire strip and waved it under the vaquero's nose.

"You filthy greaser, doin' such a mean thing to a dumb animal. . . . " He grabbed the vaquero with both hands and began to shake him. "Dis vill shake some sense into . . . Oh, mine Got!" Blood spurted from Otto's lips. The vaquero had sunk the blade of his Bowie knife upward to the hilt, cutting the lung, angling for the heart. He struck again as Otto sank to the ground, looked him in the eyes, and struck again. Swiftly, he rifled Otto's pockets, removed the wad of bills, then deftly swung onto the mule's bare back . . . and galloped toward town.

Manuela, worried over her husband's delay, headed off for the stables. From a distance, she saw her husband's blood-soaked body leaning against the corral . . . saw the men rushing out from the barn. She screamed as only a loved one can—a terrified, blood-curdling, shrill wail that could be heard for blocks around. Holding her skirts high, she ran and collapsed at Otto's side . . . he was still alive, but an unforgettable vibration was deep in his throat.

"Come close, Liebchen," he whispered.

"Oh, my darling," she sobbed while placing her ear close to his blood-spattered lips . . . faintly, hearing his last words. . . .

"Oh, mi marido," she sobbed, "you joke at a time like this?"

CHAPTER 16

SAM LEANED BACK in his chair, staring at the letters and telegrams spread out before him . . . messages of heartache and despair, anxiety and tears. At first he was shocked at reading about the loss of friends, each communiqué a painful jolt of bad news. Grief and empathy followed, concern for the wives and mothers, family and friends, loved ones lost.

Sam's brow furrowed as a curious ache swept through him, telling him something was amiss. It didn't make sense that all met with untimely deaths within such a short period of time. Wade Johnson accidentally killed in a poker game fracas . . .Sherry Arbuckle missing and wanted for murder . . . Jethro Briggs gunned down by the son of one of his victims . . . Andrew Quade falling down a mine shaft . . . and most recently sweet, gentle Otto Schmitz, knifed by a disgruntled Mexican. "Six of us shot, killed, or missing within the past year." He looked at the communiqués, picked them up, and read them again. "Every single one a violent death; no one died naturally . . . it doesn't seem right."

Sam shuffled the letters and telegrams, reading them once more, pondering the circumstances that brought this morose information to his attention. "If I hadn't lost my arm, I would never have known."

During his and Matthew's long convalescence there was little to do. Sam passed the time by practicing to write with his left hand. For weeks, balls of crumpled paper littered the room, mementos of frustrating, clumsy attempts to legibly communicate. Although he realized everyone wrote with just one hand, little did he realize the necessity of another to hold the paper still, steady the ink well, or sharpen a pencil.

Writing with only one arm was a chore. Slowly but surely his skill improved, to the degree that he felt confident enough to write his friends . . . men who served with him in the Civil War. Receiving letters in return would help pass the time. Most had kept in touch over the years.

Then the letters came, each one filled with sadness. The first he received was from Agatha, Wade Johnson's wife. Next, the incredulous letter from the mother of Sherry Arbuckle, detailing the murder charges against her son. It was a jumbled, anxious communiqué written by a parent fearful of foul play, yet defending the honor of her missing son. Last was the tear-stained note from Manuela Schmitz.

Not all of the squad members were dead, although the telegram from the Sassy Mae Mine office stated that Charlie was in a sanitarium in Colorado, dying of consumption. This information came as no surprise, remembering the violent coughing spells and the reprobate life of his former boss, but Sam was somewhat relieved to hear he was still alive. Kenneth Seymour was practicing law in Silverville; his secretary noted receipt of Sam's letter.

"The devil takes care of his own," Sam mused. "Seems good men die young but the Meyers and the Seymours live on."

There were three squad members Sam could not locate, comrades he hadn't heard of in years. Last he heard of Sean Sullivan, he was tending bar in Chicago. Clarence Devlin worked for the U. S. government somewhere in the West, and Porter Dixon had left Illinois for parts unknown. He had no idea if they were living or among the dead.

The letter that depressed Sam to the quick was Eliza Arbuckle's. She included clippings from the newspapers, detailing the crime and Sherry's disappearance. Her son was the prime suspect. His sudden departure confirmed in the minds of many that he was the culprit. To make matters worse, the articles intimated that the murdered woman had been violated.

Further devastating to Eliza Arbuckle and her daughter was the snubbing by the Edger County citizenry. She was being shunned by old friends because of what her son had reportedly done. Since no one was available to manage the farm, the surviving Arbuckles had been forced to sell and move into town, living off the proceeds of the sale.

The letter tore at Sam's heart, particularly because the Arbuckles were kinfolk; Sherry was his first cousin by marriage. They had been the best of friends . . . sat next to each other through eight years of grade school, joined the Union army together, and fought side by side for three long years. Sherry was as close as his own brothers. Nothing could convince Sam that his relative had harmed a defenseless woman, much less sexually violated her. Sherry was a Christian man, moral through and through—never vile or profane, even under extreme provocation. "Darn them, don't they know he could never do that?" Sam picked up a book from the table and threw it across the room.

Sister Keppel poked her head in the room, "Anything wrong?"

"No, nothing to worry about. I dropped a book."

The door closed without a word of response. The sisters let him stay in the hospital in order to be near his son. St. Joseph's was not crowded; the quarters and food were substantially better than the fare in town. The sisters were having a hard time keeping the hospital open. Sam's room and board helped. He was grateful, but now he was embarrassed over his loss of temper. "I need some fresh air." Putting on his coat, he left the warmth of his room for the frigid outdoors. The hospital was on a plain to the east of the frontier settlement, a good walk to the center of town. Sam ducked his head into the blustery cold wind surging out of the West. He contemplated turning back. *What the heck. I'll have it behind me coming back.*

Sam walked farther than he expected, crossing the tracks, past the coal sheds and Union Pacific machine shop and roundhouse. All the time he couldn't get Sherry's disappearance out of his thoughts. *He'd never do that, he would never run away.*

The war years came to mind. Sherry was an idealist, hating the institution of slavery, believing it to be a canker on the body of the Republic. He fervently advocated the abolitionist cause of the North and was committed to President Lincoln. Sam remembered vividly the excitement Sherry displayed upon Lincoln's reelection. Many believed he would be defeated by McClellan, but Sherry never doubted Abe Lincoln's ability to win.

"God is usin' ol' Abe to hold this land together and free the slaves; no way he'll lose to that pontificating military windbag . . . the Lord wouldn't let that happen," Sherry had insisted.

Sam also clearly recalled his friend's enthusiasm over reading a month-old issue of a Washington, D. C. newspaper. During a lull in the fighting, the squad was relaxing around their tents, enjoying the warm spring day. The Virginia hillsides were bursting with new growth; apple, cherry, and peach trees were blossoming; a warm spring breeze moved lazily through the new green grass. The balmy weather allowed the soldiers to temporarily forget slogging and laboring through muddy battlefields. As the bloody war was drawing to a close, the fighting had become more desperate and vicious. Lee's Confederates were going down hard, making the Union forces pay dearly at every turn. The assault on Petersburg was close at hand, and victory there would spell the doom of Richmond and the Southern cause.

"Sam . . . fellers . . . would you listen to this!" Sherry sat down cross-legged and began to read from the newspaper. 'Woe unto the world because of offenses! For it must needs be that offenses come; but woe to that man by whom the offense cometh.' If we shall suppose American slavery is one of those offenses which, in the providence of God, must needs come, but which, having continued through His appointed time, He now wills to remove, and that He gives to both North and South this terrible war as the woe due to those by whom the offense come, shall we discern therein any departure from those divine attributes which the believers in a living God always ascribe to Him?"

Sherry smiled and looked up, "Sounds like a preacher, don't it?"

Everyone seemed to be in agreement.

"No, it ain't . . . there's more!" Sherry read on. "Yet if God wills that it continue, all the wealth piled by the bondsman's two hundred and fifty years of unrequited toil shall be sunk, and until every drop of blood drawn with the lash shall be paid by another drawn with the sword, as was said three thousand years ago, so still it must be said, the judgments of the Lord are true and righteous altogether."

Sherry grinned at the soldiers gathered around. "Guess who said all that?"

No one volunteered an opinion.

"Old Abe, that's who! That was only a part of his Second Inaugural Address. I told you he's a man of God; those ain't the words of no politician." Sherry shook the paper above his head. "Beeootiful words! When I have youngun's, I'll read this to 'em every year to let them know what their daddy fought for, by gum—I shore will."

Sam was sure Sherry must be dead. No man with his ideals and character would stoop to killing a woman. "Gotta see the sheriff, show him the letters, and hear what he has to say."

The frigid February winds penetrated the sheepskin coat, piercing through every seam, spreading its chill with vengeance. He pulled his hat down tighter and tilted his head against the whistling wind to keep the gusts from ripping it off. The street was a mess of frozen mud and slush mixed with horse manure. Sam's boots broke through the ice and sunk to the ankles as he crossed over to the sheriff's office. Reaching the boardwalk was a comfortable relief. He stomped his feet, dislodging the chunks of half-frozen mire.

"Sorry about me trackin' up yer office," Sam said as he stuck his head through the door.

"Shucks no, Sam, come on in." Deputy Joe LeFever waved casually, "Your mud is as good as ours, only we bring in more of it."

"Where's the sheriff?"

"Oh, he's home."

"Think he would mind if I dropped in on him?"

"Can I help you with anything?" Joe politely offered.

"No thanks, Joe, I need to see Nate." Sam waved farewell and went back into the cold. The wind had picked up to gale proportions, taxing Sam's energy. His strength had only partially returned, and already he dreaded the long walk back to the hospital.

Nate Boswell lived on the corner of Fifth and Grand, just a short way from his office. Sam stepped up on the wide porch, kicked the snow from his feet, and knocked. The door was quickly opened by the sheriff.

"Sam! . . . Come on in before you freeze to death."

He gratefully stepped inside the door. "Pretty cold out there."

"Balmy Wyomin' day," smiled the sheriff. "What can I do for you?"

"Need yer help again, Boz, and yer advice as well."

Boswell couldn't help but note the seriousness in Sam's voice. He stopped smiling and pointed to the sofa. "Sit down; let's talk about it. I'll ask the wife to pour us some hot coffee."

For more than an hour, Sam explained what was on his mind.

The lawman listened intently, occasionally scribbling a line or two on notepaper. He then read and reread the letters Sam had given him, studying each one carefully. He glanced across at the one-armed cowman sitting uncomfortably on the sofa, every so often shifting his position to favor his sore shoulder.

"Still hurt much?"

"Not near as much as those letters," replied Sam.

"I can understand why. Sam, what do you intend to do?"

"Sheriff, I think there might be some connection between Sherry Arbuckle's disappearance, Wade's death, and my shooting. I have to find out best I can. I got to return to Illinois and see my kin, visit Sherry's ma, see if I can find any trace of what happened to my cousin. I'll be stopping off on the way back in Brookville, Kansas, to pay my respects to Agatha, Wade Johnson's widow. I'll be talkin' to their sheriff as well."

"Why do you think you can find out anything more than the local constables?"

"I don't know if I can, but I know I have to try. Nate, did you notice one real important fact? Not one of them killers has been caught! The cowboy that killed Wade ain't never been found . . . that boy who shot Briggs neither. Not even the Mexican who knifed Otto; all got away clean."

"Could be coincidence," commented the sheriff.

"Maybe so, but there's too many coincidences to leave to chance . . . best I check 'em out."

"I have to agree with you; only a fool could leave it be—'specially since it involves so much killing."

Sam lumbered up from his seat, "Sheriff, one more favor. Matthew's comin' along real fine. In a couple a weeks he'll be ready to travel home. If you could look in on him, I'd sure be appreciative. I should be back by the end of a month, but if anything happens and you don't hear from me by then, figure the worst. Would you see my boy gits home safely?"

"Don't worry about Matt. Upholt, Joe, and me will take good care of him. We think he's a special youngun."

Sam smiled, "Yep, he certainly is for sure."

★ ★ ★

The train ride to Illinois was uneventful. Sam's younger brothers met him at the station and took him immediately to the family farm. His mother cried when she saw him. "Oh, Samuel! Who's done this to my boy?"

"I'm alive, Mother, and by the grace of God, I'm getting on fine . . . and I intend to stay that way." He smiled and hugged her. "Besides, Mom, I've got six of your grandchildren to raise."

Her faced brightened, "Sam, tell me all about them, every last detail!"

They went into the house and talked about family doings late into the night. Not until the next morning did Sam broach the subject of cousin Arbuckle.

"None of the family and none of Sherry's close friends think he murdered that gal, but a heap of folks do. They take his running away as admission of guilt," stated Father Dodd. Everyone nodded in agreement.

"We tried ta help Sherry's mother but she wouldn't hear of it. Proud woman, that Eliza Arbuckle. Sold the farm to pay bills," added Mother Dodd.

"I'm aware of that," responded Sam. "I'm going into town and see Sheriff Wattis."

"That's not possible, Son. Saul passed away last year. His young deputy, D. B. Dills, is acting sheriff 'til the next election. Dills will be tough to deal with."

"Why's that?"

"D. B. stands for 'dumb board,'" offered brother Timothy. "He's convinced Sherry molested and killed the girl. He's promised ta catch him and bring him to justice. It's all he talks about."

"Yeah," added Mike, "D. B. is Sheriff Wattis's nephew. He gave him the job just to please his sister. D. B. was barely tolerable when ol' Saul was alive, an' now that he's dead, D. B.'s somethin' insufferable. We all think he's using the killin' as a way to get officially elected to the sheriff's vacated seat. Ol' Saul doubted Sherry's guilt, but he kept quiet 'cause all of the noise the newspapers were making. D. B. joined in, howlin' for Sherry's neck to be stretched by a rope."

"I think I remember him. Scrawny little kid?"

"Now he's a scrawny *big* kid with a badge on his chest," added Mike.

"Well, dumb or not, I have to see him soon. Pa, can I use one of the horses?"

"Take the buckboard, Son; it'll be easier on you."

"I'll hitch up the roan," offered Mike.

"Mike, thanks, but don't any of you bother. I have to get used to riding with just the one arm an' I can saddle good enough." His voice was firm, trucking no dissent . . . so no one did.

Sam enjoyed the ride into town, which brought back a slew of memories as he passed by the town's central square; the red brick of the county building still had the look of newness about it. In his youth, he played on the courthouse lawn with his friends on hot summer afternoons while the grownups shopped and chatted about the weather and crops. They were wonderful days. Several folks recognized him, waving greetings while inquisitively staring at the pinned-up sleeve.

Sam dismounted and tied up the horse in front of the sheriff's office where a deputy was leaning against the wall, biting off a chew of tobacco.

"How are you, Deputy," said Sam, cheerfully greeting the young man. "Is the sheriff inside?'

"Yes, Sir," he replied.

"Is he busy?" asked Sam.

"He's not doin' nothin' that cain't wait," answered the young deputy.

Acting Sheriff D. B. Dills was seated with both feet propped up on his desk, deeply engrossed, head buried in a western dime novel. He was startled when Sam said, "Sheriff, can I talk to you?"

"Oh, yes . . . you betcha." He put down the cheap pulp, smiled, and offered his right hand, withdrawing it quickly when he saw there was nothing to shake. "Howdy, I'm Sheriff Dills—what can I do for you?" he beamed.

He was barely thirty years old. A scraggly beard bordered his toothy smile. Splotches of skin shown through where hair refused to grow on his narrow face. The smile vanished with Sam's opening remark.

"I'm Sam Dodd, Sherry Arbuckle's cousin."

"So?" His mouth twisted into a smirk; sarcasm dripped from his lips. "Another relative protesting Arbuckle's innocence?"

"I'd like some information about the circumstances of the killing," Sam said, ignoring the ill-humor of the acting sheriff.

"What's to know? We found the body; she was last seen with Arbuckle and he's run off. There's nothin' much else a feller's got to know to see who's guilty." D. B. then picked up the book and contemptuously uttered, "I'm sort of busy, so that's all I've got to say." With that he dropped down into his chair, tilted backwards, and returned his feet to the desk.

As soon as he reopened the novel, Sam leapt forward and kicked the back legs of the chair, spilling the surprised lawman on the floor. He grasped the front of the sheriff's shirt, lifted him bodily from the floor with his one hand, then swiftly backed him into the wall and held him against it. Without raising his voice, he spoke between clenched teeth, "Listen to me, you piece of horse dung, I've come a long ways to find out what happened, and I will. I've been a deputy sheriff too, and I know about upholding the law. If my cousin murdered that girl, I'll help you hang 'em—but from what I know about Sherry, it's hard to believe he did it."

The young man's face was beet-red. He tried to wriggle away from Sam's grasp but could not. The strength in that one arm was intimidating and the determination in his voice was equally as powerful.

"I've some questions to ask, so sit down now quiet-like!"

Sam released the shirt, turned his back to the trembling sheriff, and returned to his seat. "Come on, sit! We have work to do." He motioned toward the other chair behind the desk.

"How the heck do ya think you're gonna get anythin' outa me by callin' me a piece o' horse pucky?" sputtered the crimson-faced sheriff.

"'Cause you are! You earned the reputation of being dumber than a board, and as long as you have that hangin' over your head, your chances of being elected a real sheriff is slim at best. Solve this crime and chances are ya'll can sit in that seat as long as Saul did."

D. B. glowered at Sam, knowing inwardly that the truth of what he just said made sense. He had already noticed some change in the town's attitude as more and more folks began to doubt Sherry's guilt. After all, Sherry was a wounded war hero, an up-standing citizen, and a friend to just about everybody. The pretty young woman was a stranger, her identity still unknown. This man seated across from him was not to be fooled with; D. B. was smart enough to know that. Besides, he said he was a lawman. Still, he was acting sheriff—and nobody had a right to insult him.

"I ain't a piece of . . . "

Sam interrupted, "All right, you're not . . . but until you prove different, yer still dumber than a board to me."

"You say you're a lawman?"

"Was . . . for a number of years I was in charge of security for mining interests in Silverville, Colorado, and was made a deputy for the county as well."

The young man excitedly leaned forward in his chair, "You were a real Colorado lawman? WOWEE! You were a lawman in the West . . . in Silverville . . . truly?"

"Yep . . . 'til I bought a spread an' took to ranching."

D. B. Dills was agog, completely forgetting his antagonism. Sitting before him was a real western officer of the law. He again leaned forward, shifted his head from side to side and looking out of the corner of his eye, enthusiastically whispered, "Didja ever have to shoot anyone?" Without pausing for breath, he added, "Didja ever break up a saloon brawl? Well, kiss a chicken!" D. B. sat back and slapped his knee, "A honest-ta-God Western sheriff—ain't that somethin'. Tell me," he said, craning his head over the desk, "didja ever kill anyone?"

Sam glanced down at the desk and about the office. Western novels lay everywhere—*Beadle's Dime Library*, articles by Colonel Prentiss Ingraham, Ned Buntline stories, escapades of the Wild West written by know-nothing Eastern writers littered the room.

"Well, did ya?"

"Uh, well . . . unfortunately yes . . . I've killed some," Sam hesitatingly responded.

"Some? Ya killed more 'an one?"

"Yes . . . regretfully, more than one."

"Darn . . . if that ain't sumthin'! If . . . that . . . ain't . . . *somethin'!*" Again the young sheriff slapped his knee in glee, then suddenly looked morose. "All that happens hereabouts is some farmer gets drunk on Saturday night, a fight breaks out at Smitty's Pool Hall, or some rowdy younguns tip over an outhouse, or someone steals a chicken." He brightened once more and asked, "Ever been in a gunfight? Have ya . . . huh?"

Sam looked at Dills and it all became clear; this young whelp was a romantic fiction buff living in a world of Western pulp novels. He saw Sherry Arbuckle as his ticket to glory, his place in the sun. What's better than making one's reputation by the pursuit of a rapist, a vicious molester of women? *This so-called sheriff is enraptured by the romance of law enforcement, not its substance . . . the dime novels scattered about his office are proof positive. But,* Sam thought, *his juvenile admiration for Western lawmen may be helpful in getting information about the killing.*

"Yep, I've been in some gunfights."

"Hot-darn, Marvin! Come in here!" the sheriff shouted excitedly to the deputy outside. "We got a *real* Western sheriff on our hands!"

★ ★ ★

Little was accomplished the remainder of the day, for whenever Sam tried to discuss the murder, the acting sheriff asked about the frontier. He was absolutely enthralled with it . . . hanging on Sam's every word. When D. B. realized Sam had fought and killed Indians, he became delirious with fascination, pressing for every gory detail. Sam's hesitancy to discuss the men he'd killed did nothing more than inflame D. B.'s curiosity and instigate further probing. He even took Sam into the local pool parlor and introduced him all around. Fortunately, D. B.'s deputy, Marvin McClintock, was a rational young man, quiet and competent. Sam finally talked the sheriff into letting the deputy assist him. D. B. Dills gladly complied . . . he had found a new hero.

Early the following morning Deputy McClintock met Sam at the boat dock where the woman's body had been discovered.

"This is right where we found her." McClintock pointed to a piling beneath the ramp. "She was under the water a few feet, floating face down . . . probably would have sunk to the bottom but the hem of her dress caught on that piling. The boatman saw the material and yanked . . . he got quite a shock."

"In other words, she might'a not been found fer days," added Sam.

"That's right. Normally a dead person sinks in fresh water, at least for a while. Usually, we have to drag the bottom when someone drowns . . . we've done that more than once in these lakes."

"What was her condition . . . was she molested?"

"Her clothes and underthings were torn, dress ripped down the front, with scratches on her right breast." The young deputy was uneasy; he obviously didn't like talking about it. "We took her body to Doc—he's our county coroner. Doc said . . . ," he turned his head away, then blurted out . . . "Doc said she had bite marks on her breast. That sure got folks upset! What kind of a fiend would do that?"

"Deputy . . . Sherry Arbuckle wouldn't!" Sam replied. "I'm sure of that! Who was the last person ta see her alive?"

"The boatman. He was closin' up shop after the last boat came in. Sherry and the girl were still on the dock when he left."

"Was he sure it was them?"

"Positive. The girl was real pretty. The boatman said she was hard to forget. He said Sherry and her were real neighborly."

"What do you mean, *neighborly?*"

"Holdin' hands, lookin' gooey-eyed. He said she even kissed Arbuckle on the cheek, real friendly-like. They were the only ones left on the dock when he went home."

"Was anyone else around that late?" Sam asked.

"Few stragglers, that's all, a young couple or two sparkin'."

It didn't look good. All the evidence pointed directly to Sherry.

"Let's go talk to the boatman; maybe he's remembered something," said Sam.

The man was painting the bottom of a small skiff as they approached. "Why, if it ain't the deputy," he called out. "Caught thet killer Arbuckle yet?"

"No, Burt, we ain't . . . that's why we're here; we need to ask you some more questions."

Once more, the boatman detailed the circumstances of finding the body. "I'll tell ya'll, it warn't a pretty sight."

"Are you sure there wasn't anyone else on the dock landing?" Sam asked.

"Nary a soul. They were the only ones."

"Were all the boats in?"

"Yep, all accounted for."

"Do you keep daily records of all the rentals?" Sam looked at the large number of boats tied to the dock; several were already out on the lake.

"Shore do. I'd ketch what-for from old man Frohm who owns this here landin' if I didn't. Come over to the shack; I'll show you."

Burt opened the ledger to the Fourth of July and ran a finger down the list, noting the times. "Yep, all accounted for."

Sam looked over Burt's shoulder at the entries. "What's this here? One boat returned on the sixth?"

"Oh, that was a die-hard catfish fisherman from over Metcalf way. He showed up with a pole, some blankets, a basket o' food, and a bucket o' smelly chicken guts . . . he had 'em in a bucket, showed 'em to me. Lordy, they smelled bad, but he said catfish seemed to like 'em. He said he was goin' to the end of the lake and camp there 'til he catched a batch of cat. He checked the boat in on the mornin' of the sixth, two days later."

"Ever seen him before?"

"Don't think so. Said he was from Metcalf, that's a few mile to the north of here."

"Get his name?"

"Got it right here in the book. Let's see . . . Jefferson . . . E. W. Jefferson."

"Remember what he looked like?"

"Oh . . . guess he was thirty or so, dressed like most farm hands, chin whiskers, blond bushy hair, kinda average-lookin'."

"Anything peculiar about him—scars, funny quirks, anything you remember different?" inquired Sam.

"Nah . . . yeah, now ya mention it. His eyes."

"What about them?"

"They was the palest blue eyes I ever saw. That's all I remember. Oh yeah, he weren't much of a fisherman. Folks was catchin' plenty of cats, but this here fella had a pitiful string. I joshed him, and he was good-natured about it. Matter a fact, that's when I seen his eyes . . . when he smiled. Most folks squint when they smile, but not this one."

"What do you mean?" asked Sam.

"He smiled like this," replied the boat hand. He displayed a large grin while opening his eyes wide at the same time. "Not many people smile that-a-way."

Sam turned to the deputy, "Did the sheriff look into this Jefferson fellow?"

"Frankly, Mr. Dodd, this is the first we've heard about him," said the deputy.

"Someone else was on that lake. We better have a talk with this Mr. Jefferson, but first let's go see Doc. I've got some questions for him."

During the buggy ride to Doc Uhler's, a flood of conversation developed over finding out someone else was on the lake that night. Maybe he saw something or someone, a clue that could help clear up the mysterious disappearance of Sherry Arbuckle.

The town of Metcalf was a good half-day's ride. The roads were a mass of spring mud, making the trip a chore, but the possibility of gaining new information would be worth the effort.

Deputy McClintock was sharp; the discovery of the catfish angler set his mind to work.

"This puts a new bend in the bow, doesn't it? This Jefferson fellow might have seen something."

"Sure could . . . we'll find out soon enough."

"It's strange that no one's come forward to identify the young woman. We've notified all the towns hereabout, even sent her description to the state capital, and we checked missing persons circulars . . . nothing. It's almost as though she never existed. No one seems to be looking for her; no family, relatives, friends." The deputy looked pretty gloomy, "Such a pretty lady . . . she was buried in a pine box at the cemetery with only a few curiosity seekers lookin' on; there's not even a marker with her name on it. Sure's a pity."

"Who was she? That shorely is a big part of the puzzle," Sam commented. "A very big part."

The doctor's office was small and simply furnished with plain, sturdy chairs. Doc Uhler was a family doctor who firmly believed there was no sense having good furniture for squirmy youngsters to wreck. Waiting in the outer room was an expectant mother, a teenage boy with a splint on his arm, and an elderly lady. Sam and the deputy would have to wait. Half-an-hour later they were admitted into Doc's inner office.

"This looks like an official visit," commented the physician.

"Yes Sir, it is. Doc, this here's Sam Dodd. His family's the Dodds over east of town. Lives in Colorado now and is back here lookin' into the death of that unknown girl. He's got some questions to ask."

The doctor sat back in his chair. "Ask away."

"Doctor, this ain't easy to ask . . . was she violated?"

"I couldn't tell. She was certainly no virgin though."

"Was she wearin' any jewelry? Wedding ring maybe?"

Doc turned toward his desk, "Let me have a look at the file. He found the records in a lower drawer of his battered roll top . . . then thumbed through the papers. "Ah, here we are." He studied the documents carefully. "Yes, she wore two rings, one on the little finger of the left hand and another on the forefinger of her right, both inexpensive jewelry."

"No wedding-band marks?"

"No . . . none. Hmm, interesting point. Usually wearing a wedding band leaves an indentation mark for some time . . . she had none. What do you make of that, Mr. Dodd?"

"It could tell us a little bit about her character, I suppose; lost virginity but no sign of recent marriage . . . she might have been a high-class harlot."

"Well, if she was," laughed the deputy, "she shore wasn't one of our locals. She'd a been recognized by our acting sheriff!"

"Sherry didn't hang around those kind of women," stated Sam.

"Now, gentlemen, let's not besmirch the poor girl's name unless we know for sure," added the doctor. "But it might make some sense. The bite marks on her breast could have been days-old, the scratches were fresh, but those bruises from the teeth might have occurred a few days earlier."

"D. B. never told me the teeth marks could have been made earlier," said the visibly irritated deputy.

"He never asked," replied the doctor.

"Sam sat hunched over in his chair, his mind racing. "Anything else, Doc?"

"One small incongruity—something my nurse observed during the examination."

"What was that?"

"The girl's clothes. Her dress was plain cotton like most of the ladies hereabouts wear, but her underthings was real expensive . . . lacy and silk. That might lend credence to your fancy-lady theory."

"What would a high-class harlot be doin' in Paris, Illinois?" asked Deputy McClintock.

"Good question," answered Sam. "It could tell us why no family was lookin' for her." Sam got up from his chair and thanked the doctor for his time. "Deputy, best we go see Mr. Jefferson. We can make it to Metcalf by dusk if we ride hard."

McClintock silently nodded in agreement.

★ ★ ★

They reined in the tired, mud-splattered horses at the hitch rail in front of the Metcalf General Store and Post Office, just as the proprietor, Sherman Holmquist, was locking up. As was the custom of any good country businessman, he unlatched the door and welcomed Sam and Deputy McClintock inside. Behind the counter, he lit the coal lamp overhead. "What can I do for ya'll? Before Sam could answer, he pointed at Sam and inquired, "Aren't you one of the Dodd boys? . . . Let's see . . . Samuel, that's yer name, ain't it? Heard ya were in Colorado, married the Arbuckle girl . . . Mary, that was her name, wasn't it? Gosh! What happened to yer arm?"

"Pleased you remembered, Mr. Holmquist . . . it's been a while." Sam smiled. Sherman Holmquist knew everyone within a twenty-mile radius of his store. Families for miles around traded there, bought farm machinery, collected packages, and bought stamps at the post office in the rear of the store. Sam answered all his questions and then some. It was good to see the old man. He was a contemporary of his father's, a longtime friend of the family.

"Lots of new folks about?"

"Oh, a few. Nothin' changes a lot 'round Metcalf."

"Ever know of a farm hand by the name of Jefferson?"

"Sure do. About ten years back the Jeffersons bought the old Albey place south of town . . . nice folks."

"Any of 'em in his thirties, blond hair, blue eyes?

"Yeah, that fits the likes of their oldest boy, Elmer."

"Any other Jeffersons about?"

"Nope, they's the only ones."

"Thank you, Mr. Holmquist, we better be goin'. It'll be well after dark when we git to their place."

The dogs set up quite a racket as they rode up to the Jefferson farm. They dismounted by a battered split-rail fence, then stepped up on the porch with the dogs sniffing at their heels. The house was dark.

Sam knocked hard on the screened door . . . "Mr. Jefferson, it's Sam Dodd."

A coal oil lamp flickered inside, held by the approaching sleepy-eyed farmer. The inner door opened a crack. "Whatcha want?" he grumpily barked through the screen.

"Mr. Jefferson, I hate to wake you up but it's real important that Deputy McClintock and me talk to you."

"Deputy? What's the law doin' way out here?"

"We have some questions to ask your son. Is he about?"

"Now, that'll be tough to do; all my boys are gone. Flew the coop. Left me and the wife to do these eighty acres ourselves. Hard work . . . need all the sleep I can git."

Sam was visibly disappointed. "Where's the oldest boy, close around?"

"Nah, he took off for Californy last year with his brother. Works on an almond orchard near Marysville . . . or was it a peach orchard near Fresno?" He turned and bellowed loudly, "Ma, is Elmer in Fresno and Hershal in Marysville or t'other way 'round?"

"What time last year?" interrupted McClintock.

Jefferson turned and shouted, "Margaret, when did Elmer and Hershal go west last year?"

They faintly heard a high pitched voice coming from the back of the house.

"She done said it were March 22."

"Are you sure?"

"My wife never forgits a date. I'll show ye. Margaret, when was Lincoln kilt?" He listened for a reply. "Well, I'll be doggied . . . says she don't know . . . must be the time o'night."

"Mr. Jefferson, does your son like to fish?"

"Nah, not Elmer . . . could never git him to eat what fish I caught from the pond out back."

"One last question—what's the color of his eyes?"

"That's a dern silly question . . . they're brown like mine . . . my other boy too!"

The two riders made it back in Paris just as the new day was breaking. The red rim of the morning sun silhouetted the trees. A thin patchy fog hugged the ground and hovered over Twin Lakes as they rode by. Both were too tired for much conversation. Sam looked at the serene setting and a cold shudder crept into his bones, chilling him to the marrow.

"Deputy."

"Yes, Sir."

"Did the sheriff check the railroads ta see if Sherry left town?"

"Oh yeah, we did all that. No one could figger how he got out so slick and clean, bein' so well-known around here."

Sam looked at the lake. The chill persisted.

"Deputy, I think I might know where Sherry is!"

★ ★ ★

At Sam's insistence, they dragged the lake bottom. By two o'clock in the afternoon, they'd hauled the decomposed body of Sherry Arbuckle to the surface. Around his neck was a short rope tied to a heavy weight, a lidded bait-bucket filled with stones and what appeared to be the remains of chicken guts.

Sam slept a restless night. Immediately after the funeral, he left for Kansas. An idle parting conversation with Eliza Arbuckle, Sherry's mother, weighed heavily on his mind.

CHAPTER 17

THE RAIN WAS BEATING THE GROUND into soggy submission, ricocheting off the wooden platform as the train pulled into Brookville, Kansas. A few hardy souls hovered under the overhang while others inside the station peered through the windows, waiting for the train to come to a complete stop . . . ready to board as quickly as possible.

Sam stepped down from the pullman car into the downpour. "Sam? Sam Dodd?"

The voice came from a covered buggy near the platform, a woman's voice . . . difficult to make out due to the wall of rain separating them. It had to be Agatha Johnson, Wade's widow. Sam had wired ahead, asking her to meet him at the train station. There was no time to wait for a reply; her presence at the depot was comfortable affirmation.

"Hurry up, Sam Dodd, or you'll be soaked to the skin."

He threw his carpetbag into the buggy and climbed aboard. A smiling, attractive woman sat holding the reins.

"Agatha, Agatha Johnson?"

"Who else would be out to greet you on a miserable day like this!"

Agatha's smile was infectious, friendly. Sam immediately liked her. The cold of the rain was dispelled by the warmth of her expression.

"Mighty nice of you to pick me up."

"I had to see the mighty Sam Dodd first hand. Wade talked about you a lot over the years, and how you and he were great friends. While you're here, you'll stay with us."

"Thanks, that's mighty kind of you, but I have to be moving on as soon as possible. The hotel will do just fine."

Agatha frowned, clearly disappointed. "Oh, the children will be so sorry. Their father mentioned your name often. Can't you stay just to have supper with us?"

"I'll be more than obliged. Wade bragged a lot about your cooking!"

When she smiled again, Sam thought of Mary. *How Wade must miss his wife Agatha; even heaven might be a lonely place without your mate at your side.*

"Agatha, you were right about our friendship. Wade and Sherry Arbuckle were the best pards a man could ever have."

"What do you mean, *were?* . . . Has something happened to Sherry?"

She was devastated as Sam unfolded the story of the past year. The shootings, the loss of his arm and Matthew's hand, Otto's and Sherry's murders. As he related each death, her tears increased. Suddenly she straightened up and asked, "Sam, are you trying to tell me Wade's death was no accident?"

"Agatha, I don't know. That's why I'm here. If Wade was murdered, maybe there's some clue as to who the killer might be."

"Sam, everybody thinks the cowboy who killed Wade is dead. They found his bloated horse and discarded saddle downriver, and his hat caught up on a snag. They figured he drowned trying to cross the Smokey River."

"And everybody thought Sherry murdered that girl and dumped her body in the lake, but it ain't so. Maybe this ain't so either."

"Why, Sam? Why would anyone want to kill Wade or any of the others? Wade and Otto didn't have an enemy in the whole world!"

"Don't know . . . I haven't figured that out yet, but I hope to find out before anybody else dies. I still haven't located all the squad members . . . I hoped you might've heard from some of the boys recently."

Strange you should ask. Matter of fact, I just wired Clarence Devlin's whereabouts to a Mr. P. T. Mellon, a lawyer in Denver. He said he had to get in touch with him about some legal matter."

"Where's Clarence living nowadays?"

"He wrote to Wade about a year ago—said he was working as an Indian agent in the Arizona Territory for the government."

"Did this Mellon mention what the legal matter was about?"

"No, but he did say it would be to Clarence's best interests if he located him."

"Seems a lot of folks are interested in the whereabouts of the squad members. At Sherry's funeral, Eliza Arbuckle told me that a young, fair-haired Methodist minister dropped by the house to pay his respects and then started to ask a lot of questions about his war acquaintances. He seemed especially interested in Sean Sullivan."

"What's so strange about that?"

"Nothing really . . . but he tried to find out exactly where they all were. Why would he want to know that?"

"I haven't the slightest idea," answered Agatha. "What did Eliza do?"

"She told him she didn't really know where all of us were, but she thought Sean Sullivan had moved to California and was tending bar somewhere in the gold country near Sacramento, and that some of us lived in Silverville, Colorado. All this interest in the squad and the dying makes me nervous."

"Why would a Methodist minister's questions upset you?"

"Irish Catholics ain't what Protestant ministers usually ask about. I know I'm tighter than a tick to a hound dog over this whole thing, but with that Mellon fellow asking . . . it all makes me really wonder what's goin' on. Maybe it's nothing but my imagination."

"Well, Sam . . . maybe so."

They were silent for awhile, both in deep thought.

"Sam . . . Wade used to tell me that during the war all the guys felt you could sense trouble . . . feel its presence. He actually said that you knew when the devil was near and that the men all stuck to you like dirt on a hog when the fighting started, that you seemed to keep them out of harm's way. Is that true?"

Sam smiled, "Well, we did stick pretty close . . ."

"That's not what I mean," she persisted. "Did you . . . could you tell when trouble was just around the corner?"

Agatha was deadly serious. "Wade wasn't joking when he told me."

Sam was silent . . . she waited for his response. "Yeah, sometimes I could—not always, but sometimes. I didn't care much for it; it'd make my skin crawl . . . it was pure hell feeling death was near."

"Have you felt that way anytime since the war?"

"No, I haven't, not once . . . but I feel it now, Agatha—I'm feelin' it right now."

★ ★ ★

"Sheriff Tate, I'm Sam Dodd."

"Come on in . . . we're all here except Ben Smith. He's outa town."

Sam stepped into the small, crowded sheriff's office. The witnesses to Wade's death were present . . . Mike Murphy, Zack Budrow, Ron Biron, Joe Coombs, and C. T. Meyerhoff. Each nodded acknowledgment to Sam's introduction.

The sheriff opened the conversation. "Mr. Dodd was a close friend to Wade Johnson. He thinks there might be something more to the shootin' than meets the eye. He'd like to ask ya'll a few questions."

Throughout the afternoon, all the details of the poker game were rehashed—the excessive drinking, the argument over the alleged cheating, the accidental shot while grappling for the gun, the desperate escape and the discovery of the drowned horse.

"Oh, he's gotta be dead for sure. Thet drunken cowboy run thet poor horse to death, then tried to swim the swollen river. He's more 'an likely hung up on the bottom, eaten up by the fish," offered Joe Coombs. Most present nodded in agreement.

"Any of you notice the color of the cowboy's eyes or hair?" Sam questioned.

"He kept his head down, lookin' at his cards, and never took his hat off," responded Meyerhoff.

"Yeah," added Zack, "he had his Stetson pulled down to his ears. It was a big floppy-rimmed buckeye, kind most cowboy's wear. Kept it on the whole game, hot as it was."

"Yeah, it was a dirty Stetson and it warn't cheap. We found it snagged up on a tree branch, way downriver, soppin' wet," said Don Biron.

No one remembered much about the cowboy's features except that he was of average build and needed a bath . . . not one could remember the color of his hair or eyes. It was late in the day when they all left; only Sam and the sheriff stayed.

"Appears all the evidence points to the cowboy drownin'. Don't it seem purty silly to go to all that trouble killin' somebody, drownin' a good horse, and losin' a mighty fine Stetson, bridle, and saddle too?"

"I guess you're right, Sheriff—looks like I'm crawling up the wrong hill. Best I get back to Colorado to my family . . . we've got a spring roundup just ahead, and lots of chores."

"Goin' back right away?"

"Looks like the best thing to do. Too many mixed up signals to make heads or tails of these deaths and besides, I got a family to look after."

Sam spent a fitful night at the hotel, half-dozing, half-awake, tossing and turning . . . jumbled thoughts crisscrossing, then running parallel, only to race in opposite directions. Sherry was murdered and so was the mystery lady, but it seemed that Wade was accidentally shot. Andrew Quade did drink too much and could have fallen down the mine shaft. God knows, Jethro

Briggs had a mess full of enemies, and a lot of folks wanted to shoot him down. Otto was killed by a crazy Mexican. The circumstances about Wade's death tilted the scales heavily to coincidence rather than any intentional murder plot. *Time to stop conjuring up a nonexistent conspiracy . . . go home and get to work.*

As the sun peeked over the eastern horizon, Sam slogged through the mud and ruts to the train depot. Balancing with one arm was still difficult, particularly when carrying his grip. Black clouds remained overhead and the distant rumble of thunder announced another wet day.

A young, bright-eyed clerk stood behind the dimly lit ticket counter, cheerfully whistling between his teeth. He and Sam were the only ones around.

"Where you off to, Sir?"

Sam grinned. "One-way to Laramie, please."

He took Sam's gold coin and issued the ticket while continuing to whistle an off-key rendition of "There's an Empty Cot in the Bunkhouse Tonight." His good nature lifted Sam's spirits a little. The rain had slowed to an irritating drizzle so that it was too wet and cold to wait outside.

"You live 'round Laramie?" asked the clerk.

"South aways . . . down in Colorado."

"Are you the fella that's been askin' about last year's shootin'?"

"That's right . . . how didja know?"

"Don Biron works fer us—the railroad, that is. He told me some one-armed fella, ah . . . no offense . . . was askin' 'bout the killin'. That murder shore did cause a lot of fuss around Brookville. Wade and Dandy were good folks. We're real sorry that cowboy drowned . . . we all wanted to hang 'em real bad."

He was interrupted when the door shut behind a neatly dressed drummer with his bag of samples. Then a grizzled old cowboy, toting a saddle over his shoulder, limped through the door and bought a ticket to nearby Ellsworth. The soaking-wet waddy had been carrying the saddle for quite a distance and proceeded to let everyone know about it.

"Danged horse dropped dead on me for no cause at all. My feet are all blisters. These boots ain't any good fer walkin', that's fer sure!" With a deep sigh of relief, he dropped the saddle on the floor and collapsed into one of the waiting-room benches. "Ain't no woman folks around here, I hope." Assuring himself that only men were present, the old cowboy struggled to remove his right boot. "There!" he exclaimed as the boot popped from his foot. "Lord, 'ave mercy, thet feels good." He then proceeded to struggle with the left one, grunting and groaning with every jerk. With one final yank, it too, popped off. "Glory be!" He flopped back on the bench, tattered socks elevated, wiggling his toes. It soon became obvious the boots hadn't been removed for a long, long time. The cowboy began to pick at his frayed socks and blistered feet. The salesman covered his nose with a handkerchief and headed for the fresh, damp air outside.

Relaxing, Sam smiled and lit his pipe, then suddenly got up and walked over to the ticket counter.

"Young man, were you workin' the morning after the shooting?"

"Sure was, ain't missed a day in two years . . . got a couple of kids . . . need the work."

"Do you remember any young cowboy catchin' a train outa town that morning?"

"Sure don't. I git quite a few folks buyin' tickets . . . hard to remember. But I sure don't recollect no young cowboy or any other young guy leavin' town that day."

"Thanks." Sam returned to his seat.

"Time to board!" shouted the clerk. The cowpoke struggled to put on his boots while the drummer rushed out, seeking a seat as far away from the cowboy as possible. Sam reached for his carpetbag but before he could pick it up, the clerk was beside him. "Let me give you a hand—it's pretty slippery out there." Sam didn't want the help but thought it might be rude to turn down his kind offer.

"Thanks," he mumbled as they walked silently to the train. Sam was about to board when the clerk touched his arm. "Say . . . I do remember one passenger that mornin'; he was a hard one to forget. Preacher fella—one of those circuit riders."

"Oh yeah?" Sam nonchalantly remarked, as he climbed aboard.

"Yep, I'll never forget those eyes."

Sam stiffened. "What about 'em?"

"Coldest blue . . . deadest eyes I ever seen."

Once again, Sam felt a chill convulse his body and the hair on the back of his neck bristled. As the train started to inch forward, he shouted over the noise of the steam engine, "His hair—what was the color of his hair?"

The surprised clerk was taken aback by the force of Sam's question. "Why, sorta blond—yeller-like."

Before the train picked up speed, Sam threw his bag onto the wet platform and jumped off. Catching up with the clerk, he said, "I want you to tell me all you can remember about this preacher—every last detail. I also have to send a couple of telegrams. And . . . change my ticket to Denver."

★ ★ ★

Sam sent four telegrams—one to the sheriff in Placer County, California, inquiring about Sean Sullivan; another to the U. S. Department of Indian Affairs requesting Clarence Devlin's address; the third to the Denver office of Kenneth Seymour with notification of Sam's imminent arrival; and the last—a long one—to Sheriff Nate Boswell in Laramie. In it, he asked him to see that Matthew was returned home safely and to let Mary know he had important business in Denver before heading home. He concluded, "If anything important comes up, write me care of the Denver office of Sassy Mae Mines. I'll keep checking with them."

Sam almost added, "Tell Mary I love her, ask her to pray for me, and tell her not to worry," but he knew she'd be doing that anyway, and asking her not to worry would cause her to fret all the more.

All at once, Sam felt lonely. *My, I sure miss that woman!*

CHAPTER 18

WHAT A BEAUTIFUL DAY—LIKE A SPRING morn on the Emerald Isle. As me father would say, 'Nothing cheers a Celtic heart more . . . lest it be a pint of Guinness beer.'"

The dull brown color of winter was vanishing fast and the foothills around the lower Cosumnes River were covered with bright new green growth . . . expansive fields of virgin grass, highlighted by wide patches of purple lupine, native golden poppy, and masses of yellow mustard. The barren oaks had disappeared under a new canopy of leaves. The air was cleansed by heavy spring rains and the first north wind was blowing . . . a dry wind, that spring zephyr which would again turn the hillsides from green to golden brown.

"Where's that?" asked Orville Potts, while rhythmically moving the handle on the shaker box. Orville didn't hear too well . . . last winter marked his eighty-second year.

"Where's what?"

"Thet emerald place."

"Emerald Isle? Why, that's Ireland, you ignorant English barbarian! Don't you know anything?"

"Ah ain't no Englishman; I'm American plum through! My Grandpappy Potts fought with Washington," replied Orville huffily. "I don't take kindly yer insultin' my kinfolks." He placed his hand on the wooden handle of his knife to emphasize his displeasure.

With shovel in hand, Sean Sullivan made a sweeping bow in Orville's direction. "Your noble ancestors fought the whelps of the Imperial Lion? Crossed swords with His Majesty's minions? Then I must recant—your stupidity is forgiven, my kind sir." With that, Sullivan returned to shoveling bedrock gravel into the cradle-rocker box. The affable Irishman had tired of the slow-witted, deaf old man, tired of constantly having to shout, repeat every sentence, then explain what he meant. Orville was considered by Sullivan to be a dull-minded, single-purposed old bore—but he knew how to search for gold. Sean did not . . . thus the partnership was still intact.

Orville wasn't sure if his partner had apologized or not. "Shore talks funny," he mused. "But he's a hard worker when he feels like it . . . which ain't often." He did not, could not, comprehend Sullivan . . . for good reason. Sean was a literate, fiddle-footed, self-taught, vagabond man of the world. There was little he hadn't experienced or at least tried. He had dabbled in the theater in Chicago and New York, playing the crafty and evil Iago in Shakespeare's *Othello*, and had been a member of an Irish tumbling team working the vaudeville circuit. He'd switched for the Illinois Central Railroad, was a decorated Civil War hero, even a bodyguard and bouncer. No matter what came his way, Sean cheerfully, enthusiastically took part . . . for a while. Inevitably, the itch to move on would return; then, in the middle of a successful venture, he would depart for perceived greener pastures. He left the Shakespearean company in Peoria, disappearing between acts; he parted company with the railroad midway through his night shift, causing several box cars to derail, and he quit his job as bouncer in the midst of a brawl . . . "Burn all the bridges behind and singe the ones ahead" was his motto . . . and life was never dull for the ever-wandering Celt.

The romance of the California gold fields beckoned Sullivan after reading *Roughing It*, by the newly celebrated author, Samuel Clemens. Horace Greeley's admonition to "Go West, Young Man" also caught his fancy. He was no longer a young man, having passed forty, but in Sean's mind a lad remained a lad until he indulged in the maturing process known as marriage. "Irish men don't wed as wee babes," he'd say. "We wait 'til our late thirties and then choose a sweet lass with a good dowry." Even by his own criteria, he was over-ripe . . . but the absence of a wife bothered him not one whit. Sean was a happy man . . . until work beckoned.

Orville, on the other hand, was a simple man with minimal desires. Though physically impressive, he caught no one's attention. Standing better than six feet tall and towering over Sean, he carried himself erect in spite of his advanced age; a well-trimmed snow-white beard graced his weathered face, hiding canyons of deep wrinkles. Orville was a dying breed. Most of the miners had cleared out years ago; only a few hardy souls with pan and shaker box worked the creeks to eke out a bare existence, sluicing a few ounces of flour-fine dust a month . . . if lucky.

Orville and Sean had been together for just a month, working the north fork of the Cosumnes River. They had met in the Silver Spoon Saloon, a gathering place for miners. Orville wandered in for a drink one night while Sean was tending bar . . . they were the only two in the place. Both liked to talk . . . a lot. Orville excitedly discussed the weather, the heavy rains inundating the Sierras, and the phenomenal snow pack. "Sure gonna open some new pockets and uncover new veins. Ain't seen a pour like this since '68. A few fellers got rich thet year."

His conversation peaked Sullivan's interest since gold was what had brought him to California.

What luck! Here was a seasoned old-timer, a successful prospector. Sean began to give free shots of whiskey to the old gent, while tossing down a few himself. Two hours later, they were fast friends, drunk . . . and partners in a new mining venture. Sean helped himself to his wages from the cashbox and left the saloon . . . unattended. The new partners headed up the Cedar Ravine Trail, across Bucks Bar to the Cosumnes. The placer deposits, within easy reach, had been discovered years ago, then later picked clean by the Chinese. Orville and Sean found color, panning about two dollars worth a day, for the abundant winter rain had washed down a smattering of gold dust and a few small nuggets.

"Just wait 'til the snow melts in the high Sierras! This here Cosumnes will be a rage of muddy water. In late spring it'll die down to a trickle an' by summer it'll be almost gone. Thet's when we git rich! Thet's when we can dig to bedrock."

Orville danced a little jig and threw another shovelful of gravel into the rocker. Sean thought his optimism was child-like. *How could this simpleton keep this up for thirty years? We've been at this thirty-two days and have but a few ounces for all our hard labor. . . .* He was ready to call it quits. Bartending began to look better every day, especially after weeks of Orville's incessant blathering.

Not Orville! Hope sprang eternal in the bones of Orville Potts. "Let all those other fellers dig holes in the ground like gophers an' blast away the sides of mountains with those hydraulic rigs. We'll hit a glory-hole our way!"

Hydraulic mining was the rage, but neither Orville nor Sean had the capital to begin such a venture. California mining was big business. Dredge, hydraulic, and deep-level hard-rock mining had replaced the lone miner with his long tom, pan, and shaker box. The Rough and Ready Mine in nearby Nevada County was mining below five hundred feet and going deeper every day. Orville thought tunnel mining was a disgusting way to make a living. "If God wanted man workin' underground, He'd made us look like moles rather'n the handsome upright things we is!"

"Wadja say?" shouted Sean, mimicking the aged prospector by leaning forward and cupping a hand to his ear. He had heard every word; in fact, he had heard it multiple times before. Orville knew a lot about gold mining but nothing else ever caught his attention. It was all he could or would talk about, and he talked about it incessantly. After the first two weeks in the hills with Orville, Sean was ready to stuff gravel down his throat to shut him up. He passed the time by teasing the simple-minded old miner.

"Orville, I got a brilliant idea. Recognizing me Irish connections, let's find a wee Leprechaun on this beautiful Irish day, discover where he hid his pot o' gold, sneak-up behind him, bash him with our gold pans, and steal his poke away."

Orville was not amused. He told Sullivan he didn't know who this Lee Lepperkon fellow was, but he wasn't up to jumping any man's claim or stealing his gold . . . it just wasn't right! "Ain't stealin' no man's dust!" he grumbled.

Sean looked at Orville, dumbfounded. "Why, everybody's heard of . . . ," then gaping open-mouthed at the old man, he realized, *No . . . not everyone had heard of Leprechauns after all.*

Old Potts had been a fixture in the gold country for thirty years. Unlike many miners, he was an honest man—but unlike the others, he never gave up working the Sierras.

He arrived in San Francisco by boat in 1850, bought his stake in Sacramento, journeyed up the American River, and cut south after reaching the foothills to Hangman's Creek. There he panned his first gravel, saw his first color, and it was love at first sight; the "Mother of Lodes" became his only sweetheart. He staked a claim on the creek near Weaver's Dry Diggins, known later as Hangtown. Orville took part in the lynching that gave the town its name. From Mill Creek to the north, to Sampson Flat on the south, folks knew prospector Potts.

Orville glanced over at Sean . . . he, too, was displeased with his partner. *Maybe I've hooked up with a rope-stretcher, someone lookin' to be hanged.* He'd teamed up with a number of men over the years but none worked out to his satisfaction. He swore he would never do it again, but here he was hitched up with another—so far, the laziest of the lot. *This one's a bit tetched as well, usin' words I ain't never heard, always blabberin' on 'bout his war experiences, and readin' books midday stead of shovelin'. Workin' a long tom sluice ain't no fun when yer pard ain't carryin' his load.*

Orville spent a sleepless night after hearing of Sean's plan to rob a fellow miner. What little gold he had accumulated was tucked under his bedroll; he slept pistol in hand. He was definitely coming to the conclusion that his partner was daft, the way he prattled on about the scenery, jabbered constantly about stage acting, and slept late into the morning; it just didn't add up. Now, this latest talk about robbing some fellow's poke . . . *not* the way a partner of Orville Potts should behave!

The following morning, Potts was relatively quiet while they worked a new spot upstream.

"Orville, have a look at this." Sean leaned over and picked up the glittering object from the top of the shaker box, holding it between his thumb and forefinger. He held it close to his eye, then handed it to the old miner. "No mistaking what this is."

"Find a nugget?"

"Take a look."

Orville excitedly reached for the nugget, his hand shaking so badly that Sean momentarily pulled back.

"Don't drop it!"

"Give it to me!" Orville's eyes grew bigger than the gold pan. "That's about the biggest nugget I ever found."

"*We've* found."

"Awright, *we've* found."

The excited old miner hefted the nugget in his hand, juggling it up and down. "This here's about five ounces!" A big toothless smile lit up his face. "Maybe there's more where this come from."

They had been working a narrow crevice in the large granite boulders bordering the river. The crevice was filled with gravel from the recent flooding.

"Move aside, let me at it." The experienced old miner dropped to his knees, took out his knife, and began to scrape as deeply as he could reach into the fissure; handful by handful, they cleaned the bedrock.

They sat side by side after the last grain of sand was worked through the shaker box, breathing heavily, beads of sweat running down their faces. Twenty ounces of gold had made it an exceptional day.

"Old man, what say we go to town and order up a batch of oysters and get drunk!"

"Can't see what fellers see in those slimy things, but the second idee is a good one."

For the moment differences were forgotten. Both knew there was more dust to be found along this stretch of river, and on the morrow they would find it. But tonight they would hang one on in Hangtown.

★ ★ ★

Sean went directly to Lacy's Bar and Grill to indulge his epicurean palate with oysters, potatoes, fresh green vegetables, and a bottle of Chardonnay. He was well aware of the excellent wines being produced in the vicinity; Boeger's Winery boasted an excellent Claret, while in nearby Plymouth, a distinctive Port wine was bottled.

Orville chose the Gold Pan Saloon and Eatery where he wolfed down a well-cooked steak, eggs, fried taters, and a mug of beer with a whiskey chaser. He decided to do his drinking at the Silver Spoon Saloon . . . knowing he wouldn't run into Sullivan there, since he'd left the owner in the lurch. Orville drank heavily and as his inebriation increased, so did the vitriolic verbiage he used toward his new partner. He hooked up with two old sourdough friends and some freeloaders to share a bottle. They listened attentively to their boozing benefactor, all nodding in agreement at appropriate pauses in Orville's running monologue.

"Know what he tried to do?" Then answering his own question, "Thet Mick tried to talk me into robbin' some feller's stash. Know what? I think I'm hooked up with a crook!"

"You really think so?" asked one old sourdough.

"Yep, I ain't totally sure, but one thing I know is true . . . he's teched, softer'n a marsh bog in the haid."

"No foolin'?" slobbered one of the hangers-on while pouring himself another drink.

"Yep, makes up the dangdest yarns, sez he wuz a war hero, he and some feller named Dodd went back of the Reb lines and blew up somethin' important. He sez he got a medal from Useless Grant hisself."

"Probably blew up some outhouse," chortled one listener, "Those nigger-lovin' bluebellies gave out medals fer everthing."

Southern sympathies were deep in California. Orville would have joined the Rebs, but he was over forty when the war began and he didn't want to leave the claim he was working. He took the South's loss hard. The fact that Sean was a Union soldier and bragged about it was one more reason to dislike him. As the evening wore on and the whiskey flowed, his aversion turned to fear.

One of his drinking companions suggested, "Think he might try to kill you and steal yer gold?"

Orville was shaken by the question. His eyebrows furrowed as the idea worked its treacherous way through his whiskey-soaked brain. The question was asked again.

"Well . . . do you think he might?"

"Wha . . . he just might."

"Might do what? This bluebelly might do what? . . . you drunken old sot." Standing behind the circle of listeners was a red-faced, livid Sean Sullivan. He had come to the saloon to reimburse the owner for what he had taken from the cashbox on his sudden departure. His newfound wealth, plus slightly inebriated condition, had inspired him to make amends. He would have to be deaf not to hear the vitriol pouring forth from the corner table.

Orville staggered to his feet, bolstered by the presence of his old and new acquaintances. With a hand on the knife in his belt, he profoundly sputtered, "Ah don't like you, you coon-lovin' Mick!"

Sean took a step forward, then thought better of it. He was a little drunk but not enough to take on a whole gang, and certainly not enough to jeopardize the partnership that had only recently turned promising. Arguing with the dumb old coot would be foolish. Sean turned on his heel and headed for the door. "I'll see you back at the diggins, ol' man!"

Some days later a miner was attracted by the circling of turkey buzzards and went to investigate. The *Placerville Mountain Democrat* reported the following:

> "Two miners, Orville Potts and Sean Sullivan, were found dead from multiple gunshot wounds. The bodies were discovered alongside their shaker box, guns in hand. Recently they were seen arguing at the Silver Spoon Saloon. The local authorities have concluded, from the evidence on hand, that they undoubtedly continued their heated altercation, leading to their demise. Fifteen ounces of gold was discovered in the camp, eliminating the probability of robbery."

As the train's wheels clicked over the tracks, Jacob Quinn relaxed and reviewed the past several days. "Too bad all of my business can't be close to home . . . and so ridiculously easy." No sooner had he arrived in Placerville, checked into the hotel, and made a few discreet inquiries than he found the whereabouts of Sean Sullivan. It was also a simple matter to identify where he and his new partner, Orville Potts, could be found on their weekly trip to Hangtown.

Fortune was definitely with him. He'd been in town only two nights before Orville walked into the Silver Spoon Saloon and began buying drinks for everyone. He had no trouble blending in as one of the onlookers, one of the crowd engrossed in Orville's diatribe against his partner . . . it was abundantly clear that Orville hated Sean. At the appropriate moment, Quinn raised the question, "Think he might try to kill you and steal yer gold?"

Jacob Quinn smiled, remembering how Orville bit on that verbal morsel. It was easy from that point on to play upon his anger and doubt. Once the aura of their mutual hatred had been publicly raised, the motive for Sean's death was established. Sullivan's unexpected arrival at the saloon and the ensuing argument was frosting on the cake, more than he ever hoped. After Orville and Sean left the saloon, Quinn mentioned to the remaining patrons, "Wouldn't be surprised if those two kill each other!" All nodded in agreement.

He had no difficulty following them to their diggings the next day, stripping them of their guns and then killing them both. Sean was first to be killed with Orville's gun, then Orville with Sean's.

Jacob Quinn enjoyed the short, beautiful ride by coach from Placerville to Shingle Springs. There, he caught the train through Sacramento to San Francisco.

"Sacramento—what a foolish choice for the capitol city, between the confluence of two rivers that frequently flood. Mosquito capital of California!"

Quinn was relieved at the sight of San Francisco Bay. "I believe I'll take a few days to relax before I'm off to Texas, where I'll have to contend with the heat. This job put me ahead of schedule—just one more to go."

Journeying by ferryboat across the bay and riding the trolley car from the docks to Nob Hill was always a pleasurable experience. Jacob loved the beauty of it all and found San Francisco sufficiently cosmopolitan for a western city and for a man of his taste.

"Good afternoon, Mr. Quinn," smiled the uniformed doorman as he opened the ornate entry of the Hampton Arms Apartments. "Ah, Mr. Quinn, how good to see you," beamed the desk clerk. "I'll get the keys to your suite."

"Good afternoon, Harvey—any messages?"

"Just one, Sir." Smiling deferentially, the clerk handed the telegram and the keys to his prize tenant. Tearing open the envelope, he read:

To Jacob Quinn
c\o Hampton Arms Apartments
421 Market Street
San Francisco, California

Dear Jacob:
Must see you soon. Urgent. Dodd in Denver.

Aussie

Puzzled, Quinn looked up from the telegram. His thoughts were running wild. *Dodd in Denver—how could that be? The shot was true; I saw him tumble over backward, hit hard. He should be dead!* Although his face showed little, his hands were white-knuckled as he tore the telegram into pieces.

"I hope it wasn't bad news, Mr. Quinn," said the elderly clerk.

Quinn looked down at the shredded paper in his hand. "No, not bad news, just some unfinished business that requires immediate attention. I had hoped to spend a few days at home—but alas, no rest for the wicked."

Harvey laughed, "There's not a wicked bone in your body, Mr. Quinn."

"Why, thank you, Harvey, you're very kind . . . but you must remember, there is a little evil in all of us."

Jacob's gentle voice had reassured the Hampton Arms clerk, convincing him the telegram was not that important, just as he said . . . business. Harvey gave every indication that he respected and admired Mr. Quinn, who epitomized the urbane, sophisticated, and educated San Franciscan; well-to-do, gentile, a charitable patron of the Arts. He was one of the city's most eligible bachelors; handsome, athletic, and well-bred.

"It's a shame you have to travel so much," sympathized the desk clerk. "So much moving about could just about kill a man."

Jacob Arthur Quinn, Jr. grinned. "How right you are, Harvey; it's killed more than one."

CHAPTER 19

KENNETH SEYMOUR was obviously unnerved. The blood drained from his face when his secretary announced Sam Dodd was waiting to see him. His hands trembled as he raised the silk handkerchief to his sweating brow. "Give me a minute, then show him in."

Seymour moved to the window of his second-story office and looked down on Fifteenth Street where a horse-drawn trolley was passing by. Denver was becoming a big city . . . gaslit streets, opera house, large brick office buildings, luxury hotels, a center of commerce, and now . . . trolley cars. He grabbed the drapes with his right hand to steady himself. The man waiting to see him could jeopardize all that he had worked for, his dreams of wealth . . . his reputation, his very life. He continued to gaze out the window as Sam entered, and he waited until Dodd spoke before turning to face him.

"Good morning, Kenneth, glad you had time to see me."

"Why . . . Oh . . . Good heavens, Sam! Wha . . . what happened to your arm?"

"Got in the way of a .50-caliber bullet."

Seymour unsteadily returned to the leather chair behind his desk and collapsed.

"Well, I'll be . . . Sarge, sit down and tell me what happened!"

Sam took off his coat, sat down, and proceeded to tell him of the ambush, his trip to Laramie, and the deaths of their old comrades. Seymour was visibly shaken.

"I can't believe it! They can't *all* be dead!" Seymour shook his head as if to enforce his disbelief.

"I wish it weren't true, but it is. Wade, Sherry, and Otto died within the last year. You already know about Andrew and Jethro."

"Sam, what about the rest of the squad?"

"I don't know about the others. I've been tryin' to find their whereabouts . . . they could be dead for all I know. I sure intend to find out."

Kenneth listened intently, especially when he told him of the Arbuckle tragedy. The information clearly upset him; he became very animated, waving his arms and raising his voice.

"You're sure Sherry was murdered? It wasn't suicide?"

"Come on, Kenneth, you knew Sherry. Do you believe he could kill that girl, then tie a bait bucket around his neck, fill it full o' rocks, hit himself on the head, and drown?" Sam detailed the circumstances of the death and of the suspicion surrounding the mysterious fisherman.

Kenneth leaned back in his chair, taking in every word. "Sam, Andy Quade's death was an accident and Jethro was killed by a vengeful son, and wasn't Wade killed accidentally during a poker game? All of them, other than Sherry, are explainable. Besides, who knows what enemies Sherry might have had? He was single and not bad looking; he could have been killed by some jealous husband."

"It's possible, but the odds are against it—too many deaths close together."

"Those things happen, Sam. As you can see, I'm still alive. So is Charlie. He's as close to death as a man can be and we all know consumption will get him. We saw it coming on for years. Less than a month ago I heard from Sean Sullivan. He's alive and kicking, said he needed a grubstake, and wired Charlie for a loan. Charlie wasn't around so I sent him a hundred bucks from my own pocket."

"Glad to hear Sean's all right. Where is he?"

"Some little gold camp called Hangtown in California, somewhere east of Sacramento."

"Know where Porter or Clarence might be?"

"No, Sam, I don't . . . but if I find out, I'll let you know. I'd appreciate it if you did the same."

Sam leaned back in the couch. "Slick . . . you amaze me. Why this sudden concern over your old colleagues? When the war ended, you never spent one minute thinkin' about any of us. You sendin' money to Sean is a real surprise, not like you at all. Why the interest now?"

Kenneth seemed hurt by Sam's remark. "Men change as they get older, Sam. I've reflected upon my past and I've mellowed a bit. The loss of these men touches me deeply. Maybe some of my early Christian training is coming through . . . whatever the reason, I really do care about these people."

"Glad to hear it, Kenneth," Sam smiled. "Changing spots on the Silverville Leopard?"

"You could put it that way, but let's not talk about me; tell me more about Sherry's death. Isn't his demise the only one that's in question . . . where they don't know who the killer might be?" Seymour's composure had completely returned . . . the competent barrister offering a contrary view, dissecting the evidence.

"Sam, could your wound have muddled your thinking? There are other far more plausible reasons for all this . . . even your own shooting could be attributable to other factors. Didn't you say you had a run-in with some Indians? As we both know, you were a pretty tough deputy in Silverville. Anyone you can think of who might have vengeance in mind? Didn't you kill two of the . . . er . . . what were their names?"

"The Cravens."

"That's it. Didn't their kin threaten to kill you?"

"Yep . . . thet's true."

"See? There are many other credible reasons to consider. The deciding factor is motive. What possible motive could there be? What could anyone gain?"

Kenneth let his words sink in. He could see they were having some impact. He slowly rose from his chair and walked around to the front edge of the desk, where he sat looking down at Sam seated cross-legged, buried in the soft leather couch. It was deep cushioned, forcing any occupants to look up when addressing him. Seymour purposely arranged it this way. He was sure it gave him an advantage.

"If there is any remote chance you could be right, we should all be careful. But I can tell you, I'm not going to lose any sleep over it. I don't think you should either."

Kenneth stood up and sauntered to the window and looked down on the street below.

"Denver's changing, Sam—so is the West. It's becoming much more civilized. We even have some marvelous restaurants in town." Seymour turned and grinned, "I have a splendid idea! It's close to lunch and I'm famished. I'll buy you a plate of oysters, maybe a rare steak . . . a bottle of French wine and good conversation. We can talk about old times."

Sam sat silently, deep in thought, then with some difficulty, he managed to extricate himself from the couch. "Seems like a good idea. I'm hungry myself."

Sam reached for his coat as Kenneth stepped forward to help him put it on. The formidable Sam Dodd didn't look as impressive with just one arm. Sam moved away and struggled into his heavy coat unaided.

"Thanks anyway, Kenneth, I can help myself."

"No offense," Kenneth flippantly responded.

As they walked along Fifteenth Street, Sam casually asked, "Kenneth, did you ever hear of a Denver lawyer by the name of P. T. Mellon?"

"P. T? Know him well—he specializes in mining law. I've been up against him in court a few times. He's done some work for the Sassy Mae Mines when I've been too busy. Why do you ask?"

"He wrote to Aggie Johnson asking about Devlin."

"Probably did it for Charlie. The old man likes to keep in touch with the old troops . . . now, where shall we eat?"

"Oh, I'll leave that up to you. I'm sure you know every good place in Colorado."

"In the entire West, Sam, from Chicago to San Francisco." The lunch was enjoyable. The two spent the meal rehashing old experiences, reliving memories of battles past, and commenting on friends departed.

"What are your plans now, Sam . . . going home?"

"Yep, haven't seen Mary and the kids in months. I especially want to see Matthew. I'd like to leave on the first train headed toward home."

"That's good, Sam. Go home . . . relax, forget about the killings, spend time with the family."

Sam had no intention of being specific. The silken, probing words flowing from his companion made his skin crawl. He suddenly felt as though Satan had joined them for lunch. The familiar sense of danger was back. He knew without question that sitting across the table was an evil man, lying, deceitful, and unscrupulous. Kenneth made a determined effort to convince him the killings were unrelated, that all were mere victims of circumstance. Sam knew better . . . there was a morbid thread that held it all together, a thread that encircled this man. Seymour had lied about P. T. Mellon. But why? What did he have to gain by telling him he knew Mellon, a man who didn't exist? Sam's acquaintances in Denver law enforcement had no knowledge of a lawyer by that name practicing in the Denver area. He checked the court documents, inquired of friends at the capitol, but no one had ever heard of him, nor was there any record of his practicing before the Colorado courts. The return address he had given Agatha Johnson was a post office box, now rented under a different name. Only Seymour knew of the mysterious Mellon. Why had Kenneth lied?

Sam sensed it wasn't wise to talk about anything of importance or respond to any more of Seymour's probing questions. He was anxious to go, so he intentionally kept the conversation on ranching, children, and Mary—all subjects proven to be of no interest to the self-centered counselor. It wasn't long before Seymour began yawning and found reason to leave.

"I'm terribly busy, Sam. I'm afraid I must be off. I'm already late for an appointment."

"That's fine, I got a train to ketch home."

They bid each other good tidings, expressing hope they would meet again. Seymour looked at his watch and dashed from the restaurant, leaving Sam still seated at the table.

"The bill, Sir?" The waiter was at Dodd's elbow, lunch tab in hand.

"Oh, put it on Mr. Seymour's account—I'm his guest."

"Mr. Seymour no longer has an account with us, Sir," he sarcastically intoned. Clearly, Seymour's credit was no good, so Sam, shaking his head, reached for his wallet.

"Waiter, do you think a leopard can change his spots?"

"No, Sir, I do not—not without the help of God."

"Me neither, not one durned spot."

★ ★ ★

Seymour went directly to the telegraph office and wired Aussie Walker in Silverville, insisting they meet right away, while Sam mailed a letter to Mary, care of the Rustic Post Office, telling her he would be home as soon as possible. He knew it could be a few weeks, even a month before someone might be able to deliver the letter to the ranch. He might even arrive home before the letter. He intentionally excluded information about Sherry's murder, writing only of good news about relatives and how much he missed her and the children. No need to unduly worry her, when there would be plenty of time to tell her later when he was by her side. He boarded the next train . . . to Silverville.

Chapter 20

WITH A CRYSTAL WINE GLASS IN HAND, Kenneth Seymour nervously paced back and forth in the library of the Hotel De Paris. Shifting the goblet of Chardonnay to his left hand, he removed the gold watch from his vest pocket, snapped it open, and again looked at the hour . . . two minutes later than the last time. Mumbling curses under his breath, he continued to shuffle impatiently around the room, sipping his wine. "Where is that fatuous Australian? He's hours late!"

Much to his displeasure, Aussie Walker had insisted they confer in Georgetown rather than Denver, requiring no travel on Aussie's part since he was establishing a new gambling saloon here. Seymour painfully recalled their last meeting in Silverville and was determined not to discuss matters in Aussie's surroundings again. Spitefully, Seymour insisted they meet at Louis Depuy's extravagant Hotel De Paris, one of Aussie's Georgetown competitors. Monsieur Depuy was a man of refined taste, much of which he owed to his substantial inherited wealth. By comparison, Aussie Walker was a lowlife.

In the most primitive of Colorado mining camps, Louis Depuy had squandered his fortune building the grandest hotel. It boasted a library filled with classic literature and rooms that displayed the most costly furnishings—deep red, velvet-covered divans, gilded tables, crystal chandeliers that sparkled overhead. Landscapes from the French romantic period adorned damask-covered walls . . . and to lawyer Seymour's delight, a wine cellar was stocked with the finest from France. Normally, he would have been in his glory tasting his way to intoxication, but the circumstances requiring the meeting overshadowed his refined taste. He checked his watch again . . . "Moron!"

"Monsieur Seymour, would you like another glass of Chardonnay?" The waiter stood quietly awaiting a response.

"Oh . . . yes . . . no . . . this time I'll try a red. Do you have a good Cabernet or Pinot Noir?

"Ah, Monsieur, may I suggest a Bordeaux, a Lafite Rothschild Cabernet '68 or the heady Cabernet Sauvignon from Graves."

"Delightful!" Contemplating the bouquet of an excellent imported wine, Seymour momentarily forgot his anger. The thought of a dry Rothschild Cabernet set his mouth to watering.

"I'll have the '68 Cabernet. When you return, bring me the dinner menu and your wine list." Then quietly, he muttered, "I might as well make good use of my time waiting for that Australian clod." Once more he pulled the watch from his vest pocket and noted the time.

"Are you dining alone, Monsieur?"

"No, unfortunately I'm not." Seymour's irritation was evident.

"Would your guest care for wine also?"

"Good Lord, no! Any rotgut will do for that peasant. Put some of that Mexican Taos Lightning in a wine bottle, mix in some tobacco juice for color, and he wouldn't know the difference. It would be a crime serving him any alcohol more than ten days old."

The waiter let out a roar before assuring, "Not a drop o' rotgut in this place." Then remembering his place, "Oui, oui, Monsieur." Composure regained, he quickly nodded assent and retired from the room.

Seymour was amused. The waiter's knowledge of vintage wines was surprisingly good for a miner-turned-waiter. French wines, paintings, and antiques could be imported to the Wild West but not good French waiters. Apparently, the management was trying to remold local peasants into men of taste . . . *silk purses from sow's ears.* . . . Thinking of the expression brought Seymour's attention back to Aussie Walker. *I wonder what one could make out of a sow's behind?*

Sam Dodd had shocked Kenneth with the news about Sherry Arbuckle, Wade Johnson, and Otto Schmitz. Although he suspected Aussie might plot a few fatal accidents, this wholesale slaughter could arouse suspicion and jeopardize everything. The killings had alerted Dodd to do some investigation but fortunately, Sam's qualms had been pretty well satisfied during their recent conversation. *His return to the ranch for the spring roundup should keep him busy; we should be safe for a while.* He frowned and added aloud, "Unless that stupid Australian peasant has done something *else* I don't know about."

"What Australian peasant are you talkin' about, Counselor?"

Blocking the doorway to the library, with head slightly bent to clear the arch, stood Aussie Walker. "Well, Shyster, what Australian peasant did ya have in mind?"

"None other than you, dear Aussie!" sneered the lawyer.

The huge man took a menacing step, glowering at the little man standing defiantly before him. Seymour was no coward . . . his smoldering anger, fortified by two bottles of wine, had diminished his customary caution. "In fact, I should amend my comments. *Stupid* Australian peasant is much more fitting."

Without trepidation, Seymour moved forward. "Your ignorant greed may cost us a fortune. I *told* you not to do anything that might muck up this deal! Now we have Sam Dodd snooping around . . . and he's no fool."

"I thought he was dead," angrily stated the huge Australian. When you wired that the bloody cowman was coming to Denver, it was a shock to me too."

"Aussie, the last time we were together, you told me you had no part in Andrew Quade falling down that mine shaft.

Now, I don't believe you. You said it was an accident . . . Ha! Was Wade Johnson's death also an accident? How about Sherry Arbuckle or the shooting of Dodd? Were they accidents as well? Walker . . .! What kind of a fool do you think I am? You lied to me. To make matters worse . . . Sam Dodd smells a rat!"

Seymour shook his fist in Aussie's face, his voice growing louder and louder. "What else have you done that I know nothing about, you stu—"

With incredible swiftness, Aussie seized Seymour's outstretched fist with his huge right hand . . . and squeezed. The crunch of cartilage and bone was deadened by Seymour's excruciating scream.

Louis Depuy and several of his employees rushed into the room to see Seymour, sitting on the red velvet sofa, right hand clutched to his chest, twisting in pain.

"What happened?" inquired the worried proprietor.

"He fell and hurt his hand . . . too much to drink. He'll be all right in a bit, won'tcha mate?

"I think it's broken," Seymour glowered at Walker. "I'll need a doctor. Is there one in town?"

"We have two. I'll send someone to fetch one of them right away," offered the concerned Depuy.

"Best we go up to his room 'til the doc arrives," suggested Aussie. "Besides, we have more ta talk about, right mate?"

Seymour nodded in agreement; there was much more to talk about.

In the spacious suite, Seymour sat propped up on the bed with a cold, wet towel wrapped around his injured hand and a goblet of wine in the other. When they were alone, Seymour inspected the swollen hand and winced. "You didn't have to do that," he groaned.

"I felt like doing much worse. I've killed men for a lot less than what you said. Counselor, I don't care if ya hate me guts; I got no love for ya either, but fer now, we need each other."

Aussie sat down on one of the antique chairs—which creaked under his massive weight. He leaned back, placing both hands behind his neck. "All right, if you want to know it all, I'll tell you. I've hired the most efficient shooter in the business, and the most expensive—it's costin' me a bloody fortune."

"You've hired him to do what?"

"Improve the odds. The fewer of yer old mates left alive, the richer we'll be."

"I totally disapprove; it's too risky. If anyone finds out what you've done we will lose everything! It has to stop!" He paused, shaking his head nervously, "You're taking too many chances."

"Don' worry, mate. . . . Don' git yer bowels in an uproar. There's little ta worry about. The shooter is under strict instructions ta make sure each killin' looks accidental or caused by someone other than himself. Everything has gone like clockwork, with only one small hitch . . . Sam Dodd."

"That's no small hitch. Dodd's sharp. As I told you, he smells a rat and he's snooping around. He's traveled to Illinois and uncovered the killing of Arbuckle. By the way, that was a mistake."

"What do you mean, mistake?"

"Figure it out. Arbuckle disappeared with everyone thinking he was guilty of murder . . . right?"

"That's right."

"Disappeared isn't dead. They might have never found his body if Dodd hadn't been poking around. Isn't that a fact? Isn't that a mistake on the part of your hired killer?"

Aussie's brows curled, his lips pressed together, taking quite a while to answer. "That's my fault, not the shooter's."

"Why do you say that?"

"I never told him the reason for the killin's and he never asked. I said get rid of 'em and make it look accidental. He's done it in every case, includin' Arbuckle. He wasn't told the body had ta be found."

Aussie got up and started to pace about the room. "You say Dodd went to Illinois?"

"Yes. He also stopped in Kansas and talked to the sheriff there about Wade Johnson's death."

"Did he say he found anything?"

"He asked about that phony lawyer, P. T. Mellon, the one you invented to get the information on the whereabouts of Clarence Devlin. Good thing you told me about it. I told Dodd I knew him. I think it took care of his curiosity; he seemed satisfied."

"Where's the nosey Bible-thumper now?"

"He's headed back to his ranch for the cattle roundup. He hasn't seen his family in ages and knowing Sam Dodd, that's where he will be for the next three months or so. He'll be a constant thorn in our side; we haven't seen the last of him. His suspicions might be further 'roused when Charlie dies and he discovers how few of us are left. The throbbing pain in Seymour's hand and the thought of Sam Dodd snooping around fired him up again. "Curse you, Aussie, you've got us in an insufferable mess!"

"Don' ye get high and mighty with me, you bloody shyster. You've known all along it was to our advantage to kill off a few of yer old war mates. You jus' didn't want to know any of the stinkin' details. It's cost me a bloody fortune to find all of 'em, not to mention the expense of making the killin's look like accidents."

Seymour's head snapped up. "How many did you find?"

"All of 'em."

"Seymour jumped from the bed, ignoring the pain, and raised his voice. "What! . . . you . . . you sent someone out to kill ALL of them? You must crazy! You must be mad!"

"Don't get excited, mate—I didn't know which ones would be easy to dispose of. I gave my shooter a list of all of them and left it to his discretion."

Seymour was incredulous. "You left it to his discretion?" Seething rage was burning inside him, bringing bubbles of saliva to the corners of his mouth. His face was crimson with hate; never had he loathed anyone more than this man. Kenneth saw a fortune slipping from his grasp. With great difficulty . . . voice trembling . . . he asked, "How many others have you killed that I don't know about?"

"None, mate, none. Soon as I heard Dodd was alive, I called off my hired gun and told him to wait, 'til we got a better idea of what needs to be done."

"Are you telling me the truth?"

"On me mother's head, I swear—I've called him off." Aussie lied. He was aware of Sean Sullivan's murder, but informing Seymour now would rankle him all the more. And Quinn was about to leave for Texas, where there was a lead to the whereabouts of Porter Dixon. Aussie was paying Quinn a set price for each murder. Scattered from Illinois to New Mexico to California, the chances of anyone suspecting all the deaths were related was slim to none. The only problem was Sam Dodd.

"Counselor, I gotta be honest with—" He was interrupted by a knock at the door.

"Must be the doctor . . . about time." The cold compress had done little to inhibit the swelling. Seymour's hand had ballooned into a grotesque shape.

The physician lifted Seymour's hand and felt for broken bones. After a short examination he said, "You better come to my office—we're going to have to set and bind that hand to keep it immobile 'til it heals."

"Is it bad?" asked Seymour.

"It's never good when bones are broken, especially the small bones of the hand. It will heal, but it could be a bit deformed if the knuckles are damaged. How did it happen?"

"He fell!" offered Aussie with a smirk.

"Yeah, I fell!" echoed Seymour.

"Better come along with me; the sooner we splint that hand, the better."

"He'll be along in a minute, Doc. Wait for him in the lobby."

To Aussie, the doctor said, "He better come right now."

Aussie Walker grabbed the doctor by the arm and shoved him toward the door. The doctor was a big man, but no match for Aussie's superior strength.

"Let go of me," he indignantly barked.

"Do as he says, Doctor," suggested Seymour, "or you'll have more than *my* bones to fix. I'll be right with you. Wait for me in the lobby." In a huff, the physician departed.

"All right, Aussie, what more do you want?"

"Dodd. We have to get rid of that bloody snoop."

"That won't be easy. I told you he would be the hardest to get rid of. The man lives a charmed life; he senses danger. Your killer won't be able to sniper him from a distance again; he'll be on his guard."

"Yeah? I'll pit the Deacon up against any man! I'll pit him up against ten men! What kinda trouble can he get from a cripple?"

"I'm telling you, Aussie, Sam Dodd would be hard to kill if he had *no* arms. The man is a fighter, the best soldier I ever saw, so don't take him lightly."

Walker rubbed his jaw for a moment, then begrudgingly grunted, "You could be right. No sense takin' chances. I'll put extra men on it. But you do agree, he must be killed . . . and soon."

Seymour was quiet as he thought about the fresh faces of Sam's young boys when last they met on that cold fall morning in Denver. He reached for the bottle of wine from the ice bucket and poured out the last drop, downing it quickly.

"Yes . . . he has to die. There'll be no rest for us until Sam Dodd is six feet under."

Aussie walked across the room to where Seymour was still sitting on the bed. "Lemme see your hand."

Seymour jerked it back close to his chest and suspiciously asked, "Why do you want to see it? Haven't you maimed me enough already?"

Aussie's massive paw shot forward and grasped the broken hand. He loosened his grip, then ever so slightly gave it a small squeeze. Seymour turned white with pain.

"Don't question what I do, you bloody little piece of legal horse dung, and don't you panic and muck it up either. Do you understand me, mate?" He squeezed it again, a little bit harder.

Seymour sat motionless, fearing to move. He nodded, cold sweat dripping from his brow.

Chapter 21

"Mate, this is a weird place to meet! It gives me the shivers!" Aussie shifted his huge bulk uneasily in the church pew, squirming uncomfortably on the hard oak. "It's not right meeting here, especially talkin' about . . . well, what we have to talk about."

Jacob Quinn laughed. "There couldn't be a better place, Aussie. Rarely does anyone frequent church on a Saturday afternoon. We can observe anyone who might get within hearing distance and besides, no one would suspect we're anything but devout brethren looking for salvation through prayer."

"What about *'im?*" Aussie nervously pointed to the painting of Jesus on the wall.

Quinn said, "I'm surprised at you, Aussie—I didn't think you had a pious bone in that murderous body of yours."

"I don't believe in pushin' me luck!"

"You push your luck when you are superstitious. Belief in gods and goblins imposes unnecessary and dangerous impediments on the mind, boggles the thought process, clouds clear thinking, and impedes rational decision."

Aussie's brow knitted, then one eyebrow raised. He was clearly confused by Quinn's conversation. "Wha . . . what do ya mean by that?"

Jacob Quinn smiled a most charming smile. "It's quite simple; allow standards other than your own to dictate your actions and you become captive of another man's imagination. Most people are unconscious slaves to some forgotten sage or discredited philosophy. Don't you know all gods are man-made? Take that man, for example." Quinn nodded at the image of the crucified Christ. "He followed the prophets of Jewish Old Testament law, then made the mistake of adding a few new wrinkles of His own. You know, His silly doctrine of turning the other cheek and loving those who despise you. What did it get Him and His followers for loving their enemies? Death . . . that's what! Agonizing, slow, painful death! His reward was getting nailed to a piece of timber, between two thieves. Those who continued to follow His doctrines became lion bait . . . bloody entertainment for the Romans. Reasonable men rejected such poppycock, but for centuries, slaves to His logic have erected temples to His memory. Today, within this religious edifice where killing is a sin, we plot murder." Quinn threw back his head and laughed again. "Come now, Aussie, don't you see the humor of it all?"

Aussie unconsciously recoiled somewhat from the blasphemous dissertation. "You don't believe in anything, do you?"

"Yes, I do," Quinn curtly responded. "I believe in *myself*—in my own ability to reason. I left superstition behind in college. I've learned we're in a changing world where nothing remains the same . . . and that includes moral imperatives. One must change or get left behind. The nineteenth century has spawned some great minds—men willing to challenge the myths of the past. Emerson, Hegel, Feuerbach to name just a few."

"Never heard of 'em."

Quinn smiled, contemptuously, "I'd be amazed if you had. You will never realize real freedom until you divorce yourself from religious constraints. Today's morality is tomorrow's sin . . . and the day after? Who knows and who really cares? All of our days are numbered by a biological clock and it is my desire to enjoy them to the fullest, unencumbered by any standards other than my own."

"Mate, you're the devil's own."

Quinn laughed again. "If Lucifer exists, he owns your plebeian soul as well. Besides Aussie, to appreciate this world, one must see it through the eye of the devil . . . don't you agree?"

"I've killed some, but I don' enjoy it like ye do."

Quinn examined his hands, then looked at Aussie. "To be honest, I *do* enjoy it most of the time. Kill a coward, good riddance; shoot a brave man . . . it's a challenge. Aussie, don't you know we're all predators? Man is nothing but the highest form of beast. What thrill is there in taking down a lower animal, one that has little chance of killing you in return?" Quinn smiled. "No sport in that. Man is the finest game."

"And women? I know you've killed one or two," sneered Walker.

"They're slightly different, I must admit. Reproductively useful and certainly pleasurable, but . . . troublesome. One wise old wag said that if you couldn't mess with 'em, there'd be a bounty on them."

Aussie smiled. "On that we agree." He stared at the smug face of Jacob Quinn, then grumbled, "Enough of this high-tone talk; let's get down to business." Quinn's metaphysical discussions and sly intonations made Aussie Walker ill at ease; intellectual dissertations were slippery bogs Aussie avoided at all costs.

Quinn gloried in making the Australian squirm. He basked in his own brilliance, enjoying the mental manipulation, knowing full well his command of language placed less knowledgeable souls at a disadvantage. He relished having the edge, making others feel inadequate.

Aussie was visibly resentful of Quinn's verbal prowess. During past meetings he had been the brunt of subtle barbs, understanding just enough to be offended. Once again, he grumbled, "Let's git on with it!" Then, with derision, "Think you can finish off Sam Dodd?"

Aussie touched a raw nerve. "I was sure I inflicted a mortal blow," said the preacher, now irritated. "That .50-caliber bullet hit exactly where I aimed. He must have moved at the last moment or the maggots would have feasted on his bones by now."

"Still, you only winged him and he made it out to Laramie where his right arm was cut off. He's a cripple now; he should be easy . . . simple pickin's for a masterful executioner like you."

"Don't be too sure, Aussie. You ever chased a wounded animal into the bush?"

"I don't hunt."

"I do. Injured beasts are the most dangerous, the most exciting. A wounded grizzly will wait in hiding, hoping the hunter will wander close. A bloodied mountain lion will charge when cornered; even a crippled buffalo will try to put a horn in your gizzard. Wounded animals are always on guard . . . menacing, a challenge!" Quinn's eyes burned with excitement. "Remember, I told you before which was the most perilous beast to hunt, to corner . . . to kill?"

"Grizzlies?" asked the curious Australian, totally forgetting the previous conversation.

"No . . . man. *Homo sapiens* is the most cunning, resourceful, and deadly of all predators—especially if he's been wounded. Sam Dodd lost an arm. You can bet he's alert, skinning-knife sharp. He's a fighter and he's smart. Finishing him off will take some doing."

"What are ya doin', tryin' to get more money outa me fer a job ya bungled?" Aussie guardedly asked.

"No, not at all. In fact, I'd do it for free. This one is the toughest assignment to date—a test of my mettle, so to speak."

"You really do enjoy killin', don't cha?"

"I'll delight in eliminating Dodd. But first, I have to know where he is."

"Dodd won't be hard to find; he's gone home. This time you're not goin' alone. This time yer takin' a couple of my lads with you."

The preacher frowned, then quietly but firmly said, "I work *alone*."

"Not this time, ye don't!" Aussie angrily replied. "Ye bungled the last time an' I can't afford no other mistake. Dodd has to be killed and killed quick before he stirs up any more trouble."

"Be sure you understand, Walker," Quinn vehemently whispered, "if they get in my way, I'll kill them too!"

Aussie shifted his great bulk forward and stood up, towering over Quinn. With venom in his voice, he hissed, "Don't threaten me, ya slick-talkin' assassin! I pays the freight, I tells ya where to go and who goes with ya . . . get it?"

Quinn didn't move nor did he show any sign of being intimidated in the slightest. "Aussie, have you ever heard of the expression, 'casting pearls before swine?'"

"Nah. What does it mean?"

"Forget it—it's just a bad habit of mine."

Chapter 22

Easter rituals drew near, usually accompanied by springtime weather, lavender and white lilacs in full bloom, flooding their heavenly scent everywhere. Red and velvet-blue pansies, yellow-headed daffodils waving in gentle spring breezes, wildflowers decorating open fields, pushing through the new, sweet-smelling grass, billowy clouds, trees bursting with buds of green . . . those were the radiant signs of Eastertime . . . not this! April at ten thousand feet was still hidden beneath winter. Sam looked out from the Silverville Community Christian Church and watched the sleet and snow peck away at the stained glass windows. The whistle of the wind was temporarily muted by the voices of the choir.

"He has risen, He has risen,
Christ our Lord lives forever . . . "

Sam joined in the singing. What he lacked in pitch, he made up in volume. The church was packed in spite of the bitter weather. While living in Silverville, the Dodds had been members of the congregation and a sizable number of old parishioners recognized him. Although it was good to be remembered and among friendly believers, Sam felt a loneliness; any service without Mary and the children was not quite the same; somehow their presence made the day warmer . . . and Christ's triumph over death all the more meaningful.

The sermon was powerful; then the small choir sang "A Mighty Fortress Is Our God" with vigor exceeding their numbers. Many went forward to receive communion. It had been a long time since Sam had received the wafer and wine; he was grateful for the opportunity. "Take this in remembrance of me,' said Jesus, 'this is My blood of the new covenant, which is shed for many for the remission of sins . . .'"

God turns them out to celebrate His risen Son, Sam thought to himself, *and even this miserable weather gives testimony to His power.*

"He has risen," gladly proclaimed the pastor.

"He has risen, indeed!" responded the congregation.

After the service, warm moments were spent renewing acquaintances. Sam fondly remembered his family's involvement in this church; how they missed the fellowship there . . and by the reception Sam received, the membership missed them also.

Some of them asked about the loss of his arm, and even though Sam tried to take it in stride, it was difficult. How do you tell friends someone tried to kill you without getting into a long, drawn out explanation? He had to leave sooner than he had wished, but the business at hand was necessary.

Sam's first stop was Sheriff Poole's office. Will Poole had been Lake County's sheriff for ten years . . . able testimony to his law enforcement credentials. Lawmen didn't live long unless they were tougher than the men they apprehended. Sheriff Poole was the standard by which other lawmen were judged. To be as tough as Will Poole was the ultimate compliment. His steel-blue eyes cut many to midget size, sobered drunks, and sent desperadoes packing. He carried his sixty-eight years well on his six-foot frame; flat stomach, weathered face, and firm muscles belied the mass of gray hair tucked under the broad-brimmed hat. Although Poole's speed-of-hand had diminished somewhat along with his legendary agility, he made up for it in wisdom and unparalleled experience packed into a calculating mind. Those dumb enough to question his age or speed with a gun rarely got older.

Poole was obviously glad to see Sam walk through the door, for he'd been keenly disappointed when his former deputy left for northern Colorado.

"I was hopin' you'd show up. I wanted to find out how ya lost that arm." Will's face was expressionless as he pointed to Sam's empty sleeve.

"That's what I've always liked about ya, Will—your subtle, genteel way of beatin' about the bush with small talk."

Will Poole's leathery face cracked into a smile.

"Heard you were in town, Samuel—glad you stopped by." He grabbed Sam's good left hand and shook it heartily. "Yep, glad to see ya. How's Mary and the kids?"

"I believe they're all right; it's been awhile since I've been home."

Sam spent the next half-hour telling his friend the circumstances and reason for his visit to Silverville. When Sam had finished, the sheriff went to a cabinet and withdrew a sheaf of papers, selected one, and gave it to him.

"What's this?" Sam asked.

"It's the letter Claude Dillon's boy wrote to Jethro challengin' him to come to the Kasser Mine and fight it out. The clerk gave the note to me the next day when Jethro didn't show up. I rode out to the mine and found his body. The kid must have been a good shot; he plugged Jethro right between the eyes."

"Did you ever find the Dillon boy?"

"Nope. There was too much goin' on at the time. I put out a bulletin through law enforcement channels asking for information on a Claude Dillon, but that's been the most of it. You're well aware Jethro had few friends and more enemies than a two-bit harlot has customers. Everybody thought Jethro got what was comin' to him from a revenge-minded son. Fact is, lots of toasts were hoisted to Claude's whelp the night folks discovered Jethro Briggs had cashed it in."

"Did it look like Jethro had been bushwhacked?"

"No . . . looked like a fair fight."

"Why'd ya say that?"

"The footprints in the snow and the horse tracks. It had snowed the day before the shootin' and hadn't snowed again 'til after. Jethro was there first. I could see where he'd been standing around for a time."

"How did ya figure?"

"Tobacco-spit stains scattered around one place . . . Jethro chawed a lot . . . spit marks all 'round where he stomped down the snow. Claude's boy was smokin' roll-yer-owns . . . I found only one butt where he was standin' and a lot fewer of his tracks."

"The man who shot me smoked roll-yer-owns, but so do a lot of folks. Sounds like Dillon and Jethro may have talked a bit 'fore the shootin'. That's strange, Will!"

"Now that you mention it, it sure is. Young Dillon had to be awfully good with a gun to beat Jethro to the draw."

"That's a fact," responded Sam. "Think about it. He'd been threatened by young Dillon. There's no way Jethro's guard would be down and there's no way he would have let Dillon get the drop on him. Even so, Jethro was fast enough to kill him anyway. You say he was shot between the eyes?"

"Yep, dead-center."

"How far apart were they?"

"Oh, I guess about twenty paces."

"Will, did Jethro get off a shot?"

"Yep . . . his gun was frozen in his hand, one round fired. "I'd say he cleared leather—but that was all."

"How many men do ya know that could outdraw Jethro?"

"Maybe Masterson or Sheriff Jason Sanford over Montana way . . . maybe me . . . can't think of any others."

"Neither can I." Sam nervously paced the room while the sheriff sat quietly in his chair. After a moment Sam spoke. "The more ya think about it, the more confusin' it gets. Will, what kind of bullet killed Jethro?"

"Let's see now," Poole rifled through the papers on his desk. "Here it is. The undertaker said it was a .44-caliber slug; I found a .44–.40 shell casing near where Dillon had his horse tied."

"Wade Johnson was killed with a .44-caliber slug."

"Who's Wade Johnson?"

"He's one of the men I told you about. It might be of no significance. Lots of men use .44-caliber bullets."

"Sam, I've got a question for ya. Did Claude Dillon, Sr. strike you as a man that could sire the kid who'd kill Jethro Briggs?"

"Sheriff, I thought of that as well . . . I thought Claude was a bachelor, never knew he'd ever been married. But he was in his fifties when he came to work for the Sassy Mae mines. He could'a been married before. He wouldn't be the first man to come west leaving a family behind."

"Did anyone at the mine know him well?" inquired Will.

"Yeah, Claude used to hang around with Swede Stoos; you threw 'em both in jail once for being drunk and disorderly."

"I remember. Never were two men meeker the next day. Swede is still around, repairing mine equipment. I saw him just last week."

"Well, grab your coat. Let's go find him."

★ ★ ★

Swede Stoos emerged from the mine covered with grime, wiping his greasy hands on a filthy rag. His countenance was as foul as his body, perennially dour. Swede was a suspicious grunter, not known for his communicative skills or diplomacy. "Umph," along with a nod or a shake of the head, comprised the bulk of his dialogue. He had a good memory, and the sight of Will Poole brought back the pain of a cracked skull and broken teeth.

"Swede, I'm Sam Dodd—remember me?"

"Umph." He cast a scowl at the sheriff.

"We'd like to ask you some questions about Claude Dillon's son."

This time not even a grunt was forthcoming. Swede turned and walked back into the mine.

"Hold on, Swede," called Will Poole. "I can find a good reason to lock you up; walking into any saloon will do!"

Swede stopped and slowly turned . . . burning with anger. "I do nuttin' to help ya catch Claude's boy."

"Then Dillon had a son."

"Umph," with an affirmative nod.

"Didja ever meet him?" asked Sam.

"Umph," in the negative.

"Could he have killed a gunfighter like Briggs?"

"Umph." His shoulders shrugged a *who knows,* then his head bobbed a *yes.* Much to their surprise, he offered, "Claude's boy, cavalry officer, bragged about him."

"Union or Confederate?"

"Union. Fought under General Smith."

"Swede, can you think of anything else?"

"Yeah, can I git inta a saloon without gettin' arrested?" Now it was Will Poole who grunted and nodded in the affirmative. Swede hastily disappeared into the bowels of the mine.

"What do you think?" asked Will.

"Not many cavalry officers were illiterate. Claude was an educated man, so it's fair to guess his son was too. The note written to Jethro was from someone with little or no schoolin'. Will, why don't we wire the War Department to see if they have a record of Claude, Jr.'s whereabouts."

"Good idea, Sam. Maybe Claude's boy could have done it."

"That's true—he could have intentionally sounded stupid to attract Jethro to the mine, or he could be a poor learner. I knew a few cavalry officers who weren't the best educated."

★ ★ ★

Sam expected a quick response from the War Department, but none was forthcoming. Not until he purchased his ticket to Laramie for the long trip home did the message finally arrive:

Sheriff Will Poole
Silverville, Colorado

Dear Sir:

We have no present address for a cavalry officer by the name of Claude Dillon, Jr. Stop. An officer by that name was killed in battle at Cold Harbor while serving under General Smith's command. Stop. I hope this information is of service.

Colonel D. O. Witcher
U. S. War Department

Will Poole reread the telegram, this time aloud for the benefit of Sam. "This proves Jethro wasn't killed by Claude's son. I guess Claude never told Swede his son died during the Civil War."

"If he did, you can bet Swede wasn't about to tell us," responded Sam, laughing, "That Swedish well runs deep; he wasn't about to help us catch Jethro's killer."

Will took the telegram and stuffed it in his coat pocket, then added, "Still going home, Sam?"

"No, not now. I have every reason to believe these deaths are tied together. I'm goin' to New Mexico to see Otto's widow and speak to the law about his murder. Maybe I can find another piece to this crazy puzzle. I know this fer sure—things aren't what they seem. Looks like Jethro was killed by a professional gunman. In fact, maybe the best there is. He was enticed to the mine by an impostor pretendin' to be Claude's boy . . . someone so confident in his ability that he was willin' to face Jethro in what seems to have been a fair fight. It took planning, nerve, and skill. But why all the deception? Why hide the killin' behind such a web of deceit? He could've challenged Briggs on the main street of town and shot him in front of an appreciative audience."

"That pretty well rules out some young shooter lookin' for a reputation or revenge," offered the sheriff.

"You bet. Killin' Jethro was a feather in any gunfighter's cap. We would've heard of the braggin' by now if some cocky fast gun had done the job."

"Could it have been revenge from some other source?" asked Will.

Sam rubbed the back of his neck while thinking about it. "Well . . . it's possible but not likely. Nope . . . this killin' must have been motivated by somethin' else, somethin' we don't know about. Will, all of these killin's are somehow connected. I'm gettin' closer to the answer—I can feel it in my bones."

Poole put a hand on Sam's shoulder and with concern, admonished his friend. "Sam Dodd, if this is a plot, then you'd better take care. You're still alive and so is the person or persons who want you dead." Will looked at Sam's empty sleeve. "Sam, you were the best deputy I ever had. I never worried about you then. I do now.

"Can you use a gun? You were right-handed. Can you shoot with your left?"

Sam smiled affectionately at his worried companion.

"I shoot fairly well—nothin' to brag about. I was best with a rifle, but it's real clumsy for me now. I can hunch my shoulder and sight with my left eye but it's difficult at best, 'cause my strong eye is my right one. I can twirl my Winchester and jack a shell into the chamber. Whenever I can, I practice with my pistol. Before long, I intend to get a shoulder holster."

His friend grabbed him by the coat. "You've got time right now! Let's head back to the office."

In a matter of minutes they were at the sheriff's headquarters, where Will unlocked the vault in the back room. It was crammed with all types and calibers of guns.

"These firearms," grinned Poole, "have been *donated* to this department by some of our more transient-minded citizens."

Sam laughed out loud, knowing exactly how the sheriff acquired so many. There was no ordinance against carrying a firearm, but anyone who abused the privilege was more than likely to lose his firearm to Will Poole, who took it away and added it to his collection. More than a few men surrendered their arms on their way to the Silverville cemetery. It was an impressive array of firepower—everything from repeating rifles to side arms.

"Here's an ivory-handled Remington model 1873. Jesse James packs one of these. Here's a single-action Colt 1873. This jewel is a Smith and Wesson .44-caliber American. Over there is a .44 Russian—you name it, I probably have it."

Sam reached for the single-action Colt 1873. "I'll take this one."

"No you won't, you'll take this little .32-caliber gem."

"Thirty-two-caliber? That's not much firepower, Sheriff."

"This, my friend, is the gun for you. Go on, Sam, pick it up; pull the trigger and fire a dry round."

Sam reached for the gun and, with difficulty, thumbed back the hammer . . . click!

"Now, do it again, only don't thumb back the hammer."

"It won't fire."

"Do as I say—just pull the trigger!"

Sam held the gun at arm's length and squeezed the trigger. His eyes opened wide as he saw the hammer move back and then forward . . . click!

"I'll be doggone! What kind of a fancy pistol is this?"

"It's called double-action. You don't have to thumb back the hammer, just pull the trigger. For a one-winged cowboy like you, that's important. This little five-shot nickel-plated beauty was just issued by Smith and Wesson. I took it off an Eastern tinhorn three days ago, shoulder holster and all."

Sam slipped off his coat and tried it on. The holster had a spring release, made especially for a quick draw. Surprisingly, it fit under his vest quite comfortably.

"I hope I never have to use it." Sam walked over and looked at himself in the mirror. "But I'm glad to have it."

He practiced a few clumsy draws in front of the mirror.

"Ain't very fast."

"Sam, before you slap leather, lean forward just a little, your coat will open naturally, givin' you a better draw."

Following Will's suggestion, Sam drew again, this time a little faster.

"Looks like I gotta practice a bit."

"Sam, bein' quick with a gun is important . . . sometimes! But, bein' able to kill is another matter. A lot of fast souls have been shot dead by slower men who knew what to do when the gun cleared leather. The man who put a hole in Jethro's skull was both *fast* and *deadly*—a rare and dangerous combination. I can't give ya any advice on how to handle that one."

"Good friend, I don't know either . . . so I pray a lot."

"Does it help?" asked Will.

"Yep, it does . . . we'll soon find out . . . maybe in New Mexico. I'm taking the evening train—but before I go, I'd like to talk to some folks about Andrew Quade. Do you know where he was drinkin' the night he died?"

"Sure do. He was seen drinking pretty heavy at the Lucky Dog Saloon, the town's leadin' blood-bucket."

Will had no love for the Lucky Dog, nor for the owner, Aussie Walker. It was the scene of more trouble than any of the other rowdy drinking and gambling holes. More gore had been spilled on its hardwood floors than on all the saloons on Walnut Street, the main thoroughfare.

"I checked 'round after Quade's fall and questioned the bartender. All confirmed Andy Quade was singin' and tossing 'em down with a bunch of miners."

"Was Andy still living at the Hoskin Boarding House?"

"Yes, he was. I gathered up his belongings and sent them along with his remains to his people in Moline, Illinois. They wanted him buried near home. Why do you ask?"

"The Hoskin house is in the opposite direction from the saloon. Why'd Quade head back to the mine? Goin' back late Saturday night to where he worked? Wouldn't Quade have staggered home to sleep it off over Sunday? I never knew him to have any great attraction for the mines or for work, either. We knew Andy was high-grading all along but when I brought it to Charlie's attention, he just shrugged and told me to forget it. Will, could you come with me now to the Lucky Dog? They're not about to tell me anything if you're not along."

"Sorry, Sam, I can't. Rest of the day, I'll be testifyin' at the county courthouse. I could do it later tonight or tomorrow."

"I'm leaving town today on the 4:45 to New Mexico."

"I've got an idea, raise your ri . . . left hand. Go on, do as I say."

Sam raised his left hand.

"Do you swear to uphold the laws of the United States and Colorado? Say 'I do'—go on, say it!"

Sam grinned. "Am I enlistin' again in the Will Poole posse?"

"Without pay. Here's your badge. Now your questionin' will be official business."

Sam tucked the deputy sheriff's badge into his vest pocket. "One more thing, Will. Whatever happened to the Cravens? Orville's kin didn't take too kindly to me killing him and his brother. It's possible one of them could have bushwhacked me."

"Not likely. There's only one that isn't dead or in prison an' that's Wilbur Craven. He'd like to be as bad as his brothers but he hasn't the guts for it. He puffs and blows when he has a snootful, but he's a coward through and through. He might back-shoot ya, but you'd have to be asleep when he did it. He fits his name . . . Craven. There's no way he could travel all the way to your ranch, then make a thousand-yard shot. He deals faro at the Lucky Dog and soiled doves. He's spineless."

"Well, I'd better be goin'. Will, take care of yourself."

"See you around, partner."

Sam stepped from the warm sheriff's office into the cold. The Colorado wind whipped the snow up from the ground. Sam pulled his hat down to the top of his ears and crossed Walnut Street to the Lucky Dog Saloon. The visit was not productive. No one recalled a thing; memory decay had set in, even when Sam showed them his badge. There was nothing more to do but go to the depot and wait for the 4:45.

★ ★ ★

"Mindy Lou, anything go on while I was in Georgetown?" Aussie Walker took off his massive wool coat, brushed the snow from its fur collar, and threw it in the general direction of a wall hook in the corner of his office.

"Nah! This bad weather and it bein' Easter are keepin' a lot a customers away. Nothin' unusual for this time a year. How was your trip?"

"Not so good. I had to meet with that shyster, Slick Seymour. He's all panicked over a business deal we have . . . had to set his mind at ease . . . finally squeezed some sense into him."

"What was Slick so worried about?"

"Some rancher named Dodd was snooping around back East . . . he gave up though, and went back to his ranch."

"Dodd, Sam Dodd?"

"He was in here sportin' a badge and asking questions about Andrew Quade no more than two hours ago."

At this news, Aussie's head snapped toward Mindy Lou. He sputtered almost incoherently.

"Sam Dodd . . . here? What was he . . . you're sure it was him, not somebody else?"

Aussie's favorite madam was shocked to see him so instantaneously rattled and angry. His face was blood-red and his temples pulsated as the cuss words came tumbling from his snarled lips. "That bloody lying little runt! Dodd's gone back to the ranch, has he! Git out of here—I've gotta think!" With that, he gave her a violent shove that propelled her across the room and to the floor. Though shaken, Mindy Lou wisely scrambled to her feet and quickly departed, while Aussie shouted, "Get me Wilbur Craven. Tell him I want to see him . . . NOW!"

★ ★ ★

"Ya wanted ta see me, Mr. Walker?"

Wilbur Craven poked his head through Aussie's office door and peered around the corner, leaving his quivering knees out of sight.

"Come in, Wilbur—take a chair." The huge man's voice was firm but not intimidating. Craven dutifully sat in the oak chair across from his boss's desk. "Wilbur, I have a pleasant job fer ya—an important task that should please all yer kin—a rich, rewardin' one at that."

Craven brightened. "Why sure, Boss, what do you want me to do?"

"Kill Sam Dodd!"

Wilbur turned ashen white. Sweat beads suddenly appeared on his brow while he squirmed in his chair. Nervously, he blurted, "I hate that rotten . . .!"

"I know you do," interrupted Walker. "There's somethin' you probably don't know. He's lost his right arm. He's an invalid now, not the man he used to be. Killin' him will be easy."

Joy was written all over Wilbur's face. "So! That righteous do-gooder is crippled. Serves him right. Hope it was cut off inch by inch for the agony he's caused my ma and pa. Right-handed, weren't he?"

"That's right, he was right-handed. I'll pay ya a thousand dollars for the job. I'll even send someone with ya to help."

"Was Dodd packin' a side arm?" cautiously asked Craven.

"No . . . he was in the saloon earlier today. No one saw a gun. Dodd took the afternoon train to Santa Fe. I have tickets for you and Tom Taggert for tomorrow."

Aussie rose from his chair, lumbered around the desk, and stood over Wilbur. He placed his giant right hand on Craven's shoulder and gently squeezed. Wilbur felt the immense restrained power and sensed what it would be like if Aussie were to crush his collarbone. Wilbur inwardly shuddered.

"Wilbur, you'd be doin' me a great favor and yerself, as well."

"Ah welcome the opportunity, Boss . . . ah surely do."

"Good. Tom will have the tickets. You can count on his advice . . . bring me back Dodd's scalp."

"It's good as done, Mr. Walker. Sam Dodd is good as dead or ah ain't no Craven."

Wilbur left the room with a jaunty step. Tom Taggert was one of the deadliest men in Walker's gang of cutthroats. The two of them would be able to down a cripple easy. Besides, one thousand dollars and the satisfaction of avenging his brothers appealed to him. The most gratifying thing of all would be the effect it had on his reputation . . . *Wilbur Craven, the man who gunned down Sam Dodd.* Yeah, the thought was real pleasant.

Chapter 23

Shadows had yet to appear in the early gray of morning. The sun still hid behind the Sangre De Cristo mountains, but its rays bounced red off of the thin wisps of clouds that rimmed the horizon.

The old man led the roan gelding from the barn and tied him to the hitching post. Sam had selected a sturdy horse for the ride to the Schmitz ranch.

"If you intend to ride over Chama way, you better have some others along 'cause those San Juan mountains are crawlin' with Apaches."

The stable owner took a look at Sam's empty sleeve and then at the roan, wishing he had checked the man's destination before setting the price. "Fact is, you couldn't get me outa sight of town with that Geronimo runnin' around them hills. Those Apaches could give lessons to the devil himself. Yer better off with yer long johns full a scorpions and sidewinder rattlers than gittin' ketched by a band of Mescaleros. If they get you, they bury you in sand up to yer neck next to a anthill, cut off yer eyelids, an let the sun bake yer brains. If thet don't do it, those red devils build a fire on yer belly and let the coals burn yer guts away."

"I'll try to look out," replied Sam.

The stable proprietor saw his gruesome commentaries were having no effect on Dodd. He shrugged his shoulders, resigned to the less than fifty-fifty chance he had of ever seeing his horse and saddle again.

Sam swung easily into the saddle, quite accustomed to mounting with just one hand. His spirits had risen, now that his shoulder was completely healed and full strength had returned to his body. Sam shed his jacket, even though the air still held a cold bite. It would be warm in less than an hour when the sun topped the horizon and filled the New Mexico sky.

The sandy trail by the Rio Grande looked well-traveled. Sycamores lined stretches of the river, and a morning flight of white winged dove darted close overhead. Long-eared jacks gathered in batches, scattering at the sight of man and horse. Everywhere were signs of wildlife; the wide swath of a bulky tortoise and its ess-patterns alongside spoke of a more deadly traveler. There were vee shaped tracks of mule deer among the marble-size droppings of elk. Red-tailed hawks perched atop saguaro cactus.

Sam reflected on the differences between the lush parts of Colorado and the dry, high desert spectacle of the Southwest. *The Lord sure likes variety.*

Sam was greeted warmly by Otto's widow, Manuela Schmitz. He was pleasantly taken aback by her Latin beauty and exceptional cordiality.

"Welcome, Señor Dodd, bueno amigo de mi marido, or en my not-so-good Engles, 'good friend of my husban'."

She was still dressing in black in observance of Otto's death which had been devastating to her. Manuela's sorrow was further complicated by the recent birth of their third child. Relatives had encouraged her to stay in Santa Fe until the baby was born, but she would have no part of it. She brought Otto's body back to the ranch and buried him within walking distance of the hacienda, where she visited the grave daily.

"I wanted su niña to be born here, close to her papa."

Manuela smiled, though a few tears glistened on her cheeks. "His girl—Otto wanted a little niña; he would be so feliz—so proud!"

Sam looked down on the pile of stones and sand that covered Otto's remains. The red rock and brown sand, surrounded by prickly cactus and scraggly mesquite brush, were a far cry from the place he and Mary had selected for their family burial site.

Scattered dry flowers were mixed with the stones.

"I try to keep plantas y flores for Otto but the rabbits an' deer . . . " She shrugged, "bot it is no good, at night they come and eat them."

They walked silently from Otto's grave back to the hacienda along the newly graveled trail. Sam found it difficult to bring up the subject they needed to discuss. He didn't know how much he should tell her, or how she'd react to his suspicions that Otto's death was not chance but premeditated murder. He'd wait for the right opportunity.

Supper that evening was a new experience for Sam.

Manuela had invited all the Becerras to welcome one of Otto's friends. The adults were seated along an outdoor table draped with red and white cloths which stretched across the patio, long enough to accommodate the entire family. The children were happily and noisily chasing each other around the immense red earthen vases containing a variety of bright flowers and tomato vines. When the senior Becerra called them to order, the children quickly complied and took their seats. There was barely an "amen" to the blessing before the noise level rose precipitously. Everyone began to talk at once while passing the heaping platters of food. Sam couldn't understand a word but "gracias," which he used profusely as he stacked his plate with the exotic and aromatic dishes.

Sam watched as Manuela's father held what looked like a thin flapjack. He saw that he heaped it with meat and crushed beans, added some greens and red sauce, then rolled it deftly, stuffing it joyfully into his mouth. Sam clumsily did the same . . . it was delicious! He made another, then another, spooning on more of the spicy red sauce and tossing in a couple of innocent-looking little peppers.

He was into the second bite before it hit him . . . his mouth was on fire! Sam groped for the glass of wine and, using its coolness to wash the brimstone into his stomach. Tears were running down his face as he noticed everyone was quietly watching him. He attempted to smile but only a silly grimace was forthcoming. He tried to be calm. "Manuela . . . what *is* that?" He pointed to the red salsa and the jalapeño peppers.

"Señor Sam, would you like another glass of wine?" Manuela's eyes were dancing with glee at the gringo and his first contact with Mexican peppers.

"Yes, if you please," he whispered while trying to maintain composure. Sam was finished eating, convinced the food would soon burn its way to the surface, mortifying him once more. Sam was relieved when dinner was over and the men retired to the verandah for cigars and brandy . . . and the women to the kitchen.

They talked of horses and stock, grasses and rain. The Becerras tried to communicate in English but would slip back into Spanish, when they needed to make a point, expecting others to translate. Not until the brandy was served did Sam turn the conversation to Otto's murder, and tell them he was investigating the crime. Two of the brothers, Juan and Jose, and their cousin Angel Paredes were with Otto when the mules were sold.

Juan spoke out. "I saw thees bad guy who killed Otto at de auction. I was sorprize when he bid for the mule."

"Why were you surprised?"

"He look too poor to buy una vaca—a cow—much less a good mule."

Sam asked, "Could you describe him to me?"

Juan thought for a moment, "I tink he wore a large sombrero and el ropa . . . these clothes of a poor vaquero. He was muy estupido, always slumped over like a beaten peasant."

"Sí," chimed in Angel. "He had no gun but he have a cuchillo grande in his belt."

"A big knife," offered Jose.

"Anything else? What did his hair look like?"

"Oh . . . let me think . . . sí, it was mucho negro, stringy, and came down to his shoulders," said Angel.

"How could he murder Otto so easily? Otto was fast and strong," stated Sam.

"We don know how it happen but that vaquero knew where to strike. Every stab would have killed. Otto was a bloody sight."

"Poor Manuela," added Juan sorrowfully. "She had blood here, there, all over her."

"Anything else?"

"He stuck Otto, then rode off. We found the mule later in town, tied to a post," said Jose.

"The vaquero was gone; nobody see him," added Jose.

"No one ever see him before, either," replied Juan.

"Did Otto die right away . . . did he say anything?"

They all looked at each other before Angel Paredes replied. "Sí, he talked to Manuela; he spoke some words of love to her."

"Would it be too hard for her if I asked her about it?"

The senior Becerra spoke for the first time. "Don' worry about Manuela; she is a strong woman. If she can be any help in finding who murdered Otto, she would be most pleased."

"Are you sure?"

"Señor, she is a Becerra!" proudly answered her father.

The opportunity came the next morning after breakfast. Manuela asked if the breakfast was as enjoyable as dinner. Sam laughed, "I know eggs, bacon, and beans when I see 'em, but that red sauce and those little green peppers, I'll leave to better men than me. Can't figger how we got New Mexico away from people tough enough to eat stuff like that!"

Manuela's face lit up in a radiant smile, then turned very thoughtful.

"Sam, Papa says you want to talk about my Otto. What do you want to know?"

"Manuela, I know it's painful, but what exactly did Otto say before he died? What were his last words? Your brothers said they were words of endearment; if so, I don't have to know."

Manuela lowered her head, then slowly raised it and looked Sam in the face.

"I haven't told anyone exactly what he said. His last words were er, silly."

"What do you mean?"

"Otto used to joke about our niños looking so Mexican. He said we would keep having niños until we have a blond and blue-eyed baby."

"He talked about the children?"

"Sí, his last words were 'Blue-eyed Mexi . . .' he never finish the words." Manuela's voice broke at the remembrance.

Sam stepped back in shocked silence, his body taut. Otto wasn't talking about his children! With his last breath, he was describing his assassin . . . *the knife-wielding vaquero had blue eyes*!

★ ★ ★

"Ya shouldn't drink so much! We gotta job to do!"

"Aw, shut up!" was Craven's slobbering reply.

Taggert looked with disdain at Wilbur. The last few days in Santa Fe had been disgusting; Craven's boisterousness had turned to constant whining about everything. What little confidence he had left was rapidly disappearing. Waiting for Dodd's return gnawed on his fragile nerves like a little lizard on a big bug. The bottom of a whiskey bottle became his refuge, and most of the past few days had been spent there.

They located the stable where Dodd had rented the horse and found out where he had gone. It would have been a simple matter to wait on the trail and ambush him on his way back, but Wilbur had no intention of leaving the safety of Santa Fe—not with Geronimo on the loose.

They devised a simple plan. They would keep the stable under constant surveillance. When Dodd arrived Wilbur would call him out for the killing of his brothers, then shoot him. Taggert would be close by, also covering Dodd. As soon as Dodd was down, Taggert planned to rush up and place a gun in his hand, giving Craven the excuse of self-defense. Shootouts were not uncommon in Santa Fe. Taggert was to swear it was a fair fight and that would be the end of it. Wilbur had laid the groundwork the last few days visiting saloons, asking if anyone had seen Dodd, telling all within earshot how Dodd gunned down his unarmed brothers. The stage was set and Taggert was confident it would work. If Wilbur missed, then he'd shoot Dodd himself. No one, including the drunken sot sitting across from him, would know the difference.

According to the stable owner, Dodd intended to return the horse two days ago. From their rented room, in the boarding house across the street, each took turns standing guard, waiting for Dodd to reappear. The first few days hadn't been difficult, Wilbur stayed relatively sober, but the last few had been painful; he kept falling asleep, especially in the late hours. Taggert was dead tired, tending his own watch and struggling to keep Wilbur awake as well.

"Where is thet one-armed waddie!" Wilbur reached for the bottle sitting on the table next to the window. He was slouched back in the chair, feet up on the sill, teetering back and forth.

"Lay off the whiskey, Craven!" Taggert violently snatched the bottle from his outstretched hand, sending him sprawling across the floor.

"Watcha do thet for? Gimme thet bottle!" Craven struggled to his feet, anger written on his face.

Taggert stepped forward and kicked his feet from under him, knocking him down again. Taggert seized Craven's shirt and pulled his face to within inches of his own. Saliva sprayed Craven as Taggert said with contempt, "Listen to me, you weak-kneed lush—didja ever see a man's eyes pop outa his head from bein' squeezed ta death? I have! Thet's whut Mr. Walker does ta someone who makes 'em mad. When that thick skull of yours pops, yer eyes will land across the room wit yer brains oozin' out the holes! Do ya hear me?"

Craven bobbed his head up and down in full comprehension, the thought of his brains between Aussie's massive hands graphically etched in his mind.

"Now . . . git back to the winder and do yer share of the lookin'."

★ ★ ★

Feeling apprehension and a need for caution, Sam swung the roan off the path along the Chamas River and, picking a game trail, traversed the mountainside. On the way to the Schmitz ranch, Sam had noticed the vulnerability of a trail traveler to ambush. Up ahead lay a narrow pass, a perfect spot to bushwhack the unwary. Working his way slowly, keeping to the brush as much as possible, he approached a knoll that would give him a good view of the trail ahead. Dismounting short of the rise, Sam tied the horse behind a large rock outcropping and proceeded on foot, rifle in hand. Cautiously, he found a shadowed spot to view the trail below. At first he saw nothing, but experience had taught him patience . . . to wait . . . make sure.

Movement. The tail of a horse swished behind a small scrubby growth of piñon trees, then another shifted from one foot to another. Five, maybe six horses were there. Sam hunkered down and waited. An hour or so later, Sam got a quick glimpse of a young Apache boy attending the animals, but try as he might, he could not locate the others—the band of warriors waiting below.

They sure know how to blend into the surroundings. Why not? This is their home; we whites are the newcomers. Backtracking was a possibility then circling around, but that would add a day to the trip and be equally dangerous. Sam chose to wait.

The hours dragged on, the morning sun turning into an afternoon oven. The canyon's shadows disappeared, forcing him to change his hiding place. The Apaches didn't notice the imperceptible movement above them as Sam found a better location behind some junipers.

In the late afternoon, Sam heard the clanging of hooves in the distance as a small group of Mexicans worked their way down the canyon, coming from the direction of Santa Fe. The noise they were making bounced off the mountainsides. They were laughing and talking while passing a skin of wine among themselves, unmindful of the danger just ahead.

Fools! They're goin' ta get themselves killed! Sam thought. Now was the time to leave and not be noticed. Five Indians with surprise on their side up against a party of Mexicans with undoubtedly superior armament made a somewhat even battle. Sam's neutrality was only momentary; one of the voices was a woman's.

"Dang it!" Then looking skyward, he said, "Excuse me, Lord."

Sam's thoughts were racing: *What now?* He couldn't see where the Apaches were hiding. He could shoot and warn the travelers, but they would turn and run, leaving Sam alone to cope with the Indians. Should he wait until the skirmish started? If he did, the woman could be killed. That was a chance he'd have to take . . . or should he? If he had two arms, he could sneak down and fire on the savages, but physically that was impossible. Sam laid his Henry rifle over the rock and sighted down the barrel with his left eye. The many hours of practice with both pistol and rifle over the past months had helped, but he still felt unsure firing with only one arm. He could use the arm stub for some leverage, but steadying a kicking rifle was trouble under any circumstances, made more troublesome when firing on someone who could shoot back.

The chattering voices and laughter came nearer and nearer. One of the vaqueros was serenading the lady, another joined in. Sam waited, a plan formulating in his mind.

If I were waitin' to ambush, where'd I be? Yeah . . . there, among the cactus . . . and there behind those rocks. What's that? . . . an Apache gaining a better view? Yep . . . I'd let the Mexicans get to that outcropping before I'd fire, cutting off their retreat and if any escaped, the horses would be close by for the chase.

Sam waited rock-still until the Mexican riders were just within the trap, then he fired a round at the hooves of their approaching horses. The shot caused massive confusion; the Apaches cut loose a salvo, a rider fell, a woman shrieked. Sam immediately turned and, bracing the rifle over the large rock in front of him, leveled a round at one of the Indian ponies. The horse screamed as the bullet smashed into its flank. As rapidly as he could, he clumsily jacked another round into the chamber, firing once more into the piñons hiding the horses. Another pony whinnied in pain. Just as Sam planned, the shouts of the Indian boy and the agonized cries from the wounded animals diverted their attention.

The dazed and disoriented Mexicans sobered quickly enough to return fire, compelling the Indians to beat a hasty retreat through the rocks to their horses. They double-mounted the remaining ponies and disappeared through the trees. The Mexicans hoisted up in the saddle their wounded amigo and rode off at full gallop in the opposite direction, oblivious of their benefactor.

"Wake up, Craven, you drunken sot—wake up!"

"Huh, wha . . . whacha want?"

"He's here, ya stupid lush—his horse's back!"

Wilbur bolted from his chair and gazed into the early morning light. An unsaddled roan was tied to the hitch rail in front of the stable, saddle and blankets hanging over the corral post.

"That tough old cowboy came in before light—musta rode at night! Wonder where he's gone to?"

Tom Taggert struggled into his pants, cursing under his breath. "Wherever he is, we better find him fast—before the whole town wakes up. You cover one side of the street an' I'll take the other. Check the hotel, find where he's staying. Probably he's asleep by now. We gotta figure a new plan."

Both hastily strapped on their guns and headed into the street, swiftly covering both sides, darting into boarding houses, trying not to disturb sleeping patrons. The town began to stir; a few riders moved down the street, shops were opening doors, lights came on in the windows.

"Tom, I found him!" Out of breath, eyes bugging, Craven pointed to the café down the street. "He's over there, havin' breakfast!"

They hurried toward the café, then peered hesitatingly through the dirty window. The waitress had just served a plate of food to Sam Dodd.

"I can shoot him through the winder." Wilbur eagerly drew his gun and aimed it at Sam's back.

Tom reached over and forced the gun down. "What you want to do—get us both hung?" Taggert looked around until he saw a stack of empty crates in front of the hardware store next door. He said, "See those crates over there? That's where I'll be. You wait in the street and when he comes out, challenge him to draw as loud as you can, then shoot 'em. I'll run up and put the gun in his hand . . . understood?"

Wilbur rushed into the middle of the street, his heart pounding so hard that his temples bulged with every beat. He took a deep breath and at once began shouting, "Come outa there, Sam Dodd. I'm goin' to avenge my brothers. Come out and fight like a man!" There was no immediate response from the café, so he again hollered the same words just as they had been rehearsed in the boarding house. He repeated them three times before Dodd stepped into the doorway, gun held at his side.

"I don't want to shoot you Craven . . . go away!"

The sight of the gun in Dodd's hand struck terror in Craven's cowardly soul. He whipped his head around and looked straight at Taggert, hiding behind the boxes. Craven frantically yelled, "You told me he ain't got no gun!"

Taggert peeked from behind the crates and hastily fired at Sam, barely missing. Seeing Dodd with a pistol unnerved him, as well. Sam twisted into a crouch and returned fire, sending wooden crate splinters into Taggert's face. He wailed in pain and raised his arms. "Don't shoot, don't shoot me!" The Colt revolver clattered on the boardwalk as it dropped from his hand.

Sam recognized Taggert as one of Aussie Walker's bouncers and he knew Craven worked for him too. Wilbur stood babbling an incoherent apology, as Sam strode swiftly toward him. His pleadings were cut short as Sam knocked him to the ground with the barrel of the revolver. He leveled the pistol at the tip of Craven's nose, demanding, "Who put you up to this . . . Aussie Walker?"

Craven bawled an assent.

"Why? For heaven's sake, why?"

"I don't know, Sir, but he sure wants ya dead."

Chapter 24

"Hello, Charlie."

"Who's there?" A weak and rasping voice came from the confines of an overstuffed chair facing the window.

A sallow face peered around, eyes squinting, struggling feebly to see the source of the greeting.

"It's me, Charlie—Sam Dodd."

"Who?"

Sam came closer, stepping around to face Charlie Meyers so the old man could see him without having to strain.

"It's me, Charlie."

"Sam! . . . Is it really you? Yes!" A bright smile lit his face . . . a shaky hand extended in friendship.

"It sure is, Charlie."

"Sam, you're a sight fer these sore ol' eyes."

Sam was shocked at Charlie's appearance. He was never a big man, but the ravages of consumption had shriveled him into a sack of bones held together by loose, yellowish-gray skin. His eyes were so sunken, it was like peering into two deep mine shafts with but a flicker of light inside. A soiled green robe hung loosely on his shoulders, stained with small dark specks of blood. Charlie's remaining days on earth were few.

Sam pulled a chair up close.

"It's been a long time, Charlie."

"Yep . . . too long!" Charlie's eyes were now better focused on the face of his friend. When he noticed the empty sleeve, the pleasant smile changed to a sorrowful, questioning look. His trembling hand gestured toward the missing arm.

"Sam . . . wha . . . what happened?"

"I'll tell ya about it in a little while, but first what about you?"

"Thar's not too much to tell; been cooped up here for 'bout a year. Been thinkin' a lot about Sassy Mae and my boy. I ain't had much of a family like you has an' when ya git real close to meetin' yer Maker, ya think of what coulda been. Yer mind changes a lot; ya think of things ya missed an' things thet shoulda been done."

Speaking took a great deal of his energy and even though the wheezing became much more noticeable, Charlie wanted to talk.

"Done a lotta bad things, a few good ones. I've lived longer than anyone expected, got a few more days to go, thet's about all there is to it. Now . . . what happened to yer arm?"

Sam could tell disease had ravaged Charlie's body but his mind still had a sharp edge to it. He was alive because he wasn't ready to give up the known for the unknown. Within that small, thin frame resided a granite-rock will, resisting the call to the hereafter.

He didn't want to tell Charlie of the events of the past year, knowing he would be grieved by the loss of his former friends, but tell him he must.

With the mention of each death, Charlie gave a small gasp, a sucking of air. He seemed to shrink further into the overstuffed chair. Not a word did he utter, not until Sam had finished; even then it was a long time before Charlie spoke, tears filling his eyes.

"How about the others? How 'bout Sean, Clarence, and Porter?"

"I can't answer that, Charlie—I just don't know. I do know somebody else besides me is looking for them."

"What do ya mean, somebody else?"

Sam told him about the fictitious lawyer, P. T. Mellon from Denver, and how Seymour had lied about his existence.

Charlie shuddered, his frail form beginning to twitch . . . crying and coughing at the same time. Ultimately, the coughing became so pronounced, so violent that his whole body shook and blood bubbled from the corner of his lips. Sam immediately called for an attendant. The doctor and a nurse rushed to the side of their pain-racked, bent-over patient.

"You better leave, Mr. Dodd; it will be a while before Mr. Meyers will be able to talk with you."

Between gasps for breath, Charlie waved a quivering hand to Sam. "No . . . don't . . . go!" His struggle for air became more difficult, as feebly he tried to free himself from the attempt to get him into bed. "Sam . . . forgive . . ." Charlie collapsed to the floor. The attendant easily lifted his limp body, placing the unconscious figure onto the bed.

"Mr. Dodd, please leave!" The doctor was most emphatic. Sam departed.

The rather exclusive sanitarium was located on the outskirts of Colorado Springs, which had become a mecca for the wealthy seeking better health. Even foreigners sought the healing power of the clear mountain air, the unlimited sunshine, and the rugged alpine atmosphere. Sam walked to the center of the sleepy little village, found a small café, and ordered a meal.

I've got to think it all out, so many pieces, bits of information. Sam vividly recalled Charlie's behavior before he collapsed in desperation. *What did he mean . . . forgive? Forgive what?* Perhaps the afternoon would tell.

After lunch, Sam walked back up the hill to the sanitarium. Instead of being allowed into Charlie's room, Sam was ushered into the doctor's office where the physician was very direct. "Mr. Dodd, we can't let you see Mr. Meyers in the foreseeable future; he almost died this morning. I'm confident any more attacks of that severity would kill him. What did you do that caused such severe excitement?"

"I had to tell him about the deaths of some close friends."

"Oh, I see. That certainly would be quite disturbing. When Mr. Meyers awoke, I told him that you had gone . . . that upset him terribly. He scribbled out a note and insisted it be given to you immediately. It took an enormous effort on his part to hold the pen, much less write the note. However, he persisted. I meant to have one of our attendants find you, but since you are here . . ." The doctor reached forward and handed the envelope to Sam. The note was a just a few sporadic scrawls of almost illegible capital letters and a few discernible words. With difficulty, Sam deciphered the wildly erratic scribble.

"SAM . . . SEE–WILL UND–DE–K—HOM–DON–TEL–
SLI–K.
C–L–IE

"I couldn't make much out of it," commented the doctor. "Who's Will, a relative?"

"Your guess is as good as mine. Could be Will Poole, the sheriff of Silverville," replied Dodd. "It doesn't make much sense to me either, Doctor. When can I see Charlie again?"

"It could be days before he recovers enough to have visitors. We went through this once before, and it took several weeks before he got his strength back. He may not recover from this bout."

"I'm real sorry to hear that," replied Sam. Time was of the essence . . . he couldn't wait around; there was no time to spare. Leave he must.

"Doctor, someone could be out to kill Charlie. I know that sounds silly knowing his condition, but some of his closest acquaintances have been recently murdered."

"Why would anyone try? It's doubtful he'll live out the month."

"That well may be, but the ornery die hard, and Charlie is about the orneriest feller I've ever known." Sam stood silently before the bay window. For several seconds he stared at the snow-capped Rocky Mountains. Finally he spoke. "Doctor, death must be mighty horrifying for the unbelieving. I know

Charlie could die at any time. Has he been visited by a pastor or shown a desire to seek help from any of the local ministers? I worry about his soul. Charlie's a man in need of forgiveness and the comfort of knowin' Christ."

A warm smile covered the doctor's face. "We men of medicine can sometimes help the body, but it takes the Lord to soothe the mind. This sanitarium is a Bible-based institution and Charlie has been seeing a pastor quite regularly from the local Lutheran Church. We found out Charlie's family was German stock and probably Lutherans, so we asked Pastor Mace to look in on him. Pastor said he was a hard nut to crack but with Christian persistence, a door has been opened."

"Yeah, Charlie *is* a hard nut . . . one of the hardest." Sam's face softened. "Doctor, that's good news; eternity is a long time, and where he was headed . . . Well, I didn't think there was much of a chance he'd change."

"The pastor might have agreed with you. One day Mr. Meyers was arguing with him and he said, 'The Lord must not think I'm such a bad fella; look at all the wealth He's given me.' The pastor told him, 'The devil can give it to you as well.'" The doctor laughed heartily. "That really shook Charlie up! It never dawned on him that the devil can reward those who ignore God."

"That's a fact," replied Sam. "We're easy pickin's without the Lord." They shook hands and parted at the entryway.

Sam looked back up the hill, fully aware that he would never see Charlie Meyers again, at least not on this earth. He felt an enormous sense of relief knowing Charlie was talking to a man of God . . . and listening! Sam owed a great deal to that old miner. He had given him a good job when it was desperately needed and advised the family on investing in mining stock. The Dodds were now quite comfortable . . . thanks to Charlie. He had been a loyal friend, a good soldier, and a fair boss.

The scribbled note was his parting farewell to Sam. Plainly, it must be important to Charlie. What did it mean? Sam took the paper from his pocket and read it again, reflectively. At last, the message started to make some sense. Sam was forced to sit down on a nearby bench when the magnitude of the scrawled communication sank in.

Maybe Charlie wasn't writing about anyone named Will; he could have been . . . *no . . . he could be telling me about a will, the final disbursement of his immense wealth!*

Sam jumped to his feet and began to pace back and forth, trying to put it all together. *Charlie would leave millions to somebody . . . but who? Could Charlie want me to see his last will and testament? If so, where is it? Seymour ought to have a copy.* With trembling hands, Sam went over the note again. *DON–TEL–SLI–K. SLI–K—that could be Slick. He doesn't want me to tell Seymour!* Sam remembered how stricken Charlie looked when told about the mysterious P. T. Mellon, and Seymour's lying about his existence.

If there is a will, I'll bet Kenneth drafted it. HOM, that might mean home . . . a copy of the will must be in his home in Silverville. UND—DE–K—what can *that* mean?"

Sam felt a pain in his stomach. Once more he would have to delay going home, because it was now imperative that he return to Silverville. A wave of excitement swept over him, pushing the longing to go home out of his mind. If there was a will, it could point to the killer or give a clue to the mystery of the murders. But what if there was no last will and testament and the WILL was Will Poole? Whatever the outcome, the answer was ten thousand feet above sea level in the still-frigid air of Silverville, Colorado.

Chapter 25

THE TRAIN SHUDDERED TO A CREAKING STOP. "Denver," bellowed the conductor, "All off for the mile-high city of Dennnnnn-ver!"

The aisles filled with departing passengers, all edging slowly to the exits. Sam stood and stretched—no need to hurry; a four-hour layover was in store for him before his transfer to the narrow-gauge Denver and Rio Grande Railroad for the long climb up the Rockies to Silverville; ample time to visit the Sassy Mae Mine office for any messages.

It was a beautiful summer day and since time was not a factor, Sam decided to walk. Denver continued to change daily—no longer was it a Western outpost for miners and cowboys. It was a big city, complete with gas streetlights, sidewalks, multi-storied brick buildings, trolley cars, and an opera house. The railroads had transformed Denver into a noisy metropolis with most of the wares of the more sophisticated Eastern cities. A cloud of dust comprised of fine dirt and pulverized manure hung over the city, tainting the air with the distinct essence of stockyard. People were everywhere and the symphony of city sounds bounced off new brick and painted walls.

Sam didn't like it. The noise and bustle tightened around him like an invisible shroud. He hurried his steps to the Sassy Mae offices only to find new quarters. The wood-framed building was now red brick, three stories high. Gone was the red and black, gold trimmed sign, SASSY MAE MINES, CHARLIE MEYERS OWNER. In its place was scripted S. M. MINES, INC. and below, in small print, C. M. Meyers, Chairman of the Board. Embossed letters adorned cut glass windows, encased in the polished oak doors.

Fancy, Sam thought. *Very fancy. I wonder if anyone will remember me.* He was greeted by a studious young man sitting behind a large desk. He was impeccably dressed, high starched collar, hair slicked back, gold-rimmed spectacles perched on his small nose.

"May I help you, Sir?" he politely asked. The interior of the office was beautiful. A dignified full-figure painting of Charlie dominated one oak-paneled wall; the others tastefully displayed photographs of the mining properties Charlie owned.

The carpets were a deep rich green, and the divans and chairs were appropriately covered in complimentary brocade with subtle gold thread. The office reeked of wealth.

"Yes, you may. My name is Sam Dodd; I used to work for Charlie . . . I mean Mr. Meyers, a few years back. I took the liberty of havin' my mail sent to this office since Charlie and I are old friends." Sam felt uncomfortable . . . out of place. The old office had pine benches and desks. On the walls had hung maps of claims and an occasional picture from the *Police Gazette*. He now felt forwarding his mail here had been an imposition . . . intruding on strangers.

The young man's condescending smile didn't help. "I know of no such correspondence, but let me check with Mr. Nolan. What did you say your name was?"

"Is your boss Mick Nolan?"

"Yes, Sir."

"Tell him Sam Dodd would like a moment of his time."

Sam felt much better. Years ago, he had been responsible for the hiring of Patrick "Mick" Nolan, a tough, red-headed

Celtic kid with a temper and intellectual brightness matching his flaming hair. At the time, he could barely speak English; what few words he knew were hard to understand sifted through his Irish brogue. An empty belly had taught him a hardy work ethic while his sharp mind recognized the importance of book learning. Nolan's temper had cost him two jobs and when he applied for work at the Sassy Mae, his reputation as a trouble-maker preceded him. Sam took him on because of his personal cleanliness. He stood out from the rest of the grubby men lined up seeking employment. He put Nolan to work with jovial Otto Schmitz, taking care of the stock, cleaning stalls, and dumping manure. In the winter, the warmer jobs were underground. Even though sub-zero weather was the lot of those who labored above ground, the lad never complained.

"Don' vorry, Sam; aye take dis Irish und teach 'em to speak Inglish goot!"

Sam hoped Nolan would remember him, as the receptionist disappeared through the inner door. There was no doubt when the chubby, red-bearded, middle-aged Mick exploded into the room, grabbed Sam in a giant bear hug, and lifted him from the floor.

"Sam Dodd!" he boisterously exclaimed, "How the heck are ye!" As abruptly as he had lifted his former boss, he let him go. "Sam, what happened to your arm?"

"Mick, it's a long story." Sam smiled broadly and affectionately gripped Nolan's shoulder. "I don't know all the answers myself . . . but . . . if you have some good Irish cheer to share, maybe I'll tell ya what I know."

Nolan grinned. "By gora, a good jolt of Irish joy does limber the tongue. Come on into me office and rest a spell."

Before either had a chance to sit down, Mick Nolan rummaged around in his desk and brought out two envelopes, explaining "Afore they slip me mind, these came for ye—a letter from your dear Mary and what looks to be one from the Bureau of Indians in Tucson. I've been keepin' 'em for ye."

Sam had almost forgotten he had telegraphed requests to the Bureau of Indian Affairs and Arizona law enforcement, inquiring into the well-being of Indian agent Clarence Devlin. The requests had been made months ago. That could wait; the letter from Mary took precedence. Sam eagerly tore the envelope open, excited about news from home—but before he could read more than 'everyone is fine,' Mick's office filled up with old acquaintances. Sam stuffed the messages back in his pocket as concerned friends gathered around, curious about the loss of his arm and wanting to know all the details of the last few years. The letter, he would read later when he was alone and could enjoy every word. The telegram could wait, as well. Mary's letter had already eased the misery of having to return to Silverville.

It was difficult breaking away from Mick and the others; Sam barely made the train. The Irish whiskey and the friendly reception created a warm glow inside . . . and it felt good.

As soon as the train began to pick up speed, he reached for the communiqués. Curiosity led him to read the business letter first, having seen enough of Mary's letter to sense that everything was all right. *I'll save the best to last; it's a long ride to Silverville.*

Mr. Sam Dodd
c\o Sassy Mae Mines
Denver, Colorado

Dear Mr. Dodd:

Forgive tardy response to inquiry about agent Clarence Devlin. At time, no information available. Devlin disappeared January 1880. Recently learned of death. On expedition into White Mountains, he and companion captured by Apaches. Devlin tortured. Companion still missing; fear worst. Apaches show no compassion for clergy. Cavalry detail found and identified Devlin. After months, given up hope of finding other man alive. Sorry to send sorrowful news.

Respectfully yours,
R. R. Winiecki
Director of Indian Affairs
Tucson, Arizona

Devlin's dead as well . . . killed by Apaches! Sam shuddered and tried not to think about the way Clarence must have died . . . but he couldn't help the image of his friend buried up to his chin in sand, baked by the sun with his hair and his eyelids removed, or hot coals heaped on his stomach, sharpened sticks placed in the rectum to embellish pain. Apaches enjoyed making their captives suffer . . . an excruciating death . . . the slower the better. Sam crumpled the letter and threw it to the floor.

Wait a minute! Sam quickly reached down, retrieved it, and smoothed the wrinkled paper on his knee. *What's this? The Apache has no respect for the cloth? Was Clarence's companion a minister? How come his body wasn't found? Apaches rarely take male captives; they're too much trouble.* Questions flooded Sam's mind. *This is the third time a member of the clergy has surfaced in this puzzle. In Illinois, a young minister was asking the whereabouts of Sean Sullivan; there was the blue-eyed circuit rider in Brookville, Kansas; and now, a minister travelin' with Clarence Devlin. The mysterious, blue-eyed fisherman in Paris, Illinois . . . the blue-eyed killer of Otto . . . could it be the same assassin posing as a man of God?* Sam laughed to himself, *Get yourself together, Dodd—you're imaginin' things! No. It couldn't be, too far-fetched, too coincidental. I must have had too many Irish whiskeys!*

The train was chugging along mightily, well within the mountains, before Sam reached for Mary's letter. His heart warmed just seeing her handwriting.

My dearly beloved husband,

Everything is fine with us; we are all healthy and in good spirits. However, we miss you so very much and can't wait until the day you ride into view. The girls and I will cover you with kisses and your sons will hug you gladly. You would be so proud of the job the boys are doing, especially David. Since you've been gone, he is the man in charge. Our good neighbors, the Wilsons and the Herbertsons, have loaned us the use of some of their men. Tom Chastain, Amos Wilson's top hand, spent weeks helping us round up strays. Tom has been a great help. The cattle wintered well in the lower pastures. We lost very little stock, in spite of the heavy snows.

Matthew is doing very well; it is surprising what he can do with only one hand.

Sam lowered the letter as he thought about the love he had for that brave little boy and the terrible price he had paid to save his father. It was hard to keep the tears from welling in his eyes. He continued to read:

The girls are fine. Asa, the oldest Herbertson boy, is by the ranch quite often, offering to help. I think he has an interest in Sarah and she in him. He's a fine lad—good manners, hard worker, and good Christian upbringing. Sarah thinks he's handsome and blushes a lot when he's around. I wouldn't be surprised if we gain a son-in-law. Sweetheart, come home soon—we miss you dearly.

Your loving wife,
Mary

P. S. We have been very blessed lately; a Methodist circuit minister has been by on several occasions. He is a wonderful, kindly young man . . . so intelligent! We talk about the Good Book and many other things. He is anxious to meet you and asks when you will be home. So do we all!

Sam hurried up from his seat and into the aisle. With lips pressed tightly together, he jerked open the pullman door and stepped outside onto the frigid platform before he vomited. "My God," he gasped as he clutched the rail, "He's there!"

★ ★ ★

The cold mountain air helped clear Sam's head, diminishing the panic somewhat. There was little doubt the circuit rider Mary mentioned was the flaxen-haired assassin. His first impulse was to pull the cord, stop the train, and head immediately for home.

Sam breathed deep through his clenched teeth. *Think! . . . I've got to think real clear!* The thought of a vicious, cold-blooded killer in the midst of his unsuspecting family pushed him again to the edge of panic. In spite of the cold, he felt the chilled sweat down the middle of his back, the stomach contractions, the desire to vomit again which had to be suppressed . . . he had to think . . . reason and remain calm.

He asked out loud, "Lord, what'll I do?" James 1:4 came to mind. Sam reentered the coach, reached into his carpetbag and brought out the small Bible he carried with him. He read . . . "Let patience have her perfect work, that ye may be perfect and entire, wanting nothing."

The passage calmed him . . . *Be patient, Sam . . . think it out . . . you will want for nothing.* With trembling hand, he reread Mary's letter . . . then once more . . . then again, digging for additional information, trying to read between the lines. Mary stated the minister had been to the ranch more than once. That was encouraging; if he intended to do them harm he wouldn't have waited around, visiting on several occasions; he would have killed them and left. *No . . . he has a reason to wait, he's after someone else . . . me . . . he's waiting for me. I'm the target. So far, there's been no mention of the families of his other victims having been harmed, just the squad members themselves.*

The fear was beginning to subside; the strong desire to throw up was gone but the bitter taste of bile remained. *I wonder if he knew about Mary's letter? Can he know I suspect him as being a murderer posing as a minister?* Sam twisted this important thought around, turned it over, viewed it from every angle. *I doubt if he suspects—he probably feels safe. I've told no one but Will Poole of my suspicions. I didn't broach the subject with Seymour.* The thought of the lawyer triggered another tightening of his jaw, a melancholy of friendship betrayed. *Kenneth . . . or should I call you Judas? I know you're mixed up in this, right up to your crooked elbows, and I bet there's more than thirty pieces of silver involved.*

The more Sam mulled it over, the more confident he felt that his family was in no immediate danger. *The killer has already had ample time to harm them. They could be in more trouble if I were home. I wonder if the preacher is working alone. He's bound to try to kill me again, this time up close! To keep his identity secret, he'd probably murder anyone nearby. Mary and the kids might actually be safer with me away. What could I do if I were there anyway? Wait for him to shoot or knife me as he did poor Otto? What good is a one-armed rancher against this cunning madman? He mutilated Clarence Devlin, drowned Sherry and that girl, gunned down Jethro, and he's got to be the best gunfighter around to come within inches of killin' me from over a thousand yards. What good could I do against that? I'm no match for him and I can't put David or the younger boys up against him either . . . that'd be leading lambs to slaughter. I can't have him arrested—the evidence is too circumstantial and impossible to prove. What jury would believe a minister is a professional killer? I'm not even totally sure that I am right . . . what if this pastor visiting Mary is a real circuit rider? I have to find out . . . I've got to be sure.*

Sam couldn't sit still; he stood up in the weaving, jostling train and paced. *If he is the killer, I've got to get him away from the ranch. But how? He's bound to wait 'til I return but if I delay too long, he could hurt one of the children or Mary, knowing danged well that would bring me running.*

The other passengers watched the tall, one-armed man pacing ever faster up and down the centerway, mumbling to himself. Sam was oblivious to their stares, his mind and soul at the ranch. "He'll stay 'til I get back or maybe discover where I am, then come get me. That's it! Make him come and get me!"

The idea of enticing the killer away from his family struck Sam like a thunderbolt; he visibly stiffened. Still deep in thought, he sat down again and gazed through the window, interrupted by a hand on his shoulder. An elderly gentleman sitting behind him asked. "Are you feeling all right?"

"Yes . . . yes Sir, I'm fine . . . thank you for your concern." Sam settled back in his seat, watching the landscape race by. Silverville was just minutes away; passengers shifted about in their seats, seeing to their luggage and coats. Awakened riders rubbed their eyes and the ladies adjusted their hats.

"Silverville, next stop," barked the conductor.

Chapter 26

The wind whipped wet particles of snow around Sam's legs as he stepped down from the pullman car to the frozen ground. He pulled his coat tighter about his body. "Mid-May and still blizzarding—a fit place for Eskimos and penguins!"

Silverville! An untamed, hot-blooded town perched on a frozen bonanza of silver ore. The bustling mining town lay 10,187 feet above sea level, yet was dwarfed by the surrounding mountains. Hunkered down under a thin layer of gray wood smoke, Silverville was a dirty speck in the middle of pristine white ranges jutting thousands of feet skyward. To the east and west were impressive snow-covered peaks and to the north, pushing 13,000 feet, was lung-busting Horse Fly Pass. The headwaters of the Arkansas River were to the south. Dominating the rugged skyline, towered Mammoth Mountain, a granite behemoth, dwarfing, intimidating, and dazzling all who gazed upon its majestic white face.

Many passengers crowded into the small station, seeking warmth around the potbellied stove. Sam contemplated joining them inside but time was of the essence. He turned into the cutting wind and started down the hill to the center of town. A familiar voice drew him up short.

"Well, if it ain't Sam Dodd himself. I didn't expect to see you back here so soon. Figgered you would be at the ranch roundin' up yer cows."

Sam turned at the sound of the genial greeting, immediately recognizing the rich baritone voice of his friend, Sheriff Will Poole, emerging from the shadows of the depot.

"Howdy, Will . . . you can bet yer buckboard I'd rather be there than in this God-forsaken icebox. I won't be around any more than I have to. What are you doin' lurking around in the cold shade?"

"I'm jest naturally curious an' neighborly about who wants to visit our fair city. You can meet some real interesting folks on incomin' trains."

Will's eyes never left the scurrying passengers as he lightheartedly addressed his friend. The sheriff observed each one, noting luggage, dress, mannerisms, and especially their faces. Will Poole missed nothing; his memory for people, dates, and places was legendary.

"Wait a spell while I look over this bunch and I'll buy yer supper; shouldn't take but a few minutes."

Sam knew it would take more than a few minutes; the train was crowded to overflowing. Miners, salesmen, emigrants, prospectors, gamblers, ladies of questionable—and some of unquestionable—reputation had boarded the narrow-gauge Denver and Rio Grande in Denver. In a few short years the town's population had exploded to well over 30,000, many heeding the siren-song of silver. Entrepreneurs, medicine men, all form and substance of humankind could be found crammed into this alpine mecca, each seeking their fortune by fair means or foul. Will Poole's work was cut out for him, sifting through the plenitude. Although Sam was in a hurry—desperate to look for Charlie Meyers' last will and testament, find it, and head home as fast as possible—he didn't want to rush off and be rude to his good friend. A few more hours would make little difference.

"Happy to wait while you do your job, Will. Take your time."

They waited for all the passengers and until those departing had boarded.

"All aboard!" called the conductor. The train groaned and shuddered, wheels spinning, then lurched forward as the ejected sand brought friction between rail and wheel. As the steam energized the pistons, the train started to move.

Will's eyes were still searching when unexpectedly, a carpetbag thudded to the platform and a dapper little man nimbly alighted, looking furtively in all directions.

"I'll be right back, Sam." He leapt up the steps and in one fluid motion, picked up the carpetbag in one hand and with the other, gathered the coat jacket of the startled passenger. Will shoved him toward the moving caboose. Sam could not hear the conversation over the noise of the engine but the passenger was obviously not pleased, waving his arms about in violent objection. The sheriff threw the carpetbag onto the deck of the caboose and let go of his coat. The frustrated man looked at Will, then at his departing clothes. As the locomotive picked up speed, he stumbled down the slippery tracks after his belongings. In the distance, Sam could see the man on the rear platform, waving his fist wildly, apoplectic with anger and screaming at the top of his lungs. Just as well, he couldn't hear a word over the noise of the train.

"Friend of yours?"

"Nah, just an old acquaintance. Mighty handy with a deck of cards. Let's go eat!"

"Yep, good idea. I haven't eaten since Denver." Sam didn't bother to tell Will his last meal was never fully digested. "We have lots to talk about. I sorely need your help."

On the walk to the restaurant Sam related the whole story, the qualms, the facts, the myriad of conjectures, his gut feeling that a minister—or someone posing as a member of the cloth—was potentially a mass murderer.

"A circuit rider who's a killer? That's hard to swallow, Sam."

"Will, the most beautiful of God's angels was Lucifer." Sam reached into his coat and extracted the two letters. "Read this first." He handed the telegram to Will.

"Is this Devlin another of your comrades?"

"Yes. Now read this." He passed Mary's letter across the table.

Sam watched Will's face soften as he read Mary's warm, affectionate letter. Halfway through, he looked up and smiled. "That's good news about Matthew."

"Read the postscript, Will."

He saw Poole flinch as the message sunk in. "Merciful saints, Sam, do you think it's him?"

"There's no reason to think otherwise. We live in too remote an area to attract even the most evangelical minister more than once. This one has been there several times asking about me. There's not enough ranchers there to warrant his preachin' time. I doubt if he suspects I know about him."

"Have you told anyone else about your suspicions?"

"Nope. You're the only one I have ever talked to about it."

"Darn!" Sheriff Poole cursed, "What a slimy character! He probably feels perfectly safe. Who would ever suspect such a villainous disguise? I know I wouldn't."

"Will . . . he's there now, close to my family . . . waiting for me."

"Friend, you must be dyin' a thousand deaths. What are you doing here?" Poole pulled his chair closer to Sam. "What can I do to help? Sam, I hope you're wrong!"

"So do I."

"Maybe we should telegraph Laramie and have Sheriff Bedlow send a few deputies to protect them."

"I thought of it . . . but that would alert the killer and possibly endanger my family. Anyone who could gun down Jethro would have no trouble with a deputy or two. Besides, what would we say? Go arrest a minister of God because of our hunches? Nate Bedlow would think we'd lost our senses. No. It could put Mary and the kids at great risk."

"You're right, Sam; Nate *would* think we were teched. What do you think we oughta do?"

"First, let's go to Charlie Meyers' home and look around." Sam dug into his pocket once more and handed Charlie's scribbled note to his agitated friend. "Look at this. Whatever is at Charlie's could possibly be somethin' important."

The lawman frowned as he tried to decipher the scrawls. "Will, could Charlie be talkin about *you*? Could *you* be the *Will* in the note?"

"Hardly think so. Charlie and me was just passin' acquaintances. I didn't run in his circles, especially since he got richer than Midas."

"Don't think so either," said Sam. "Does Charlie's place have a deck?"

"Why do you ask?"

"Look at the note, DE–K, that could be deck. UND—that's German for *and*. Could it be, *and* deck? That doesn't make much sense."

"No, it don't. Besides, ain't no deck at Charlie's—just one big porch front and back. Could it be *desk*? That makes more sense."

"Could be. Yep, it sure could be."

"One way to find out," remarked Sam as he got up from the chair. "Let's go take a look."

"Right now?" exclaimed Will. "It's turning dark."

"Right now. There's no time to lose, knowing who is hangin' around my ranch."

They stepped out into the twilight. The snow had stopped and the prevailing westerly winds had pushed the clouds away. The western sky was rose-tinted by the setting sun while pinspot stars cut diamond holes through the eastern blue.

Beautiful, Sam thought, *but still bone-chilling cold.* "Will, do you ever get used to this icebox weather?"

"I don't much care for the winter, but I do love these balmy summer evenings."

"Yeah . . . balmy." Sam couldn't help but grin. People didn't come to Silverville for the weather or to build permanent homes with white picket fences; they came to make money and get the heck out. The walk up Walnut Street warmed the bones. Any walk at ten thousand feet was an exertion, especially if one wasn't used to it. Both were breathing heavily when they arrived at the darkened mansion. No lights anywhere; the house was locked-up tight.

"What do we do, break in?" asked Sam.

"Nah, there's a caretaker out back, lives over the carriage house."

"When did Charlie build this?" Sam was visibly impressed by the huge three-storied Victorian.

"Gossip is Charlie wanted to show up Horace Tabor and that other Meyer over in Leadville. Both have mansions. Charlie wanted to show them he was the real Colorado silver king. You think it's fancy outside, wait 'til you see what's inside. Too bad Charlie didn't have much time to enjoy it."

A light could be seen in the carriage house window. Will climbed the stairs and knocked on the door. "Elmer . . . it's me, Will Poole."

A small elderly man with a coal lamp in hand opened the door. Grumpily he asked, "What do you want, Sheriff, at this time of night?"

"Get the keys, Elmer, we have to get into the mansion."

"What fer?"

"None of your business . . . get the keys."

"Who's that with you?"

"None of your business."

"Can't. Come back tomorrow. I got to get permission from Mr. Meyers' lawyer, Mr. Seymour, before I can let you in. He was real firm when he told me that. He ain't gonna like this."

"Elmer Smith, what are you going to tell him about the broken window in the back door?"

"There's no broken winder in the back door."

"There's goin' to be in about two minutes if you don't get the keys!"

"Oh . . . you wouldn't," then noting the grim look on Will Poole's face, "Yep, guess you would . . . be right with you . . . I'll put on me pants." He turned away grumbling, "Mr. Seymour ain't gonna like this!"

Mumbling under his breath, the caretaker led the way to the rear of the mansion, opened the back door, and stepped inside. "Well, here you are."

Sam spoke for the first time. "Does Charlie have a desk?"

"Yes, he does. Upstairs off the big bedroom. He has a small office up there."

Sam and Will looked at each other in relief. "Lead the way," directed Poole.

Elmer lit the gas jets inside the kitchen door, then methodically lit each one as they moved through the house to the spiral stairs. At the head of the stairwell was the door to Charlie's bedroom and office. Elmer selected another key from the ring and opened the door. "Mr. Seymour ain't going to like this!" Another gaslight was ignited, illuminating the room and a large roll top desk in the far corner. It too was locked.

"Will, hand me that poker next to the hearth," said Sam.

"You can't do that!" exclaimed the caretaker. "Mr. Seymour'll have your job, Sheriff."

Without hesitation, Will seized the poker and jammed it under the latch and popped up the roll top, exposing the small drawers inside.

Sam quickly pulled each one open and systematically reviewed the contents; old letters, invoices, shipping orders . . . nothing peculiar, nothing that shed any light. Sam shrugged his shoulders. "Looks like we may have read Charlie's note wrong."

"Mr. Seymour was just here the other day sorting through the papers. He locked that desk and he has the key. Look what you done to it!" Elmer pointed to the shattered wood and the bent lock. Both ignored him.

"Whatever was there, looks like ol' Slick got it," Sam said dejectedly.

"Let's not give up so easy . . . Sam, let me see Charlie's note again."

Sam got out the scribbled message. The constant folding and unfolding hadn't improved the legibility.

"It's very hard to make out," commented Will.

"It confused me—it still does in part. I could make out my name and Charlie's. The SLI–K is obviously Seymour. SEE is clear—he wanted me to see something or somebody. At first I thought he wanted me to find some guy named Will but you're the only Will I happen to know. Then I figured maybe he had a *will* he wanted me to *see*. A last will and testament could sure tell us who might have a motive to kill. When Charlie meets his Maker, someone on this here earth will be very rich. I figured HOM meant *home*, and that had to be this place. I reasoned he didn't want me to *tell Seymour*. That was strange; Seymour's been his legal advisor for years. The UND I couldn't figure out. Looks like German, or it could be part of a word; the other letters you can't read."

"Was Charlie a secretive kinda person?" Will asked.

"He sure as heck was! He was always fearful of repeating his early years of poverty. Charlie hid money in the dangdest places, stuffed it into the toe of boots, sewed it up in the lining of his jackets, hid it inside coffee cans in the kitchen, and only *he* knows where he's buried thousands of gold coins. We found over ten thousand dollars under a loose floor board in his office. He was real distrustful of banks. Only in the past few years, after he served on the boards of several banks in Denver, would he put any of his money in one. Why'd you ask?"

"Old habits are hard to break. He might have hid the will in his desk. The UND—in his note, could be tellin' us where, it could mean *under*. How about lookin' under the desk?"

"Or under one of the drawers!" exclaimed Sam as he leaped out of the chair and toward the desk. "Eureka!" Sam shouted. Tacked to the bottom of the middle drawer was a brown envelope filled with official-looking documents.

"What did ya find?" asked an excited Will Poole.

Sam didn't immediately answer. He took the envelope's contents close to the gaslight and became deeply engrossed in reading papers.

"Well . . . what does it say?"

Sam turned towards Will with a pained look on his face. "It says a lot. It's Charlie Meyers' Last Will and Testament." Tears came to his eyes as he handed it to Will. "Big-hearted old fool. He wants to give the members of our squad his fortune. Instead, it's become a death warrant for those he cares about. No wonder he was so shaken when I told him about all the dyin'."

"This explains the motive for the killings," said Poole, after he had finished the document.

"It explains just about everything. The will is real carefully drawn, so the money only goes to the men in the squad who survive Charlie. None of their wives or the families get a dime if the husband is deceased."

"Why would he do that?"

"Charlie hated women, and Seymour knew it. He must have taken advantage of Charlie's dislikes when he drafted the will. Seymour is the executor." Sam dejectedly sat down, the vitality drained from his body. He felt old . . . very old and very sad. "I knew Kenneth had a lot of bad in him, but plotting the deaths of all his fellow squad members? It's too much to take. It's hard to believe he'd do such a thing."

"Didn't you say a couple of Aussie Walker's boys tried to kill you in Santa Fe?"

"Yeah . . . what of it?"

"The rumor around town is that Seymour is heavily in debt to Walker. He could be involved. He could know about the will. Aussie would destroy the whole Union Army if profit was involved."

"That makes a lot more sense, but under no circumstances can Seymour be absolved of his share of guilt. We were to be murdered, making the pot bigger for those who were left. All the names are in this will—there were twelve of us squad members who survived the war. Norm Moore died from old battle wounds in '68, leaving eleven of us. We know six died within the last year, and who knows about the rest."

"One thing's for sure, it'll be hard to prove Seymour was guilty of the murders," commented Poole. "From what you have told me, the killer covered his tracks pretty well. I bet it'll be next to impossible to prove Seymour had anything to do with it. He likely isn't the gunman and neither is Walker. Just because slick Kenneth is a beneficiary doesn't prove his guilt."

"You know and I know he has blood up to his crooked elbows," exploded Sam, angrily.

"You shouldn't be sayin' such rotten things about Mr. Seymour," shouted a high, shrill voice. A nervous Elmer Smith had been listening intently from across the room. The accusations made against his employer were too much to take. In the excitement, his presence was totally forgotten. What he had heard was shocking information . . . and he didn't believe a word of it.

"Elmer," threatened the sheriff, "you forget everything you heard. Open your mouth and I'll lock you up and forget where I put the key! . . . Do you hear?"

"You bet, Sheriff."

"Do you understand? I mean it!"

"Yes, Sheriff, I won't tell a soul, not even my wife. You have my solemn promise . . . not a word!" Elmer cowered in the corner until neither Sam nor Will was looking, then noiselessly slipped through the door, crept downstairs, and headed toward town as fast as his skinny legs would carry him.

Chapter 27

THEY WERE WORSE THAN HE EXPECTED. *Birds of a feather*, Quinn thought to himself. One could hardly expect Aussie to hire anyone smarter than himself. *Birds of a feather hire each other is more appropriate.*

For weeks, he had been putting up with these two bores and as each day passed, they grew more disgusting. It had turned into a loathsome journey to the Dodd ranch; the long train ride to Denver, the transfer to Laramie, securing horses and equipment, then the rugged climb into the high country. Neither Clem nor Abel Jebson had endeared themselves to Quinn on the arduous trip. Quinn was fastidious, while both Abel and his older brother were walking grime, failing to wash either themselves or the cooking utensils. After the second day, Quinn prepared his own food and ate alone.

Shedding their blood will be pure joy, but for now, they're more useful to me alive, Quinn admitted to himself.

Aussie Walker had signed their death warrant when he sent them along. Jacob Quinn had warned him that the fewer people who knew his identity the better, especially if he had to don the garb of a circuit rider. At the appropriate time he would dispose of them, when their usefulness was over. Presently, he had them guarding the two passes into the Dodd valley; one was stationed on the bluffs overlooking the upper stretches of the Laramie River, watching the approach from the north. The other was covering the trail from the east, over Deadman's Pass from Rustic on the Cache la Poudre River. Another route from the south was by the headwaters of the Laramie around Chambers Lake, but the chances of a rider making it to the ranch through the snow-covered passes was remote, at least until summer.

Clem Jebson was a wiry, stoop-shouldered Faro dealer who doubled in whatever dirty work Aussie wanted accomplished, from collecting debts to roughing up whores who didn't share their full take. In his younger days he had been a cowhand, rustler, train robber and, supposedly, he rode with Quantrill during the war. Although both he and his younger brother were competent with firearms, Clem's specialty was a knife. He enjoyed cutting people. Sharpening the sizable hunting blade sheathed in his belt was his favorite pastime. Whetstone in hand, he'd sit by the fire, honing the edge. Most of the hair on his forearms was gone, dry-shaved by testing the blade's sharpness. He wore a hat at all times, pulled tightly down, almost covering his eyebrows. This was an attempt to hide the large scar on his head and the absence of the upper half of his ugly left ear, mutilated in the only knife fight where he had emerged second best. A dour look constantly marked his face, magnified by a drooping handlebar mustache; the tips dangled below his chin. His mentality matched his left ear.

The younger Jebson, in his late twenties, wore an unkempt, wispy blond beard, very sparse. Where Clem was usually silent, Abel possessed a perennially open mouth, emitting incessant noise or babbling chatter. When he wasn't talking he was humming, singing out loud, or whistling through his well-spaced teeth; intermittently, he belched, spat, or was flatulent. A wad of snuff swelled his lower jaw and the stained teeth and lips were hard to ignore since his mouth was eternally open. Abel considered himself quite a gun hand; when eighteen, he killed a drunk in a barroom shoot-out. His victim had a bad reputation so Abel inherited the glory of gunning down a wanted desperado. For his gallantry, he received a small reward. Talking about his notorious exploit was his favorite subject; the story had acquired numerous embellishments over the years. The gunfight took place in the Silver Dollar Saloon in Leadville, where Abel's job was wiping tables, emptying spittoons, and sweeping the floor. His broom happened to hit the boot of the drunken desperado, who immediately took offense. He pulled out his six-shooter and shot wildly in Abel's direction. Abel ran around the tables, darting, skipping from one foot to the other, while the bleary-eyed gunman blasted away.

"Stand still, you dirty dog!" demanded the drunk. Abel was in no mind to comply. Finally, in terrified desperation, he took a dive for the floor behind the bar only to hear the sottish bully shout, "Now I gotcha!"

The barkeep's loaded sawed-off shotgun was handy, right before Abel's eyes. In mindless panic, he grabbed it and fired both barrels through the bar. Silence. The smell of gunpowder filled the air, but there wasn't a sound.

Abel peeked over the bar and saw his assailant sprawled outstretched in a pool of blood . . . dead! No one had witnessed the shooting. The few patrons beat a hasty retreat after the first wild shot; not a soul came forward to refute Abel's later embellishments. His picture was taken by the local press standing next to the dead body of one Roscoe Strate, wanted by Wells Fargo for armed robbery and the shooting of a guard. There was a $500 reward, dead or alive. The story made the Denver press and the young Jebson's reputation. He carried the photo and clippings with him at all times.

Abel was constantly practicing, drawing his Colt single-action .45 and dry firing. "Bang!" he would say. "See that draw? Purty fast, wouldn't ya say?"

Quinn swore he would kill him first.

Weeks together had lulled both Clem and Abel into passive tolerance. They followed Quinn's orders out of fear of Aussie. They had no reason to be afraid of the baby blue-eyed, flaxen-haired young man who was about as pretty as they come and who was so fussy about keeping clean. He never raised his voice, never seemed to get angry, and always wore a sly grin on his velvety face. Quinn was too uppity to suit either of them. Wouldn't drink from the same bottle, bathed at every opportunity, didn't even chew or cuss.

"Clem, Aussie has this guy all wrong." Clem nodded his head in agreement.

Quinn had expected Sam Dodd to be at the ranch and was surprised he wasn't. He and the Jenkins brothers set up camp deep in the timber, miles from the Dodd spread, observing from afar.

"Where do you think he is?" asked Abel after the second day.

"Who knows," Quinn responded. "He could be anywhere close abouts. He could be visiting neighbors, rounding up strays, getting supplies in Laramie or, now that the passes are open, he could be over the mountains in Rustic. Maybe he's selling cows in Fort Collins. We can't do anything but wait and be patient."

They were patient for two weeks. They made fun of Quinn when they saw him for the first time, dressed as a minister.

"Well, looky here! If you don't look saintly in that outfit. Whatcha goin' to do, pray 'em and slay 'em?" Abel fell to the ground laughing at his own humor.

Quinn just smiled. "I have to pay a visit and find out where Dodd is. No stranger can ask questions without raising suspicions. People won't doubt the sincerity of a reverend or suspect that his inquiries are anything but godly. Both of you are to stand watch at the two approaches. If you can be assured of dry-gulching Dodd successfully, then do it; if you have any doubts, come back here to the camp and tell me. No long shots . . . take no chances. Do you understand?"

Both nodded in the affirmative. Aussie had lectured them about strict obedience to whatever "Mr. Smith" wanted. Neither had any fear of Mr. Smith, even though Aussie had intimated he'd be deadly to cross.

"What do you want us to do when the sun goes down?" asked Clem.

"Come back to camp every night after dark. Not much chance Dodd will travel at night. After I find out what I can, I'll meet you back here tomorrow night. In the meanwhile stay covered, stay out of sight." The brothers again nodded, saddled their horses, and rode off. Quinn checked his garb once more, secreted a small derringer in his boot, and headed for the ranch house.

"Ma . . . lone rider's coming up the valley," shouted Matthew.

Mary went to the door to have a look. At that distance, all they could make out was the dark figure of a rider on a bay horse.

"Know who it is, Ma?" asked Sarah. Quietly she had slipped up behind her mother, curious about the approaching horseman.

"Who's coming Ma?" asked Betsy, pulling on her mother's apron. "Who is it?"

"Don't know. Matthew, run down to the barn and let David and Daniel know someone's riding this way. Girls, you know what to do."

"Yes, Ma." Both girls disappeared within the house and moments later, the thick wooden shutters began to close with bars dropped across them to hold them in place. Mary moved back a few steps to where she could easily reach for the rifle just inside the door.

"Sarah, baby John inside?"

"He's in here, playin' under the kitchen table."

"Keep him inside."

The dogs had scented the rider and began to bark. Mary looked toward the barn in time to see David in the loft, gun in hand.

The rider stopped at the bottom of the knoll. "Mrs. Dodd," he shouted. "I'm Reverend Smith, riding a new circuit. Do you care if I come up and talk about the gospel and our dear Lord?"

"Reverend Smith," Mary joyously called, "You come up here right now! You're as welcome as can be!"

Mary hurriedly walked down the hill to greet the minister, who swung down from the saddle only to remount quickly; both dogs growled viciously and lunged at his boots. They circled the bay, growling. As Mary grew near she called them off and extended her hand. The Reverend brought the mare to a halt, leaned over, and grabbed Mary's hand, squeezing it gently. "Peace be with you." His smile was warm and friendly, infectious, trustworthy. Mary returned it in kind.

"This is a great occasion, Reverend; you are the first real minister to visit us here and we are deeply honored. I apologize for the behavior of our dogs."

"Think nothing of it—after all, I'm a stranger."

Mary was thrilled! The very idea that a learned man of God was visiting delighted her immensely. When he entered the house, he removed his black hat, displaying a tousled, full head of yellow hair. He moved like a man in his early thirties— agile, light on his feet. His voice, however, was of someone older, deeply resonant and controlled. His use of language denoted a good education. Mary could readily see that this was no *typical* backwoods preacher called by God to minister to the frontier. She looked forward to a good talk about Scripture. To her disappointment, there was little of it. He seemed much more interested in discussing the family, the ranch, the immediate neighbors, the cattle operation, and news of the outside world. Even so, the conversation was extremely stimulating; little Sarah was fascinated, soaking up every word, sitting on the edge of her chair as her mother answered question after question. The afternoon passed quickly.

"Reverend Smith, could you stay for supper? The boys have had their chores and haven't had the opportunity to know you. Would you like to stay the night? We use our old sod house for storage and a bunkhouse. It's better sleeping than on the trail."

"You sure I'll be no trouble?"

"No trouble at all," laughed Mary. "In fact, you can work for your supper. After the dishes are out of the way, we can have a Bible lesson. It's not often we get a pastor to lead us. Do you accept the job?"

"Of course, I would be delighted."

"Supper won't be anything out of the ordinary—just what we have on hand, mostly leftovers."

"I'm sure it will be wonderful."

Supper was indeed special. Sarah and Mary bustled around the pantry and kitchen, preparing an extraordinary meal. Bean soup, elk steak, mashed potatoes, gravy, dandelion greens, fresh bread, and apple pie. It was delicious . . . and a welcome relief from the awful grub prepared on the trail.

"Where did you attend divinity school?" asked Mary.

"Harvard."

"Where's that?" asked Susan.

"Back East—Cambridge, Massachusetts," grinned Jacob Quinn. "You have never heard of Harvard?"

"No, Sir." Susan was embarrassed. The way he had cocked his eyebrow made her feel ignorant. "Is it a big place?"

Mary interrupted, "No, Susan, but it is the oldest. It was established just sixteen years after the Pilgrims landed in Plymouth. Godly men built it as an institution to promote Christianity. The first major contribution to the school was by John Harvard, a minister. It was named after him."

"My, my, Mary Dodd—you surprise me!" exclaimed Quinn. "Where did you learn so much about Harvard?"

"My pastor back home in Illinois graduated from Harvard Divinity. He was very proud of it. You should be too."

"I am; the ideas I was exposed to changed my life."

Quinn reflected on his first year at the college. It was a slow transition from belief to disbelief. Some of the more contemporary professors brought to light the theories of Charles Darwin, the writings of Ralph Waldo Emerson and his disciple, the brilliant Nietzsche. The young German philosopher's two papers, "The Antichrist" and "Behold Evil and Good," swept through the campus like wildfire. His ethical nihilism appealed to Jacob Quinn, who found it to be a philosophy which gave little reason and purpose to man's existence, condemning Christianity as a source of man's troubles. Quinn adopted this new logic, which unshackled him from any previously accepted moral constraints.

But all this talk about Harvard was leading nowhere; it was time to ask about Sam Dodd.

"Mary, do you and the children run this ranch alone?"

"No," Mary sighed, "I have a husband, a good husband; we expect him home any day now. In fact, when we saw a rider approaching in the distance, we hoped it was him. Instead, it was you."

"Yeah," piped in Matthew, "we really miss him."

"Where is he then?"

"It's a long story," Mary responded sadly.

In his best pastoral voice he comfortingly offered, "I have time . . . tell me."

When Mary had finished, "Reverend Smith" asked, "How do you know he'll be home soon?"

"Well, mail delivery is nonexistent back here but over the mountains in Beaver Flats, there's a post office servicing all the men timbering for the railroad. Sam has sent us several letters and when somebody heads this way, we get the mail.

"Last week, our neighbors, the Herbertsons, brought us two letters. One was pretty old but the other was sent from Denver this past April. Sam said he had a bit of business to attend to, then he would be right home. I expected him weeks ago, since several of the passes are open."

"You must be very anxious. I can't wait to meet him; he sounds like quite a man."

"We love him very much," Mary quietly stated. Heads nodded all around.

"Enough of this wishful thinking." Mary stood up and went over to the bookcase for the thick family Bible. The leather cover was worn from constant use. "We've been studying the Old Testament this month. We're now in the Book of

Deuteronomy, chapter 28. These are difficult passages, so we could surely use your counsel."

"Certainly. Let me go out to the barn and get mine, it's in my saddlebags."

"Oh don't bother—you can use ours." Mary handed the huge volume to Quinn.

He hadn't opened the Bible since leaving college. For Quinn, it was just a prop, a part of his ministerial clothing, another article of disguise. The one in his saddlebag had pages stuck together from misuse and smelled of mildew, beef jerky, and spilled whiskey. *Holy Bible, King James version*, was clearly legible on its leather binding, which was all that was necessary. He fumbled a bit finding Deuteronomy but no one noticed.

"What chapter did you say?" he asked.

"Chapter 28, verse 4—that's where we stopped yesterday," piped in Daniel.

"Yeah, that's where they were talking about cows," added Matthew.

Quinn noticed the Bible was well marked, with passages underlined, words and sentences circled. These people were biblical fanatics. He made light of Matthew's comment. "Let's see about those cows."

Everyone giggled.

"Here it is. 'Blessed shall be the fruit of thy body, and the fruit of thy ground, and the fruit of thy cattle, the increase of thy kine,'" Quinn hesitated. "Matthew was right." His well-placed quip brought about more laughter.

"Let me continue . . . 'the increase of thy kine, and the flocks of thy sheep.'"

"That last part was for sheepherders. We don't raise sheep," said Matthew wrinkling his nose. "We're cowmen!"

"That's enough of your interrupting, young man," admonished Mary. "Read on, Reverend."

"'The Lord shall cause thine enemies that rise up against thee to be smitten before thy face: they shall come out against thee one way, and flee before thee seven ways.'" He looked up at Mary, "Do you believe that, Mrs. Dodd?"

"Of course I do. I believe every word is divinely inspired."

"That's the right answer," he said, smiling at them all. "Read on, please."

"All right, let's read on. 'But it shall come to pass, if thou wilt hearken unto the voice of the Lord thy God, to observe to do all of his commandments and his statutes . . . all these curses shall come upon thee and overtake thee.'"

Quinn glanced up again. "What have we learned so far?"

Susan raised her hand. "God has told us of the blessings if we believe in Him; now He'll tell us what will happen if we don't." Jacob Quinn was ready to move on to another subject. "Don't you all think it's time to turn to the New Testament and learn of God's love?"

"Let's finish the chapter first. Please continue . . . you read so well," Mary said.

"Very well." He read on, this time a little faster. He literally sped through the curses God promised to all who forsake Him. "'The Lord shall send upon thee cursing, vexation, and rebuke in all that thou settest thine hand unto for to do, until thou be destroyed, and until thou perish quickly; because of the wickedness of thy doings, whereby thou hast forsaken me.'"

The curses became progressively worse, promising boils on the body, incurable diseases, cannibalism, plagues, insect infestations, mothers eating their children, fear, panic, desolation.

After he had skimmed through the last verse, Quinn asked, "Do you believe a loving God could let all of this horror happen?"

"Sure do," affirmed David, the oldest child. "Don't you?"

"I tend to believe the Old Testament passed into oblivion at the birth of Christ. Love instead of hate was borne into the world. Later, the veil was rent at Calvary and the old God became the new, through Christ's teachings. The New Testament clearly states, 'God is love.'"

They were all silent for a moment; this was a different way of looking at the Old Testament. Mary was fairly stunned; here was a minister of God teaching new doctrine.

Mary asked, "How then do you interpret Christ's comment in Matthew 5:18, 'Till heaven and earth pass, one jot or one tittle shall in no wise pass from the law, till all be fulfilled,' how do you explain it? Isn't that clear confirmation from Christ Himself on the importance of the Old Testament law?"

Quinn hadn't run into anyone this scripturally knowledgeable before, nor had he been confronted so directly. He had to think of something fast to say to Mary to shift her away from scripture and win her confidence once more. He glanced about the room for inspiration . . . his eyes finally resting on the empty cuff of Matthew's tan shirt sleeve.

"Sorry about your boy's hand, Mary," Quinn said, feigning sympathy. To the boy, he said, "Son, I know the good Lord will reward you in the hereafter for what you are now suffering. . . . "

The words rang hollow and were followed by a hush that reverberated around the room. Mary rushed in to redirect the conversation.

"Matthew does a fine job around this ranch with just one hand . . . don't you, Son? I'm real proud of you."

Then to Quinn, she said, "About that passage of Scripture . . ."

"Mary, I'm sure there is a scriptural answer, but it's not on the tip of my tongue. I'll pray about it and have an answer for you in the morning. It's been a long ride today and I'm bone-tired. Can it wait 'til tomorrow?"

"Oh, Reverend, I'm so sorry—we've kept you up too late. Plenty of time to talk again at breakfast."

"I intend to spend a lot of time in this valley, with lots of folks moving into the back country. We'll have *years* to talk about Scripture."

"David, show our guest to the bunkhouse."

"Yes, Ma." David led the way, past the two dogs lying on the doorstep. Their eyes and their deep, low growls followed Quinn into the night.

★★★

The Dodd kitchen filled with the aroma of fresh-baked biscuits and ham. As Mary greased the griddle for flapjacks,

Sarah cracked the eggs and little Betsy spooned out the wild berry jam.

"Matthew, go down to the bunkhouse and fetch the Reverend. Tell him breakfast will be ready in a couple of minutes. Here . . . take this coffee with you."

Matthew grabbed the cup and trudged down the slope, sloshing coffee on the way. Before Mary had flipped the first batch of hot cakes, Matthew burst through the door.

"He's gone, Ma—so's his horse."

Chapter 28

MINDY LOU LEANED OVER the back of Seymour's chair, displaying her ample bosom to the players seated around the private poker table in the back room of the Lucky Dog Saloon. "Someone wants to see you, Slick."

"Hah," guffawed one of the gamblers, "we see you, too, Mindy Lou."

The house madam was pleased by the comment, "Look all you want but don't touch, boys." As if anyone would; she was Aussie's private property. Broken bones were a sure bet, messing around with Big Mindy.

"Well, Slick, what should I tell 'em?"

"Mindy, tell 'em I'm busy . . . see me during office hours." Seymour had been losing and drinking heavily, so his mood was anything but hospitable.

"Whatever you say," she cooed, swinging her hips provocatively as she strolled toward the door.

"Wow, wow wee!" one muttered under his breath. "Did ja ever see anythin' like that?"

"Yep," answered an old miner. "Ever been to a zoo and seen one of them there giraffeys from Afriker?"

No one had.

"Well, I seen one in a zoo in New York City. I seen the south side of one of 'em long-necked buggers headen north . . . that's how Mindy Lou walks."

"Sorta like two possums fightin' in a burlap bag?"

"Yep . . . only slower." Everyone but Slick laughed.

"Let's play poker," he said.

"Whose deal is it?" the miner asked.

"I forgot," exclaimed another. "I'm still thinkin' about giraffes."

"Yeah, an I know which giraffe yer thinkin' about!"

The laughs continued as the door opened and Mindy Lou appeared once more.

"Mindy Lou, guess what we been talkin' about!"

"Girls and fun." She smirked.

"Nah! Animals . . . possums and giraffeys!"

"Yeah," piped in another, "and burlap bags."

With a confused expression, she turned to Seymour. "He won't go away, Slick, sez it's real important."

"Who is it?"

"Said he's the caretaker up at the Meyers mansion."

Seymour's brow knitted. He sat still for a moment, thinking . . . readjusting his thoughts through the haze of booze. *What in the world does Elmer Smith want with me at this time of night?* He shook his head, trying to clear the bourbon fog. He got up from the table, weaving. "Don't fill my seat, boys—I'll be right back."

Seymour staggered, squinting into the bright lights of the packed saloon, looking for the caretaker. Loud boisterous voices mixed with the untuned piano, grating on his nerves. Elmer stood by the entrance and as Seymour approached, he stepped outside on the boardwalk. Seymour begrudgingly followed him into the cold.

"What do you want?"

"Mr. Seymour, you told me to let you know if anybody wanted to get into the mansion . . . remember?"

"Yes, I remember," he disgustedly replied. "Couldn't this wait until tomorrow?" He started back into the warm saloon.

"Be a good fellow. Go home. I'm busy."

"It was Sheriff Poole and someone I don't know."

Seymour turned to face Elmer. "Poole, what did he want?"

"He and this other fellow wanted in the mansion."

"Did you tell them to come back after they got permission?"

"Yep."

"Then go tell them that; they have to see me first."

"That's what I told 'em but the sheriff threatened to break in if I didn't get the keys."

"You didn't let them in, did you?

"Yep, I did . . . but . . ."

"Idiot!" Seymour was sobering up fast. "What did they want—why were they there?" Obviously, they were looking for something—but what? He had cleaned out Charlie's desk; any real useful information was now in his office safe.

"What did they do . . . did you go in with them?"

"Yes, Sir. They asked to see Mr. Meyer's desk."

Seymour suddenly had a sinking knot in his stomach. "Did they find anything?"

Elmer became very excited. "I didn't want to let them in—really I didn't—but how could I . . ." Seymour interrupted Elmer's whining reply by grabbing him by the coat and furiously repeating the question.

"Did . . . they . . . find . . . anything?"

"They found Mr. Meyers' last will and testament tacked to the bottom of a drawer."

"That secretive old sot! I should have known Charlie'd do something like that." Seymour's mind was racing; blood surged to his head, clearing out the cobwebs, forcing him to forget all but the subject at hand. He paced back and forth in front of the saloon windows, the light casting buttermilk shadows on his pasty face. "You said somebody else was with Poole—who was it?"

"I don't know; never seen him before tonight. He didn't give his name."

"What did he look like?"

"Maybe forty or so, musta' been over six feet, mustache, no beard. One thing about him . . ."

"What was that?" Seymour broke in.

"He only had one arm."

★★★

Sleep was impossible; not until the morning sun touched the horizon did Seymour nod off in a stupor. He never returned to the poker table; instead, he kept company with his favorite Kentucky bourbon. It wasn't until the last drop was coaxed from the bottle that he collapsed onto his bed, fully clothed. He was awakened at eleven-thirty by a knock on the door.

"Mr. Seymour, are you there? It's me, Robert."

Seymour rolled over and forced his eyes open. He recognized the voice of his young law clerk, Robert Gaston. He stared at the ceiling for a moment before answering hoarsely, "Wha . . ." clearing his dry throat, "what do you want?"

"There is somebody to see you over at the office. I think it's important."

Seymour slid his legs over the edge of the bed and sat, elbows on knees, scratching his head, running his tongue over his teeth, rubbing his eyes. Finally he asked, "Why do you think it's so important?"

It was a moment before the law clerk responded. "Well, Sir, he said he was from Colorado Springs and he had something to tell you about Mr. Meyers. I thought you would want to see him."

Seymour sat up straight. "Charlie Meyers . . . *our* Charlie Meyers?"

"Yes, Sir . . . that Charlie Meyers."

"Tell 'im I'll be right there, as soon as I get dressed."

"Yes, Sir." The footsteps faded down the hall.

"So!" he grinned, "Charlie finally kicked the bucket." Seymour stood up, swayed to one side, caught his balance, and staggered to the wash basin. With eyes partially closed, he poured water from the pitcher, sloshing some on the rumpled suit. Cupping two handfuls of water, he buried his face in the cool liquid, scrubbing vigorously. He gazed in the mirror at the stubbled, puffy-faced, red-eyed reflection. "I've been worse." He looked again. "Maybe not."

Shaved and dressed in a pressed suit, Kenneth Seymour went downstairs to the hotel restaurant and got a cup of black coffee. Once fortified, he was ready to leave for his Silverville office, then stopped to look at the luncheon menu, then at his gold watch. "Eleven fifty-five. Time for a bit of lunch and a glass of good wine. I have a right to celebrate. The messenger, whoever the heck he is, can wait."

Seymour poured over the menu, saw nothing that appealed to him, and finally ordered soft boiled eggs, hash browns, buttered toast, and a bottle of white wine. When the food arrived, he picked at it, pushing the eggs to one side, eating only the potatoes.

So . . . Sam Dodd is still alive and he knows about Charlie's will. So what! Charlie's dead. The reprobate must have hidden a copy and told him where it was—how else would he know? Will Poole knows too. That could be trouble but . . . there is no way they can trace the killings back to me. I don't even know who Aussie hired to do the dirty work.

The thought of Aussie caused his anger to surface. He flexed his right hand, still sore and bruised from Aussie's vise-like grip. *Stupid greedy fool. He came close to trashing the whole deal. Fortunately, Charlie has already put his foot through death's door.* Seymour felt the telegram within his coat pocket and patted it affectionately. He received it several days ago, informing him that Charlie had entered a deep coma and was not expected to recover. The doctor wired that if he wished to see him before he passed away, he should come immediately. Kenneth chuckled, "I'll see him now that he's in a pine box." He poured himself a glass of wine and held it up. "Here's to you, Charlie, my good ol' friend—may your bones rest next to the ashes of a good-looking wench."

"Mr. Seymour?"

Kenneth turned sharply in his chair, surprised by the voice behind him, spilling wine in his lap. "Look what you made me do!"

"I'm sorry, I didn't mean to startle you. My name is K. K. De Chambeau . . . my card."

Seymour snatched it from his hand while wiping his lap with the table napkin. He glanced at the card which read, "Jackson, Bell, Hodson and Neilson. Attorneys at law."

"I'm a junior partner in the firm," he quietly stated. K. K. De Chambeau was quite proper; a dignified air encompassed him. "May I sit down?"

Seymour waved a hand to the chair across from him. "Help yourself. What do you want? Are you here to tell me Charlie died?"

"No. Mr. Meyers was still alive when I left the sanitarium but, alas, I fear he has but a few days to live."

"He's *not* dead?" Completely perplexed, Seymour asked, "Why, then, do you want to see me?"

De Chambeau reached into his briefcase and took out a sealed envelope. "It's a personal handwritten note to you, from Mr. Meyers."

Seymour tore open the envelope and read the barely legible words:

> "I know what you did, you Judas! May God forgive you!"
>
> Charlie.

Seymour sat in shocked silence.

"Mr. Meyers also requested that you receive a copy of this. De Chambeau now brought out a much larger envelope. Seymour didn't reach for it; he just asked in a low monotone, "What is it?"

"Mr. Meyers retained our firm to draft a new will, which, as you know, takes precedent over any other like document."

"I know . . . am I in it?"

"Yes, you are—quite handsomely."

Seymour perked up. "Are you at liberty to tell me what Charlie left me?"

"I am. You should be happy to learn Mr. Meyers came to the Lord in the last few months, repented of his sins, and asked forgiveness."

"Oh yeah . . . delighted . . . Hallelujah," yawned Seymour, "Get on with it."

The lawyer continued. "Our firm is a Christian body of men; many of our clients are God-fearing, as well. We represent the sanitarium where Mr. Meyers lives and at his insistence, redrafted his will. He left half of his fortune to his son and the other half to the sanitarium to care for the needy."

"I thought you said he left me something?"

"He did; he forgave all of the debts you owed him. It was a sizable sum. You should be very pleased."

"Was that all?"

"No. One thing more." He reached again into his briefcase. "Mr. Meyers wants you to have this. He said you would need it more than he."

"What is it?"

"You should be honored. It's his personal Bible."

★ ★ ★

Long after De Chambeau left, Kenneth sat in the dining room, staring first at the large envelope containing the new will, then at Charlie's Bible. He ordered another bottle of wine, this time gulping down one glass after another. He clenched the frail wine glass with his aching right hand. The stem snapped, leaving a deep gash in his palm.

He cursed Aussie Walker . . . then cursed him again.

Cramming the envelopes into his coat, Seymour rushed to his room, tossed the Bible on the bed, then quickly washed and wrapped his bleeding hand in a white handkerchief. Without wasting a moment, he headed for the door . . . his system demanded another drink, this time something with more body. "I need some whiskey before I break the good news to my pal, Aussie Walker," he spat out bitterly.

★ ★ ★

"Are you comfortable behind your big desk?" Seymour sarcastically asked after boldly busting in to Aussie's private office. "Well, I sincerely hope you are. I've got something to read to you." Seymour had trouble standing erect without teetering from side to side. He braced himself by leaning on the edge of Aussie's desk.

"Yer drunk!"

"Not as drunk as I'm going to be, my dear Australian peasant. Listen to this." Dramatically, he fumbled to his inside coat pocket and with a flourish, removed the document. "Ta daaa . . . The *last* will and testament of Charlie Meyers."

"I've read it before . . . git out of me office ya drunkin' sot."

"Aha! You stupid, overgrown aborigine. You haven't read THIS will!" Hatred seethed from every pore in Seymour's body as he spoke. "Read every word of it, you primeval ape!" He wadded the will in a ball and threw it into Aussie's face. "Read it, you idiot!" he screamed. "It's a new will, a new one, do you hear?" Seymour was foaming, froths of saliva oozing from his mouth as he demanded, "Read it!"

The import of Seymour's words finally began to register. "What do ya mean, new will?"

"Let me put it in language that even a dumb jackass like *you* can understand," ranted the enraged lawyer. "Charlie changed his will and we won't git a dime . . . not one red cent! To make matters worse, Sam Dodd's in town and Will Poole undoubtedly suspects the two of us are guilty of multiple murders."

Seymour's rage was consuming him. The disappointment, the fear, everything he had hoped for . . . crushed by the greedy foreign hulk sitting behind the desk. Seymour's white knuckles dug into the top of the desk as he leaned across it, spewing out epithets. Abruptly he stopped, moved closer, and spat in Aussie's face.

Before he could back away, Aussie's massive hands grabbed him by the throat.

Until Kenneth had expectorated, Aussie was somewhat ignoring his blatherings, trying to smooth out and read the crumpled document, concentrating on the horrible news Seymour had given him. Now, the anger rose within him like an erupting geyser. Spittle trickling down his nose, Aussie rose to his feet, dragging Slick Seymour across the desk and off the floor.

Seymour, legs kicking, gasping for air, reached inside his coat and pulled out a small derringer. He placed it at the base of Aussie's throat and pulled the trigger. POW . . . POW . . . ! Thunderstruck by the realization of what Seymour had just done, Aussie squeezed with all his might . . . the snap was sharp and clear.

The door to Aussie's office flew open and a small crowd, aghast, saw Aussie leaning against the wall in a large pool of his own blood, a death rattle reverberating from the gaping hole in his neck. Seymour's lifeless body lay across his lap, his broken neck still cradled in Aussie's massive, lifeless hands.

Chapter 29

These past months have been the most painful period of my life . . . until now. This is worse!"

Today was both heaven and hell for Sam. After eight long months, he finally had the chance to see his wife and children, but through a telescope from a distance of half a mile. He'd never felt such a longing, an indescribable, agonizing passion to hold his wife and children and shout out how much he loved them. He watched Mary walk about the porch, lean against the rail, stare up the trail he and Matthew traveled those many months before. Sam wanted to rush down the slope, sweep her up in his arms, and squeeze her 'til she yelled. He looked away. His whole body ached. Should he sneak down during the night and see her? No . . . too dangerous. Somewhere, nearby, were people plotting to kill him, desperate men who posed a threat to him and his family. One had to be the most diabolical killer imaginable—the devil incarnate—the only man who'd ever made him sick with fear. He was out there right now—cunning, crafty, deadly . . . waiting. There was little doubt the killer had to be enticed away from his family. Under no circumstances could his wife and children be involved in the final meeting between the two of them. Sam knew the confrontation had to come, and if it must, his Armageddon would be at some other place than this beautiful valley. "If I'm to die, let it be far from my loved ones."

Sam was hiding above, in the dark timber, the horses well away in a little hidden grove on the high flats below the western rim. For three days Sam secretively scouted the valley and ridges surrounding the homestead. He located two armed men, one watching the ranch while the other covered the main entrance to the valley. Neither had flaxen hair, blue eyes, or wore the garb of a minister, but within their camp were the boot prints of three men.

The carefully thought-out letter that he and Poole drafted together was delivered to Mary yesterday, right on schedule.

My dearest Mary,

I can't tell you how desperately I want to see you and the children but I can't come home right away. I have some very unpleasant business to attend to. Several of my old war buddies have died, some mysteriously. I hate to tell you bad news, but your cousin Sherry is dead . . . murdered, we believe. Also, sweet lovable Otto was fatally knifed by a Mexican. I have been trying to locate some of my other comrades and warn them to be careful. Somebody is trying to kill us, but I have no idea who or why. I finally found Porter Dixon; he's a mining engineer now and his business is investigating old mines. Next week or so, he will be in Gold Diggins, Colorado. From what I hear, the town is deserted since the placer mining days ended. Porter thinks there is still gold to be found in hard-rock mining. He said he was terribly busy but he could see me in Gold Diggins. I have to find out. Charlie's in Colorado Springs. I hear he hasn't long to live. I worry about his soul. Also, I better stop by some doctor's office on my way back and have my arm checked. It hasn't healed as well as expected. Don't worry though; it will be all right as soon as you, my sweet, can give it your tender loving care. Give my love to the children; I miss all of you so much.

Yours,
Sam

As Mary read the letter on the porch, Sam watched her through the telescope. She sat down on the steps, pulled her apron up to cover her face, and sobbed, with Sarah and Betsy trying to comfort her. He ached all over with love for them and watching Mary cry tortured his soul. Once more, the desire to run down the hill and cry out, "I'm home!" overwhelmed him . . . but patience ruled; he had to sweat it out. Their lives depended upon it.

Would the preacher take the bait? He had to wait and see. It took two days.

★ ★ ★

"Where have you been?" sneered Abel, as the preacher emerged from the trees.

Quinn, alias Reverend Smith, swung gracefully down from the saddle, "Tending to the flock, my good man, tending to the flock."

"Whata ya mean?" inquired brother Clem.

"It means, I had to establish myself as a circuit-riding minister. I visited several other ranches over the past few days, spreading the gospel far and wide."

"What do you know about preachin' the Bible?"

"More than enough to get by. Most people believe in God, but they're too lazy to read much about Him. Their ignorance is my bliss. Dress up in this garb and what I say becomes the gospel—the gospel as interpreted by Reverend Smith. That is, unless I run into someone like Mary Dodd."

"Did she tie a knot in yer tail?"

"No, but she had the rope in her hand . . . I just didn't let her throw the loop." Quinn had gone back to the ranch several times, spending afternoons pitching hay with the boys and talking about Eastern city life with Sarah. But he made sure he departed before supper, for he wanted no more Bible lessons with Mary Dodd around. Most of the time, he talked about his visit with the Herbertsons, the Pezoldts over in Beaver Flats, and the Haneys, the other side of Aukum Creek. Quinn knew he couldn't fool Dodd's wife for any length of time.

"Either of you have any news to report?" he asked.

"Yeah, we sure do. Some old guy with a load of supplies stopped by and delivered some packages to her. Then he went on toward the Herbertson spread."

"Did he deliver any mail?"

"Couldn't tell, too far away."

"Best I visit them again tomorrow and find out."

Quinn took the wool blanket off the back of his saddle and moved to the far side of the fire, close as he could comfortably get, yet far up wind from the gamy Jebson boys, unbathed since Laramie . . . or before. Quinn thought of tomorrow and another visit with the Dodds. What if there were no news of Sam? Some action had to be taken soon . . . they had been here too long already. It might be necessary to get rid of one of the children . . . that would bring Samuel Dodd running home. But which one? Pretty Sarah? *No, not her. I've other plans for that sweet virgin.*

The oldest boy, David? No. It should be one of the younger children . . . but which one? Quinn smiled. Of course. *Yeah, that should do it.* He could shoot the crippled boy, pick him off from long range—he'd be the most expendable and invoke the greatest rage. Afterwards, he could perform the funeral services, maybe even carry the sad news to Sam Dodd. *Yes, it's vital to have an alternative plan.*

★ ★ ★

It was a long crawl in the dark, bellying through the open meadow at night, worming around and over sage. Sam had to get close, real close. Finally a rider appeared through the trees; the third man had joined his comrades. It could be him, the preacher. The distance was too great to hear them clearly; only an occasional word could be distinguished rising above their mumbled voices. The new man was obviously in command; he did most of the talking while the others nodded in agreement. Sam watched them move around the fire, casting shadows on the surrounding trees. He leveled the Henry rifle over a large rock and placed the sights on the chest of the new arrival. One hundred and seventy five yards . . . easy shot.

There, he's perfectly still, hold the rifle steady, squeeze the trigger, and blow a hole through his chest big enough to drive a team of Belgians through! Sam's finger tightened on the trigger, the aim steady . . . he couldn't fire. *What if it's not him? I can't see his eyes or his hair. By this light I can't even tell if he's dressed like a minister. What if he's just another hired gun?*

Sweat broke out on Sam's brow. *I gotta be sure.* He watched two of them bed down while one stood guard. They were taking no chances. *Smart.*

Soon as they go to sleep, I'll move out. Come dawn, I'm back to observing the ranch. Tomorrow will tell if my plan is working; I should know for sure. Sam turned in the dark and rose to one knee. No need to crawl.

"Snap!" The dry twig broke under Sam's foot; in the quiet of the night, it sounded like a rifle shot. Sam turned and dropped to the ground facing the encampment. All three men were on their feet. The new arrival rose like a cat, gun in hand. He kicked dirt on the fire, extinguishing the light.

"What was that?" exclaimed the youngest.

"Shut up, you fool!" his brother hissed. The third man disappeared into the darkness.

Sam knew it was time to move or he would be trapped between them. Crouching low, he angled toward the camp, pretty sure they would never suspect he'd travel in that direction. Two of them thrashed about to his right, not straying far from the campsite. Both made too much noise for Sam to consider them much of a threat. Where was the third . . . the one who who moved quiet, like a cat? The feeling of eminent danger crept over him, and Sam's skin began to crawl. It was him, after all! *I had him in my sights and could have killed him dead . . . now he's stalking me.* Sam wet his finger and held it aloft. The wind hadn't changed—it was still in his favor. Lifting his head, he inhaled deeply through his nose. There. Upwind, he could smell him. He was close. Sam worked himself into the edge of the pines and under some dead fall and brush. There was no way he could be seen in the dark. It was now a waiting game. The man sat quietly on a log nearby and waited as well, listening.

If he stays put to first light, he'll find me. Sam felt defenseless, paralyzed by the knowledge that the slightest movement would be heard, so that even reaching for the rifle beside him would be extremely difficult—and besides, it wouldn't be much use at close range. A losing proposition, especially if an adversary were armed with a handgun. Sam bit his lip, bringing blood. Insects were crawling over his body, under his pants leg, biting . . . the desire to scratch was intense.

Off in the distance came the sound of snapping wood. Something heavy was moving through the trees. "Haw! Lookee here, Smith, it's just a cow moose!" Abel shouted. "Come on back; let's git some sleep."

The man on the log waited another fifteen minutes, lit a cigarette, then went back to the camp where the fire had been rekindled. The three talked for a while before settling down. An hour before dawn, Sam finally worked his way out of sight and sound. He resumed his watch over the ranch.

★ ★ ★

By break of day, Quinn was awake. He made coffee then kicked the feet of both brothers. "Time to get up." Both rolled out of their blankets, scratching. Quinn looked toward the noise he had heard during the night and started off in that direction.

"Where ya goin'?" smirked Abel, "Goin' to piddle?"

Quinn ignored him. He circled about the area, then bent over, searching the ground, checking for sign. The rocky gravel showed little. He found the tracks of the cow moose and a fresh pile of dung. Within spitting distance of the camp, much closer than the sound of the snapping twig, he discovered the print of a boot heel. Quinn traipsed quickly back to the Jebson boys. "Let's see the bottoms of your boots—lift 'em up!"

Both complied. "What fer?" asked the older brother.

"There's a footprint out there . . . just checking your boot heels. Hummm, it doesn't look like one of ours."

"Where abouts?" asked Abel. Quinn pointed.

"Oh, that was one of us. Too close to the camp anyways. If a body was out there, they woulda lit out in the opposite direction."

"You're probably right," answered Quinn. He tried to put it from his mind, but it kept buzzing around in a corner of his brain, a mental gnat that wouldn't go away. *Could someone have been out there listening, watching us? If so . . . who?*

Sam watched the lone figure unhurriedly ride up to the house. He saw Susan run out and greet him, then Betsy. The boys waved from the barn. It was the circuit rider.

Mary was on the porch, waiting, as the preacher tied his horse up to the rail. They talked for a bit, then went inside. Sam's mouth filled with the taste of bile, knowing the devil's own disciple was in his house. Clenching and unclenching his fist helped, the thought of his hands around his neck . . . hands? What hands! Overwhelming frustration gripped his heart. *Oh God, I'm half a man.* He felt helpless, knowing he was no match for the killer. His only hope was to somehow get him out of there . . . if nothing else, make sure his family was safe.

Late in the afternoon, the preacher rode off, heading back in the same direction. Sam waited until he was out of sight before cautiously circling the ranch and going back to where the three were camped. It was midnight before he could crawl his way close. Their fire was low, nearly extinguished;

no one was on guard and all seemed to be sleeping. This is my opportunity. Sam looked up to the stars and prayed, "Lord, I have to kill them while they sleep." There was no doubt in his mind that the third man was the minister and the other two were there to back him up. Slowly, noiselessly, an inch at a time, Sam crept nearer. He'd never shot a sleeping man before; the thought bothered him but there was no alternative. *There's little chance I can capture them alive.* Sam moved ever closer. Something was wrong! Only two were there. Both were lying down but without blankets; one was sleeping in a grotesque position. Neither stirred. There was no sound at all, nothing. There were no horses.

Sam stood up. He had seen men "sleep" like this before, twisted, contorted bodies scattered across battlefields from Vicksburg to Richmond.

The moonlight cast ghostly shadows over the corpses. One had been shot through the mouth, eyes still wide open in shock, staring at an unseen sky. The other lay in a pool of blood that circled outward from the small hole directly over the heart. In death, he clutched a knife.

The preacher and horses were nowhere in sight. Sam waited for first light, then followed their trail which lead out of the valley north, toward Laramie. Sam rode back to the campsite to bury the bodies. It was the Christian thing to do and it preserved the evidence of their murder. With just one arm, it took most of the morning to cover them with rocks. When he felt the remains were sufficiently protected, he pulled his Bible from the saddlebag and read a few words over them.

Sam mounted and turned south, for one last look at home.

Chapter 30

Just a little while longer. Sam knew he must leave, but just a few moments more. It might be and in all probability, *could be* the last time he would ever see his family. He wanted to drink it all in, indelibly brand into his mind every move, every gesture of Mary's as she tended to chores. He watched her shaking dirt from the throw rugs, sweeping off the porch, watched little John and Betsy playing in the yard, the boys poking each other as they romped for the barn, the dogs joyfully yapping at their heels. He wanted to remember it all . . . burn it in his brain like a brand on a steer's hide. The Lord's advice to not count the years but the days was good indeed—drink in each minute because tomorrow may never come. Sam thought of the last few years, vintage moments, voluminous hours of love and affection.

"I've been blessed. Thank You, Lord."

The wind shifted ever so slightly. The dogs quieted down, lifted their noses in the air, and sniffed. They started to amble up the slope and as Sam's scent became stronger, their pace increased to where they were excitedly racing up the hill in search of their master. Sam greeted them affectionately, even though they had practically bowled him over. He scratched their ears and fondly petted each one. Both lay down beside him.

Slowly he got up and commanded the dogs to go home. "Rusty! Moose! Git!" With both heads hung low, they dutifully but begrudgingly obeyed. Sam turned and took his first step on the long trail to Gold Diggins.

★★★

For centuries, the upper reaches of the Laramie River to the northern high plains was prime buffalo country and the home of the Cheyenne. Now, the bison were gone and the Indians forced onto reservations. In their place were cattle and small ranches, homesteads that popped up like gophers, wire fences, red barns, and an occasional schoolhouse.

"It'll be awhile before these sodbusters venture as far as the Dodd ranch," Quinn predicted. "Maybe another decade or so."

The demise of the Jebson boys crossed his mind. Quinn looked toward the sun and continued out loud, "Going to be a hot day; they should ripen up real quick. By the time the birds and the wolves get through, they'll be just rags, bones, and boots."

When Quinn had arrived back in camp, both were there, eagerly awaiting any news. Abel was practicing his fast draw. "Bang!" he said after each attempt.

"Learn anything?" asked Clem.

"Bang!" repeated Abel, as he drew and pretended to shoot Quinn. "Yer dead, Preacher!"

"Yes, I learned two things," replied Quinn as he dismounted.

"Whut was that?" asked the perennially open-mouthed Abel.

"I discovered Dodd won't be back for more than a month." Quinn walked around the rear of his horse and faced both brothers.

"Whut was the other thing ya learned?" asked Clem.

"I don't need either of you anymore." With unparalleled dexterity, Quinn drew and shot Clem in the chest, who staggered backwards, drew his knife, then collapsed to the ground.

Abel stood in shocked disbelief at the smoking gun leveled at his head . . . and for the first time he was speechless. He looked at his dead brother, then back to Quinn. Trembling, he blurted out, "Yer goin' to kill me too?"

Quinn casually holstered his gun. "That all depends on how fast you are."

Abel had just witnessed Quinn's blinding speed. He knew he wasn't good enough. His lower lip began to quiver.

"I ain't that fa-fa-fast," he stuttered.

"I know you're not." Quinn smiled, "So, let's give you an edge."

"Whut do ya mean?"

"Reach down and draw your gun real slow, cock the hammer back, and hold it to your side. Be a good boy, do as I say!"

With hand and body shaking, Abel did as he was told.

"Now, slowly, bring it up until it points at my feet. There, that's fine. When I draw, all you have to do is bend your wrist up and pull the trigger. You might get lucky."

"I don't wa . . ."

Before Abel could finish the sentence or cock his wrist, Quinn drew and fired. The bullet, appropriately, entered Jebson's open mouth.

Jacob Quinn holstered his Colt and sauntered over to the lifeless body. Quinn drew out his gun and pointed it at Abel. "Bang!" he said . . . smiling.

In 1858, Will Russell discovered gold along Dry Creek in the mountainous western section of the Kansas Territory, later called Colorado. A rush to find this precious metal began, drawing a hundred thousand fortune seekers from both East and West. Most were disappointed; however, a few of the rugged, persevering souls made worthwhile discoveries. Slow-talkin' Lon McElvaney was one of them. A mile climb up Elk Creek, near the headwaters of the Arkansas River, ol' Lon struck it rich. The boom town of Gold Diggins came into being. At the height of its brief existence, five thousand lived and mined on the steep slopes of Elk Creek. As quickly as the town had grown, it shrank. By 1875, only a few hardy souls had stuck it out, scratching a bare existence out of the hard rock. After the deadly winter of 1877, no one was left. All that remained were the quickly-built wood structures that once housed saloons, hotels, livery stables, and a sundry of other commercial ventures. The hillsides were dotted with abandoned mines. Most of the residential shacks on the eastern high slopes had burned to the ground during one of the frequent, wind-driven summer electrical storms. Main Street had miraculously escaped the blaze, however, several roofs were caved in from the massive snowfall of '77. Trees on the slopes were gone so that only their stumps remained, stark reminders of the need for firewood and mine timber. Higher up Elk Creek were scraggly stands of aspen, somehow left untouched by the wood-ravenous miners. Gold Diggins was a ghostly eyesore of weathered wood, cracked brick, and faded paint on awkwardly tilted buildings, the victims of sliding earth, minor quakes and heavy winters. The ghost town was on the way to nowhere, deserted . . . out of sight, out of mind.

Sam approached the town from above, making his way down Elk Creek, the most direct route from home. Traveling south, over the high mountain passes, crisscrossing the Great Divide, he figured to arrive days before the preacher. The snow had been deep over Mosquito Pass and along the high ridges, adding another twenty-four hours to his ride.

Sam mulled over the plan he and Will Poole formulated back in Silverville. They first had to determine whether or not the circuit rider was the killer or a real minister carrying the gospel to the isolated area. Getting his letter to Mary via the deputy was essential, so Sam could circle back to the ranch and secretively keep an eye out for the preacher, knowing he would leave if he were really the assassin. Then Sam would telegraph Will and his deputy to meet in Gold

Diggins, where Sam was sure the three of them, assisted by the element of surprise, could apprehend the killer.

Finding the bodies of the two men had confirmed the assassin's guilt. No longer were they dealing with circumstantial facts, conjecture, and suspicions. Solid evidence was now on hand—more than enough to arrest him, convict him before a jury, then hang him by the neck.

Sam was relieved that he wouldn't have to shoot him down from ambush. Let the law take care of it. He and Will still had a lot to go over. They had to find the best location to get the drop on him, then put him under arrest. They must gain the advantage, select the most strategic position, and maintain maximum cover. He remembered the old Deluxe Hotel located in the middle of town; it had a high window on the second floor overlooking a balcony, allowing an excellent view of Main Street in both directions . . . an ideal cover to brace the Henry rifle over a window sill while Will and his deputy waited below.

The aspen grove was just ahead, a good place to conceal his horse. Sam dismounted, watered the gelding from the creek, then tied him up short, secure to a tree. He stashed the saddle in a nearby mining shack. With dusk settling, there was just enough time to reconnoiter the town before dark. Sam removed his bedroll from the saddle, then reached for his Winchester and hiked toward the deserted town below.

It was an ugly sight, denuded of trees, ripped up by mining, tailings dumped everywhere. On the canyon walls, scorched scrub brush and sage. No birds, not a sign of wildlife . . . a dead valley.

Psalm 23 came to mind. "Yea, though I walk through the valley of the shadow of death . . ."

Better be wary, Sam thought. Years of living on the edge had structured his cautious nature. Out of habit, he kept to whatever cover was available, working from stand of high bush to tree to rock outcropping, always in the shade, halting to listen, using all his senses. At the edge of town, there were the distinctive and familiar smells of sage, rotted, burnt wood and . . . fresh horse manure.

New horse dung, here? Sam stopped in his tracks, then melted further into the shadows of a nearby structure. *Where's the horse now? Who did it belong to? Will Poole and his deputy shouldn't be here 'til tomorrow.*

Sam moved stealthily along the dark sides of the buildings, quietly, cautiously, taking advantage of the dusk light . . . rifle in hand.

The odor of horse and leather grew stronger; it seemed to be coming from the left. Then he heard a muffled snort and the rustling of an animal, coming from the barn downhill.

It was still too light to safely cross the open space between the shade of the buildings and the barn, and a broken-down, barbed wire fence was in his path. *Gotta wait . . . just a few minutes more.* Sam's heart was racing. Whose mount could it be? *Is some prospector grubbing around these old mines?*

A myriad of questions ran through his mind. One caused his stomach to contract, forcing a bitter taste in his mouth. *Could it be the circuit rider?* Possible, but highly improbable. *The letter clearly stated I wouldn't be in Gold Diggins for several days. There'd be no reason for him to rush.*

The sun finally dipped behind the western ridge. Sam sped across the open space and surged over the downed fence, catching a trouser leg on one of the barbs. He slammed noisily to the ground. Frantically, he kicked at the tangled wire, tearing himself loose. He paid no heed to the cuts on his leg as he scrambled to the shadows of the barn. Out of breath, gulping in air, he waited.

Did anyone hear me? Sam hugged the side of the barn, trying to disappear from view. Waiting a few minutes more, he silently worked his way down to a shattered window where he could see inside.

Grinning, he shook his head and heaved a deep sigh of relief; it was Sheriff Poole's buckskin gelding alongside a roan mare, no doubt the deputy's horse.

Why am I in such a panic? Sure no need to be, not with Will and his deputy down at the hotel, waitin' for me. Sam looked at the lacerations on his right leg. *That's what ya get for gettin' yerself too excited.*

Still keeping to the shadows, Sam slipped through the old blacksmith shop into the alley, crossing over to the back staircase of the Deluxe Hotel, then quietly climbed to the second floor. The long, narrow hallway was dimly lit by a good-sized hole in the roof which let in the fading light. Sam carefully stepped around the fallen debris and worked his way to the room overlooking the street. The door was wide open. Will was seated in silhouette against the window with his double-barreled shotgun across his knees. The handlebar mustache and hat were unmistakable.

"Will, it's me, Sam." Then, a little louder, "Will . . . wake up, it's me."

Sam walked over to Will, leaned his rifle against the wall, and lifted the shotgun from his lap. Waking his friend from a sound sleep could be dangerous. He gently poked Will's shoulder with the butt of the gun. "Wake up, friend, this ain't the time or place to snooze."

Will Poole crumpled over to the floor.

"My God, Will . . . what the . . ." Sam quickly dropped the shotgun on the floor and felt for a heartbeat. Nothing but the sticky substance Sam knew so well . . . coagulated blood.

From the dark corner of the room came a silken voice,

"Well, if it isn't Mr. Dodd. We fina . . . "

POW! POW!

"Before the sentence could be completed, Sam lunged for the shotgun, thumbed back the hammers, and fired in the direction of the voice. Almost simultaneously, he dove through the shattered window onto the balcony. Shots followed him. Without hesitation, Sam rolled violently across the boards, smashing through the rail and . . . fell heavily to the ground below, knocking the breath out of him. Gasping, he twisted under the balcony and up against the wall. The preacher was overhead, craning to see over the edge. He began firing down through the wooden floor, the shots perilously close, ripping into Sam's clothes, cutting a cruel welt across his thigh. He groped inside his coat, searching for his .32-caliber Smith and Wesson. Gone! It must have slipped out in the fall. Reaching back, he fiercely pawed over the dusty ground . . . to no avail. Above, the preacher was reloading, then more shots punctured the floor! Bullets kicked up dirt in Sam's face, landing all around him. The killer emptied his gun, then cursed and clumsily reentered the upstairs room. Sam rolled over and scrambled to his feet. He had only seconds to make it across the street before the assassin made it down the stairs. Sam tripped part way, falling to his face, but desperation gave him the energy to crawl his way under the dark boardwalk ahead, just as the limping figure emerged from the hotel.

From the dark confines of his hiding place, Sam watched the man look in every direction. In obvious anger, he dramatically reloaded his six-shooter, slamming new .44–.40 shells into the chamber. Then, something on the ground caught his attention; stooping over, he picked up the pistol. An ache of helplessness welled up in Sam's chest, *Oh, Dear Lord, he found my gun.*

With a smirk on his face, the preacher hobbled back to the hotel.

Watching his assailant limp away, Sam knew he had winged him with the shotgun blast. *I've got to get to my horse and the .44 in my saddlebags or I'm a dead man.* Sam scanned to the left and then to the right. The boardwalk had caved in on the left, denying him passage. He couldn't go back in the street without being seen. The only possible escape lay to the right, the opposite way he wanted to go. If he could belly under the sagging wood to the end of the street, he could go around and make it back upstream. Very slowly, as quietly as possible, he inched his way. He wasn't alone; the frightening buzz of a rattlesnake came from directly in front of him, barring his path. "There's a bigger snake than you out there, pard. Git away!" he whispered. Groping about, he found a loose board and briskly waved it back and forth. Sam moved forward a little at a time, poking it blindly ahead. Shortly, the rattle stopped, the snake obligingly slithered away, leaving the way open to crawl around the corner of the building.

Sam kept to the shadows. Shots! Then the violent screaming of horses pierced the night.

"That rotten swine! He's killin' the mounts! I gotta get to my horse before he does," muttered Sam as he worked his way through the dark. Sam anxiously retraced his steps back up the creek, his thoughts racing. *Where's the deputy? . . . probably dead. If he could kill Will Poole, no deputy could give him much trouble.* Sam thought of his good friend Will, lying in a bloody heap on the hotel floor; an emptiness swept over him. Fond memories of the good times they had spent together flooded his mind. They were immediately replaced by the burning hatred he held for his assassin.

What was that? A sound just ahead; something was moving slowly through the brush ahead of him. *Could it be an animal? The Colorado mountains are full of game.* Sam wet his finger in his mouth, then held it in the air.

Good, the wind is coming down the creek. Sam moved quietly to his left and crossed the creek. The scent was unmistakable . . . man.

Dear God, he's between me and my horse. Just then, Sam's gelding whinnied. There was no doubt the preacher heard it too.

★ ★ ★

"Slippery devil!" Quinn had been totally caught by surprise by Dodd's reaction to his voice. The following shotgun blast and his subsequent leap through the window caught him off guard. The blinding flash of the muzzle blast and the pain of being hit threw Quinn's aim off. He limped to the window as fast as he could, hearing Sam's body crash through the rail and hit the ground below.

★ ★ ★

"Why . . . that psalm-singing waddie nicked me!" Quinn's right leg was bleeding from two of the double-0 shotgun slugs that had penetrated his left boot, one just grazing his ankle and the other buried in the calf of his leg. It hurt like fire! Quinn's boot was oozing with blood.

He angrily stuffed a handkerchief down the boot and headed for the stairs as quickly as his wounded leg would allow, furious with himself for not shooting Dodd first . . . then talking later. *He fell hard from the balcony and should have been on the ground. One of my shots must have hit him. Where did he go?* Quinn's anger was somewhat moderated by finding Dodd's pistol.

I know he's unarmed or he would have returned fire. Hurting, he limped back inside, sat down, took off his boot, and sopped out the blood. *Blast his luck!* Tearing off the tail of his shirt, he tied up the wound, stopping the flow. *I must have hit him too. That one-armed cowboy shouldn't be feeling so good, either.*

Frustrated, Quinn hastily reviewed the past few days. *Things haven't been going so well.* As soon as he had reached Laramie, he telegraphed Aussie Walker, informing him of a change of plans. The telegram read:

> Mr. D not at ranch. Know where he is. Should I head there now?
>
> Quinn

The immediate reply from Mindy Lou told him of Aussie's demise and that "Mr. D" was recently in Silverville visiting with Sheriff Poole. Then he rented horses and went home to his ranch.

Aussie dead! Dodd headed for his ranch weeks ago? Something was amiss. What was Dodd doing in Silverville visiting the sheriff? His letter had said he was going to Colorado Springs, then to Gold Diggins. What if Dodd *did* go back to his ranch? *If so, where was he; why didn't we see him? Why would he go back and not see his family?*

That boot print near our campsite . . . could that have been Dodd's? The noise in the night . . . was it him? Had the three of us been seen or overheard? The letter to his wife . . . why did he not tell her where he really was? Quinn shook his head. Too many unanswered questions.

The only way to find out was to travel quickly to Gold Diggins—but go early, enter at night, and expect the worst.

Quinn frowned. For the first time in his life he felt threatened. He had looked upon Sam Dodd as a challenge, but no more. The rancher now posed a threat to his very existence, possible exposure . . . or worse, failure and death. That one-armed Bible-thumper epitomized everything he hated . . . he had to die . . . his family too. Yeah, even sweet Sarah, but she would be last.

Quinn made all haste to get to Gold Diggins. He waited until dark before he silently stole into town. He wasn't the first; Sheriff Poole and a deputy were already there. Their horses weren't hard to locate and the glow of a cigarette from the hotel window announced exactly where they were.

Thinking of the sheriff, he smirked. *Old Poole thought I was Dodd! He even greeted me without turning around. "Hello Sam," he'd said. "About time you arrived."*

Quinn dropped the smirk when he remembered Dodd's silent arrival, like a cougar in the dark. *I didn't even know he was in the hotel until he called out to Poole. Anyone else would have turned to listen when I spoke to him, giving me a clear shot. Not that cowboy. Aussie was right; that one lives a charmed life.*

The challenge had now gone out of the hunt. It was no longer a game, a test of ability. A grim determination to quickly exterminate Sam Dodd was foremost in Quinn's mind. *Shoot him on sight, no playing around. But first, I've got to find his horse and prevent his escape. In all likelihood, he'll be heading there now. I have his rifle and pistol—all I have to do is find him. Come light, it shouldn't be too difficult. Better move fast and find his mount. He must have come in from above; otherwise I'd have seen him ride in. His horse must be somewhere up creek.*

★ ★ ★

The ominous low rumble of thunder resounded through the night, webs of lightning lacing the sky. Sam slackened his pace and looked up into the black as a few drops of rain touched his face. *Lord, what'll I do?* Once more Psalm 23 came to mind: "I will fear no evil: for thou art with me." Sam took a deep breath . . . *I should fear no evil for You are with me.* He was almost back to the edge of town when, in the distance, another shot was fired, almost blotted out by thunder and the crack of lightning. Sam knew it was the wanton destruction of his gelding.

Sam felt uncontrollable hatred for the false man of God. He loathed everything about him, particularly his viciousness and cruelty. For the first time in his life he passionately wanted to kill a fellow human being, wanted to see him suffer and die. Sam knew there could be no leaving this ghost town for one of them. "Thou preparest a table before me in the presence of mine enemies . . . my cup runneth over. . . ."

Black clouds massed above, blocking out the moon. Streaks of light criss-crossed the heavens, momentarily illuminating everything in ghostly white. The storm seemed to be centered overhead and with greater frequency, the stark light flashed over the town again . . . then again. Off to the right, he saw the barn where Will had stabled the horses, suddenly highlighted by lightning. *Will's saddlebags! Maybe he packed an extra gun!*

No time for caution. Sam ran toward the barn and burst through the door where Will's dead horse was jammed in the stall. The saddlebags were exposed on just one side. Sam rammed his hand inside, frantically searching for a gun . . . nothing of use! The deputy's gear was gone.

Of course, the preacher must have checked! The other side of Will's saddlebag was wedged in against the wall. It was impossible to move the dead animal in order to get at it. Sam grabbed a fallen beam and wedged it between the dry boards. With extreme effort and drenched in sweat, he pried one loose . . . then another, enabling Sam to lie on his back and thrust his arm through the slats. Straining, he unstrapped the leather thongs and stuck his hand in the bag. No gun. Nothing! *What's this!* Two round objects at the bottom. *Shotgun shells!* They didn't have the feel of double-0 buckshot. *Oh, blast it . . . bird shot!* He shoved them in his pants pocket. Sam remembered Will always carried several shells of small bird shot with him in case he came across any grouse or quail. The heavy loads must have been in the other side. Bird shot could inflict mortal damage, but only up close . . . very close.

What happened to the shotgun? Think, Sam, think! He rubbed his jaw. I had it in my hand when I jumped through the window. It could be on the balcony!

Sam climbed awkwardly to his feet and once more began to run through the night. There was not much time!

Sam ran into the hotel and up the stairs to the room overlooking the street. He peered out the window. Too dark to see anything. Nothing to do but crawl out on the balcony and hope it was there. Sam felt around frantically for the shotgun. Again, lightning lit the sky. *Dear God, there he is!* Quinn, limping up the middle of the street, stopped at the sight of Sam and drew his gun. Lightning flashes came one after another so that it was impossible not to be seen. Sam rolled back out of sight as shots tore into the roof. He felt cold metal pressed against his cheek . . . the shotgun! For a moment the lightning ceased, giving Sam time to scramble to his knees and dive back through the window, landing on Will Poole's dead body. With his quivering thumb he broke open the action and holding it between his shaking knees, he loaded both barrels.

I gotta get out of here! Sam slipped into the hall, only to hear the preacher's halting ascent up the stairs. He opened the first door and moved inside, stumbling over the cold, still body of the deputy.

Trapped! The room was cramped, with just enough space for one cot and a wash table. The roof had caved in, littering the floor with debris and jagged glass. Heavy rain pelted on what remained of the galvanized roof, drumming in his ears, drowning out any possibility of hearing his assailant in the hall.

Where is he now? Down the hall? Outside the door? Sam stood in the center of the tiny room, shotgun in hand, muzzle just a few yards from the door. The whip crack of thunder was deafening. Bolts of lightning continued to lace the sky, one flash after another, casting black shadows across the room and on the door. Sam was paralyzed by the vivid image of a cross as it appeared again and again against the weathered old wood. Tiny hairs rose on the nape of his neck and his skin prickled as if a thousand ants were moving over his body.

Unconsciously, his hand jerked, firing one round, then the other, through the center of the cross.

Sam sat immobile in the dark room, dripping wet with his back against the far wall; the empty shotgun lay across his legs, muzzle aimed at the splintered hole in the door. The last few gusts of wind were clearing away the storm, passing as quickly as it had begun; the silence was almost as deafening as the violent deluge that preceded it. Sam dared not move for close to an hour.

"Dodd . . . Sam Dodd? Can you hear me? I'm wounded bad . . . the bleeding won't stop. I need your help."

Sam remained silent.

"You're a Christian man." The preacher groaned in pain, "For God's sake, man . . . help me, I'm bleeding to death."

Sam sat stock still, speechless.

"Some Christian you are . . . a hypocrite!" Now, the voice was much weaker.

Sam knew that if he uttered a word he'd betray his position in the small room. Blind shots fired at the sound of his voice could kill him.

The feeble pleading persisted from the hallway. "You have nothing to fear. I don't have a gun and I couldn't even use it if I did. You shot it out of my hand, you crippled my fingers. For the love of God, man . . . help me!"

Silence.

"Is there not a good Samaritan?" Quinn began to sob softly. "Don't you believe in your own Bible?" The pleas were barely audible; then they stopped altogether.

Hours later, Sam threw a piece of glass to the other side of the room. He heard nothing. With one of the fallen boards, he touched the door. Nothing. Slowly, carefully, with the barrel of the shotgun, he nudged the door open.

Quinn was seated rigidly upright across the hallway, back to the wall, blinded by the bird shot, bleeding from the abdomen. His arms were extended out, braced on his knees. Both hands were wrapped tightly around the grip of a Colt .44 . . . hammer back, finger on the trigger.

The false man of God was dead.

Sam finally answered, aloud, "The Bible teaches me to judge a tree by the fruit it bears." He then kicked the gun from the dead man's grip. "And nowhere in the Good Book does it call upon me to be a fool."

EPILOGUE

"Pa!" hollered Matthew, "Mr. Wilson's ridin' up."

Sam stuck the pitchfork into the hay, wiped the sweat from his brow, and climbed down from the loft as his good friend and neighbor rode into the clearing. Sam waved a greeting and walked toward the approaching rider.

"Welcome, Amos, get off that critter and have a cool bit of well water with me."

"Howdy, Sam, don't mind if I do. It's hotter'n blazes ridin' over from Rustic." Amos Wilson dismounted and tied the reins to the hitching rail, then pulled out a red bandanna and dried the damp from his mustache and goatee.

They shook left hands vigorously. "Dang it, Sam, it's shore good to have ya home."

"It's good to be here. Come on around to the back of the house and I'll pump us a cold one. What brings you over our way, Amos?"

"Got a letter for ya from Texas, some gent named Porter Dixon." He handed the letter to Sam then drew it back. "Want me to open it for ya?"

Sam smiled. "Be obliged, but first let's have a drink."

Sam poured some water into the top of the pump for priming, then rapidly jacked the handle up and down; soon, a gush of clear, cool mountain water spewed out.

"Grab that tin cup, Amos, and help yourself." His neighbor filled it to the brim and drank heartily; what little was left he poured over the back of his neck. "Ah . . . that feels good. Now, let's see what this letter is all about." Amos carefully opened the envelope, just as Mary emerged from the kitchen door.

"Thought I heard some adult voices out here." She cheerfully said, "Glad to see you, Amos."

"Likewise, Mary," he tipped the brim of his hat and handed the letter to her. "Better you read it."

"What's this?" she asked.

"Our good neighbor here has brought us a letter from Porter Dixon, Honey. I sure hope he's all right."

Mary opened the letter. "At least he's still alive or he wouldn't be writing. Let me read what it says—it's not a very long letter."

"Dixon never was too much for talk," Sam remarked.

Mary added, "He's not too much for spelling either."

Dere Sam,

Got yer letter months back. Took a wile fer it to find me. Mabel and the kids are fine, so am I. Hope ye are too. Sorry to here about Wade, Otto an Sherry. What's all the fuss about someone wantin' to kill us all? Hogwash. Why wood anybody want to do thet? I'm a thinkin thet cold Colorada air makin' ye teched in the hed. Sam, ye worry to much.

Dixon

P.S.—If yer ever by Texas we wood like to visit with ye. These Rebs ain't to bad wonst ye git to no them.

"That man doesn't know how lucky he is. He'd probably be dead too, if it weren't for you," commented Wilson.

"Luck had nothing to do with it," responded Sam. "It was the hand of providence."

"What do you mean *providence?*"

"Amos, the Lord has a hand in all the affairs of men, and nothin' passes His notice. Christ Himself said not a sparrow falls to the ground without the Lord's will."

"Not even a sparrow?"

"Nope, not even a pesky little bird. What happened to me was no exception. It was providence that I lost my arm, and it was the Lord's will that I survived."

"That's hard to accept, Sam. Why should the Lord will that anyone suffer?"

"Why not?" His Son did—He suffered and died for us. Pain is a sorrowful but able teacher. Trouble is our earthly lot along with the good we receive. Some get more of one than the other."

Amos Wilson removed his Stetson and wiped his brow with the back of his sleeve. "I swear Sam, it's hard to figure."

"Reckon it is but that's where faith comes in, believin' when human reason fails . . . and fail it will."

Sam turned and looked down the valley and took a deep breath, inhaling the cool, pine-scented air. "Besides, my good friend, when you look at the blessings side of the ledger, it's bountiful . . . not much to complain about when you compare the two."

"Not much, when you think about it," reflected his thoughtful neighbor. "Not much to ask for, except maybe another cup of water."

Sam laughed heartily and primed the pump again.

About the Author

H.L. Richardson is a former California state senator. He has authored numerous articles, columns, and books. An avid outdoorsman, he is president of Gun Owners of America.